HANNIBAL'S
FOE

BOOK ONE IN THE REPUBLIC OF ROME TRILOGY

EDWARD GREEN

Copyright

A Windheim Book
Published by Windheim Publishing Inc.
8 The Green
Dover, DE 19901

http://windheimpublishing.com/

TRADE PAPERBACK Edition v. 1. October 2018

ISBN-13: 978-1-7327920-1-2

First Windheim Publishing Printing: November 2018

For Jana, who believed in me

ACKNOWLEDGMENTS

When I began this book, I knew how every step of the story would go. Reality crashed in the next day when I found that describing history and making it fun was a lot easier as a reader than a writer. If you enjoy this book, it is because of so many other people than the name on the cover. Here, I have the opportunity to thank some of them for the magic they added to my story.

To Jane Dixon-Smith from JDSmith-Design.com, whose cover designs blew me away when I despaired of finding someone who could see into my mind. You should see the ones we didn't pick. Those were awesome too. And the advice on writing, editing, and life were spot on. Next time our families go on holiday, we'll meet you in Spain.

To Kristen Tate at theBlueGarret.com, who asked the questions that made me go back and actually explain what was in my head rather than assume the reader could read my mind. And who corrected every comma error (because I suck at commas), thank you for sweeping up behind me. You held my hand through the editing process, making it, well... if not fun, then less painful than shoulder surgery. And you can still be jealous I get to drink wine while you drink coffee during our Skype sessions. I could not have done this without you.

To Perry Iles my final reader before publication. You caught all the mistakes Kristen and I could no longer see after reading the book fifty-seven times. You made my writing more concise and clearer than I could have possibly imagined. And you did it on a shortened schedule caused by my personal problems. This book is out on time because you made the time for me. I can't thank you enough.

To Derek Heaman at Historia Civilis on YouTube. You bring the Roman Republic to life with every video. Your visualizations of Scipio's and Hannibal's battles gave me the foundation for describing the action from the ground level. Keep making those videos, they are the highlight of my day every time you post a new one.

To Ernie Jones at History Den for also making great YouTube videos that inspired me. Your work gave me a starting point to research some of the tiny details of each battle and the lives of Roman soldiers. Keep up the great work. It gives me a reason to procrastinate on writing the next book.

To Nikolas Lloyd, or Lindybeige, on YouTube, your videos on Trebia and Lake Trasimene were exciting and detailed. But I really want to thank you for having ridiculously long discussions about SONAR and submarine warfare during the Battle of the Atlantic when I should have been writing. You too were an inspiration, and I hope your graphic novel about Hannibal is as excellent as your videos. I can't wait to read it. And I'm still suspicious of the whole ballroom dance thing.

To Joanna Penn, from the Creative Penn, who took the time from her busy schedule and multiple personalities (i.e., Penn Names) to encourage a new author. Your podcasts are the highlight of my week. I have learned so much from you and hope to learn so much more. Thank you for having done it all and then taking the time to share it with the rest of us. Now would you please write something fictional that doesn't give me nightmares?

And to all the others I failed to mention that supported, guided, and educated me on this journey.

And finally, and most importantly, to Jana. For every night you struggled to read my words while we snuggled on the couch. You helped me catch my own silly mistakes. For all the exasperation I caused when I get too focused on my writing to pay attention. I will get around to cleaning the flat. For forcing me to have a life when I thought mine was over. I thank you from the bottom of my heart.

Edward Green
Bonn, Germany
September 2018

AUTHOR'S NOTE

Dear reader,

At the end of this novel, I have included some information you may find useful in understanding the offices, ranks, and workings of the Army of the Roman Republic. Along with the maps, I believe they provide a useful reference to help you understand the differences between the Roman Republic and the much better known Empire. I hope you find them informative and helpful as you follow Appius, Decius, and Scipio on their journey across the ancient world.

Happy reading,
Edward Green
Bonn, Germany
September 2018

CISALPINE GAUL

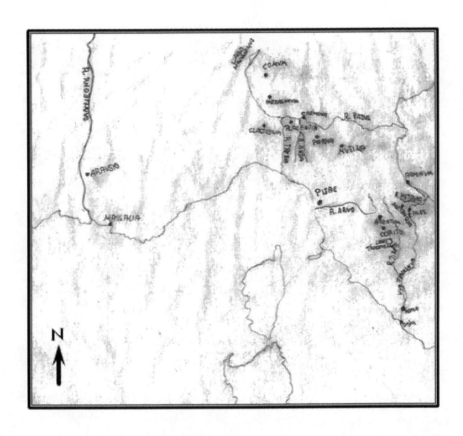

I

ELECTION

The still morning air lay heavy with moisture. The sun was just below the horizon, but its glorious radiance lighted the foggy sky like the heights of Mount Olympus. The grass crunched with frost beneath nearly ten thousand feet as the legions paraded before the colony of Pisae. The golden glow of the mist gave centurions and optios light enough to inspect the infantry while decurions inspected the cavalry. The general observed the core of his consular army preparing to march.

Publius Cornelius Scipio, Consul of Rome and Commander of the Northern Legions, sat on his roan stallion, back stiff and hands resting lightly on the reins. The four-pommeled saddle had been polished to a mirror shine that revealed the intricate embroidered patterns in the leather. I knew he was a man accustomed to privilege and wealth, for I had served him for seven years now as military tutor to his scion. The general's crested galea, the helmet of a legionary, bore red-dyed ostrich feathers as a tribute to Mars, god of war. I could follow his eyes inspecting the officers of his legion as they in turn ensured the readiness of his men.

I sat upon a gelded gray horse with a much less ornate but more practical saddle, next to my general and his seventeen-year-old son. I say my general, but that was inaccurate at this point. I had yet to join this army. In the past, I had served as decurion of a turma, leading thirty cavalrymen into battle against the Illyrians and Gauls when I was but three years older than Scipio's young son. Scipio had picked me above all other centurions and decurions seeking the patronage of a great family to teach the art of war to his son. At twenty-eight years of age I was a seasoned veteran

1

of battle on foot and in the saddle, but I had no desire for accolades or decorations. I wanted a simple life, untroubled by war or strife.

The quiet boy next to me enjoyed art and poetry but never faltered at the tasks I set before him. He had mastered the gladius and scutum, horsemanship and hastae. While not gifted, he was able to defend himself against an armed foe. At seventeen, he was readying himself to enter the legion in his first military office. Today, he would join a turma, and I would be there to guard, protect, and guide him.

The primus pilus called the formed men to attention and received reports from each century and turma. Then he turned to the general, saluted, and made his report. "All present and accounted for, sir!" he said in a gravelly baritone comfortably pitched to carry across the parade field.

General Scipio returned the salute and thanked the man. He pushed his horse forward to take the position of the primus pilus, who jogged to take his place at the head of the First Century. Scipio's trained voice raised so every man could hear. "You men have done heroes' work these past six weeks. The Insubres and Boii Gauls rebel no more against their lawful masters. You have saved the cities of Mutina, Mediolanum, and Placentia from certain destruction. You have crushed the Mutina rebellion. You should be proud."

A cheer erupted from the younger soldiers. Some slammed their fists against their shields. But I could see by the expressions of the older legionaries that they knew more was coming.

"My fellow consul, Gaius Sempronius Longus, leads his army, equal in strength to this noble host, to Sicilia. With one hundred sixty ships, he will invade Carthage and end this war." General Scipio paused to allow the men to absorb the scope of Roman operations. "Our task is to meet the spark of this war and extinguish its light for all time. We march to destroy the one who sacked Saguntum, the vile ogre, Hannibal Barca!"

The entire army roared its approval of the mission. The noise echoed across the parade ground and flowed over and through me as I watched the general sit calmly in the storm of approbation. He waited for it to subside with no movement at all. His horse was well trained, and barely flicked its ears at the noise.

"Our scouts report he moves from Iberia through Gaul with an intention to invade Rome. We will meet him before he has a chance to step one sandaled foot upon Roman soil. We will meet him and defeat him with the help of the gods. And Hannibal will be sent back to the dark gods of his people to pay for his crimes against the Senate and People of Rome!"

I saw the eagerness in the eyes of the infantry as they raised their voices in another roar of approval. The older men, those who had campaigned before, knew what the general was doing. And yet they too cheered him.

"Primus Pilus!" the general shouted as the men quieted at last.

"Yes, General," came the instant reply.

"Take charge and get these men ready to march."

"Yes, sir!" The primus pilus moved back to the center of the formation as the general turned his horse to face the boy and me. A stream of orders came from the senior centurion, and General Scipio walked his horse the few paces required to regain his reviewing position, then turned to face the men again. When the primus pilus finished shouting orders, he made a perfect about-face and saluted the general.

General Scipio returned the salute and asked, "Which of the turmae needed replacements?"

"Third and Seventh, sir," the veteran soldier responded immediately. "Third lost all three of its decurions and two other men in an ambush, sir. Seventh lost three men, but no officers."

"Very good," said the general. "I will see Third Turma now. You may carry on."

"Very well, sir," said the primus pilus, who then turned back to the formation. "Third Turma, fall out and form to my right!" He paused while the horsemen turned their horses and filed into a new formation separate from the gathered men. "We march in one hour. Centurions, take charge of your centuries and carry out your orders!"

The parade ground changed from a fairly quiet assembly of men into a rumbling roar of low voices. Centurions and their seconds, the optios, issued orders to their men, and several hundred trickled out of the formation to retrieve gear or rations for the march. All the legionaries grounded their marching yokes at the first opportunity. These burdens carried their gear, food, and some small personal effects when on the march and were the bane of every legionary's existence.

The general kicked his stallion into motion toward the men still formed to our right. The boy and I followed, coming to a halt before the small formation of mounted men. The general received the salute of the man serving as decurion today and returned it crisply. "Gentlemen," the general addressed the assembled men in a low but commanding tone, "you have been sorely used these past weeks."

The general referred to their ongoing battles with the Gallic tribes of the Insubres and Boii that had been conquered four years earlier by the general's brother, Gnaeus. The Gauls had rebelled against the Roman colonization of their lands, diverting this army from its purpose of defeating Carthage to subduing the Gallic rabble. General Scipio was now six weeks behind schedule, but that did not color his voice as he addressed the cavalrymen.

"I understand you have taken some losses recently. I provide you with these replacements." He waved his hand toward his son and me. "Asprenas served as a decurion in the Illyrian Wars, with distinction." He pointed to the two round discs affixed to my armor. "Those phalerae were earned in battle under Lucius Postumius Albinus at Apollonia and later under Lucius Aemelius Paullus at Issa. He is a brave man and a fine soldier."

Some of the cavalrymen seemed impressed by the general's recitation of my battle honors. I remembered earning those honors, so I was much less impressed by them. I recalled the gut-wrenching fear as, unhorsed and separated from my men, I had faced an Illyrian cavalryman bearing down on me. Desperately, I had slashed at the horse's mouth before the Illyrian's spear reached my chest. The horse reared in agony, blood spraying across my face, and the rider fell back, off his saddle, slamming into the ground. As he gasped for breath, I picked up his spear and used it to gut him. Then I ran into the nearby woods and hid until nightfall, all the while terrified that some enemy would discover me.

The general continued, "And this is my son, Publius. This is his first campaign, and I would see him and you successful in it."

The impressed looks turned stiff as the import of what the general had just said penetrated. Technically, all the cavalrymen came from the Equestrian class and were therefore equals. The three officers in the turmae were elected by the men. The acting decurion barely reacted, but I could see eyes widening and faces falling as these men realized their chances of promotion had just been cut by two thirds.

The general had placed these men in a quandary. Electing me, an experienced and decorated former decurion, would be an easy task, but the general quite obviously wanted the men to elect his son as another decurion of the turma, which was not so easy. These men hoped for elevation into the Senatorial class, and General Scipio was a very influential politician who could provide patronage. But his son was a seventeen-year-old boy with no experience. I could see by the looks passing between the men that they wondered what risks the inexperienced boy could inflict on them.

"I wish you Jupiter's blessings and the wisdom of Minerva," said the general and then, "I take my leave of you. Good day, gentlemen."

The decurion saluted as the general rode back toward his staff.

The younger Scipio looked at me, took a deep breath, and stepped his horse forward a pace to face his new comrades-in-arms. "Good day, sir," the boy addressed the decurion. "I am Publius Cornelius Scipio," he said, beginning the formal introductions. "This," he made a small gesture toward me, "is Appius Curtius Asprenas."

"Sir," said the decurion, "I am Marcus Decius Mus, acting decurion of the Third Turma."

"You have a proud name, Decius. A century ago, your ancestors may have saved the Republic."

"We are all lesser men now, Scipio," he said modestly. "With the addition of you two gentlemen, our number is complete. We lost all of our decurions and two other men to the Boii a week ago. Ambushed while on patrol."

"We grieve for your loss, Decius," Scipio said solemnly. "They were brave men doing their duty, as should we."

Decius nodded, but he was wary of the young man. I could see his eyes searching for a childish smirk or sarcasm; finding none, Decius continued. "We number thirty men. Let the nominations begin."

There was a brief pause, then one of the men said, "I nominate Decius for the post of decurion."

Another voice said, "I nominate Asprenas for the post of decurion."

Two other men were quickly nominated, then there was a brief lull. Decius cleared his throat and said, "I nominate Scipio for the post of decurion."

Quiet fell upon the men as Decius had decided the issue for them. For a minute, no one spoke. Then another man said, "I move that nominations be closed."

This motion was seconded and approved.

Decius again took charge. "Candidates, please space yourselves," he said, spreading the nominees apart with his arms. "Let the vote begin."

There was a brief pause while the remaining twenty-five men decided who to vote for. The men looked at each other with uncertain glances and shifted in their saddles, not wanting to commit to a decision. Then two men moved their horses into a file behind Scipio. Another fell in behind me.

A man took a deep breath, then moved behind Scipio, bringing his count to three. Another man moved behind Decius with a dark glance toward Scipio. Another moved behind Scipio, then another. Two more voted for me. Decius glowered at a block of four men, who reluctantly moved to Scipio. He had won his post, achieving nine votes. I sighed in relief.

Then another man moved behind me and one behind Decius. Decius caught the eye of the leader of a group of five and tilted his head toward me. They moved to stand behind me, securing my office.

The remaining five were not enough to decide the vote for the remaining post, though all but one filed behind Decius.

One of the other candidates said, "I remove myself from consideration" and moved his horse behind Decius.

With that, the last man finally voted for Decius and the remaining candidate conceded.

As the first selected, Scipio was now commander of the turma, with me and Decius as his deputies. I could see the men were not happy about this turn of events. But they knew the general's son must be given command. There was no other political choice.

As the election had been concluded, Decius and I turned and saluted our new commander. "What are your orders, sir?" I said with as much gravitas as I could manage.

"Decurions, appoint your optios," the young decurion said firmly.

He was prepared with a response, good. "Yes, sir." I gave him a nod of approval and turned to face the men.

Decius picked his man quickly. "Tanus," he said, pointing to the candidate who had removed himself from consideration.

I chose the final candidate as my deputy and found his name was Quintus. Scipio considered his choice for several moments, then chose the man who had first voted for Decius.

"What is your name, sir?" the new decurion asked.

"Marcus, sir," the man replied.

"Marcus, please report to the general with my compliments. Inform him that Third Turma of the First Legion is prepared in all respects for march and battle," Scipio ordered crisply.

"Yes, sir," the man said, surprised that the young man had such understanding of command responsibilities. He saluted and rode toward the staff officers surrounding the general.

"Decurions, inspect your men," Scipio ordered. "Make certain my report to the general was accurate, if you please."

We saluted, then dismounted to inspect our sections. Scipio did the same. I noted that he learned the name of each man in his section. Within a few minutes, he had gained a tentative trust with the soldiers of the turma.

Scipio had combined my military training with his native intelligence to achieve the proper distance from the men he now commanded. Years of living in a senator's household had given the boy experience directing servants and slaves, but now he had demonstrated the same light but commanding touch with men far more experienced.

It was a good beginning.

II

MASSALIA

General Scipio rode a mottled gray stallion perhaps eighteen hands high. His rust-colored traveling cloak covered glistening armor and a scarlet tunic. Ahead of him trod the vanguard of his legion. Behind were the First Legion and over ten thousand Gallic infantry. The shadows of cavalry scouts could be seen flickering amongst the trees. It had been eleven days since we marched from Pisae.

As we crested the final rise, the Gallic city of Massalia came into view. The general turned to his staff and said, "Get the camp built. I willwant all decurions and cavalry prefects to report to the forum at sundown. I will be meeting with the Chieftain of Massalia until then. Third and Sixth Turmae will escort me."

A chorus of affirmative responses came from the staff. Riding only a few paces behind the general, I looked at his son. The boy seemed not the least awkward in his perfectly formed armor, the best Scipio's immense wealth could buy, as he raised his voice to arrange the Third Turma into a double column of fifteen riders. He conferred briefly with the senior decurion of the Sixth, then allowed them the honor of leading the way into the city. The general moved his horse in behind the trotting cavalrymen, and Decurion Scipio gave the order, "At the trot, advance!"

We rode toward the wall surrounding a dun-colored city whose buildings lay in a haphazard arrangement along the sinus Gallicus coastline, what the locals called the Gulf of Lion. The wall, really a wooden palisade atop a twenty-foot-high embankment, encircled the city with both ends touching the coastline. The Volcae Gauls had used entire trees to construct the wall. We approached a massive, oaken gate hung on iron hinges between two reinforced gateposts that stood open at a span that allowed four horsemen to ride abreast.

Just inside the wall, a few citizens were building new storehouses for the Roman grain and equipment that had been arriving by ship daily, in advance of Scipio's army. The walls were made of interwoven birch or hickory branches hung horizontally between rough-hewn wooden frames. To this mesh, the villagers applied a combination of straw and clay. The roofs were sharp-peaked and high, covered in thatch. The peaks themselves were insulated with good soil, covered in grass to help keep out water. The bright green of the grass was the only contrast in a city colored in muted browns.

The streets, what there were of them, were dirt tracks winding between buildings and hills toward the docks. Most of the people stood aside as we passed, but some just stood staring at the sight of General Scipio and the rest of us riding through the city. One had to be prompted to move his cart from the road, so the general could pass. I found it all quite amusing. Rome was an orderly and clean place, if much more crowded, than this crude mud-covered city. *These are our allies?*, I thought. Decurion Scipio seemed not to notice the city or citizens, intent on his father and entourage. His eyes followed the scribes and messengers that inevitably trailed the general everywhere. *Good*, I mused, *he's watching the internal threat and trusting us to watch for external dangers.*

We rode on until we reached a large building facing an open square alongside the docks. The square was alive with activity as the crews of the quinqueremes and triremes tied to the quay wall were busy unloading sacks and crates. General Scipio dismounted and entered the building, flanked by an escort of twelve soldiers.

Decurion Scipio looked over his shoulder and said, "Dismount. See to the horses. Set a guard, then let the men relax."

"Yes, sir," I said and heard Decius echo the same. "My piles thank you for taking pity, finally," I said sotto voce.

Scipio rolled his eyes as he pretended not to hear my oft-voiced complaint. He led his horse to a water trough and let the animal drink. The men around him tended their mounts and splashed water on their dust-caked faces.

"Any idea how long we'll be here?" Decius asked me.

"The general didn't confide in me," I said. "Funny that. He usually checks his schedule with me daily."

Decius looked at my face for a moment before deciding I was joking. "Well, if he does tomorrow, please ask him to let us sleep late. I need a rest after twelve days in the saddle."

"I'll see what I can do," I said. I walked to the four men posted to watch for danger. "Stay alert, men. I don't trust these Gauls as far as I can spit."

Optio Tanus, in command of the detail, said, "Decurion, after the way Ducarius treated us, I don't think any of us trust Gauls."

"Ducarius?" I asked. "Who's he?"

"One of the Insubres rebels," Tanus said. "He's the one that ambushed us and killed the officers, sir. Big man with a red mustache that covers his whole mouth. Looks like a shaggy red bear." Tanus shuddered in remembered horror. "We'd heard stories about him from the men at Mutina. Apparently, he had a run-in with a Legate Flaminius some years back, during the conquest. He developed a serious hatred for Romans, especially officers."

"What happened, Optio?" I asked.

"Well, sir," Tanus said, "two of our decurions survived the ambush but were unhorsed." He paused for dramatic effect and said, "Then this Ducarius comes along and chops their heads off." He slashed his arm through the air twice. "Just like trimming the hedge. Like it was no effort at all. Then he gets down off his horse and collects the heads. He's got a collection of Roman skulls hanging off his saddle, you see?"

"Tanus," I said, "you're an optio now. Don't go scaring the men with wild stories."

"It's no wild story," Decius said from a comfortable seat atop a low wall at the edge of the square. "I saw it happen. And I saw the skulls hanging from the bastard's saddle."

"Even so," I said, "let's not dwell on it. Better to stay out of ambushes and away from Gauls."

Decius chuckled. "Appius, I couldn't agree more."

Scipio sat with his back against the water trough and his eyes closed against the sun. I saw his mouth twitch as Decius laughed. *Good*, I thought, *he's paying attention, without seeming to pay attention.* Now if I could just get my back to stop aching...

* * *

"Gentlemen, we have a problem," General Scipio said. "Since the fall of Saguntum last winter and the declaration of war against Carthage, we have been overly lax in tracking our enemy's movements."

The cavalry leaders of the legions under General Scipio's command shifted uncomfortably in the forum outside the command tent called the Principia. This large area set aside for ceremonies and briefings accommodated the seventy or so men and the general's attending staff easily. The space could hold an entire legion if necessary. Our group stood between two braziers filled with hot coals against the evening chill while the general stood on a small dais illuminated by several torches. The general's son stood just in front of me and Decius. We waited for the general to continue.

"We know Hannibal departed Carthagos Nova in May with ninety thousand men and some number of elephants." He allowed the magnitude of that number to penetrate his audience.

"Gods, we number but twenty thousand at best," Decius whispered, his eyes wide.

Scipio turned and quieted him with a glance.

General Scipio continued, "Our estimate, for we have no reports from reliable sources, is that Hannibal will have to subdue numerous Volcae tribes on his march to the Rhodanus. He will undoubtedly take losses and be forced to leave garrisons to protect his line of march." He turned as a group of Gauls exited the Principia. "These men have volunteered to guide our patrols and act as translators with the locals."

He turned back to the assembled officers. "I need information. That is your task, gentlemen. Find Hannibal's main force and report that location to me. Then stay in contact, reporting any movements. I will hold a third of the cavalry in reserve for rapid reinforcement. Tribune Linnaeus will have your specific assignments." General Scipio stepped off the dais and walked the few paces into his quarters.

Linnaeus stepped forward and began calling on individual decurions. When he reached Scipio, the three of us stepped forward. "Decurion, your orders are to patrol upriver to where the Volcae chief Araxes is camped, just south of the village Aurasio." He turned to point at a large Gaul who stepped forward to loom over the tribune. "This is Micah. He will be your guide."

"Hello, Decurion," the Gaul said in heavily accented but clear Latin. "I am cousin to Araxes and was raised near Aurasio. I will show you the best way there."

"Your Latin is quite good, Micah," Scipio said.

"Thank you, Decurion. I learned from some Roman traders when I was a child," the large man said with a toothy grin. "My uncle encouraged us to learn the languages of our neighbors."

"Well, I am glad he did." Scipio turned to Decius and me. "We leave at first light. Ensure we have a mount for our friend here and show him where we will form in the morning."

"Yes, sir," Decius and I said. I tilted my head and let Decius take charge of our new Gallic guide. I followed Scipio as he walked back toward our quarters down the Via Praetoria.

Scipio glanced over his shoulder and saw me following. He asked, "You have something you wish to discuss, Appius?"

"I just wanted your opinion on our new friend, sir," I said.

"If he knows the area as well as he says, we will be in good stead," he said.

"And why did we draw this assignment, do you think?" I asked.

"Testing again, Appius?" Scipio stopped in front of the horse pen in front of the tent we shared. He fed his horse a bit of sugar and stroked the beast lovingly. Then he said, "Father wants to send a message to this Araxes. Rome is here to fight our mutual enemies. I am the message and the messenger."

"Good, sir," I said. "I didn't think you had missed that double meaning."

Scipio turned to look me in the eye and said, "And he gets a professional opinion of the state of Volcae forces in your report."

I blinked. "I am sure your father trusts your observations, sir."

"Perhaps." Scipio released my eyes with a last caress of the horse's nose. "But he will want it confirmed by you." He walked toward the tent. "Make sure the guards are posted, then get some rest. We have a long ride tomorrow."

"Good night, sir," I said, then turned to find the triarii assigned to guard the horses for the evening.

* * *

The sun sparkled on the river and dazzled my eyes. We were a few hours into our patrol. The river Rhodanus flowed toward the sinus Gallicus, emptying the waters of Gaul into the vastness of the Mediterranean. The city of Massalia controlled the mouth of the river and the coastal passage past the Alps into the Roman territory of Liguria to the east. The river delta, a broad area of marsh and water some tens of miles wide, provided the city with a convenient moat to the west, while the Alps acted as a barrier to the north. It was an ideal base of operations for the Roman army.

I rode beside Scipio the younger, along the bank overlooking the river. He was quiet today. As we walked the horses, he pulled off his helmet to run a hand through sweat darkened hair that was already thinning. Scipio looked out across the river with eyes seemingly not dazzled by the bright reflections.

"Appius," he said.

"Sir?"

"We are late in arriving. I fear too late. Hannibal will not have tarried despite what our Gallic allies have been telling us."

"That is likely, but he will have had to fight through. The Gauls may be disorganized, but they fight well individually."

"True. But what if he didn't have to fight?" he asked.

"Nasty thought, that."

"Indeed." Scipio swatted absently at a mosquito that was pestering his horse and said, "While we scout north, I am afraid Hannibal has already crossed the Rhodanus and marches for Liguria."

"He would have to pass your father's army first or climb the Alps."

"Yes, and we have had no reports of Hannibal's army I know," the young man said, thinking aloud. "Is it so hard then, to climb the Alps?"

"His men would have to be part mountain goat," I said. "It's late autumn and already snowing in the passes. No place for men and beasts from Africa to march."

We rode on in silence.

* * *

The late afternoon sun glowed orange a hand's span from the horizon. We led the horses along the riverbank. Our Volcae guide, Micah, seemed unconcerned, strolling as if on a picnic instead of a military mission. It annoyed me.

"Noble sir," Micah said to the decurion. "These are my uncle's lands. Another hour to his camp."

"And the Volcae army?" Decurion Scipio asked.

"Camped on the island where the river splits and rejoins. It is the only crossing within a day's march."

"Why is the camp on the island?" Scipio asked.

"It is a good position to defend the crossing in either direction," Micah explained. "You have to cross the island to stay on firm ground. Very marshy to the north and south along the river's edge. I will show you a small path to the island from the south, but we must ride single file."

Scipio nodded his understanding.

We rode north, angling northeast and staying out of view from the western bank of the river. *No need to advertise our presence if Hannibal is actually nearby*, I thought.

We rode into the trees, the setting sun deepening the shadows to a murky twilight.

III

THE VOLCAE

We reached the Volcae camp just after sunset. It was a crude affair with campfires dotting the landscape randomly. But there was an air of tension as men sharpened weapons and seemed to be preparing for battle. Micah led us to a large tent. The guards apparently recognized him, for they did not move as he entered the tent and motioned for Scipio, Decius, and I to follow.

The tent held a large table; seated around it were several gray-bearded Gauls, one of whom greeted Micah.

"Uncle, these are the Romans sent to aid us," Micah said.

"Decurion Publius Cornelius Scipio, sir," the young decurion said, coming to attention.

"I am not familiar with your ranks. You are a bit young to be the commander of the Roman army, but that is the name I was given as the general," the large Gaul said.

"My father, sir."

"Ah! The general honors us then. He sends his blood to fight with us." The Gaul stood and embraced the decurion. "I am Araxes. We kill many Carthaginians tomorrow."

Compared to Micah's educated Latin, Araxes's thick accent was nearly incomprehensible.

"Tomorrow, sir?" Scipio said. "I was told Hannibal had yet to be seen."

"This morning, large Carthaginian army, maybe thirty thousand men, camped across river," Araxes said. "We guard ford and prepare for fight. Messages have been sent to Massalia."

"Hannibal is here? And preparing to cross?" Scipio asked.

"Yes. Probably at dawn tomorrow or the next day." Araxes grinned. "Will be a bad day for Hannibal. River is high, and crossing is narrow. They must build rafts."

"What else can you tell me about his army?" Scipio asked.

"He has some giant, gray beasts. About twenty. They make noises like the sound of a hundred horns. He has lots of horses too. Maybe five, six thousand."

"Decius," Scipio said, turning to my fellow deputy, "take your section. Inform the consul of our location and the presence of thirty thousand Carthaginian infantry with six thousand horse and twenty elephants on the west bank of the Rhodanus just south of Aurasio. Advise him that an assault across the river could occur as early as tomorrow morning. I will continue to observe and report, as ordered. My recommendation is to move the main force of the Army north immediately."

Decius read the message back to the decurion, saluted, and departed. Through the sides of the fur-lined tent I heard the sounds of men mounting and riding away.

Araxes sat again and said, "I have reported this to General Scipio already."

"Perhaps, but an additional emphasis on the gravity of the situation might inspire the general to move with a bit more alacrity," Scipio said diplomatically. "In any case, it will not slow their response. Might I see the disposition of your forces, sir?"

Araxes pointed to one of his lieutenants. "Show him our preparations." With that, we departed the tent and took a tour of the Gallic fortifications.

* * *

The riverbank sloped to meet the water in a gentle hill. Upstream and down were marshy areas of uncertain depth.

"This is where they will cross, Roman," our Volcae lieutenant said. "Only solid land wide enough for an army's crossing is three days march to the north."

"And if they wait, Roman forces from the south will smash them," Scipio said.

"Yes, Roman, but we will smash them here first," he said, grinning from beneath his bushy red mustache that reminded me of Tanus's story in Massalia.

"What if they swim the crossing?" Scipio asked.

"They die wet and tired." The lieutenant laughed loudly.

"This is an island, right? What about the other crossing?" Scipio asked.

"There is a crossing there." He pointed to the north of the Volcae camp. "But they must cross the entire river and along the north bank to get there. We have scouts posted and archers ready if they come."

"Thank you. We will walk a bit and check on our horses," Scipio said.

The lieutenant nodded once sharply then strode off toward the command tent.

"Appius, let us see this crossing to the east bank," Scipio said after the lieutenant was out of earshot.

I shrugged and followed as he led off.

* * *

The eastern crossing looked much the same as the western, with a well-worn path between the two across the island. The island itself was hardly a mile wide. Obviously, this was a path much used by the locals, for it was broad – perhaps two hundred yards wide. The only difference was the lack of several thousand Gauls guarding this crossing.

Scipio pointed to the squad of four Gauls watching the crossing by a small campfire. "Half asleep and night-blind from the fire, wouldn't you say?"

I agreed with a nod. Scipio knew, as did I, that the fire was more of a hindrance than a help as the light only reached to the water's edge and marked the position of the picket force. The main camp was half a mile distant to the southeast, and lighted by hundreds of fires.

We walked back to our horses. There we found our men picking hooves clean of stones and grooming unsaddled horses with loving care. One man handed us bowls of a thick stew and a small loaf. We ate, enjoying the rich taste of venison gravy.

After dinner, we each saw to our horses, although our men had already done so while we were away. It paid to check your own mount, usually by saving your life.

Scipio motioned for me to join him by a small fire. I sat and waited for him to begin.

"Orders for the turma. All mounts to be saddled and provisioned. Post five guards per watch. All of us to be up and mounted two hours before dawn. Questions?"

"Sir. You expect trouble?"

"These Gauls have Hannibal right where they want him," Scipio said.

"And that's a problem?"

"They underestimate him. There is no reason for Hannibal to cross here with a direct assault. It simply does not make sense."

"What do you think will happen tomorrow?"

"I do not know, but it won't be what Araxes expects," Scipio said. "The Gauls have what – five, maybe six thousand men on this island?"

I nodded at the estimate.

"Even behind walls and a river, Hannibal outnumbers them sixty to one," Scipio said. "Araxes's only hope of survival is the arrival of father's army."

"He thinks he can bottle them up at the water's edge and hold," I offered.

"Yes, and from everything we know about Hannibal, does it seem likely that he does not know Araxes's intentions?"

"I see your point, sir."

"Good. I want to be able to move at a moment's notice. Set the watch please."

"Yes, sir," I said and moved off to give the orders.

* * *

We didn't get to sleep long. About three hours after midnight, the Carthaginians began loading the rafts across the river for an assault.

"Noisy, aren't they?" I said.

"Quite," Scipio said.

We watched as the Volcae formed ranks at the riverbank to meet the Carthaginian flotilla. From the far side, arrows and slingshot launched into the night air. Screams of pain announced their arrival on our side of the river.

Our position just south of the crossing and a bit closer to the camp gave us a good angle to watch the assault force coming across the river. Mounted, we could see over most of the Volcae troops.

"They're anchoring rafts filled with archers to the south of the crossing," said one of the men.

"Assume they have a similar disposition to the north. How many?" asked Scipio, looking at me.

"Make it four hundred archers. Maybe some slingers, but they need more room and can't fire over the heads of their assault force," I said.

"Hannibal had ninety thousand men, according to our intelligence," Scipio said. More screams in the Volcae ranks announced the arrival of another volley of arrows. "He should be swarming over this crossing in the thousands, not hundreds."

"A feint?" I asked.

"Perhaps, or just probing. Seeking hidden reserves or waiting for more rafts to be constructed."

We watched as the Volcae withstood the arrow and slingshot barrage behind their round shields for half an hour. A dozen rafts were now anchored midstream, and their archers began to add arrows to the fire from across the river.

"I see what they're doing," Quintus exclaimed.

I looked at my optio for an explanation. He pointed at the line of rafts coming across the river in a single line, well north of where the Volcae waited. "Those are dismounted cavalry. You can see their horses following behind the rafts. They're building a breakwater."

"Quintus is correct, I think," Scipio said. "The horses slow the water so the rafts with the attack force can reach this bank as one force. Good eyes, Optio."

Quintus's teeth shone in the darkness as he smiled at the compliment. We all continued to watch as the battle developed. Soon the line of horses in the water was complete.

From the Carthaginian side of the river, more rafts, this time full of heavy infantry, poled into the river. At first there were two, then three, and soon there were twenty – each carrying thirty men across the river. Each raft had high sides covered with hide or wooden shields, protecting the soldiers within. Volcae arrows began to fall from the night sky, and now the Carthaginian infantry suffered and covered their heads with their shields. As the Carthaginian rafts reached the arrow platforms they had anchored midstream, a light from the northeast rose from the marshy woodland like the rising sun.

As one, we turned to see horsemen, silhouetted by the beacon, climbing out of the river. Hundreds followed, swimming alongside their horses with inflated hides buoying them against the weight of their armor and weapons. The bodies of the four pickets we had seen earlier at the eastern crossing lay where they had fallen around their campfire, their killers already mounted and forming for the charge. I saw their black skin reflecting the light from the fire. Each lighted a torch, then raced toward the Volcae camp.

Scipio shouted, "You and you," pointing to two men. "Ride south. Find the Army. Tell my father to hurry. Hannibal is crossing the Rhodanus now. He will be across by nightfall today at the latest with thirty thousand men. Move!"

The two men saluted and rode south at a gallop.

Scipio turned his mount to follow them and kicked the beast into motion. "To the south crossing! We must get to the far side before the Numidians cut us off!"

We raced to the narrow crossing and coaxed the horses into the river, water rising to our knees. Behind us rose the cries of battle as the Volcae were attacked from two sides at once. We made our way to the riverbank and watched as, on the other bank, Carthaginians pulled hundreds of rafts that had been hidden in the trees into the water.

"Appius, two men to guard the crossing. We observe until detected. Then we ride south to rejoin the legion," Scipio ordered.

I instructed two men to go back to the crossing we had just used, then turned back to the decurion. "Sir, we are abandoning the Volcae?"

"The Volcae are defeated," he replied. "Hannibal has trapped them on an island with cavalry behind and at least two thousand infantry in direct contact and thousands more reserves. The Volcae had perhaps six thousand men on that island. Surprised and surrounded, they have no chance."

"But they could hold for a day, surely? The legion might relieve them."

"The legion, unless I miss my guess, is still staging at Massalia. It will take them two days, perhaps three, to get here. We must maintain contact with the Carthaginians. See where they go from here."

"Yes, sir."

Scipio had made a decision, and had given orders that he expected to be obeyed. The boy had learned my lesson on indecision well. Now we would find out if we survived the consequences of his decision.

At a shout from the crossing, I realized that maintaining contact with Hannibal's army was likely hopeless. On the island bank, a group of Numidians sat on their wet horses, looking at us.

"Now the race begins," I said to myself, turning my horse south.

IV

FALLING BACK

Trees whipped past our heads as we galloped south along the bank of the Rhodanus. We had been galloping for ten minutes and walking for twenty, attempting to save the horses' strength. I think Scipio assumed that the Numidians' horses would be tired after a long ride the night before and the swim across the river. It was a logical assumption. But it was wrong.

A Numidian patrol caught up to us about two hours after we first sighted them across the river. There were only six of them. Their white eyes contrasted with the dark skin of their faces. They wore light leather armor and carried javelins that stabbed upward toward the sky behind each rider like the spines of a lizard. We charged them, only to realize our mistake as the first two fell, surprised by the unexpected attack.

From the thick trees and underbrush behind them erupted dozens of horsemen alerted by the sounds of our weapons striking Numidian armor. I cursed and wheeled away from the river, following Scipio into the nearest tree line to the south with the rest of the men. We rode full tilt, ignoring the low branches and protruding roots, praying for Fortuna's grace.

One of the horses to my left stepped into an unseen hole, and I could hear the bone snap as the screams of horse and man merged. I ducked lower and urged my mount to keep pace with the decurion.

We broke into a clearing perhaps two bowshots wide. Our horses, lathered and straining, raced for the far side. If we could cross the field and get into the dense trees again before the Numidians caught us, perhaps we could lose them long enough to rest the horses again. We all

21

leaned into the gallop and willed our mounts faster. As we reached the edges of the trees, I risked a glance behind. Nothing.

We slowed to a canter for a minute, then a trot after a minute more. Scipio led us deeper into the wood and angled away from the river. Five minutes later, he slowed us to a walk. I turned to count my men. I had lost two, and Scipio's squad had lost one. Now we numbered seventeen including the decurion and me. I pulled alongside his horse.

"What now, sir?" I asked.

"We rest the horses at a walk for ten minutes, then canter for ten," he said. "It's the best we can do."

I nodded, agreeing with his logic.

"Hannibal must have circled a force south to prevent the Volcae from escaping to the legion in the south. They undoubtedly have orders similar to our own. Move south and locate the Romans."

"They'll have a blocking force behind for the Numidians to fall back on," I said.

"Maybe. I'm not sure Hannibal wants to fight here though. Too easy to conceal an ambush."

I looked at the dense forest around us. "He might want to ambush the legions marching north."

"True," Scipio said. "Though our efforts may prevent that eventuality. Let us see to it then." With that, he signaled the trot and we moved south again.

* * *

We sighted no more patrols that day. By sunset, the horses were nearly blown, and all were footsore. We watered and fed them. Each man grabbed a morsel of hard beef or biscuit and a swallow of wine. Then we led the horses ever southward, into the darkening forest.

By midnight we were ready to drop. Scipio, though unused to marching afoot, seemed none the worse for wear. He posted pickets and set a watch rotation. We slept for four hours, using a crude clepsydra fashioned by Optio Marcus to keep time.

The clepsydra was a water bag with a wax stopper at the bottom that allowed only a drop of water to escape. A bowl, hung in a rope mesh below the water bag, caught the escaping water. When the bag had emptied, half an hour had passed. The guard then woke his relief, who filled the bag and began the process again. I had seen more accurate devices constructed of bronze in Scipio's home, but Marcus's contraption worked well enough for our purposes.

The final guard woke us at the end of his rounds. I chewed a hard piece of bread as breakfast. Then we watered the horses again and led them south until the sun's light brightened the eastern sky.

With the approach of dawn, we mounted and rode at a walk. I recognized some of the farms we had passed two days ago and realized we were nearly to Massalia. Either we had passed the marching legion in the night or they were still encamped at the mouth of the Rhodanus. Traveling through the forest to avoid contact with Hannibal's patrols, I couldn't be certain which.

* * *

A few miles later, the sunrise answered my question. The legion was marching north but had only just departed camp. The bright red tunics and bronze armor shone in the morning sunlight. We could see them from our hilltop vantage as they followed the course of the Rhodanus northward.

Scipio angled his horse toward the consul's standard and increased his pace. The rest of us followed, only slightly behind. Then a shout from behind let us know that we were not alone.

I looked over my shoulder just in time to see a javelin flying toward my face. Somehow it missed me, but I could feel the wind as it passed by my head. "Numidians!" I shouted.

We careened down the hill through the trees. I had lost sight of the approaching army, but I kept pace with Scipio. I rode alongside Quintus, ducking my head to my horse's mane in hope of avoiding any tree limbs. I could see his eyes were wide with fear as the hill steepened, and we had to angle to keep the slope shallow enough so the horses wouldn't stumble. We came out of the tree line onto the floodplain only to realize we had veered off course. We were still a mile or more north of the Legion.

"Make straight for the river!" Scipio shouted.

I thought he was crazy – the river was west, the army south. But I had no breath nor any time to voice the question. Scipio had made the decision, and we would live or die because of it.

Seconds later, we heard another shout from behind. I chanced a glance over my shoulder and saw twice our number of Numidians galloping to catch us with javelins in hand. The river was close. When we reached it, we would have no choice but to stand and fight.

Just as I thought Scipio would give the order to turn and face the enemy, I heard a roar to my left. I turned in time to see at least a hundred cavalry crash into the Numidians.

I reined in without orders and turned to watch. The Numidians had been so focused on chasing us that they hadn't seen the Roman cavalry cover the distance to Third Turma – just as I hadn't seen the troops because I was too busy running from the Numidians. They were caught completely unprepared for the sudden attack. I saw Decius grinning like a loon as he stabbed a Numidian who was attempting to flee.

"I am glad father was paying attention," Scipio said near my elbow.

I started, then relaxed. "I'm glad someone was. Should we go help?" I asked.

"Our horses are blown, and we have tempted Fortuna enough for one day, no?"

"You should build a shrine to her. Gods, that hill was steep. One stump or root in the wrong place and—"

"And we survived," Scipio finished. We watched as our cavalry pursued the Numidians north along the river until they disappeared into the trees. "Let us go see Father now."

As we approached the army, a patrol of Gallic cavalry met us. Scipio acknowledged their presence with only a curt nod and passed them by. I motioned for the turma to join the column behind the consul's guard as we rode up to the general himself.

Scipio and I saluted properly, and Scipio began his report. "Father, Hannibal has crossed the Rhodanus."

Scipio the elder noted the travel-worn state of his son and said, "With how much of his army?"

"He had at least a thousand light cavalry at the back of the Volcae yesterday morning that we saw. Twice that in infantry assaulted across the river, and we saw hundreds more rafts being dragged to the shoreline before we were driven off."

The General looked at me. "Your assessment, Appius?"

The boy looked at me with an impassive face that hid any detectable feeling of resentment.

"They had enough horse to send more than a hundred just to drive us off only two hours after the battle began. And obviously they are patrolling south looking for you, sir. The Volcae are no longer a threat to them. Hannibal probably has the majority of his army across the river by now, crossing unopposed."

General Scipio looked grim. "What of the terrain?"

His son answered, resuming his role as leader of the scouting party. "Dense forest with some sparse clearings. Good for concealed approaches but bad for moving formations. Skirmisher and light cavalry country, sir."

"Still, our allies count on us to come to their aid," the general said.

"Sir, our allies no longer exist," his son said quietly.

"Be that as it may. Perhaps we can catch Hannibal by the tail and harry him into the mountains. Good work, gentlemen. See to your men. Join the supply train as a close guard and get something to eat. Work enough for us all tomorrow, I think."

Taking that as our dismissal, we saluted and moved back to our men. We marched north until dusk, then established a marching camp.

* * *

Mid-morning the next day, we reached the island crossing to find... nothing. The Volcae camp was burned to the ground. Thousands of dead Gauls lay in heaps, obviously moved to clear a path for the army that had passed here. The earth was trodden bare of any grass or other vegetation. The Carthaginians were simply gone. The only indications of their losses were a few dead archers floating in the river, caught by the tall grass just south of the crossing. Any others must have floated downstream, I thought.

Decurion Scipio walked beside me as we explored what had been the Volcae camp.

I asked, "No sign of Araxes or his officers, I take it?"

"None," he said. "Any survivors must have fled into the swamp. Not that there were many, I think."

"From the number of bodies," I said, "a few hundred at best."

Scipio nodded slowly as we walked past the charred remains of Araxes's tent. "What a waste." He used his foot to push over a charred stub that had once been part of the tent frame.

"They were surrounded and fought bravely."

"They were overconfident and stupid."

I stopped and waited for him to turn and face me. "Give the dead their due, for they paid for their foolishness with their lives." I pointed to a pile of bodies waiting for the funeral pyres. "Those men fought bravely. They fought where their leaders told them to. They earned the respect of all warriors. Save your contempt for their leaders, who chose this place for them to die."

Scipio cocked his head as if my words had struck the side of his helmet. We stood there, facing each other, for several seconds. "A new lesson, Appius?"

"No, sir, an old one. A leader must make a decision and stick to it, for the lives of his men depend on it. Indecision kills, usually those being led."

"But these men are dead due to a poor decision," Scipio said.

I nodded. "That happens too. But a leader must have the fortitude to accept the consequences of his decision."

The boy looked around as if comprehending for the first time the reality of his responsibilities. "A hard lesson."

"One some never learn," I said.

Later, a group of mounted scouts returned from patrols to the east, reporting no sign of the enemy. General Scipio ordered the construction of a camp and the burning of the dead. Our Volcae guides searched through the bodies for kin or friends. Their grief, as we helped with their funeral rites, kept the mood in camp somber.

We spent the next day searching for the enemy. Only a single patrol found a hint. A village to the northeast had been burned to the ground and the survivors scattered.

* * *

The consul's tent overflowed with every officer from the First and Second Legions that evening. Save the two centurions in charge of the camp guards, all had gathered to hear the latest intelligence and the consul's guidance on what the legions would do next.

I sat with the other decurions at the right of General Scipio's dais. Ten tribunes sat on camp stools in the first row in front of their nearly one hundred sixty centurions representing the Roman infantry. To the left of the dais sat the officers of the Alae, the allied Italian and Gallic infantry and cavalry units numbering the same as the Roman contingent. At the rear, stood the mensures and archetectii, the engineer officers responsible for construction of fortifications, roads, and siege equipment.

The loud murmuring of hundreds of individual conversations ceased as the general mounted the dais followed by the primus pilus and two senior tribunes. The consul took his seat and motioned for the other officers to begin.

Tribune Marius of the Second Legion began. "Gentlemen. Our scouts have reported very little this past day." His voice was pitched to carry to the officers at the rear, so all could hear him clearly. "All indications are that the Carthaginian army passed this crossing and moved northeast into Belgae or Germanian territory. We assume they have arranged or seek further allies in their war against Rome." He summarized the scouts' reports, then sat, and the general nodded to Tribune Linnaeus of the First Legion.

He stood and spoke clearly. "Hannibal's numbers must have been reduced drastically during his opposed crossing of the Rhodanus. He must need to bolster his numbers before moving back to the coast and into Roman territory. His army cannot move far from his line of communications to Carthage and line of supply to Iberia and maintain his campaign this year." Linnaeus took his seat.

Decurion Scipio said in an uncompromising tone, "Sir, I was here two days ago and saw the Volcae preparations for battle. From what I saw, Hannibal's forces were hardly reduced at all."

General Scipio rose, with a quelling look at his son. "Officers, I would appreciate your candor and opinions at this moment. The options before us appear to be to pursue Hannibal into the north or fall back into Roman territory and await his assault next spring. I would hear your thoughts." With that he resumed his seat and waited for the discussion.

A young tribune rose at once. "General, we have the chance to corner the Carthaginians against the mountains and destroy them. We should pursue."

Another tribune spoke. "Which direction? We know not where they have gone."

And then the discussion commenced as every position was explored, torn apart, and raised anew. I found it quite tedious but remained impassive and composed as the obvious points were debated. There was only one decision and the consul had already made it. It was not a realistic option to lengthen our supply lines and pursue a winter campaign in possibly hostile territory. This discussion was pure theater. I noted that Decurion Scipio sat quietly during the entire discussion after his initial statement. He observed the interactions of the officers but took no part in the discussion. He looked like his father, interested but apart.

Finally, General Scipio raised a hand and the arguments quieted. "Gentlemen, I thank you for your rigorous examination of the possibilities." He stood and stepped to the edge of the dais. "We march for Pisae by way of Massalia at dawn. We must consolidate our forces with the two legions in the Padus Valley. There we can meet any threat next spring and shorten our lines of supply. Primus Pilus, see that all is in order for the march."

As the general departed, the primus pilus called us to attention and began issuing orders for breaking camp on the following day. I followed Decurion Scipio back to our billets when we were at last dismissed to our duties.

"So now we march for Massalia?" I asked as we walked.

He looked at me and said, "I think it is the right decision for the wrong reason."

"How so?"

"Hannibal planned this campaign carefully. You saw the assault, as did I."

I nodded.

"Do you think he lost enough men to warrant seeking new allies to bolster his forces?" Scipio asked.

I thought for a moment and said, "No. You said so at council."

"Exactly. This was his plan. And it is going according to or even ahead of schedule." We reached our tents. "And we are failing to see that."

"So, we fall back on our forces in Cisalpine Gaul and prepare for next year?" I asked.

"With confidence that he is running from us." He paused. "What if instead of running, he is herding us?"

"That would mean he is confident that he could defeat four legions in the field," I said, unconvinced. "He would need far more numbers than what we have seen."

"That or unmatched mobility and superior morale," Scipio said. "I hope he has neither, but I fear he will have both if we do exactlywhat he expects."

I pondered this a moment. "I still don't see how Hannibal can defeat us in the field with the force he has available."

"Neither do I," Scipio admitted. "But that does not mean he does not see a way." He ducked under the flap of the tent we shared. "And that is what worries me."

Scipio's observations kept sleep at bay long into the night. It would be a long march in the morning.

V

MEDIOLANUM

Thirty-seven days later we arrived in Liguria. The River Padus flowed by our marching camp, icy and fresh, waiting for the first snows of winter. The Alps loomed like snowy walls to the north, and all of Italy stretched to the south. We were met near Clastidium by a delegation from the Senate headed by Gnaeus Cornelius Scipio, the general's older brother. After a day of discussion, the elder brother departed at the head of the Second Legion, moving south toward the coast.

Our forces now halved, we camped outside the walls of Clastidium. General Scipio began the process of dividing the army into groups that would garrison the Roman villages and forts in the Padus Valley in anticipation of the rapidly approaching winter. Daily, centuries marched away from camp until only four remained, along with the cavalry. Scipio had dispatched the allied cavalry troops to serve as messengers and scouts for the outlying villages, but he retained the equites as messengers and scouts to gather his own intelligence.

Several days after our arrival at Clastidium, Scipio was ordered to report to his father at the Principia. Decius and I attended him. As we entered the tent, a servant announced us to the general. "Decurions from the Third Turma to see you, sir."

The general looked up from the scroll he was reading. "Gentlemen. I have work for you," he said, returning our salutes. "Stand at ease."

We adjusted ourselves to an attentive but less formal stance.

"First, you should know that Gnaeus has been named proconsul and assigned to Iberia. He intends to occupy Emporiae and move south to

Tarraco. He has taken the Second Legion and a newly raised Seventh Legion there to carry the war to Carthage."

"That should occupy any reinforcements for Hannibal, sir," the younger Scipio said.

"Such was the thinking of the Senate," said the general. "Now to you. Your assignment is to patrol the communication lines to Mediolanum and up to Comum. Make a loop, following the Ticinus, and return here in a week," said the general. "Any questions?"

"Any Insubres activity expected, sir?" Scipio asked his father.

"Not since Mutina, but maintain your vigilance."

"Of course, sir," Decurion Scipio said.

"While you are in Mediolanum and Comum, meet with the local dignitaries. Try to get the feel of them. I know Lucius Manlius is a bore, but try not to offend him overmuch."

"Yes, Father."

The general frowned at the familiarity of his son. "Decurion, you will investigate any rumors of trouble or discord and report them to this headquarters immediately," he said in a much more formal tone.

"Yes, General," his son answered, unruffled by the chastisement.

"Leave before first light. Dismissed." He returned to reading his scroll.

We saluted, then exited the tent to find our men.

* * *

The turma had been ordered to patrol northeast into the lands of the Insubres, Gauls from northern Italy. In the dawn light, we mounted our horses and trotted through the gate. The wind was fresh and biting and the ground frosty, crunching beneath the horses' hooves.

"We'll head across the Ticinus and on to Mediolanum," Decurion Scipio said to Decius and me.

"We sleep there then?" I asked.

He nodded. "Then we strike northwest along the river until we reach Comum."

"Where from there, sir?" Decius asked.

"Depends on what we find there. Perhaps back to camp, maybe up into the mountains a bit. I'll decide then."

He motioned to the file of cavalry following behind us as we exited the small village that was establishing itself outside the camp walls. "Flankers out!" he ordered.

The village would support the legionary and alae soldiers through the winter. It would provide a place for goods, food, and other forms of recreation. In turn it would receive the benefits of the army's protection and the gold the soldiers would spend. Such villages were common around armies in winter quarters. Until March or early April, the soldiers would be a captive clientele for the ambitious Gallic and Roman merchants.

The decurion led us forward to Mediolanum.

* * *

An uneventful journey brought us to the outskirts of a small city with a sturdy stone wall, newly constructed judging by sharp edges on the stonework and the lack of moss. Mediolanum served as the capital of Cisalpine Gaul – 'Gaul on this side of the Alps.'

"Wasn't it your cousin that captured this city, sir?" Decius asked Scipio.

"My uncle, Gnaeus. He has two legions moving into Iberia now," Scipio said.

"Good man, your uncle," I said.

"Yes, and a good general," Scipio agreed. "Let us speak to Praetor Lucius Manlius Vulso and see what information he may provide."

We rode through the gate and up the high road to the praetor's residence in the city center.

* * *

"Ah, my friend Publius," Praetor Lucius Manlius Vulso said in a high-pitched voice, rising to embrace Scipio. "So good of you to visit. Who might be these... gentlemen?" He looked at us as if we were a particularly ugly pair of cockroaches.

"Lucius." Scipio received the embrace, returning it only slightly. "These are my officers, Decurions Asprenas and Mus."

Manlius nodded curtly to each of us, then returned his attention to Scipio. "Can you stay long? We have so much to discuss."

Scipio responded coolly, "We can only stay the night. We are for Comum at first light."

"Surely you can delay for a day or so? I would so love to hold a feast in your honor and hear about your late adventures in Gaul."

"My apologies, Lucius. We are on patrol and must return within two days. Orders."

"Well, duty must come before pleasure." Manlius turned to a servant and motioned for the needs of his guests to be met. "We will, of course, provide anything my humble house can afford for your comfort, dear Publius."

Scipio accepted a goblet of wine, sipped, and nodded appreciatively. "The only thing we require at the moment is information. What news from the north?"

"We have had a few reports that something is stirring up the Gauls in the hills," Manlius said before taking a sip of his own wine. "No details really. Just that a mountain tribe, Centrones I think is the name, have been fighting with their neighbors to the north."

"Can you show me where their territory is, sir?" Scipio asked.

"Certainly." He turned to one of his scribes. "Patrarchus, fetch me the map of Cisalpine Gaul and the Northern Reaches."

A balding Greek slave scurried into the next chamber and returned shortly with a long scroll. He unrolled it onto a nearby table, weighting the corners with some smooth, polished stones to keep it open.

"Here we are," said the praetor in his high voice. "The Centrones live in this plateau area in the Alps. Quite severe weather, but the area provides enough grazing for their livestock, I suppose."

"When did you learn of this fighting?" Scipio asked quietly.

"Perhaps a week or ten days ago. Reports were sent to the Senate, of course. But with no details, it was not prudent to weight them with any special significance."

"Did you also send messengers to my father and my uncle Gnaeus?"

"Yes, of course. But with no details, the reports simply do not merit any attention." The praetor, sensing the vein of this questioning, began the process of shedding himself of this well-connected but decidedly junior officer. "Rest now. My servants will see to your needs. Dinner will be served in one hour. Please join me then."

"Of course, Lucius," Scipio said, understanding the situation at once. "Decius, Appius, attend me in my quarters after you have bathed."

With that, we were led away to the baths by a slave.

* * *

Scipio's quarters were a spacious set of chambers, decorated in the opulent style favored by our host. Rich tapestries hung on the walls, and deep cushions lined every divan and bench. Scipio seemed to ignore the luxury, preferring a simple stool near a low table.

"Gentlemen. We have little time. Please, take seats." He motioned to a bench across from him. "Appius, what did you think of the intelligence provided by our host?"

We sat on the deep cushions lining the bench, and I replied, "Very slim on detail. If that's an example of his agents' thoroughness, it's not hard to see why Mutina revolted so... unexpectedly."

"Decius?" He turned to my neighbor.

"There's a problem in the pass to the north. We should investigate," Decius said.

"I agree," the decurion said. "At first light we will depart, as I told the praetor. Once out of sight of Mediolanum, Decius will break off with two men. You will be able to move quickly and perhaps reach my father before midafternoon."

Decius nodded his understanding. "What message do I take the general?"

"I will have a message written for you to deliver. Your report will be that message and what you have heard today and this night. No embellishment or supposition. I will make the recommendation that the consul consolidate Roman forces in the region. Tell him only that further information will follow as we continue north."

"I understand, sir."

"Then see if you can pry loose additional cavalry and lead them north to reinforce us. He will probably support that course given our current information."

"And the rest of us?" I asked.

Scipio looked toward the mountains. "We go to Comum. Then we see what is afoot in the mountains." He turned back to Decius. "In any case, I'll leave word for you in Comum on where to rejoin the turma. Head directly there along the east bank of the Ticinus. At the great lake, turn east to the city. I'll have any messengers follow the same route."

"Gauls fighting each other in the mountains concern us how, sir?" I asked, probing more bluntly this time.

"This region revolted less than four months ago," Scipio said. "Our orders are to investigate any trouble in the region. I would say fighting between tribes that may spill into this valley qualifies."

I nodded. "I would say yes to that, sir."

"Good. Any more questions?"

I looked at Decius and saw only confidence. "None, sir," I said.

"Good, then let us partake of the good praetor's largesse and get a good night's rest," Scipio said, rising and moving toward the entrance.

* * *

As we rode through the city gates, I regretted the third decanter of wine I had consumed during dinner. My head ached, and I moved as if I were twenty years older. Scipio glanced at me, smiled, and ordered the trot. He was an evil bastard sometimes.

"Lucius sets a fine table, does he not, Appius?" he asked, laughing over his shoulder at me.

My only response was a quiet groan as the bouncing trot echoed the throbs in my skull.

He laughed again and led the turma along the road to Comum.

Once deep into the trees north of the city, Scipio called the halt. I motioned the flankers deeper into the wood as we three officers met for a quick conference.

Scipio asked, "Decius, you have my message?"

"In my saddlebag, sir. I'll see it to the general."

"Good. We will not change passwords until the entire turma is whole again. Your men are all clear on challenge and reply?" Scipio asked.

We said, "Yes, sir!" in unison.

Scipio smiled. "Good. Then on your way. See you in Comum in a few days."

Decius saluted, turned, and called for his escort to join him. He rode southwest, back toward the Ticinus. I watched him ride into the forest, then turned back to the decurion.

Scipio turned north and said, "Now, let us see what has these Gauls stirred up, eh?"

"Right, sir," I said.

He motioned for the turma to form for the march, and we moved at a canter deeper into the forest.

VI

COMUM

The local Insubres Gauls gave the turma as much space as possible along the road. We passed merchants pulling carts or riding wagons laden with late-harvest crops toward the city, but all cleared a path for Roman horsemen as they saw us approach. The day was cool, but the sun shone brightly and our passage was uneventful. As the sun lowered to the western horizon, we approached the small city atop rugged hills at the southern tip of its namesake lake. The road rose into the hills, twisting through switchbacks, giving the place an impression of security.

The guard at the gate passed us through with an escort of infantry and a centurion to guide us to the official residence. A runner had been sent ahead, so by the time we arrived at the impressive residence, the prefect stood ready to meet the turma. He stepped down from the portico to greet the decurion.

"Decurion. Welcome to Comum. I am Prefect Publius Lucilius Gamala," he said formally.

Scipio dropped from his horse and stood before the prefect. "Decurion Publius Cornelius Scipio, the younger, sir."

Recognizing the name, the prefect bowed slightly. "My home is honored to host you and your men. What other service may I provide?"

Scipio returned the bow and said, "Only provisions and lodging for the night. We shall be off again at first light."

"Certainly, you are welcome in my home." He turned to some servants. "See to Decurion Scipio's men." He turned back to Scipio. "If you and your officers would care to accompany me, I'm sure I can find us a cup of Falernian to quench your thirst after your journey."

36

"That would be most welcome, sir." Scipio motioned me to follow.

Gamala turned back to the steps and led the way. "You came along the south road. You were recently at Mediolanum then?"

"Yes, this morning."

"Moving quickly, I see."

"We had word of some troubles to the north. We are a patrol from the First Legion near Clastidium, recently returned from Massalia."

Gamala led us into a spacious but simply furnished chamber and invited us to sit. A servant brought a decanter of deep amber wine and three goblets. As the wine was poured, Gamala said, "Yes, the Centrones have been fighting up in their central plateau. We had a patrol up there about five days ago. We were due to send another tomorrow."

"What did the patrol report?" Scipio asked with an intensity that surprised the prefect.

"Only that the Centrones were preparing fortifications and moving men into positions to guard their passes. Their village is located in a low valley – well, low for the Alps – guarded by two narrow passes at either end. When threatened, they bottle up the passes and wait for the snow and ice to kill their enemies."

"And word of this was sent to Mediolanum?" Scipio asked.

"Of course. I knew we weren't threatening them. The Insubres, Cenomanii, and Boii" – the Cisalpine Gaul tribes of northern Italy – "have been more concerned with Rome than their neighbors to the north. It seemed probable that one of their northern neighbors was threatening their borders."

"How many in your patrol tomorrow?" Scipio asked.

"Ten men and a decurion to lead."

Scipio glanced at me then back to Gamala and said, "I would be glad to accompany your patrol, Prefect."

Gamala looked a bit nonplussed at this diplomatic phrasing but said only, "That is certainly possible, Decurion. Your rank would make you senior, I believe." Legionary ranks always superseded provincial garrison ranks in practice.

"Your man knows the terrain and the people, sir," Scipio said skillfully. "I would be happy for his knowledge and guidance."

"And he will be quite happy with your numbers, I am sure," Gamala's shoulders relaxed and he turned to signal a messenger. "I will inform him of your intentions."

"I would be grateful." Scipio said smiling.

"I believe dinner is ready. I'm sure it is not quite up to your standards, but it is the best we have here in Comum," the prefect said, rising.

"Appius and I have been eating nothing but camp fare or hard tack for three months. I'm sure it will be delicious."

And it was. Roast lamb, vegetables, and a warm bread that smelled wonderful and tasted better. The food was accompanied by very good wine that more than satisfied our appetites. The conversation was genial as Gamala was a pleasant host. Though I drank only a single goblet of the wine, it was delicious. Scipio's eyes twinkled as he noticed me switch to water. We turned in early to rest in modest but comfortable rooms. It was a good evening.

* * *

In the morning, Decurion Cato met us in the stables. His men were properly turned out in full kit. Obviously, he was trying to impress his legionary counterparts. The decurions exchanged salutes.

"Good morning, sir," Cato said stiffly.

"Good morning, Decurion Cato." Scipio ran his eye down the line of Cato's men. "Your men look to be in excellent condition."

Cato noted the lack of condescension in Scipio's voice. "Thank you, sir."

"You would not be Marcus Porcius Cato?" Scipio asked.

"The same, sir," said Cato with surprise.

Scipio said, "Our fathers served together. I remember his stories. It is a common name, but I thought you looked familiar."

"I am sure we know many of the same people in Rome, Decurion."

"Shall we enjoy a morning ride then?" Scipio asked with a grin. "We can discuss our mutual acquaintances to pass the time."

Cato, unable to resist the effort to be won over, said, "Of course, sir. If your men will follow us. We'll see you up to the Centrones' village."

Cato led the way toward the city gate at a brisk walk. His men followed in two files, and we followed in kind. Once out of the city, we turned west along the foothills and increased pace to a quick canter, enjoying the morning sun as it burned away the low fog over the lake.

Sparse lines of trees bordered neat farms that covered the rolling hills in every direction. It was beautiful country, no doubt. All the fields had been turned after the autumn harvest, so the earthy smells of loam and wood smoke from the small farmhouses gave a pleasant aroma as we passed quickly along the path to the Ticinus. By midafternoon, the horses were lathered and we climbed a fairly substantial hill, revealing a lovely view of the River Ticinus.

"We can camp at the lake's edge, sir," Cato said, pointing to trees hiding the river's path to the northwest.

"That will be good enough, Decurion," Scipio said, still formal to ensure Cato's men understood he respected their leader. "I will send off a report from our campsite, and by morning my last messengers will have rejoined us."

"There's a small village nearby. Perhaps we can buy a haunch or some wine for the men," Cato said.

"Excellent suggestion. They may have more current news of their neighbors."

We rode on for two more hours, slowing as we entered the thickening wood near the lake. Finally, we entered a large clearing containing sheep pastures and a cluster of houses atop a small hill, fenced and tidy. Apollo's chariot descended behind the snowcapped mountains across the lake.

"Decurion Cato, have the men establish camp where you think best. Then if you would join Appius and me, I think we should pay a call on our Gallic friends there." Scipio indicated the houses.

Cato rapidly gave orders to establish a secure campsite by the river, set the watch rotation, and detailed four of his men to act as escort for the decurion's party. "Ready, sir?" he asked Scipio.

Scipio nodded and turned his horse toward the nearby houses.

As we rode up at a walk, it took a few minutes for anyone in the village to take note of us. The first to do so was a small boy throwing rocks at a pile of blocks he had piled up as a target. At the end of one of his throws, he turned and saw the seven of us and his eyes went wide. He yelled something in the Gallic tongue and ran into the nearest house. By the time we reached the house, four adults had emerged from inside. Stepping forward to meet us were three large men and a woman, who sent the boy off to the other houses in the village – no doubt to spread the alarm.

The escort peeled away in pairs to guard the approaches to the village, while keeping their officers in sight. We dismounted and led our horses to meet the villagers. Cato, who had been here before, whispered, "The large man in the middle is Doiros – the other two are his brothers. The woman is his wife. I know them slightly."

Scipio nodded, then stopped the party five paces from the villagers and removed his helmet. He ran his fingers through his sweat-dampened hair before saying, "Good day, gentlemen, lady." He addressed the large man with a beard, matted and graying, covering his thick chest. "I understand your name is Doiros, sir?"

The man nodded in assent. He wore a rough-spun tunic of mottled brown, leather breeches, and ankle boots. His arms were strong, though not defined – as if they were small tree limbs made of oak.

Scipio smiled. "I am Decurion Scipio of the First Legion. I would speak with you if you can spare the time?"

"We know Cato. We don't know you, Roman. What is your purpose here?" Doiros asked Cato in thickly accented Latin.

"We merely patrol our borders. We seek conversation, perhaps a bit of trade if you have some food or wine to spare," Scipio said, interrupting Cato's reply. "Would you allow us to secure our horses to that tree?" He indicated a small tree, obviously used for climbing by the village children given the scuffed bark and low, wide limbs.

Doiros nodded. I gathered all the reins and led the horses to the tree. With a quick loop, I secured them to a branch with a slipknot, in case we had to leave quickly.

Scipio continued, "We'd be interested in a few jars of wine, if you have any?" walking closer to Doiros with his hands well away from his weapons.

"We have some. Maybe a haunch or two of lamb as well," Doiros said, relaxing as the Romans continued to offer no threat.

"Good. Our patrol will be glad of it. Hard tack and biscuit are good for survival, but not so good for morale." Scipio's smile grew broader. "Cato here has told me of the beauty of this part of Insubres territory, but one must see it to truly understand. Your farm has a wonderful view."

"We are fortunate in our land, Roman. Which is why Romans take it."

"I will not debate you on this topic. I only admire the landscape and your beautiful farmland," Scipio said, trying to allay the recent wounds of the conquest which his uncle had made only four years prior. "Perhaps you would be good enough to show me the best vantage point from which to view your home and farm?"

"We were about to have our meal. Let us be done with trade, Roman," Doiros said, directing the conversation back to business.

"Of course." Scipio turned to me and said, "Appius, see to it."

I stepped forward and introduced myself. I haggled for about five minutes over two lamb haunches and six jars of wine. In all it cost me twelve sestertii, and I counted out the silver coins into the hands of Doiros' brother Vectitos, who led me off to the smokehouse to the side of the house. By the time I had given my load to one of the escorts and returned, the decurions and Doiros had entered the house and sat around a large rectangular table. Vectitos motioned for me to sit next to him, and he poured me a cupful of the local wine in a wooden goblet. I sipped and found the wine surprisingly good. Apparently the local Gauls knew a thing or two about grapes.

"What news have you since my last visit, Doiros?" Cato asked politely. "It has been more than ten days since my last trip through here."

"Ducarius visited a week ago," said Doiros.

"Is he not a leader of the Insubres that rebelled not long ago?" Scipio asked.

He had been paying attention to the stories his men had been telling, I noticed. *Good.*

"The same. He is a cousin to my wife, but no friend of mine, Roman," Doiros said, spitting on the floor. "He had a meal and was off to hide in the north. Out of reach for the Romans, I think."

Scipio smiled politely but did not rise to the bait. "I am sure it is better for everyone if he stays outside of Roman territory." The silence lingered after that statement. Doiros and Scipio exchanged bland glances while everyone else eyed one another warily.

Cato, obviously uncomfortable, broke first. "Any news of your family, Doiros?"

"My cousin Bimmos and his wife visited here two days ago," Doiros said. "They fled after a fight with some black-skinned cavalrymen and some northern Gaul warriors that passed through their lands." Scipio's eyes went sharp at this statement. "He said their numbers were endless. It took two days for the entire lot to pass his home."

Cato, nodding understanding, asked, "They came in this direction?"

"Only direction to come from the north. Unless they be mountain sheep," the Gaul said gruffly.

Cato looked at Scipio and back to Doiros. "Did he say where they went after passing?"

"He thought they camped at the north end of Verbanus."

Scipio looked confused and turned to Cato.

"The big lake, sir. They are on the other side of the lake from us."

Scipio turned to me, eyes narrowed in thought, and said, "Hannibal is here in the Padus Valley."

"And your father has dispersed the army to winter quarters," I said.

"If Hannibal moves south in force, Father will not be able to withstand the attack," Scipio said. "He will need time to recall the garrisons." Turning back to Doiros, he said, "Sir, it is likely a battle will be fought near here in the coming days. I would advise you to take your family elsewhere until the issue is decided."

Doiros scowled at that. "I will not do that. No man will drive me from my home."

"Sir, if what you say is correct, Hannibal Barca and his army are but a few miles from here." Scipio lowered his voice a bit and tried to soothe the Gaul's ego. "Doiros, you may be a brave man, but only an army can face such numbers. A month ago, I saw a Gallic army utterly destroyed by that same force. You cannot hold here and survive."

Doiros looked down at the table. "We will not leave."

"Good luck to you, sir." Scipio rose, and Cato followed suit. "I wish you well. Our thanks for your hospitality."

With that uncertain end to the conversation, I opened the door and followed Scipio and Cato from the house. We mounted.

Doiros asked, "You will not stay for a meal, Roman?"

Scipio said, "I thank you for your information, Doiros, and your hospitality. I apologize for not staying for dinner, but I must see to my duty."

"Farewell, Roman," Doiros, said standing on the threshold of his home.

We turned our horses toward our camp and spurred them into a gallop. Minutes later, we reined in. "Appius, get everyone together," said Scipio.

It was a sign of his agitation that he failed to notice the men gathering of their own accord at our abrupt arrival. "Yes, sir." I raised my voice, "Optios, form the men, on foot here." I indicated a line in front of me.

In seconds, the men fell into a rough formation and Scipio began. "Men, we have just learned that Hannibal and his army are only miles north of us." He paused to let the shock of those words sink in. The only response was stunned silence. "Tomorrow morning, we will begin scouting. The general sent us here to investigate anything unusual – I think a Carthaginian army qualifies as unusual."

Marcus, bless him, chuckled at the poor jest.

Scipio continued, "We must remain undetected for as long as possible." He turned to Cato and said, "Decurion Cato, I am assuming full authority over you and your men."

"I understand, sir," Cato said. "You have our full support."

"Thank you," he said. "Appius, pick two men. Send them south along the route we discussed with Decius. Tell the general that Hannibal is in the Padus Valley, encamped at the north end of Lake… what was the name again?" he asked, looking at Cato.

"Verbanus," Cato supplied.

"Verbanus. I intend to scout and report this force. I request immediate reinforcement. Specifically, I request the cavalry reserves. I need them to scout effectively."

I chose two men and had them repeat the message verbatim. "On your way then," I said. "And don't spare the horses."

Cato posted the guards for the evening. I slept fitfully, knowing it was going to be a long day tomorrow.

VII

LAKE VERBANUS

The sun rising in the eastern sky transformed the morning fog into a brightness of rose and gold, fighting the efforts of the cavalry soldiers to remain concealed. Two of Cato's men led the group, staying just within sight of the others, while the majority trailed in a loose wedge formation spread to ensure support to any individual while giving a wide view of the countryside. Two more followed the main force, guarding against any overtaking force. We were in enemy territory now.

Each man rode at the walk, straining to hear sounds that would reveal enemy scouts nearby. The closer to the reported camp, the more strained our senses became. Scipio gave no indication of stress or anxiousness. He sat his horse as if taking a ride on his father's estates in Campania. But his eyes saw everything. He slowed as part of the line entered denser underbrush and adjusted spacing when passing through open clearings. During his training, I assumed he had been going through the motions when we performed this most difficult task with his father's household guards. But Scipio had obviously retained my lessons. He controlled the turma as well as experienced men twice his age.

Cato and I took turns patrolling the line of advance and checking the flanks. One of us was always near Scipio and the other pushing out. I was forward when one of the point scouts signaled halt. I watched him slowly dismount behind a small, densely wooded hill. I checked behind to ensure the signal had been passed, then dismounted.

The scout had tied his mount to a tree and walked deeper into the forest. His partner led his horse to a tree nearby and did likewise. I moved forward and did the same. Both men had disappeared within moments of passing the outer line of trees. I waited, not wanting to disrupt their practiced drill. I looked back to see Cato adjusting the men to create a secure perimeter for the brief halt.

Scipio remained mounted, observing the turma with impassive patience. I caught his eye and his only response was a slight nod. *Good*, I thought, *he remembers that silence before contact is the key to surveillance.* I turned back to the point men and saw one waving for my attention.

He signaled enemy in sight and the need for silence. I passed this to the others. Scipio approached at a walk, dismounting as he reached my position. Cato moved to the formation's center as was proper, I noted.

Scipio motioned for me to accompany him, and we walked to the scout. He led us to a point just below the crest of the small hill, then lowered to a slithering crawl. At that pace, we made our way to the top, behind some dense brambles between two large birch trees.

I caught a flash of color to our left, and we found our guide's companion. Carefully, we slid abreast of his position. He slowly raised a hand to point ahead and slightly to the right.

I saw nothing for a few moments. Then a distant flash of motion revealed the Carthaginian position. As my eyes adjusted, I saw perhaps two dozen infantry, encamped and looking quite the worse for wear. Several were bandaged and moved stiffly or with limping strides. I saw no guards or pickets.

After a few minutes, Scipio motioned us back. We crawled back below the crest, then crouch-walked back to the horses.

"Soldier, return to your fellow. Report any changes," he ordered in a low voice. Then he signaled Cato to join us. When Cato arrived, Scipio gave his orders. "Each of you take ten men. Appius, spread your section west to the edge of the lake. Two-man teams. Penetrate the pickets if there are any. I want a count of numbers and type, condition of enemy troops, and anything else that you see that is out of character. Cato, your men know the terrain better. Circle east and do the same. I will remain here with the rest as a reserve. We will watch them until nightfall, then fall back here. I want as wide an observation as possible without compromising our position. Take no chances – fall back quietly if you must. Questions?"

Cato asked, "How far do I take my men east and north?"

Scipio said, "As far as you think prudent. The general needs an accurate assessment of the force Hannibal has assembled before us. All of our information is vital." He paused for a moment, thinking. "Don't cross the Alps."

Cato blinked, then a smile lit his face as he realized the decurion had made a joke. "I'll try to remember that. Those are the big hills to the north, right?"

"Correct, Decurion." Scipio returned the smile with one of his own. "Both of you, be careful, be quiet, and get us intelligence. This is likely to continue for some days. Make sure your men know to rest in turns. See you at midnight."

Scipio looked at the optio holding the reins of our horses. "Marcus, set up that clepsydra. We will be here for a while."

The optio nodded and began assembling the water clock with the help of the signifier, who planted the turma's standard into the soft ground with a soft *thunk* before getting to work.

We each moved to our sections and gave orders. Then we moved off to our new tasks. Scipio stood beside his horse, absently stroking the smooth neck without any apparent concerns that Hannibal's army was over the next hill.

* * *

"They don't have pickets out at all, sir," Cato reported that evening. "It looks as though they've been mauled."

"No reports of elephants or siege equipment either," I added.

"Let me understand this, gentlemen," Scipio said. "Hannibal has ten thousand men that we can see here, most wounded or showing signs of rough handling, no pickets to speak of, and no indications of an intention to move?"

Cato said, "He probably has more numbers. I just couldn't go further without missing the return deadline."

"Noted. Get your men back in place before dawn. Appius, give Cato two of your teams. Cato, push a bit further north. See if you can find an end to them. I want to know where their cavalry is."

"Did I see Decius as I arrived?" I asked.

"You did. I sent him up the hill with a relief team for Cato's men watching the first camp we saw."

"What word from the legion, sir?" I asked.

"The general has ordered the garrisons at Mediolanum, Cremona, and Placentia to assemble and join him on the banks of the Ticinus about half a day's march south of here. He has recalled all of the First Legion from winter quarters," Scipio said. "The legion broke camp yesterday morning and will arrive there tomorrow evening at best, the following day at worst. Most importantly, he has asked the Senate to recall Consul Sempronius's army from Sicilia."

"We are still a bit outnumbered until Praetor Manlius's men and the rest of the legion arrive," Cato said.

"True. Still, we have an advantage at the moment. Now is the time to push. I think my father will, once his forces are concentrated again."

"What now, sir?" Cato asked.

"I shall send another messenger south tonight with your reports, gentlemen," Scipio said formally. "Do you have anything to add?"

We both responded, "No, sir."

Scipio nodded. "Dismissed then. Get the men in position, get back here, and take a nap. I'll need you both tomorrow."

* * *

I spent the next day moving between the lake and Scipio's command post, checking on the men. Around midday I walked with Decius toward the hill.

"Scipio seems a good man, if a bit stiff, eh?" he said to me.

"That's his father's doing," I said. "It's hard to be a great man's son, I suppose."

"How long have you served the Cornelii gens?"

"Since my grandfather's time. He was a centurion in the consul's father's legion. He rose to the rank of primus pilus. The consul promoted him on the death of his father as a reward for faithful service. My father married into the Cornelii, and I have served the consul for eleven years."

We walked for a while in silence, then Decius asked, "So you've known our decurion his whole life?"

I nodded. "His father made me guardian and teacher on the boy's tenth birthday," I said. "What of you, Decius?"

Decius shrugged, "My family is and always has been of Equestrian rank. My father's estate is south of Rome along the Tiber. My wife and son live there. It's a lovely place, full of olive trees and rolling hills. A good place to raise a family." Decius smiled longingly, then asked, "And you, Appius? Do you have a wife?"

"No," I said. "Never had the time."

"A wonderful thing, a wife." Decius chuckled. "It's nice to have someone make a fuss when you come home, cook you meals, make you feel like a man. You should try it sometime."

I cocked my head at him and said, "I'll keep that in mind when I no longer feel like a man."

Decius stopped and looked at me for a moment. I kept my face impassive. The he laughed again. "Your jokes are going to take some getting used to, my friend."

"A pity," I said, and Decius laughed some more.

We trod the now worn path into the camp and toward Scipio's headquarters, which consisted of a low table with three camp stools arranged around it. We saluted and Scipio invited us to sit with a small gesture.

"Gentlemen, your reports," he said quietly.

I went first. "The enemy are tending their wounded and pack animals. They show no signs of organizing for a march."

"Perhaps they are waiting for something," Decius said.

"And our men?" Scipio asked.

"They are doing well considering the cold camp and lack of movement."

"We will have to move the horses if we stay another night," Decius said.

A horse at the gallop rode straight to the decurion's table. The soldier dismounted and saluted quickly. "Sir, Decurion Cato reports enemy cavalry moving this way. Looks to be in force. At least a hundred."

Scipio stood. "Any further information, soldier?"

"Cato said they were Gauls, sir."

"See to your mount. Dismissed," Scipio said. The soldier moved off to brush down his lathered horse. "Decius, pull your section back here and prepare the mounts for withdrawal."

"Yes, sir." Decius saluted and moved east at a run.

"Appius, your men will stay in place. When Decius returns here, I intend to fall back along the Ticinus until I find a defensible location or the legion."

"I understand, sir."

"Cato will fall back on your men and together you will fall back on my position. The Numidians will be hunting soon – this Gallic rabble is just to flush us out." Scipio swept his hand in the direction of the approaching cavalry. "Do not allow yourself to be pinned against the river and stay in front of them. I'll need you when Father arrives."

"Yes, sir. I'll keep them off our backs."

"Good. I know you will, old teacher. I trust you to control the men during a retreat. It will be a difficult task," Scipio said, clapping a hand to my shoulder. "Now send Cato's man back to him. Tell Cato to fall back slowly toward the Ticinus, maintaining contact with the Gallic cavalry. If he sights Numidians, he is to send a messenger at once. Otherwise, he is to continue observations only."

I saluted and went to give the assignment to Cato's messenger. Then I went to check my mount personally. I checked my section's mounts alongside the man assigned to care for them. By the time we finished, Decius had returned with his men.

After ten minutes of packing and tending to the horses, Decius's section was mounted and prepared to ride. Scipio climbed into his saddle and walked his horse to my side. "Appius, when Cato arrives, it's likely to become quite interesting here. Send them on ahead of your men. You'll have a better chance to pull back since your men will be better rested."

He's nervous or he wouldn't be pointing out the obvious to me. "I'll play rear guard, sir. Those men of Cato's are good, but they aren't legionaries. I'll make sure we play our part." I knew my men would be sacrificed if Fortuna failed to smile upon us.

"Very good," Scipio said, and then raising his voice slightly, "We ride!"

The force left at a walk, angling southwest toward the Ticinus. I watched them until they moved into a canter and quickly disappeared into the brush. Then I turned to the soldier guarding the horses. "Optio Marcus, take your mount. Lead ten horses toward Cato's position. I want him to be able to retreat quickly when it's time."

He grabbed the lead line and fastened ten horses to it quickly. Then he mounted and rode off at a walk, leading the garrison cavalry's mounts behind him.

I did the same for my own men to the west, hiding pairs of mounts in copses of trees just south of each observation post. It was better to take the risk of the horses being seen and having them closer to the men than to have them muffled by distance from the enemy camp. With that task accomplished and my men informed of our assignment, the trying part began. Waiting for the enemy to act went against the training instilled by years of military practice. It was always difficult to do something against the grain.

By the time night had fallen and a dim quarter-moon had risen, every sound seemed to be an enemy looming in the darkness. Finally, Marcus returned. He led his horse, walking quietly to the base of the hill where I was stationed. Together we waited for news from the east.

VIII

AMBUSH ALONG THE TICINUS

The moon reached its zenith and sank toward the western horizon. It was perhaps two hours before dawn when movement caught Marcus's eye to the east. I hadn't seen it, but his hand upon my shoulder showed me where to focus my searching eyes. A moment later, I saw shadows cross before trees in the distance. We stood motionless, weapons long drawn and resting loosely in our hands. Finally, we heard two snaps and a scrape of leather against wood. It was the entry signal.

Marcus responded with three snaps. "Come in one at a time," he said softly.

Shadows approached and soon became men, leading their horses by the reins. First one, then two and so on until Cato stood before me. "Good to see you, Appius. Our friends are close behind us."

"Do they know we are here?" I asked.

"Don't think so," he said. "They started moving an hour ago. We keep two men back to watch them as they approach. Gauls are good at moving in daylight, but they don't do well on horseback at night. Lots of noise."

I pulled Marcus in with a tug on his reins. "Leave one of your men with Marcus here." To Marcus I said, "Show him the drill." I turned back to Cato, "Move your men south and west to the Ticinus." I waited while Cato assigned a man to stay with Marcus. "The decurion will have found the Legion or a good position by now. Be looking for him and Decius."

"Understood," Cato said and grasped my arm. "May Fortuna smile upon you."

"Likewise," I said, returning the embrace. Cato moved off with his men. "Marcus, when you see movement, follow Cato's men. I'm pulling the rest of the section south along the river. Meet us there."

"Yes, sir," he said softly.

I led my horse westward to the next observation point. By the time I reached the last team, the sun was brightening the eastern sky. With nine men, we mounted and headed south a bowshot from the banks of the river.

* * *

Marcus raced across the clearing on his dappled gray horse with his companion close behind. They entered the tree line just before a dozen mounted Gauls broke through the trees on the far side. The two riders pulled up as they passed our horses. We had spaced ourselves wide, just inside the wood line, to give the best view across the clearing.

Marcus saluted. "Had to chance the noise, sir."

I nodded. "Understood. Head south and report to Cato or one of the other officers. Take Cato's man. We are pulling back but maintaining observation."

"Pulling back but maintaining observation. Right, sir." Marcus turned his horse and they rode south at a walk with my report.

I turned back to watch the Gauls. They had obviously heard something, but their gazes around the darkened clearing told me they didn't know what the noise was or where it was coming from. After some discussion, a big Gaul with a bushy mustache slammed his fist into the shield of one of the others. That seemed to end the discussion. They broke into two groups and began to patrol the perimeter of the clearing.

"That's enough," I said. I signaled the section to form up, and the men moved closer in two files. We walked south to the next clearing to repeat the process.

* * *

Things were going smoothly. On the fourth repetition of sighting the enemy, withdrawing, and finding another concealed position, Marcus rejoined us.

"Sir, Decurion Scipio says he has established an ambush position. We are to withdraw to his position and act as a blocking force to the south."

"You have seen the position?" I asked.

"Yes, sir. He's in a dense tree line near the top of a good-sized hill overlooking the river. We're to leave a trail that will lead the Gauls along the banks of the river. At his signal, we turn and give them a sharp rap on the nose. Then he'll attack their flank." Marcus slapped his fist into his palm in demonstration. "All of us withdraw south to the legion's marching camp about half a day's ride south."

"Understood. Good report." I busied myself informing the section of the plan. When that was complete, I said, "Marcus, lead off."

We started at a trot and soon advanced to a canter. In a short time we came into view of a lovely wide bank along the Ticinus, with a steep hill to our left. Our horses left unmistakable prints in the soft turf. Behind us, the sounds of horses at the gallop and shouts told me that the Gauls had finally realized that Romans were nearby. I raised my hand to order the gallop and we raced south under the warm sun and puffy white clouds that would have been perfect for a summer outing with fine ladies in this beautiful countryside.

I chanced a look over my shoulder and saw the first Gaul to break cover in sight of my men. He was a large man with a dark beard, wearing a metal helmet. His legs hung down nearly touching the ground on his stout black and white horse. His round shield had a metal boss and was painted black and white. I saw him open his mouth wide and pump his right hand into the air before drawing a long sword. Then I was around a bend in the hill and the Gaul was out of view.

Marcus led us toward a heavy copse of trees along the riverbank. He pulled in hard as the last of the section passed behind the dense trees. "This is it, sir!" he said over his shoulder, grinning. We were hidden from the sight of our pursuers. It was time to turn the tables.

I quickly organized the men into two even files of five. "When the signal sounds, follow me and stay tight. Form a wedge as soon as we clear the trees. We attack and pass through the enemy line. We will turn after Decurion Scipio's force strikes from above. Then we retreat south."

The only sound now was the horses and men trying to catch their breath. I searched the hillside for the man assigned to signal the attack but saw nothing. We waited. I thought of another day long ago – when a newly promoted decurion led his turma in an ambush that went horribly wrong – then firmly suppressed the rising terror. I looked at my men and forced a smile to my face. They were good men and deserved a calm, competent commander. They had me instead. So I gave them my best facsimile.

After a few minutes, everyone's breathing had calmed to something like normal. Then a Roman soldier, the signifer of the turma, appeared on the hillside waving a scarlet pennant. "There's the signal!" I said drawing my sword. "At the trot – forward!"

We advanced around the trees and spread into formation. I checked both wings and signaled canter. Then I saw the Gallic cavalry – about fifty men in various combinations of armor and fur, some carrying long swords alone and some bearing shields. All were riding along the river toward my men, perhaps a bowshot distant, in a clumpy line of threes and fours. I locked eyes with the leader of the first group of three. It was the same man I had seen over my shoulder before. In the sunlight, I could see his mustache was a fiery red. I aimed my sword for his face and yelled, "Charge!"

I could see the surprise on my target's face as my horse closed the gap between us. I felt more than saw my section accelerate to stay with me. I could see the bright green moss churned to clumps of mud as the horses' hooves dug into the ground to push forward. Then I noticed the white decorations, bouncing from leather thongs on the Gaul's saddle. They were skulls.

My target looked over his shoulder to shout something, then waved his sword in a quick circle before kicking his mount into a faster pace. I could see some matted grease in his gray speckled beard. His eyes were crystal blue, shadowed by a heavy black brow and unkempt flowing hair. His sword's point lowered to the charge and he leaned forward, urging his mount to close the distance.

I ducked low over my horse's mane and felt the breath of air as the Gaul's sword passed over my head. I thrust my sword into his armpit and felt the impact throughout my body as it ripped free. Then I was past the first group and racing toward the next.

The mossy bank was wide enough for about ten horses side by side. The Gauls struggled to form a line as my men cut through them. We may have been outnumbered five to one, but surprise was on our side. I chose a new target and forced my mount to stay at a gallop. I knew speed was the key to this attack. This Gaul carried only a sword and was much younger than the first. His sword brushed aside my attack, and I felt my horse stagger as it struck home on the saddleback at the base of my spine. Only the hard leather of the saddle saved me from having my back broken.

Then we were past the last of the Gauls. We continued at the gallop for another ten heartbeats. I looked right and saw an empty saddle and left to see another Roman face spattered with blood. I pulled up and wheeled. Two of my section had been unhorsed. One was a headless corpse I could see a few yards distant. The other was standing, facing three mounted Gauls. It was Scipio's optio, Marcus. He was backing toward the river. As the Gauls approached, he jumped into the river to avoid their attack.

The remaining Gauls were turning their mounts to pursue us into the trees to the north. The horses snorted, and we readied ourselves to receive their charge. The Gauls had recovered from their initial surprise and were coordinating their attack this time.

We stood our ground, giving them time to form three ragged lines. This time, there would be no passing through for us. The battle would devolve into a melee of individual fights and the enemy numbers would finish us – if Scipio's maneuver was not perfectly timed. The Gauls shouted and began their charge.

From the hillside, the rest of the turma roared a war cry and charged down upon the Gauls before they had covered ten paces. While the Gauls were well formed for an attack on my section, the three lines were vulnerable against this flank attack. Scipio's men crashed into the Gallic cavalry, who could not turn in time to meet the new threat.

"Charge!" I shouted, slamming my heels into my horse's flanks. I chose the young Gaul who had nearly killed me earlier as my target. He was engaged in a melee with two Romans by the time I arrived. My horse crashed into his, and he was thrown by the shock. One of Cato's men stabbed down but missed his stroke as the Gaul rolled under his horse, stood, and stabbed upward with his long sword. Cato's man died but had distracted the Gaul long enough for me to turn and thrust my sword into his eye as he whipped around to face me.

Scipio had remained on the hillside with the signifier to observe the ambush. I glanced up to see him shout and point to the south. I assumed he was signaling the retreat, according to the plan.

"On me! Withdraw!" I shouted, and the order was echoed by men around me. The Gauls had run north or into the river. I saw Marcus dash from the river to grab the reins of a Gallic horse and mount it to rejoin the fight. He had retrieved a sword from a Gaul and was making his way to my side.

I pointed my mount south and coaxed him through the dead and dying. We had done well. We had killed or wounded perhaps half of the Gauls for the loss of five men dead. Others were wounded but still able to ride. We formed into two files and trotted south as Scipio joined us.

"Numidian cavalry to the south!" Scipio shouted as his horse pulled alongside mine.

I stared uncomprehendingly at him.

"Do you hear me?" he shouted. "There are Numidians to the south of us!"

"How… why?" I said dumbly.

"It does not matter. We must pass through them and then continue flying south to the legion," Scipio said more calmly.

"Halt!" I ordered, and the horses and men came to a stop, struggling to regain breath and composure in equal measure.

"How many do we face, sir?" I asked as Cato and Decius joined us.

"I saw at least a turma of Numidians pass around us to the east as you engaged the Gauls," he said. "Expect two to three times as many that I did not see."

"They outnumber us three to one?" Decius asked.

"Yes. And the longer we tarry here, the greater their numbers grow. There must be more to the east, and the Gauls to the north. Our only chance is to break through their line to the south. That is where they are weakest and where Father's army marches."

"What are your orders, sir?" I asked, not wanting to hear the answer.

"We charge them. They will not stand," he said. "We sling shields over our backs and run for the camp."

Cato interjected, "They'll slaughter us with their accursed javelins, sir."

"I know. But the longer we wait, the more they concentrate their forces," Scipio said. "We must go now."

Realizing that Scipio was correct, I said, "At once sir!" and turned to the other section leaders. "Form your sections on mine. Three files. We'll pass through them easily enough." *Then they'll have our backs as easy targets for their javelins,* I thought, knowing better than to say it aloud.

Scipio took position at the head of the column, with the signifier at his side. He drew his sword and adjusted the long shield on his left arm before taking the reins. "At the walk, forward!"

We followed him toward the enemy.

IX

NUMIDIAN CAVALRY

We passed the narrow riverbank and entered the forest at a walk. I noticed Marcus's pale face focused on Scipio's back. He looked ridiculous on the back of the Gallic horse. Its mane was braided with dyed thongs, making a line of spikes down its neck. The bridle was Roman, but the saddle was a crudely carved piece of wood held in place by two strips of leather. Marcus's eyes never left Scipio's back.

Then we moved into a trot that was bone jarring, but saved the horses for the desperate gallop coming soon. In the periphery, we started to see flickers of movement, shadows in the trees that moved in parallel with our line. We all knew that it was time for the ambushers to be ambushed in turn.

Ahead was a small rise that drew us away from the river to avoid some dense underbrush. I dropped back to check the last men in the formation. I watched as Scipio crested the hill. His back tensed before he raised his sword and disappeared over the rise.

I reached the top of the hill and looked down on a grassy field, browned by winter frost. The river bent away to the west, and I could see it curve back toward our route five miles hence. Dotted across the plain were groups of horsemen, each group equaling our force. We were outnumbered not three to one, but ten to one. Scipio pressed on, knowing the only path to survival lay ahead.

I spurred my horse forward to regain my place at the head of my section. Maneuvers would come soon, I was sure. As I regained my place, Decius banged his shield against my knee and said, "That lot looks like the mating of a horse and a porcupine."

He was right. The Numidians eschewed the use of bridles and saddles but carried javelins that stuck up behind the rider like porcupine quills. Feeling nothing but dread, I instead forced a laugh and said, "Then we'll tickle their bellies and turn them into balls." It was a poor joke, but the men needed something to keep their spirits up.

"Decius," Scipio said over his shoulder, "where is the marching camp from here?"

"Just on the other side of the far bend of the river, sir."

"They will try to cut us off," Cato said.

"We will maintain this pace until first contact," Scipio ordered. "Then we gallop to the camp."

That was a death sentence to many of the men and horses. A five-mile gallop was too much for horses that had been pushed so hard. And we could not outrun the Numidians' light horses and unarmored riders.

Decius said what all of us were thinking. "We'll not make that distance, sir. The horses can't do it."

"Gentlemen, we have been enveloped by the enemy. The only way out of the trap is through the enemy," Scipio said. "Jupiter will preserve us if we can reach sight of the marching camp."

"The time for discussion is done," I said. "The enemy comes, now!"

All eyes turned to follow my gaze. To our left and a bit ahead, a group of the Numidians crossed the open field toward us with javelins raised to throw.

"Shields up!" Cato shouted as the first volley arced toward us.

One javelin pierced the rump of a Roman horse. It reared, and the rider was thrown.

"Straight at them, men!" Decius shouted, veering his horse toward the enemy.

"Decius!" Scipio shouted angrily, "Get back here! We ride to the camp!"

Six of Decius's men followed him as they tried to catch the Numidians. The short desert horses had no saddles or bridles, only a rope around the neck for the rider to grasp. The Numidians danced away, easily avoiding the heavier Roman horses.

As Decius and his men closed, one Numidian rider reached back to pull another javelin from his quiver. He turned and threw a perfect arc into a Roman face.

Decius realized he could not catch the nimble horses and turned to rejoin the Roman formation.

More javelins flew. Only Decius made it back. The others fell with javelins in their backs. Now we numbered twenty-nine.

With no time for recriminations, Scipio pushed on. A quarter of the distance was covered, but the marching camp was not yet in sight when the next attack came.

The Numidians had decided to come from our left again. Javelins fell from the sky, and we did our best to swat them with our shields. To take a direct hit was to chance a puncture. The shield would be useless with a javelin stuck through it. We had to take the incoming fire at an angle, which left us vulnerable to the next javelin.

Four more men fell to the relentless barrage of missiles. We made it to a field that had been freshly plowed. Scipio moved right, alongside the turned earth, to avoid the furrows and stay on harder ground. It proved an effective measure as the Numidians had to slow in the deeply churned earth or go around the field.

Now half the distance was covered. The horses were lathered and blowing hard. And still we could not see the Roman camp. Ahead was another group of Numidians with their javelins ready. We had tightened into a compact formation that was a perfect target for them. They loosed and scampered back to reset for another volley. Scipio halted abruptly, causing his horse to rear. The javelins, aimed for where we would be, fell harmlessly to the ground. The abrupt halt caused the horses behind to falter and nearly threw me over my own mount's head. I slid hard against the pommels of my saddle and grasped desperately at my horse's mane. With a struggle, I pulled myself upright again.

Pushing forward took much kicking and lashing, but finally the horses moved again. Another volley of javelins and two more Romans fell. More Numidians closed behind us. There would be fire from two directions now. As we crested a small rise out of the plowed field we saw hope – at last. The Roman marching camp lay behind a small copse of trees bordering another turned field. The sight renewed our efforts to push the horses faster.

Scipio aimed for a hard track along the edge of the field, but it was blocked by perhaps ten Numidians. These had apparently used all their missiles as they had short curved blades in their hands. This fight would be close and personal. The Numidians would try to delay us so their fellows could spear us from behind.

Scipio aimed his sword at the first Numidian and charged. The rest of us followed. A volley of javelins from behind felled another horse, and as it went down it took another with it. The rider was unharmed, but without a mount was doomed to capture or death.

The rest of us flanked our leader and attacked the black-skinned men before us. Scipio missed with his passing stroke as the nimble desert mount danced away from the larger Roman horse. He passed on, not slowing to engage. My blade struck true as the rider that avoided Scipio's blade moved toward mine. The man screamed, but I had no time to finish him. To stop and fight was to risk death. We pushed on. The Numidian attempt to slow us had worked, and more missiles came from the rear, felling another of our number. We forced our lagging horses down the hardened track toward the edge of the woods.

Finally, we heard a beautiful sound – the buccinator's call rousing the garrison of the marching camp. The deep bellow of the horn was followed by the opening of the gate, and a century of infantry marched out toward the fight. I aimed my horse for them and whipped his flank bloody.

Even at the gallop, our horses were barely moving at a trotting pace. The last distance would be a roll of dice against Mors, god of death. The Numidians launched yet another volley behind us. One of the missiles struck Cato's thigh and he lurched from the saddle, landing in a rolling heap on the soft, turned soil.

"Leave him!" Scipio ordered.

I saw Cato's remaining four men slow as if to stop for their decurion.

"Get to the infantry!" Scipio shouted, and the four thrashed their mounts forward again. One, not quick enough, caught a javelin in his spine and fell with a limp thud into the loamy field.

Cato leaped up and struggled with one good leg to regain his horse. I lost sight of him as the Numidians swarmed past him, trying to kill us before we could reach the safety of the legion. Another volley of javelins killed another man, and the Roman cavalry finally emerged from the marching camp.

A sigh of dismay could be heard behind us as the black-skinned warriors veered west to avoid this fresh threat. We slowed our mounts to a walk as we reached the marching infantry. I looked back, seeking any sign of Cato, sure that he would be a bloody heap in the field behind.

Scipio rode into the gate and straight up the Via Praetoria to the consul's command tent. I watched him dismount before I turned to speak to the optio of the guard. "Send a patrol to see if any of our fallen are still alive."

"Yes, Decurion," said the optio, saluting.

I followed Scipio through the gate and then stopped to count the men that entered after me. Of the thirty men that departed the legion a week ago, only thirteen remained. Of Cato's men, only three.

"Decius, see that the horses and men are cared for," I said. "I will make the casualty report to the decurion."

Decius nodded and watched me stumble into the command tent.

* * *

Cato had been found by the centurion's men. His wounds were severe, but the Roman cavalry had driven off the Numidians before they could finish their work. I visited him in the infirmary that evening.

"You must have kissed Fortuna's ass," I said. "You are lucky to be alive."

The surgeon was checking Cato's bandages and testing the sutures. He had removed a piece of spear point that had broken off against Cato's femur. The surgery had taken most of the afternoon. The wound had been washed in wine and packed with boiled honey. The other wounds were bruises and a few cuts inflicted by Numidian swords, not long enough to finish the decurion completely.

Cato stirred a bit and replied groggily, "No thanks to your man Scipio."

"What do you mean?" I asked.

"He left me to die," Cato said angrily.

"He made a decision to save the rest of us."

Cato tried to roll over but couldn't get his limbs to work. "He's a cold bastard who only saved himself," he said, finally giving up on turning away from me. "He didn't even join the ambush. He stayed behind where it was safe. He's a coward."

"He is not!" I said, forcefully pushing him back into his cot.

"He's a coward and I'll see him punished before the legion for it!" Cato shouted, struggling to sit up.

"Here now!" yelled the surgeon. "I'll not have you killing my patient after I've put him back together."

"I'd like to see him try," Cato said with a surly and reddening face.

"Out, Decurion!" The surgeon herded me off my seat and out of the tent. "And don't come back if you are going to agitate my patient!"

I walked toward the tent I shared with Scipio and Decius. This news, on the heels of the general's displeasure at his son's loss of half a turma, would not be welcome. The general did not need infighting when Hannibal was here in Liguria.

I entered my tent and sat on my cot. Scipio looked up and nodded a greeting.

I returned his nod and said, "Sir, I have news."

"Cato?" he asked. "I heard he was brought in alive."

I nodded.

"How is he?"

"He will recover from his wounds," I answered. "But there is more. He intends to accuse you of cowardice to the general."

Scipio raised his eyebrows at this. "How so?"

"He says you left him to die and stayed safe in the rear during the ambush. I don't think it's enough to convict you, but it's enough to start some nasty rumors throughout the army."

"Well, he can do what he likes, but it will only add to Father's anger at me at the moment."

"Surely he can't blame you for your decision to push through that last ambush?" I asked.

"He says I should have withdrawn a day earlier. Before the Carthaginians began moving. I should have been back on schedule, in fact."

"Then he wouldn't even know Hannibal was at Lake Verbanus."

"No matter. It will only increase his ire. I cannot change that," he said. "I can only prepare the men for the next engagement. Defending myself against decisions I made while in contact with the enemy is something I will not do. That is a lesson Father taught me, even though he seems to be forgetting it today."

"Sleep. We need sleep, and tomorrow will see to itself," I said.

"Agreed," he said, and we pulled off armor and lay upon our cots.

"Sir," I said after the lamps had been extinguished.

"Yes, Appius."

"I would have made the same decision."

"I know. It is a lesson I learned from you," Scipio said quietly. "Good night, Appius."

"Good night, sir," I said and closed my eyes and let dreams take me.

X

TICINUS

Scipio and I entered the command tent the next morning to hear a Gallic voice speaking heavily accented Latin.

"The Taurinii are destroyed, noble lord." A haggard-looking Gaul with rough bandages covering seeping wounds on his head and left arm was saying.

"Surely not the entire village, man. He would not kill the children and women?" General Scipio asked.

"Only those of us who fled into the forest and hid survive. My wife was caught by those black-skinned devils and raped before my eyes."

I could see the man was close to breaking. I grabbed a nearby flagon and filled it with wine. He accepted the cup with eyes dead to any emotion.

"When they were through with her, they cut her throat," he continued in a voice hoarse with rage. "One of the ones holding me loosened his grip. I attacked him, but his fellow hit me with his sword. They left me for dead, I suppose. I woke in a pile of corpses on a pyre. Rain had caused the fire to smolder."

I imagined this man, bloody wound blinding him, struggling to free himself from the pile of dead. Then walking miles to reach this camp. It was incredible bravery or determination, I thought.

"And you found no one alive in the village?" the general asked.

The Gaul shook his head. "No one. The village was burned and everyone I knew is dead."

"Thank you for your report, Narbo. My man will see to you." One of the general's servants led the man away.

Scipio and I saluted. "Good morning, Father," Scipio said.

The general turned to face us. "Nothing good about today, Decurion. That man just informed me that the Taurinii, our staunchest allies among these Gauls, defied Hannibal when ordered to join him." The general drained a glass of wine and said, "He destroyed the village and killed every man, woman, and child who lived there."

"A powerful message to the other Gallic tribes," I said.

"Indeed," the general said, much calmer than the previous day.

"He has moved from Lake Verbanus then?" Decurion Scipio asked.

"Of course he has. He is recruiting Gauls to his banner to replenish his numbers before we can defeat him," General Scipio said. "The Senate is recalling Sempronius Longus from Sicily. He will reinforce us by way of Arriminium."

"It will take a month for him to arrive at least, sir," the decurion said.

"Yes, and Hannibal will attempt to besiege Placentia, Mediolanum, or one of the other northern cities soon. He needs men to do that. He needs men and time. It is a race to determine who can be seen to be winning first," said General Scipio.

"We should seek battle now then, sir."

"Of course we should," the general said in an irritated voice. "I need no lectures on tactics from a cowardly boy pretending to be a man."

"Sir?" his son asked without stating the question.

"Cato told me of your cowardice, boy." The general glared at his eldest son. "You are an embarrassment. Hiding behind your men in battle and running from the enemy to save your own skin."

I stepped forward to stand beside my decurion. "Sir! That's not how it happened—"

The general cut me off. "And you! I ordered you to teach this boy the art of war. And in his first fight he runs away like a woman! If I didn't need every man for the coming battle, I would send both of you packing! But at least I can put you where you can do no more harm to my army's morale. You, Decurion Scipio, will command the cavalry reserves. Your turma will guard our line of retreat back to camp. I am certain you can accomplish that task at least."

"Father, I should be with you," the younger Scipio protested.

"I need no cowards on my staff." The general turned his back on his son. "Dismissed, gentlemen," he hissed.

We both saluted and left the command tent.

We walked toward the stables in silence. We checked the horses and inspected the tack to ensure no frays or cuts had been missed by the men entrusted with caring for the leather and brass.

"I see Cato made his report," Scipio said finally.

"The general is under tremendous stress, sir," I said.

"He taught me to gather all available information before reaching a conclusion. It appears that he fails to follow his own admonition, Appius."

"Hannibal is on this side of the Alps, an ally has been destroyed, and the Senate is up in arms with these events or they would not have recalled Consul Sempronius Longus. Can you not see he spoke in anger, sir?" I said, trying to soothe the decurion.

"He is a Consul of Rome. He cannot afford anger," Scipio said coolly. "The legion is exposed here."

"I am sure General Scipio knows that, sir. We will be moving out soon."

"Father will seek battle soon," Scipio said. "He has no choice. The Gauls will flock to Hannibal, and that will cause problems in our own ranks as our allies begin to question Roman strength."

"Then we'd best see to the men, sir."

Later that day, Decius joined us in the tent we shared. "The engineers are building a bridge across the Ticinus just north of the confluence with the Padus," he said.

"What of the legion?" I asked.

"We are to establish a fort on this side of the bridge to guard the crossing."

"Then we will seek out Hannibal for a decisive battle," Scipio stood up from his pallet.

"It would seem so, sir."

"The legion will need scouts and escorts. Tell the men to pack up. I expect orders to move presently," the decurion ordered before leaving the tent and walking in the direction of the command tent.

"That Cato is a fool," Decius said as soon as the decurion was out of earshot.

"Why is that?" I asked.

"He might have a stick up his ass, but anyone who thinks that boy is a coward is an idiot."

"Maybe so. But the general seems to agree with Cato at the moment."

"Maybe. But he was very relieved to see the boy return even so," Decius said. "Maybe the general is smarter than we give him credit for, eh?"

"I'll not gainsay you on that. But Scipio is upset."

Decius's eyes widened. "How can you tell? He looks the same to me."

"The boy has always been shrewd and calculating. Anyone brought up in a noble family like him is. But he's always thinking. He thinks the general is making a mistake," I said. "He doesn't care a whit about the charges. He's worried about the vulnerability of the legion and his father isn't listening to him today."

"The boy thinks himself a better general than his father?" Decius asked.

"You were with him the past week." I lifted the tent flap. "Did he make a decision – any decision – that you, ten years his senior, would not have made?"

"There is that. But it's a far cry from leading a legion."

I looked toward the command tent. "May be. But I'll keep following him just the same."

Decius grunted as he lifted himself off his cot. "Let's go get the turma moving," he said. We headed toward the tents of our men to rouse them for whatever orders came next.

* * *

At dawn the next morning, the legion began construction of a wooden fort on the floodplain north of the River Padus and east of the River Ticinus. The engineers had completed work on a wooden bridge spanning the Ticinus, complete with guard towers and walls for archers to guard the crossing. The fort was well back from the crossing, but close enough to cover the near side with ballistae. By nightfall the main fortifications had been constructed. A thick palisade surrounded the legion's marching camp, and a deep trench lined with wooden spikes circled the wall. Platforms to mount artillery and archers would be constructed along the inside of the palisade. The gates would be guarded by tall towers that provided good vantage points to survey the approaches to the bridge in every direction. The legionaries would improve on the defenses daily by clearing fields of fire and cutting back any brush that could provide cover for an approaching army. Now, the cavalry just had to locate Hannibal's forces.

It was approaching the last days of November. Frost covered the ground most mornings. Supplies from Mediolanum and Placentia were rolling in on long wagon trains daily. Soon the fort would be prepared for a long siege.

Two days later, a patrol returned and the decurion in charge hastened to the command tent. Having been assigned no other duties, Scipio, Decius, and I lingered near the command tent and followed the patrol leader into the general's chamber.

The decurion saluted, and Scipio told him to report. "Sir, Decurion Marcus Flaminius. I was in charge of the western patrol."

"Are you related to Legate Flaminius by any chance?" I asked, earning raised eyebrows from Decurion Scipio.

"My uncle was a legate a few years ago," he said uncertainly, obviously not understanding why he should be questioned about his relatives.

"Go on, Decurion," General Scipio said with a glare at me.

"Yes, sir," Flaminius continued. "We sighted the Carthaginian army twenty miles west of here sir. We saw heavy infantry, as well as Numidian and Gallic cavalry in the thousands, sir. Our position was concealed, and I do not believe they saw us. They gave no pursuit in any case. I spent two hours observing them before returning."

General Scipio's lips tightened. "You believe this to be the main force then?"

"Yes, sir. I saw at least two thousand cavalry, sir. The infantry more than doubled that number. They were camped but were making preparations to move."

"Good report, Decurion," General Scipio said. "See to your men. Prepare them for departure in two hours. You will lead us to the enemy."

The decurion saluted and departed. The primus pilus said, "You will take the cavalry to attempt to pin them down until the infantry can join you, sir?"

"Yes. I believe that is the proper course. I'll send a messenger once I've located them. You will then leave a century as garrison here and join me with the rest of the legion."

"At least take the velites," the veteran soldier advised. "They can flush out ambushes and cover you if you need to re-form."

"Good idea. Have them and all the cavalry alerted. We march in two hours."

The old soldier saluted and departed to execute his general's orders.

"Decurion Scipio," the general turned to his son, "you will take what is left of your turma and guard the line of march as the trail party."

"Yes, sir."

"Dismissed."

We saluted and left the command tent at once.

As we approached our quarters, Scipio said "Get the men paraded and inspected. I want them ready to march in one hour. Pack rations for three days and full kit."

Decius and I said in unison, "Yes, sir." We saluted and walked into the turma's area to rouse the men.

* * *

Two hours later, the general led the cavalry out of the gate. The velites had paraded by the bridge. They were all young men, unarmored except for tough leather and animal pelts covering their heads and backs. They each carried a short sword and a bundle of seven veretae, the short iron-tipped javelins. Their role was to skirmish with the enemy. They approached the enemy in a ragged line and lobbed their projectiles into the massed infantry to disrupt the formation and probe for traps before the Roman infantry could close with the enemy. They were not intended to stand in the line of battle. The sword was only a final defense for when the last veretum had been thrown. The velites would then retreat behind and to the flanks of the heavy infantry until the battle had been decided. It was rare for them to be deployed without heavy infantry, as they would be in this case, but they were the only troops that could expect to keep up with the fast-moving cavalry.

The centurion in charge of the velites brought his men to attention and saluted as General Scipio approached.

The general returned the salute and ordered the centurion to lead the way. The centurion turned and bellowed with a perfectly pitched parade ground shout. At once the velites turned and marched toward the waiting bridge. Once across the bridge, the light infantry spread into a wide skirmish line and marched west toward the enemy. The cavalry followed, led by the general himself. Decurion Scipio, Decius, and I brought up the rear. The legionaries guarding the bridge shouted good-natured insults and begged us not to kill all the Carthaginians before they arrived.

We marched an hour past sundown, then camped without a marching camp. *The general thought two hours of extra marching was more important than the security of a fortified camp*, I thought as I inspected the velites pickets guarding the camp. The nine hundred Roman cavalry circled General Scipio's command post. The two thousand alae, Gallic cavalry allied with Rome, surrounded the Romans, and the seven thousand velites surrounded them. It was a powerful force to face the Carthaginians' two thousand cavalry and four thousand infantry.

The army was perhaps five miles from the crossing north of Pavo where the fort had been built. Just before midnight, a column of Roman cavalry numbering a hundred and led by Decurion Gaius Laelius joined the camp. Laelius was a childhood friend of Decurion Scipio, and I had taught them both from time to time when they were boys.

Laelius made his report to the general and then found his old friend at our campfire.

Scipio greeted his friend with a fond embrace and said, "Good to see you, Gaius. What brings you here in such a timely manner?"

Laelius returned the embrace and then greeted me with a nod. "Appius! Are still inflicting endless gladius drill upon our friend here?" He laughed at my nod. The boy had an infectious humor that brightened our small group. "I bring good news. Praetors Manlius and Atilius have brought their garrisons to the lovely fort your boys built. There's another six thousand heavy infantry and ten thousand Italian infantry to face that beast Hannibal."

Scipio sat next to his friend and offered wine. "Good news indeed. That should hearten the men here this night."

"Your father ordered my men into the reserves. I hear you are their commander?" Laelius asked politely.

"Yes. He is keeping the youngsters out of the way, it seems," Scipio said a bit sourly, then shifted his voice to a more cheerful tone. "It is good to see you, Laelius. I am glad you are with us. I'll be happy to have you as my second if you would agree?"

Laelius glanced in my direction and seeing my nod said, "Of course, Publius. I would be honored."

"I'm for my bedroll, gentlemen," I said, rising. "Don't stay up too late gossiping. We have a busy day tomorrow."

The two young men laughed and said in unison, "Yes, mother."

I smiled fondly at the two and listened to them catching up on family and friends back in Rome as I drifted off to sleep.

XI

RECONNAISSANCE IN FORCE

We woke before dawn. As the sun's first rays broke over the rolling hills, we were marching west seeking Hannibal's forces. The mood in the ranks was bright. Many of the men joked with their fellow cavalrymen, be they Roman or Gaul. Our turma, now reinforced by Laelius's replacements to a full three turmae, made a proper rear guard for the army.

In less than an hour, the velites crested a small hill and sighted Carthaginian heavy cavalry approaching from across a small plain. Signifiers signaled the column to spread out to meet the enemy. Our reconnaissance in force had made contact.

Scipio ordered Decius to organize the men. Then Scipio, Laelius, and I went to the general for instructions. We had to wait as he issued orders to the centurions, decurions, and prefects in command of the velites, Roman, and alae cavalry.

While we waited, I examined the Carthaginians arrayed across the field. I could see a single rider passing in front of the enemy ranks. From his gestures, he seemed to be encouraging them. I realized that the man must be Hannibal Barca.

"Gods, that's him," I said in a low voice.

Decius and Scipio followed my gaze. What we saw was a man dressed in flowing sand- and gold-colored robes. A white cloth covered his helm, revealing only a rounded spike at the peak. His face was olive-skinned and his beard black as night. His teeth shone through the beard like a beacon as he spoke to his men. When he finished, he pulled back on his reins, causing his horse to rear. With his sword held aloft, he cut a dramatic figure.

"They seem to enjoy his speech," said Decius.

I looked and saw the spears and swords of the Carthaginians held high overhead. We were too far to hear anything, but they looked impressive. "He's brought them across a continent and through an impassable range of mountains. I'd be impressed too," I said.

"Look there. That must be one of his brothers, Mago or Hasdrubal," said Scipio as another rider approached Hannibal. The two figures conferred for a few minutes. Then the brother, if that was who he was, rode toward the left of Hannibal's line to position himself with the cavalry there.

When General Scipio finally noticed us, his face grew stern. "Decurions. You will remain on this hill and observe the battle." He looked toward the marching camp. "You will guard the route back to the fort and provide a safe place for wounded men to retreat. You will not engage the enemy this day. You are to learn what battle is and how it is conducted through your observations. Are your orders clear?"

Decurion Scipio advanced a step and said, "Understood, sir. We will guard the line of retreat. If I may, sir, may Jupiter guard you this day."

"And you, son." The general's gaze softened a bit. "Gentlemen, may Fortuna's gaze be upon you. Dismissed."

We all saluted, turned, and rejoined our men. They had formed mere yards from the command post, so the journey was short. We had an excellent view as the velites descended the small hill into the plain below.

Seven thousand men moved forward, spreading into skirmish order. Each held a pilum ready. The Gallic cavalry, our allies, formed a line behind the light infantry, and the Roman cavalry extended the line to the right. General Scipio and his staff rode at the center of the line.

There was motion across the field as the Carthaginian cavalry abruptly lowered their spears and charged, immediately launching into a gallop and crossing the distance to the velites before they could loose even one veretum. The Carthaginian spears tasted Roman blood as they rolled through the light infantry like a wave across a beach.

Then the charge was through the velites and upon the Roman cavalry an instant later. Two thousand heavy cavalry had routed seven thousand light infantry in mere seconds. The survivors fled back, mingling with the enemy cavalry, and jammed into the Romans, who were unable to form an effective counter charge.

The Romans found themselves fighting in tight knots, disorganized and cut off from support. The velites continued to stream past the cavalry fight, running for our hilltop viewpoint. Then the Numidians charged. From both flanks, the leather-armored horsemen charged from concealed positions in the woods surrounding the field and chased down the fleeing velites. Numidian javelins pierced leather and pelt with ease. Some drew short swords and rode down the panicked infantry.

Decius turned to Scipio and said, "We have to help them, sir!"

Without turning, Scipio said with unnerving calm, "We have our orders, Decius." His eyes were locked on his father's position.

Decius looked at me, and I shook my head helplessly.

I looked down at the battle. Some of the Gauls had dismounted and were using their spears and longer swords to stave off the Carthaginian assault. Here and there were knots of Roman and Gallic horsemen fighting back to back as if they were infantry. All were surrounded. It seemed that all were doomed.

I saw the general fighting with a swarthy Carthaginian horseman. The Carthaginian's small round shield missed a parry, and the general's sword point thrust into the man's eye. General Scipio was a good swordsman, but he and his staff were surrounded and now outnumbered. It was only a matter of time.

The velites continued to run and soon passed our position. The Numidians halted at the base of the hill and re-formed. Then they launched themselves at the Roman and Gallic cavalry from the rear, their short swords and javelins adding to the mayhem below. It was too much. At first, one or two Gauls turned and fled only to be caught by the fleet Numidian horses. Then the rout began. The flanks caved in. Romans and Gauls fled in terror from the Carthaginians, who seemed to be everywhere now.

General Scipio tried to organize a fighting withdrawal, but his horse stumbled and he was thrown. A Carthaginian saw the general fall and charged him with a lowered spear. The general rolled to his knees just in time to take a glancing thrust to his side. The Carthaginian wheeled for another attempt but was met by a Roman blade in his throat as one of the general's guards threw himself at the threat. That guard fell to two Numidian javelins. There were only three Romans around the general now.

I felt Decurion Scipio's tense inhalation as the general tried to stand. Blood poured from the wound in his side, and he fell back to his knees. He reached for the reins of his horse, but the animal shied and fled.

Decurion Scipio looked over his shoulder at Laelius and me. He drew his sword and ordered, "Aid the general!"

Scipio was halfway down the hill before the rest of us could react to the command. A Carthaginian made a lunge at the general with a falcata, but the heavy-ended curved sword crashed into a Roman shield as one of the general's guards intercepted the blow. Decurion Scipio struck the Carthaginian from behind, thrusting his sword deep into the kidney of the man attacking his father. Then he threw himself from the horse to his father's side, dropping his shield in the process.

By then, the three decurions and a hundred men of our turmae had driven off the Carthaginians around the general. Scipio helped his father onto his dappled gray horse, then climbed on behind. Decurion Scipio shouted, "Retreat!"

The command echoed through the remaining riders, and we fled up the hill. I looked over my shoulder to see the Carthaginian cavalry re-forming at the base of the hill. Then I lost sight of the enemy as we galloped east toward the fort. We caught up to some of the velites and slowed our pace.

Decurion Scipio rode up to a centurion whose crest had been hacked nearly off his helmet. Its remnants hung by a single bent piece of bronze to the left side of his head. Wide eyes met Scipio's calm face. "Centurion. Organize a litter for the general. We must get him back to camp at once."

The centurion stared up at the decurion uncomprehendingly for a moment. Then he shook himself. He looked back into Scipio's face and said, "I'm sorry, sir. What did you say?"

"I need a litter for the general here. He has been wounded," Scipio said calmly.

The centurion looked around and grabbed two velite soldiers that were running wildly eastward. "Here now! You two. Make a litter with your veretae." The soldiers, comprehending someone in authority was in charge again, stopped and hastily created a litter by sliding their wolf pelt armor over two javelins. Then they laid the general on the litter and lifted him gently. The centurion stopped several more of the velites and organized a guard force.

With a hundred horsemen and a growing number of light infantry, the legion marched back toward the previous night's camp.

* * *

Arriving at the camp, the centurion, whose name was Marcus Septimus, organized the construction of a proper marching camp. Within two hours, the trench was dug, and the palisade walls were erected. The men could feel safe within the strong defensive walls. Decurion Scipio organized the defense as soldiers straggled into the camp throughout the day. For some reason unknown to us, Hannibal had chosen not to pursue us back to camp. Fortuna smiled on us at last. Scipio named Septimus senior centurion as few of the officers had survived. Septimus then organized the duty rotation and gathered a count of dead and wounded.

Decius and I took turns tending to General Scipio, who faded in and out of consciousness. Laelius managed the surviving officers and organized a meeting of senior officers as the sun approached the horizon.

All officers stood as Decurion Scipio stepped to the front of the formation. It was a sign of respect for the man that decurions and prefects years his senior deferred to his command. Scipio had earned their respect this day. None here would gainsay any of his commands.

"Gentlemen, it has been a dark day," Scipio began. "Our dead or missing number two thousand one hundred seventeen. Another thousand or more are wounded. And tomorrow, Hannibal will be between us and the bridge to the fort on the Ticinus before we can pass the distance between here and there."

There were downcast looks as the realization that tomorrow could be worse than today dawned on some faces. There was some shifting and grumbling as fear grew in their hearts. But before that fear could find voice, Scipio continued. "Therefore, we will not march tomorrow. We will march tonight." Confusion and dismay at the thought of another march after the battle today warred with hope that they might avoid Pluto's demesne for one more day. "I want cooking fires stoked and fed to last until early morning. We march at midnight. I need thirty volunteers to be rear guard. They will remain here for two more hours, tending the fires. Then they will ride as if Cerebos nipped at their heels to the bridge."

I looked at the faces around me. Scipio would have no problem finding volunteers. I looked at Decius and he smiled. Scipio was in command.

"I need the men fed and readied for the march." Scipio scanned his audience. "Get them rested as much as possible. The pace will be hard tonight. Dismissed."

The officers dispersed to attend their duties, and Scipio headed to the pallet where his father lay. The wounded man was conscious and grimaced at a flash of pain as his son reached his side. "I will not cross the River Styx this night, son. Appius tells me you have assumed command?"

"Yes, Father," the boy said, grasping the older man's arm. "It was necessary."

"It is necessary," the older man said. "You must get my men back to the Ticinus and safety."

"I will, Father."

The general winced as he shifted on his pallet. "Jupiter, Minerva, and Mars will guide you. Have faith and trust yourself, even if others doubt you."

The younger Scipio bowed his head at the blessing.

"Go, attend your duties. Appius will see to my needs."

I nodded my agreement to the son.

Decurion Scipio gripped his father's arm tighter for a moment then stood and said, "Laelius, Decius attend me."

* * *

At midnight we crept out of camp, heading east as quietly as possible. We led the horses, whose hooves had been muffled with leather coverings designed for the purpose. Only about half the cavalry still had mounts. Those that did guarded the flanks and served as a vanguard. We knew that to be discovered now would doom us all. We assumed the Carthaginians had scouts in the woods observing the camp. We stayed alongside the Ticinus as much as possible.

We moved at a fast pace. I walked at the side of General Scipio's litter, leading my horse. The cavalrymen on foot suffered while the younger and less armored velites hardly noticed. By the time the sun lightened the sky before us, we were crossing the floodplain before the bridge.

Scipio motioned for me to mount and we rode together into the fort, where he advised the guard commander of the approaching army. Then we rode up the Via Praetoria to the command tent and handed the reins to an infantryman guarding the entrance. "Soldier, have them watered, fed and brushed down at once."

The legionary saluted and said, "Yes, sir."

We entered the tent to find a man seated at General Scipio's table.

"Sir," Scipio said coolly as the man rose at the intrusion.

"And you are?" the man asked.

"I am Decurion Publius Cornelius Scipio, currently in command of this army and castra," Scipio said without a hint of apprehension.

The man's eyes widened at the recognition of his name. "Decurion. I believe command of the army is your father's assigned duty." His lips thinned and his cultured voice only partially hid his contempt. "You are his son, I suppose?"

"I am." Scipio returned his questioning gaze stonily for a moment. "The general, my father, was wounded in battle yesterday. I have assumed his duties for the moment."

"I see, young Publius," said a high-pitched voice from behind a curtain. Praetor Lucius Manlius Vulso entered. "This is Atilius. How is your father, lad?"

"You will address me as Decurion or sir," Scipio said coldly and waited for the reaction from the two noblemen.

"Of course, Decurion," said Atilius in a soothing voice. "We meant no disrespect. It is just that you are a trifle young for your current duties."

"My age is of no consequence. I command here until my father or Consul Sempronius Longus relieves me," Scipio said, then turned to me. "Appius, have the prefect of engineers report here at once. We have to destroy that bridge."

I saluted and turned to leave.

"Destroy the bridge? Whatever for?" Manlius asked.

I ordered one of the runners to fetch the prefect, then turned to hear Scipio's reply.

"Because in an hour, the Carthaginians will ride across that bridge and kill us all if we don't," he said in an icy tone.

"Surely you jest. We have three legions here. Nearly thirty thousand men," Manlius said with growing irritation in his voice. "Hannibal is barely in the field here, by all reports."

"The reports are wrong, gentlemen," Scipio said, moving to seat himself behind his father's desk. Atilius moved aside without comment. "Hannibal routed our army yesterday with more than twice our numbers in cavalry." He paused to allow that information to penetrate. "He has recruited the northern Gauls to his banner. When last I saw his army, it numbered twenty-five thousand infantry alone. With allies flocking to his cause, that number will surely double."

"That is not possible lad... er... Decurion," Atilius corrected hastily. "He cannot have fifty thousand infantry in Liguria."

"I do not intend to take the chance, gentlemen," Scipio said. "Now, if you will excuse me, I have to accomplish my current task. Please assemble your staff officers for a briefing in two hours. That will be all, gentlemen."

I held the curtain aside as a pointed hint that the two nobles were dismissed. When they departed, I waited for a few heartbeats before saying. "That was a bit rough on their noble sensibilities, sir."

"Appius, you yourself taught me that the chain of command must be well defined from the beginning," he said with a sly smile. "They would have questioned every order if I hadn't shocked them so. I need to have unquestioned authority until we can reach Placentia. Then father or Sempronius can deal with those two."

"Well, you certainly shocked them. But I wouldn't count on them staying shocked."

"I know. But if we can get the bridge torn up, we can slow Hannibal down long enough to reach the castra at Placentia," he said, taking up the papers on the desk. "Stone walls make a better defense than wooden palisades. And we can resupply by sea if necessary."

"We fall back to Placentia? What of the rest of Liguria?" I asked.

Scipio looked into my eyes and said, "If we fail to hold Placentia, Liguria is lost."

XII

DECAMPING

The prefect of engineers arrived. As he entered, he looked confused at seeing the boyish decurion seated at the general's desk. He was a balding man with graying hair and a round paunch that made him look out of place in his legionary officer uniform.

"Ah, Paulus. Good. I need you to destroy the bridge. Take what men you need and do it at once," Scipio began. "Tie a rope line for my rear guard to use crossing the river. They should be along within the hour."

The prefect's eyes were bulging as the boy behind the desk rattled off orders. "What? What do you mean, destroy the bridge? My men just finished building the bridge!" he blurted out finally.

"My orders are perfectly clear, prefect. Destroy the bridge at once," Scipio said calmly. "Unless you'd care to face the Carthaginian army not an hour from here at the head of the front line?"

I took the prefect's elbow and nodded at the decurion. "I'll see to it, sir," I said to Scipio. "Come on, sir," I said to the prefect, coaxing him out of the tent. "We really must get this job done now." Once outside, I quietly explained the situation. The man finally gathered his wits and marched off to find his men.

Within fifteen minutes, a century of legionaries was at the far side, tearing up planks from the sturdy bridge with pry bars. Prefect Paulus supervised the rigging of a rope across the river. It dipped into the water but would suffice to help the rear guard cross the river, if they arrived before the Carthaginians.

Twenty minutes later, I stood with Scipio on the tower guarding the gate overlooking the river. We could see Roman cavalry forcing exhausted horses toward the river. Behind them were short desert horses ridden by Numidian warriors. Periodically, one of the desert men would loft a javelin at the fleeing Romans. There were only a dozen Romans remaining. As they approached the river, the Numidians launched a final attack in mass. Scipio and I watched helplessly as dozens of javelins flew at the desperate Romans. The last man leapt into the water from his horse's back. A Numidian pulled up by the bank and threw his spear in a perfect arc, landing in the fleeing man's back. The rear guard was dead. I would remember them in my prayers that evening.

I saw Paulus walk to the rope he had rigged to help the men who we had just watch die. With a deep breath, he drew his sword and cut it. The river current caught the rope and I watched as the end slid along the bank and into the water to drift downstream. I eventually lost sight of the line as the water pulled it beneath the surface.

The Numidians gathered on the far bank of the river. I could see several of them pointing and their teeth gleamed in stark contrast to their ebony faces. They seemed excited as they surveyed the destroyed bridge from across the river. One of the men, who seemed to be in charge, pointed at the fort and soon several of the horsemen rode off at a canter back toward Carthaginian lines.

Laelius joined us on the redoubt. "Publius, the primus pilus would like a word with you."

"Yes, of course," Scipio said, then descended the stairs to the ground. "Have him come to the command tent. I will meet with him after I see Father."

"Appius, will you see to my men?" Laelius asked.

"Of course, sir," I said. "I'll have them ready to march by nightfall."

Scipio looked over his shoulder and said, "Then come meet the primus pilus. I'll need you there. Bring Decius too."

"Yes, sir," I said, moving toward the tents shared by the cavalry.

* * *

Half an hour later, I ducked under the flap into Scipio's command tent.

"Decurion, this fort can withstand any assault from the Carthaginians," the primus pilus boomed in a voice more suited to parade grounds than intimate conferences.

"I am well aware of the defensive capabilities of this fortification, Plinius. What I am concerned with is our supplies," Scipio said reasonably, in sharp contrast to Plinius's voice. "We cannot withstand a long siege here, and I can see no means of resupply once Hannibal crosses the river."

"What about the river, sir?" Plinius asked.

"It is a ballistae shot from the fort. Would you care to unload enough supplies to support twenty thousand men, under fire, while Hannibal sits out of range?" Scipio said in a cool voice. "It would trap us here where we could not join with Consul Sempronius Longus."

"But to abandon the fort, sir?" Plinius said.

"Is necessary," Scipio said simply. "We must move behind stone walls with a secure line of supply. That means Placentia. I'll brook no more discussion on this topic. Plinius, I know your men did the work of Hercules on this fort. It will be retaken. But here and now we must face the military reality that we cannot hold this castra against Hannibal's army."

Plinius nodded his defeat. "I'll have the camp struck, and the men will be ready to march at nightfall."

"That will do. We will move an hour after darkness falls. I want cavalry flankers, but close in," Scipio said to the senior officers. "I'd rather not have any skirmishes with those Numidian mercenaries. Their horses are too quick for us to deal with effectively." Scipio turned to his staff officers. They were tribunes of senior rank to him but they deferred to him out of respect for his father's wishes. "Legions will march out in order of precedence. Roman cavalry to provide the inner screen, alae cavalry to form the outer screen. Alae infantry to act as rear guard. Are there any questions?"

None of the gathered officers spoke.

"Very well then. Gentlemen, you have your duties. I'll see you at parade, which will be at nightfall. Until then, good day."

The officers left in knots of twos and threes. Decius and I allowed them to pass by us to the exit. Then we approached Scipio's desk and saluted.

"Gentlemen, I'm glad you heard that little conference," Scipio began.

"The primus pilus seemed a touch annoyed that we are giving this castra to Hannibal without a fight," Decius said.

"It rubs him wrong, I'll grant. But he understands the logistics as well as I do," Scipio said. "Father trusts him to speak his mind. I will do the same. So long as he follows orders. Now to you, gentlemen." He picked up a small parchment scroll from the desk. "I have written a message to the Senate advising them of the plan to fall back on Placentia. I expect them to shift our supply chain from Pavo to Placentia. I need one of you to deliver this and the other to deliver a similar missive to Placentia."

I said, "I'll take the message to Placentia. Decius, you haven't seen you wife in months. Go to Rome."

Scipio added, "And bring back some replacements for our losses. The Senate will back your authority to levy more troops. I will include a letter signed by father to ensure it is legal. See the primus pilus before you depart. He will have the numbers you need."

I asked, "When do we depart, sir?"

"At nightfall," Scipio said. "Decius, take the turma as escort. Appius, you take Laelius's men. That should get you both to Placentia before midnight. Decius, leave there before dawn."

We nodded our understanding. "You want Decius out before the army arrives, sir?" I asked.

"Yes. And more importantly, before Hannibal's scouts arrive. He'll have two rivers to cross, but I can't tear up the stone bridge over the Padus near the Trebia. I can only delay him. I expect him to besiege us at Placentia within three days."

"Perhaps when Sempronius arrives, we can retake the initiative, sir," I said.

"That is the plan." Scipio smiled and picked up another scroll. "If you will excuse me, gentlemen, I have a meeting with Paulus shortly. I'll have the messages delivered to you as soon as they are ready."

We saluted, turned, and exited. We had a long night ahead to prepare for.

* * *

Decius and I led the turma out and onto the road for Placentia. With a hundred men on horseback, we made good time and were in sight of the town in only a few hours. The castra or stone fort dominated the countryside from its position along the Trebia and Padus rivers. The castra had been constructed the year before to guard a new colony of six thousand Romans, mostly veteran legionaries who had been promised land in return for years of service to Rome. These colonists received ius Latinus or Latin rights, meaning full citizenship in Roman society. With land scarce and expensive near the capital, spreading Roman culture to other parts of the Italian Peninsula was the new policy of the Senate.

The risk to those Roman citizens in the hinterlands was the often rebellious inhabitants of the newly founded colonies. Earlier this year, Boii and Insubres Gauls had attacked the Roman colonists bound for Placentia and Cremona. That arrogant ass, Praetor Manlius Vulso, had been dispatched with half of Scipio's army to deal with that threat as the survivors had huddled in Mutina. The delay had given Hannibal time to cross Gaul and make it to the Alps.

We came to the city just before midnight. The gates were closed. I could see men guarding the walls, so I called out, "Open the gate!"

"And who might you be?" said a deep voice from the wall above the gate.

"Appius Curtius Asprenas, Decurion of the First Legion," I said. "Now open the gate!"

"I have orders to open the gate to none until dawn."

"Orders that supersede a consular order?" I said, growing angry.

"You're no consul." The words were arrogant, but the voice was uncertain.

I took a deep breath to regain my composure. "Friend, I am the consul's messenger with dispatches for your officers and the Senate," I said, conveniently forgetting that my messages were actually from the consul's son. "In less than six hours, a Roman army – that is retreating in the face of a far larger Carthaginian army – will be camped outside your walls. Let me ask you this, do you think your officers may want to have some advance notice of these imminent events?"

"Open the gate!" the voice said after a moment's hesitation.

"I thought not," I said sotto voce to Decius.

He grinned. "We have to meet this intellectual giant guarding the gate here."

"Later. Get your men billeted and get some rest," I ordered. "I'll deliver the messages and get the garrison ready to receive visitors. I'll have someone wake you and your men when it is time for you to depart."

As we passed the gate, Decius grasped my arm for a moment and then led his turma toward the cavalry billets. I turned my horse toward the Principia that was at the center of every castra. There I would find the garrison commander and hopefully someone useful in preparing for a siege.

* * *

"We do not have room for two legions, Decurion," Senator Flaminius said, exasperated. "We barely have room for our current garrison." I had woken him with the unpleasant news of the legion's imminent arrival.

"I understand your problem sir, but the consul and his army will be here in less than six hours. We must prepare a defensive position for them at the very least." Flaminius, one of three patrons of the new colony of Placentia, took me on a tour. He showed me foundations of barracks blocks and a few tents, but the lack of permanent or even temporary structures to house troops was quite obvious.

"We have been concentrating on completing the walls and the emporium, you see," he said, indicating the massive walled docks that dominated the southeast side of the walled city. "We will certainly be able to resupply the army, but housing them will give us no room to construct the barracks themselves."

"Then I need your mensures to lay out a marching camp alongside the city walls. Your garrison can begin construction of the camp tonight. It must be complete, or nearly so, when the legions arrive, Senator."

"Of course, Decurion. After the Boii insurrection, I'd not leave any Roman unprotected against Gallic treachery."

"You were at Mutina then?" I asked.

He nodded. "I was. Our relief column was cut off and we had to flee to the nearest defensible place," he said. "Fortunately, Praetor Vulso managed to drive them off eventually. But it put us behind in our construction of this place. I'm sure Cremona is in a similar state." He referred to the other newly established colony in Ligurian territory, which was now called Cisalpine Gaul.

"Our mistakes compound. If we had not been delayed because of that uprising, perhaps Hannibal would have been stopped on the other side of the mountains."

"I'll have my men begin working at once," the old man said with a hint of command in his voice.

"Thank you, sir." I watched as he walked back to the Principia. Flaminius was perhaps sixty, gray and stout, but he walked with a straight back and head held high. He had been a senator and former consul. He obviously remembered his years fighting against Carthage twenty years ago. He seemed a good man, and I trusted him to make sure everything was put in place.

I examined the emporium. Foundations for warehouses led down to mostly completed docks along the stone quay wall. The docks protruded into the river, and I could see where the river mud had been dredged to make a deep harbor for cargo vessels. Two biremes stood at the last quay, manned by sailors and marines, ready to close the entrance with metal cables. The wall that guarded the docks pushed into the river nearly to the midpoint. Every thirty yards, a tower rose to provide a platform for ballistae and archers. Obviously, the colonists' recent experience had given them sufficient incentive to concentrate on defense before comfort. This place could withstand almost any assault, I calculated.

The docks themselves were empty, apart from a single trireme. I assumed that to be Flaminius's personal transport. Perhaps it could be of some use.

I walked toward the northern wall, noting with approval the rousting of what looked to be the entire garrison. Those men would grumble about the lost sleep, but Flaminius would see them complete the legionary marching camp before dawn. Scipio could ask no more. And Hannibal would not attempt an assault against two such imposing structures within supporting distance. The army would be safe until Sempronius could arrive with his reinforcements. I watched the soldiers work by torchlight until it was time to wake Decius. I woke him myself and saw him to the gate. Then I resumed my position on the wall, awaiting the arrival of Scipio and the army.

XIII

MISSIONS AND HONORS

"Rest here, father." Scipio helped the general onto some luxurious cushions prepared by Flaminius's servants in a spacious chamber. Flaminius and I hovered anxiously. General Scipio looked haggard and gray, but he made himself as comfortable as possible on the cushions and relaxed enough to take in his surroundings. "Gaius. Is that you?" he asked in a weak but steady voice.

"Yes, Publius," the stout counselor said at once. "You've looked better."

"I dare say you have that right." He laughed for a moment then winced as the pain in his side made him gasp. "Not as spry as I should like, but well enough."

"Father, you need to rest. I'll see to things here," Scipio said.

"You seem to have done well enough. How did you cow those two popinjays, Vulso and Atilius?"

"I told them you put me in charge, and I had an army to back up my word." The young decurion sat on a stool beside his father. "They fussed a bit, but lacking imagination or a plan of their own, they decided to let me hang myself. Fortunately, Appius and Decius were here to keep me out of too much trouble."

Laelius entered and saluted the supine general. "Sir, the marching camp is complete, guards posted, and the men are resting."

"Good, Laelius. But make your reports to Publius here. He's in charge apparently," said the general with a grimace of pain. "He's not very good at following orders, but seems to be doing well giving them."

The younger Scipio reddened a bit and started to protest.

"Enough, boy!" the general said with some of the strength back in

85

his voice. "You've done well. Let the humor pass. It can't hurt you, and it shows the men that you know the difference between attack and jest."

"Yes, father," Scipio said in a voice resigned to yet another lecture by his demanding father.

"As to the other thing," he gestured to his side, "I shall honor you with a Civic Crown."

I'm sure my eyes were as wide as Laelius's. The Civic Crown was the highest individual award that could be given to a citizen save one.

"I will not accept the crown, Father," Scipio said at once. "I saved my father, disobeying my general's orders. I deserve no recognition."

"You can't refuse, Publius," blurted Laelius. "You led the charge that saved the general."

"The guards around you deserve the crown. I merely put you on a horse, father."

"Certainly more than that, boy!" the general snapped. "You saved my life. And you saved the army."

"Yes, Publius, you took command and acted to save us all," Laelius said.

The younger Scipio took a deep breath, then said, "General, I will not accept the award. Please save us both the embarrassment of a public refusal."

The general held his son's eyes for what seemed an eternity. Then he blinked and said, "Very well, Decurion. You may carry on."

With that dismissal, Scipio saluted his father and walked out of the chamber.

"Appius, see to him," the general said softly.

I saluted and looked toward Laelius, and we followed our decurion from the room. I heard the two older men begin to reminisce as we left. Scipio waited by the rooms cleared for his use.

"Gentlemen," he began, and we followed him into his chamber, where he seated himself at a low table and poured a goblet of wine for each of us. "We must get in contact with Sempronius Longus. He needs to know that Hannibal is between our two armies."

"How do you know that, Publius?" Laelius asked.

"I don't. But it's what I would do in his place, so I assume he will try to keep us separate until he can defeat us in detail."

"The consul could be anywhere from here to Arriminium," I said.

"Yes, but he was supposed to be there a week ago," Laelius said. "He could be quite close."

"And his legions?" I asked. "He dismissed them all in Sicily. Will they fulfill their oaths to travel on their own to Arriminium?"

Laelius glared at me. "Appius, do you have to be so negative? Those men swore a holy oath to Jupiter and Mars. They will be there."

"Still, it would be better to know for sure," Scipio said.

"Decius is on his way to Rome. So I suppose it is up to me to find General Sempronius and see he makes it here?" I said, knowing the answer.

"Thank you for volunteering," Scipio said with a broad grin. "Some exercise will do you good, old man."

"Shall we have some practice with the rudius before I go, young master?" I asked with an evil glimmer in my eye.

Scipio shuddered in mock horror. "No, indeed. Be beaten by you with a wooden stick filled with lead? I'd rather take that crown father wanted to give me."

"Shall I tell him then?" I asked with a grin of my own.

His face grew grim. "No. That award is much too important to the legion to be cheapened so," he said. "Following so soon after Cato's accusations, it would look as if father were trying to cover up my disgrace."

My eyebrows raised at that. "His charges worry you then?"

"No," he said, "but I need no rumors of that nature whispered in the barracks, nor the halls of Rome. Let the charges stand and let them stand alone."

"When do I depart, sir?" I asked.

"Tomorrow morning will suffice," Scipio said. "We shall hold a ceremony this evening to honor the dead and the heroes of the battle. I will want a phalera for that centurion, Septimus, that led the velites."

"I'll see to the arrangements, sir," Laelius said.

"Good. Appius, please tell Father and Flaminius. I am sure both will wish to attend."

"Of course, sir. And I'll have your servant bring you a fresh tunic, so he can polish your armor. It's a bit worn at the moment." I gestured to the smears of blood and mud on the metal.

"Very good," he said, sitting behind the desk. "Dismissed, gentlemen."

We saluted and left the office.

* * *

Parade that evening was in full dress. Every man in the legion was turned out in perfectly polished armor. If there were some bandages scattered through the ranks, they did not detract from the display. On the dais prepared for the event sat the three patrons of Placentia, Flaminius in the middle. To one side lay General Scipio, propped up on red and blue cushions in a warrior's tunic and belt, if no armor.

Laelius and I stood before our cavalrymen to the right of the dais and prepared ourselves for a series of long speeches from the politicians. Decurion Scipio was noticeably absent. We waited in ranks for the ceremony to begin.

A priest of Jupiter entered from the rear of the formation and climbed the dais slowly. Acolytes carried braziers of burning incense across the front of the legionaries and came to a halt on either side of the dais. The sweet smoke drifting from the braziers tickled my nose, and I had to strain to keep from sneezing.

The priest gave an invocation and blessing to the legion and to Rome. He blessed the shades of the departed and wished them well on their journey across the River Styx and into Elysium. He intoned a long sermon about the trials of Perseus, which I suppose was meant to remind us of the virtue of perseverance in the face of insurmountable odds. I found my mind wandering as the politicians took the place of the priest and began the speeches. I schooled myself to attention again when Flaminius, the last speaker, stepped to the front of the dais.

"Legionaries, soldiers of Rome, hear me now," he said in a booming voice trained for oratory. "This evening, I speak not for myself, but for your general. He asked me to convey his deep and undying respect for you and your unstinting resolve in the battles to come. You are the heart and soul of Rome – its mighty fist that will strike down that barbarian Hannibal and his entire Barcid ilk. They are a plague upon this earth and will be burned out by your hands." He paused to allow his words to penetrate. "For myself, I swell with pride to see your faces set in the direction of the future, unthinking of past privations and hardship. It does you credit, and you honor Rome with your dedication to duty. Some among you deserve greater recognition than mere words. Centurion Marcus Septimus, come forward!"

The centurion came to attention and marched to the dais, stopping before Flaminius. He saluted and stood waiting.

"Centurion Septimus led velites during the late battle. As the retreat sounded, this man organized an escort for our wounded general and saw him safely to camp. For this service, at the recommendation of General Scipio, I award Septimus this silver phalera." He affixed a small silver disc bearing the face of Minerva onto the centurion's harness. "Wear this with pride and honor, Centurion," Flaminius said, then turned the soldier to face his fellows. The soldiers of the legion banged their pila against their shields in a deafening show of pride in recognition of the centurion. At last, Flaminius sent the man back to his unit.

Flaminius presented several lesser awards and recognitions. When the last of them had been given, two legionaries walked onto the dais from behind and helped General Scipio to his feet. Flaminius turned and nodded, yielding the speaking area to his friend. Supported by the strong arms of the young men at his sides, Scipio walked painfully to the center of the dais.

"Men of Rome, hear me!" he began in a commanding voice, but all could hear the stiff pain beneath. "I owe another man my life this day. One who has refused any award or recognition for his service to me personally and Rome. One who threatened to refuse the crown of oak leaves in public if I dared present it."

There were murmurs in the ranks of the legion at that statement.

"But he cannot avoid my praise completely. Decurion Scipio, come forward!" the general commanded.

From behind the dais, the younger Scipio stepped up and to his father's side, taking the place of the legionary at his right.

"This man, Decurion Publius Cornelius Scipio, at great risk to his life and the lives of his turma, led a charge to drive off the Carthaginian mercenaries that nearly took my life. He placed me on his own horse and then organized the retreat in the face of great pressure from the enemy. He has commanded the entire legion in my name since then. And though he will not accept formal recognition of these deeds, a son cannot refuse the pride of his father." With that, the general embraced his son warmly, kissing each cheek.

The men erupted with loud cheering and banged their pila against shields once more. It seemed as if the cloud of loss and pain from the previous day's battle had lifted. The men understood the pride of a father for his son and the honor deserved by the young decurion. I smiled and cheered as loud as any of them. For he was my decurion.

XIV

MUTINY

We celebrated our newly decorated heroes well into the evening. Laelius and I escorted Scipio back toward our tents in the marching camp around the midnight change of the guard. We overheard the guard commander as we approached the porta principia.

"Quintus, you're drunk!"

The legionary in question swayed a bit, then steadied himself to attention. "I'm not, sir."

"You've had your head in a bloody barrel of wine!" the centurion bellowed. "You're on a charge."

"Sir?" Quintus said with a pleading tone. "I've had no more than the rest of the lads."

I nearly giggled as the legionary doomed his entire section.

"Is that so?" the centurion said evilly. "Then you're all on a charge. Latrine duty for the next six days."

Quintus started to protest but was interrupted by an elbow from his companion. "Yes, sir," he finally gasped.

The optio, second-in-command of the guard century, noticed us walking toward the gate. "Quiet! Officers," he hissed a little too loudly.

The centurion brought his men to attention and rendered a salute. "Good evening, gentlemen," he greeted us, trying to divert our attention from whatever we might have overheard.

"Good evening, Centurion," I said cheerfully, ignoring the swaying legionaries behind the centurion.

"Do you require any assistance, sir?" The centurion asked, grateful that we had not interjected ourselves into his command.

"No, we can manage on our own," Laelius said, taking the hint.

We passed on, to the relief of the gate guards, who were hoping that the brief interruption would spare them any more of the centurion's wrath. We heard his bellowing chastisement begin again once we turned the corner toward our tent, much to the disappointment of the legionaries, I'm sure.

"I believe our legionary friend will be sorry for having been caught out," Laelius said, chuckling.

"He will be after his squad mates are done with him."

Scipio, who had been silent through all of this, suddenly stopped. "Do you hear that?" he said.

"What?" asked Laelius.

"It sounded like sandals slapping... as if someone were running." Scipio pointed toward the infantry tents. "Over that way."

"Someone making a dash for the latrine?" I said.

"No, it was more than one," Scipio said.

"Let's go see," Laelius said.

We walked toward the noise but saw nothing. Just row upon row of orderly tents, some occupied by snoring legionaries.

"Maybe it was your imagination," I said.

"Perhaps," Scipio said reluctantly.

Then we heard a muffled slap and a grunt from a tent nearby.

"That was not my imagination," Scipio said.

"No, I heard it too," Laelius agreed. "That way."

We ran to the tent opening and caught a glimpse of shadowy men running through the opposite entrance. I ran after, followed quickly by Laelius. We chased the shadows into the next tent, where we found four Gauls stabbing sleeping legionaries before they could wake to the danger.

"Sound the alarm!" I heard Scipio's voice shout. "Guard century to me!"

But we had no time to wait for the guards. There were four armed Gauls with bloody swords coming toward us with murder in their eyes. We drew our swords and prepared to fight.

I flipped an empty cot into the air, distracting the closest Gaul. As he caught the frame, I charged and thrust my sword through the canvas and into his stomach. The stink of intestines and half-digested food filled the tent as he screamed.

Two of the Gauls attacked Laelius, but his youthful reflexes saved him from immediate death. He parried their blows and forced them back with a few vicious thrusts.

The fourth Gaul bellowed his rage and began to charge me, but one of the stabbed legionaries tripped him with a bloody hand. The Gaul attempted to roll away as I stabbed down, but my sword found his guts. I twisted the point inside him, seeking his heart. Blood flowed as I fell upon the man, trying to immobilize his sword arm while my blade sought his life. Finally, I cut something important and I felt his struggles cease.

I looked up to see Laelius pinned against a tent pole by a hulking Gaul while his mate staggered back from a blow to the side of his head. I shoved the disoriented man into another tent pole and the impact felled him. Then I seized the sword arm of the Gaul attacking Laelius and jerked back hard, spinning the man toward me.

Laelius did not hesitate and thrust his gladius into the man's back, twisting sharply. I turned to find the wounded legionary atop the other Gaul. It was a moment's work to cut his throat.

"Legionary, are you alright?" I asked the wounded man.

"I'll live. Bastard missed his stroke," the man said, coughing. "Got me in the side instead of my stomach. Broke a rib I think. Maybe two."

"Good man," I said, handing him a tunic drying on lines between the tent poles. "Use this. Bind your wounds. We must alert the camp."

"Scipio's seen to that, I think, Appius," Laelius said. "He's a bit smarter than us, chasing into the dark after gods knew how many men. We're lucky to be alive." He was realizing how close he had come to dying.

"Fortuna smiled on us," I said. "But we're alive and they aren't. Let's rejoin the decurion and see to the security of the camp, eh?"

"Right," Laelius said.

We left the tent, headed back toward our own. Torches had been lit by legionaries waking in their tents. Eerily, the walls seemed unchanged. But we were in enemy territory now.

We found Scipio at the center of a knot of perhaps twenty legionaries, variously armored, but all carrying scutum and gladius. He looked at us and said, "Gods! You look as if you've bathed in blood, Appius." He hid his momentary surprise at our appearance and said, "Report!"

"Gauls, sir. Four of them. All dead now. They were killing sleeping men. We're fine." I looked at the legionaries surrounding the decurion. "The guard century?"

"Dead, I believe," Scipio said. "At least none of them responded to my alarm. We'll see as we pass through the gate."

"The gate?" Laelius asked.

"Yes. We must alert the garrison and retake this camp. Laelius, you will take two men and make for the castra. Most of the legion is there and drunk I am afraid, but send back as many armed men as possible. Make sure you tell Flaminius what is happening."

"Yes, sir," Laelius said.

"Appius, lead half the men here to the gate as an escort for Laelius. Then come to the Principia. Find me there."

"You men, from here to here," I waved my arm in a semi-circle, "come with me." I moved toward the main gate at a walk, and the soldiers arrayed themselves around me. Laelius fell into step beside me, and we made our way to the gate we had entered only minutes before.

We found the guards at the gate. All were headless. "They must have waited for us to pass before attacking," Laelius said.

"We were fortunate then," I said. "You and you," I said, pointing to two legionaries. "Up on the tower, tell me what you see."

They climbed up the stairs warily, swords low and ready to thrust. When they reached the top, one of the soldiers shouted down, "Just more of the same sir. All without heads."

"What about toward Placentia?" I asked.

"Looks clear, sir," the legionary said after a quick survey. "No movement and it's well lit. We can watch your man all the way to the gate."

"Good. Stay there and do so." I turned to Laelius and said, "Off you go then, sir," and indicated two legionaries should follow him.

"Good luck, Appius." Laelius gripped my arm for a moment then ran out the gate with the two soldiers close behind.

After a few minutes, one of the legionaries on the wall shouted down, "He's at the gate, sir!" A moment later he said, "They're inside now."

"Come on down then," I said. "Let's get back to the decurion."

* * *

Scipio had found another thirty men and was busy organizing a defense of the Principia as I arrived. "Laelius made it. We watched them go through the gate," I said with a perfunctory salute.

"Good," Scipio said. "Then we should have some assistance soon. The gate guards?"

"Dead to a man," I said. "Their heads were taken."

"It seems some of our Gallic allies decided to defect to Hannibal," Scipio said grimly. "Apparently, they wanted to take some proof of their loyalty to his cause."

"Hence the heads," I said.

He nodded grimly. "And now we have no choice but to push all the others out of the walls. But until we have some reinforcements, the fifty of us are hardly enough to mount an offensive."

"Agreed," I said. "We wait then?"

"Yes." He thought for a moment, then said, "Take your men and check the perimeter. Reinforce where you deem necessary. Then report back to me."

"Yes, sir." I gathered my eight remaining men and made a circuit of the Principia. It was a large tent, with several chambers divided by tapestries of wool. Scipio had posted a pair of guards at each entrance. Nearby was a small squad of men to respond to any incursion, but they were far enough away to make it difficult to attack both groups at once. I placed a pair of men with each of the reaction forces, then went back to Scipio.

Minutes later, we heard a buccinator sound his horn. The legion was marching to our aid. Scipio and I both walked to the main entrance, from where we could watch the main gate. Soon we saw a century in formation pass through the gate and march up the Via Praetoria to the headquarters building. The centurion in command halted the formation at the center of the forum and shouted orders to his sections to block each avenue. Behind him came another century and then another. The first went left and the second right. They efficiently began the task of clearing the tents in each row as more legionaries entered through the main gate. Finally, Laelius walked through the gate. Beside him came Flaminius, carrying a gladius at the ready. The pair approached the Principia.

Scipio stepped forward into the light of the torches. "Flaminius, Laelius. Thank you for coming so promptly, Senator."

Flaminius looked up grimly. "What happened?"

"We don't know numbers for certain, but some number of our Gallic allies decided to take Hannibal the gift of our guard century's heads," Scipio said briefly.

"Roust and parade them all?" Flaminius asked.

"Without weapons, if you please, sir. No need to provide arms to possible enemy troops."

"Indeed." Flaminius turned to his garrison prefect. "Sextus, see to it."

The prefect saluted and began shouting orders to his men.

Within an hour, it was over.

* * *

We sat in Scipio's chamber and drank his father's wine as Prefect Sextus entered. He came to attention and saluted.

"Report," Flaminius said.

"Two hundred twelve men killed, thirty-seven more wounded, sir," he began. "One thousand twenty-three Gallic infantry missing, presumed deserted to the enemy."

"Can the survivors tell us anything?" Laelius asked.

"Only that they were sleeping when men came into their tents and attacked them. Most of the survivors were left for dead when the alarm went up. All of the dead had their heads taken."

"Any prisoners?" Scipio asked.

"None, sir," Sextus said. "We found tracks heading southeast from the marching camp but did not follow them in the dark."

"Good, we need no more ambushes after tonight's business," Scipio said.

"The camp was clear by the time my men arrived. I had a century at each gate to seal the camp. No one left after we arrived," Sextus said.

"We surprised them in the act," Laelius said.

Scipio nodded. "Good work, Prefect. Have your men search our allies for any messages or Carthaginian silver."

"After that, sir?" Sextus asked.

"Post a guard on them and send them back to duty. Any not fled are not Hannibal's allies. But we'll watch them closely to be sure."

"I'll post a guard on the camp and get started cleaning up, sir," I said.

"Yes. And get cleaned up yourself," Scipio said. "You look as if you rolled under the carving table at butcher's shop."

With that, I saluted and left with Sextus. "Thank you for coming so quickly, sir," I said to him as we walked to the entrance.

"Fortuna blessed us this evening. It could have been much worse," Sextus said.

"True enough," I said as we passed through and onto the parade field. "But I'm damned if I can see how at the moment."

We walked in silence until we reached the gate. "Decurion, I'll leave you here. You should be safe enough walking back to the city to retrieve your men."

"Thanks again. I'm sure I'll have to nearly drown most of my legionaries to get them in condition to march over here," I said.

"One look at your uniform should sober them up, I think," Sextus said grimly.

I nodded and walked toward the city gate.

XV

MUTINA

The mutiny delayed my trip by a day. Scouts had verified that Hannibal was moving south of Placentia along the River Trebia, probably seeking a crossing. But three days later I was within sight of Mutina, and to my relief I saw two legion marching camps on the plain near the city walls. Sempronius Longus was within three days' march of Placentia.

I led my cavalry troop down the hillside toward the city. Ninety horsemen coming out of the hills elicited an immediate response from both legion camps. Within minutes, twice our number of cavalry rode out to intercept our path.

I brought my troop to a halt and waited for the decurion in command to approach. I saluted and said, "Good to see you keep a watch. There are some nasty fellows in these hills, I hear."

The decurion halted and returned my salute. "Name and unit," he said abruptly.

"Decurion Appius Curtius Asprenas, First Legion," I said politely. "And you would be?"

"Decurion Lucas Meridus, Fourth Legion," he said, adding in a snide voice, "And of course we of the Fourth keep a good watch. Wouldn't want to be ambushed, would we?"

"I bear dispatches for General Sempronius," I said, ignoring the insult. "Could you be so kind as to tell me where I might find the good general?"

I must have irritated him by not rising to his bait, for he said, "The general is where he pleases and does not confide his plans to every passing decurion."

"Or at least not to the ones he has guarding the latrines, I suppose," I said, done playing this game. "I'll just apply at the Third Legion's camp then, as the general's presence would be known to the privy guard if he were in camp." I spurred my horse past him and enjoyed the gaping mouth that was still searching for a retort.

* * *

I discovered that the general was in the city but was due back at the Third Legion's Principia momentarily. I decided to await Sempronius in his headquarters. About twenty minutes later, he arrived with a large group of staff officers and scribes. He walked straight past me as I stood and saluted. He continued into his chamber and I made to follow him.

"You can't go in there," said a man wearing the tunic of a scribe, stepping in front of me and barring my path.

"I am a messenger from Consul Scipio, and I must see Consul Sempronius," I said politely.

"You may give the message to me," the small man said. "I am the consul's personal secretary, Gracchus."

I examined the man. He was a Greek from his accent. He wore the curly black locks of his people, oiled and perfumed. His hands were soft, with splotches of ink spattering his right hand. "I have orders to see Consul Sempronius," I said.

"Let me see your orders," the functionary said.

"They are verbal orders."

"Oh, I see," said Gracchus, with a disappointed shake of his head. "In that case, I am sorry. You will have to wait until the consul has time in his schedule."

I stared at the man for two heartbeats. Then I turned as if to walk away defeated, allowing my cloak to cover my arm. I heard the scribe inhale for a parting jibe as I departed. Then I continued my turn, stepped back toward the man, and punched him solidly in the solar plexus. The explosion of air from his lungs made a *whump* sound that gave way to a clatter of writing desks, tablets, and scrolls as Gracchus landed among them.

The guards posted at the entrance started toward me, but I ordered them back with a glare.

"Here now, what's this all about?" said a voice from the next chamber.

A tribune walked in and saw Gracchus huddled on the floor and me standing calmly over him.

"Gracchus seemed to think a message from Consul Scipio could wait," I said. "I disagreed."

"Oh my," said the tribune, understanding my meaning. "And you are?"

"Decurion Asprenas, First Legion," I said.

"I see," said the tribune. "Titus Manlius Torquatus, Senior Tribune of the Third. And we seem to have a bit of a problem here."

I stood impassively, waiting for the tribune to continue.

"The general gave orders to not be disturbed, you see, Asprenas," said Torquatus pleasantly. "And you have apparently assaulted a member of his staff who was only trying to follow the general's orders."

I stared into the eyes of the tribune, not trusting myself to speak.

"The message is important?" he said. Then he continued without awaiting my response, "Of course it is. It comes from Consul Scipio. Perhaps a report of yet another defeat at the hands of the Carthaginians?"

With that remark, Torquatus had my undivided attention.

"Let's have it then, Asprenas," he said. "What is your message?"

"Sir, I have orders to give my dispatches into the hand of General Sempronius. If I would not give my dispatches to that," I said, indicating Gracchus, who was now trying to restore order to the scrolls and tablets, "what makes you think I will give you my messages?"

"Because, Decurion, I can arrange for you to see Sempronius," he said coolly. "And I promise, if you assault me, I'll have you hung."

I took a breath and decided to relent. "Sir, what I can tell you is that Hannibal's army is between this army and Scipio's. It is larger than expected and growing."

"I see. I suppose that information is relevant," Torquatus said mildly. "Gracchus, clean up this mess. Come with me, Decurion." He turned and passed back through the opening into the headquarters of Third Legion. I followed him through several rooms until we came to the guards before the general's chambers. "Wait here," he said and disappeared past the legionaries.

I stood passively, observing the scribes and functionaries at work. Scipio kept most of these people outside his headquarters, except for a personal secretary and two scribes. This building teemed with civilian bureaucrats.

Torquatus reappeared and motioned me to follow him. We passed the guards and went into the general's chamber. There were rich tapestries hanging on the walls and an iron brazier radiating warmth to ward off the winter chill. The general sat behind an ornately carved wooden table, polished and dark. Obviously, Sempronius enjoyed his comforts.

The general himself wore a red tunic of expensive cloth, trimmed in gold. A rich blue woolen cloak lay about his shoulders, to ward off any lingering chill in the air. His face was narrow with thin lips. His gray eyes read a wax tablet he held out at a distance, revealing a bit of farsightedness.

I came to attention and saluted. Before I could report myself, Torquatus announced me in a sour voice. "This is Decurion Asprenas, sir. He has important dispatches from Consul Scipio for you."

"I see. Let's have them then," Sempronius said extending, a long-fingered hand toward me.

I opened the leather pouch at my side, breaking the lead seal that had been affixed to the knotted end. Under the flap, I found three scrolls of parchment. These I carefully placed into Sempronius's waiting hand.

"Anything else, Decurion?" Sempronius asked.

"Just what I told the tribune, sir. Hannibal's army is between you and General Scipio. We believe him to be southeast of the city itself, sir," I said.

"Very well, wait outside while I read these," said the general.

I saluted again, then allowed Torquatus to lead me to another chamber with several benches and a table bearing food and wine.

"Have a seat, Asprenas. You might have a bit of a wait, depending on what's in those dispatches," he said pleasantly.

I took a seat on a bench facing the entrance and asked, "How long have you been here at Mutina?"

"Just arrived yesterday," he said. "Planning on a two-day march to the River Arda starting tomorrow. Then on to Placentia."

"Moving at a rather leisurely pace, aren't you?" I said.

"I believe moving too fast got several thousand of your men killed, did it not?"

I bit my tongue on a hot retort. "The only thing moving too fast that day was the Numidian and Carthaginian cavalry," I said neutrally. "We were lucky to escape the trap."

"True. But that is the past, and now Consul Sempronius is here," he said. "Perhaps he can manage to close with these barbarians, so we may finish this war quickly."

"I wouldn't count on it," I said. "Hannibal is a crafty and daring general."

"You sound as if you admire him."

"I've seen his army destroy a tribe of Gauls in an assault across a river in early winter, fight their way across the Alps, then rout two legions worth of cavalry in little over a month," I said. "He's not an enemy I would care to underestimate, nor should Consul Sempronius."

"I'm sure the consul will take your opinion into account, *Decurion*," he said, emphasizing my rank in a tone that meant he was sure the consul would do no such thing.

Gracchus walked into the room and said, "The consul has finished reviewing the dispatches. He will send for you this evening with his reply. You are to hold yourself ready within this camp and leave notice where you will be with my office."

"Very well then," Torquatus said. "You seem to be dismissed for the moment, Asprenas."

I stood and saluted the tribune. "With your permission, sir, I'll inspect my men and horses, and find my own cot. I expect I'll be leaving this evening."

"We shall see," he said, with a strange half-smile. "Join me for dinner. I'll send a man for you."

"Of course, sir. Thank you," I said.

"Dismissed then. See to your men," he said.

I turned and found my way out of the Principia. My men were caring for the horses in the stables. As I groomed my horse, I thought about Torquatus's smile.

* * *

Dinner was served after evening parade. Torquatus's servant brought me to the triune's tent, which was appointed with simple but luxurious tapestries and cushions. The man was wealthy, his father being one of the two consuls elected the previous year, so luxury was to be expected. But the simplicity of the décor demonstrated something else, a willingness to forego ostentatious display. I seated myself on one of the cushions and suffered my hands being washed by the servant.

"Ah, good. You've arrived, Asprenas," Torquatus said, entering the tent and shedding his armor. "I'll be ready in a moment. I look forward to more of your scintillating observations."

I smiled, not knowing how to respond to the obvious barb. I was a messenger from the consul, not a toy for this one to play with. I admonished myself to control my temper.

"There!" he said shedding the breastplate and leaving it carelessly on the floor. "Much better. Now we can enjoy ourselves until your meeting with Sempronius Longus."

"Thank you for the invitation, Tribune," I said.

"That will be enough of that rank nonsense. I am Titus and you are... Appius, isn't it?"

I nodded my agreement.

"A good memory for names is so important for politics," Titus said enthusiastically. "Some people get so unreasonably offended if you forget their name."

I had no idea what the man was going on about. "Yes, sir... Titus," I said, catching myself.

"Take yourself, for example," he said. "Asprenas is a good equestrian name. You must enjoy quite a view of the political intrigues of the senatorial class."

"My family has been allied with the Cornelii gens since the marriage of my grandfather to a daughter of Consul Scipio's grandfather," I said. "My view of politics is that the senators play for blood, and it is best to be on the winning side."

"That is true," he agreed. "But determining the winning side is always a challenge. I do so enjoy a challenge. Don't you?"

"I enjoy staying alive," I said. "For that, I trust my sword, shield, and wits."

"A soldier then?" he asked.

"Always," I said.

"Ah, here is Timius with dinner," he said, distracted by the entrance of his servant with two silver platters.

Upon one were two small bowls filled with wine-soaked oysters sprinkled with herbs. The other held some flatbread and olive oil. The servant placed the trays between us and departed again.

Titus lifted a jug of wine and handed it across to me. "To a successful campaign," he toasted.

I raised the jug in salute then tried the proffered wine. It was a mild, dry wine and delicious.

"Do try the oysters. I found them in Arriminium," he said. "They were brined, but I find that a good soaking in wine gives them a piquant flavor."

The oysters were indeed delicious, and I said as much. I chose some bread to dip into the olive oil and followed it all with another sip of wine. "You set a fine table, Titus."

"Why thank you," he said. "One tries when roughing it in the legions. This small repast would hardly be an appetizer at one of my father's cenas."

"True," I agreed. The elaborate dinner parties of the wealthy could last hours and have dozens of dishes served, "but it is nice to have such delicacies occasionally on the march."

"So it is," he said cordially. His eyes narrowed a bit, then he said, "What have you seen of Hannibal then? Is he the seven-foot-tall ogre we've been hearing rumors of?"

I thought for a moment and said, "I've only seen him once. Across the battlefield on the Ticinus. He seemed a normal-looking man. Swarthy, as all those Carthaginians are."

"Not a monster, then?"

"I wouldn't go that far," I said. "He certainly slaughtered the people at Saguntum and utterly destroyed the Taurinii. Those are fairly monstrous acts."

"But he himself? Just a man?" Titus said.

"From what I could see, yes," I said. "He's a very cunning general. He saw our velites forming in skirmish order while he was deploying his cavalry. Before all his men were deployed, he ordered the charge and was on us before the velites could throw a single veretum."

"Poor deployment on General Scipio's part."

"In hindsight," I said. "But seven thousand men, supported by cavalry, routed in seconds. It was unexpected and something I won't forget."

"And what happened to the cavalry support?" he asked.

"The Carthaginians were upon them before a charge could be mounted," I said, remembering the fight. "The velites blocked the cavalry and broke the formation. It became a general melee. Then the Numidians appeared on the flanks and began slaughtering the fleeing velites."

"It was a rout from the beginning then?" he said.

"As much as any I've seen," I said. "Our cavalry was surrounded and outnumbered, and the velites were fleeing in terror."

"Was General Scipio gravely wounded?" he asked.

"It was a serious wound, along his hip," I said. "It could have been fatal, but he'll mend."

"Praise the gods for that," Titus said. "Here is Timius with more wine and a bit of dessert."

We enjoyed the dessert, which turned out to be honeyed plums and quinces, until the general's servant came to fetch me. I thanked my host for sharing his largesse and followed the servant to Sempronius's chamber.

XVI

SEMPRONIUS LONGUS

"Decurion Asprenas, would you care to explain your actions in my head-quarters this afternoon?" Tiberius Sempronius Longus said in his most senatorial voice.

I hesitated for a moment, unsure as to what actions he was referring. Then I saw Meridus smirking at the side of the room. Beside him stood an equally smug Gracchus. I could see where this was heading, so I decided to dive in headlong. "I found your decurion rude, condescending, and not forthcoming with pertinent information. As for Gracchus, he impeded my access to you during my mission. I am not in the habit of allowing plebes, no matter their lofty placement on your consular staff, to delay my military mission, sir," I said bluntly.

"But you delayed in finding me upon your arrival, Decurion, did you not?"

"I was informed that you were expected back at your headquarters presently and decided to await your return since I had no knowledge of your route or exact location, sir."

"I see," he said sourly. "You have an answer for everything then?"

"I do my duty, sir," I said stiffly.

"Do you?" He pursed his lips then said, "Do you indeed? If you were on my staff or in my legions, I would have you demoted and sent home in disgrace for striking my scribe. And delaying those messages, of which you knew the import, was almost criminal."

"Sir," I said, acknowledging the statement but not adding any more fuel to the fire.

"You think you are above reproach, Decurion?" he snarled. "My men were expressing well-justified contempt for cowards and incompetents who cannot even see off a rabble."

"Hannibal's army is hardly a rabble, sir."

"We'll see to Hannibal soon enough." Sempronius raised himself from his stool. "As it is, your commander's incompetence has already delayed the conclusion of this war by at least a year. I should be invading North Africa now, not saving northern Italy from barbarians."

"As you say, sir," I said, knowing that nothing could change the general's mind. I saw Titus enter the room. His knowing look was all I needed to understand his smile earlier. *Giving the condemned one last meal, were you?* I thought.

"I believe I'll let General Scipio deal with you," Sempronius said, then turned to his guards. "Seize him and place him under confinement in his quarters."

Strong hands grasped my arms. A centurion took my sword and knife. The three men led me back to my quarters.

The centurion came inside with me and said, "Sir, you are to remain here until we march in the morning. You will be brought food. We march at daybreak. Do you have any questions?"

"What of my men?" I asked.

"They will be assigned under one of Third Legion's officers until we join First Legion," he said.

"Very good then. Good night, Centurion," I said.

Surprisingly, the man saluted then turned on his heel and left. I didn't need to check to know there were two men guarding the entrance to my tent. I decided to rest. It would be a long march back to Placentia.

* * *

Sempronius decided to make the journey as humiliating as possible for me. He denied me access to my horse and made me march at his side while he lectured me on battle tactics and strategies. I supposed he thought the foot march would have me begging for a mount, but the pace was leisurely and I found it relaxing.

Disappointed by my lack of complaint, he had me served only puls, the watery porridge made from emmer, at meals. It was bland, but they let me eat my fill, so I was not unhappy with anything except the indignity of being separated from my men.

One of them tried to see me and was run off by a tribune before we could speak. There was murder in my man's eyes as I saw him ride away to the rear of the formation. After being in the van of every movement First Legion made, being relegated to rear guard was another insult to my men.

The march to the Arda took two days, but nothing of consequence happened. A day later, scouts reported the enemy fleeing northwest at our approach.

"See there, Asprenas," Sempronius said to me after the messenger departed, "Hannibal fears my approach. He knows there is a competent general here to lead the armies of Rome now."

"Yes, sir," was my only response.

Two days later, we came into sight of Placentia. I saw with approval that the legionary marching camp in the hills to the south of the city had been improved with more outer works and sharpened stakes. I assumed that the trenches had been lined liberally with iron caltrops as well. The First and Second Legions would halt any attack from the south.

Four days' walk had done little to improve my mood. I was not looking forward to the coming meeting between Sempronius and Scipio. If Consul Scipio was not up and about, this hothead would be in charge of the Roman army.

"Titus, please inform the senior tribunes of the Fourth Legion that we will establish camp at the confluence of the Trebia and Padus," Sempronius said. "We will patrol both sides of the rivers before locating our fleeing prey."

"Yes, General," Torquatus said, riding forward to the headquarters detachment of his legate.

"You see, Asprenas, concentrating your forces is necessary for victory," Sempronius lectured me. "Splitting your army in the face of the enemy invites defeat."

I ignored him.

"Come, man! Surely you have some military advice for me. Are you not the military tutor to Scipio's scions?" he asked.

"Reconnaissance in force is best conducted with light and mobile troops," I said, mollifying the general.

"Of course. There it is," he gloated. His eyes lighted as he said, "It is time to conduct our own reconnaissance. Shall we pay a visit to your commander?"

I offered Sempronius a stony glare.

"I am certain Scipio will want to reward you for your actions," he said. The general's party diverged from the main column at his signal and headed for Placentia's gates.

* * *

We marched to the Principia and were led to the Patron Council's chamber. It was a large room, reminiscent of the Forum Senate chambers in Rome, but much smaller. Around the room were benches for notables to sit in consultation with the three patrons of the city. It was lighted by sunlight from small openings near the ceiling and oil lamps around the room. The senate banner and the banner of the new colony hung on the far wall.

Today the three patrons sat in their designated places at the head of the room, Flaminius at the center. To their right Scipio reclined on a palanquin covered with cushions. He was pale but seemed alert, though I could see blood seeping through the bandages around his hip.

"Consul Sempronius, it gives me pleasure to welcome you to Placentia," Flaminius said formally.

"Gaius Flaminius, my thanks for your greeting," Sempronius said. "It is good to know that some uphold proprieties even during such dark times."

"I believe you are acquainted with Consul Scipio?" Flaminius said, turning the conversation over to the consuls.

Sempronius smiled an ingratiating smile at his co-consul. "Publius, how are you recovering from your wounds?"

"Well enough, Tiberius," Scipio said in a steady voice. "Your legions are a welcome sight to us all."

"I noted that the Carthaginian dogs ran as we approached."

"They decamped and moved west. I doubt they fled. More likely they needed food and supplies."

"I think you overestimate their strategic abilities," Sempronius said. "They feared being trapped between two Roman armies, I think."

"A possibility, to be sure," Scipio admitted, "but that army outnumbers both of us together now. It is far more likely Hannibal needed to secure a source of food for his growing numbers. Every Gaul in the north is flocking to his banner after his slaughter of the Taurinii for their defiance."

"Yes, a pity you were unable to aid them. Still, our forces are sufficient if properly led."

"Sufficient for whatpurpose?" Scipio asked.

"For destroying the Carthaginians, of course," Sempronius said. "The Gauls are fickle. They will scatter and run as soon as Hannibal is seen to be losing."

"True, though I underestimated him once. I will not do so a second time. He is a sly one. Never does what you expect."

"Then one must plan better. Shall we adjourn to your headquarters that I may survey the status of forces here?"

Scipio grimaced. "I am afraid that I am not quite ready to resume my role as commander of the consular army assigned me. My son has been acting as my deputy and keeping me apprised."

"That boy? He's, what, sixteen?" Sempronius looked shocked.

"Seventeen," Scipio corrected. "And he's turning out to be quite good at managing everything."

"No wonder your man here had to be arrested." Sempronius gestured toward me. "You have children running the army. No discipline."

Scipio finally noticed the three legionaries accompanying me were guards, not an escort for Sempronius. "Arrested? On what charges?" Scipio asked.

"Insolence and striking one of my staff," Sempronius said. "And he has been confined and on basic rations for the past four days. Since he is your man, I thought I would let you handle the discipline."

Scipio looked into my eyes. I don't know what he saw, but something must have given him a clue to the true events. "Release him. Appius, we will discuss your punishment before cena. Report to me directly."

"Yes, sir," I said, coming to attention. He wanted to talk, but not in front of these men. Before the evening meal would suffice. "Shall I report to headquarters now, sir?"

"Yes. Go now," he said.

"You intend to let him walk free?" Sempronius asked, appalled.

I hesitated, waiting for the consuls to come to a consensus.

"I intend to discuss the matter with him and decide his fate after that discussion," Scipio said calmly. "His family has served mine for generations. It is the least I can do. He will not wander. Appius is a soldier first and foremost, as was his father."

"I begin to see why Hannibal has bested Rome so far," Sempronius said coldly, "if this is how you maintain discipline in the ranks. That man should be confined until he is drummed out of the army in disgrace!"

"Hannibal has not bested Rome, nor will he. He has surprised us and moved rather more quickly than expected. With both our armies present, he cannot harm us." Scipio paused for a moment to control his temper. "As for Appius, as you have said, he is mine to punish. Leave him to me, Tiberius."

"Gentlemen," Flaminius interrupted, "I am sure Consul Sempronius needs to rest after his journey and you, Scipio, are still recovering from your wounds. Perhaps we can reconvene in two hours at First Legion's Principia?"

Scipio nodded his assent.

"Of course, Flaminius. I look forward to seeing the state of the army," said Sempronius with sarcasm dripping from his tongue. Then he turned and stalked from the room, followed by the three legionaries.

Having waited for dismissal from General Scipio, I remained at attention.

"Appius, go tell my son what has occurred," Scipio said. "Tell him to prepare a briefing on the state of the army and all intelligence we have on the location of Hannibal's army."

"Yes, sir." I saluted and left to find the younger Scipio.

* * *

Two hours later, we stood around a map on a large table in the First Legion headquarters. General Scipio, lying on his palanquin, left the briefing to his son. Sempronius had brought his two legates and the prefects of the two alae infantry legions assigned to his army. The senior tribunes of First and Second Legion were present, along with a smattering of staff officers. Decurion Scipio gave a concise description of Hannibal's army, its probable location and intentions. Then he described the state of the consular army assigned to his father. It was a clear and pleasantly short briefing for my tastes, but I was sure it was about to become interminable.

"You say you have reports that the enemy has moved west, Decurion?" Sempronius asked in a dry tone, laced with condescension.

"Yes, General. Toward Clastidium, from the last report," Scipio said in an even voice.

"He might be returning to Spain now that we have concentrated our forces," a tribune from Third Legion suggested. "He must know he cannot defeat us now."

"He will not leave Roman territory without a decisive battle," General Scipio said from his elevated position.

"If he cannot achieve a decisive battle, what will he do then?" asked Torquatus, perfectly comfortable in the company of these senior officers.

Decurion Scipio said, "He will live off the land and terrorize Roman colonies and our Gallic allies."

"You seem very sure, Decurion," Sempronius said. "What makes you so?"

"Only logic, sir. He must be the knife at our throats that concentrates our attention here rather than Iberia or Africa. Those places are where the Carthaginians are vulnerable."

"Which makes my consular army's presence here a victory for Carthage," Sempronius said. "Do you not agree?"

"Of course, sir," Scipio said, standing his ground under Sempronius's disapproving gaze. "But until the Senate decides to concentrate on those vulnerabilities and raise more legions, we must obey our orders, sir.."

"So, the Senate is wrong to defend Roman territory?" Sempronius asked, incredulous. "Boy, when you have gained enough years to take a seat in the Senate, perhaps you will understand that Rome must defend what is rightfully hers."

"The question is how best to defend it, General," Scipio said, ignoring the condescension. "Winning the war would end the threat to Rome. We cannot do that fighting on our own ground."

"So we should abandon our Italian and Gallic allies, leave Rome defenseless, and hare off on some wild scheme to invade Africa?" Torquatus asked. "That would violate our oaths as citizens of Rome!"

The room erupted in shouts. Some were in favor of the decurion's position, but most abhorred the possible cost to the unprotected Roman populace. Scipio's analysis forced the men in this room to face the harsh realities of war. Sometimes the defenseless must be sacrificed.

Flaminius borrowed a spear from one of the guards and banged the butt against the wooden floor until the shouting subsided. "Gentlemen! You forget yourselves. This is a council of war, not the forum for endless debate," he said, when the roar of voices subsided. "Decurion, please confine yourself to the present situation."

Slightly chastised, Decurion Scipio nodded. "We expect a report from our scouts this evening with more details, as the current report is two days old."

"Until then, my army will remain camped at the joining of Trebia and Padus as a ward against Carthaginian troops approaching from that direction," Sempronius said. "Publius, would you direct your engineers to construct a bridge across the river, that supplies may flow more easily?"

The elder Scipio said, "Of course, Tiberius," then glanced at his son, who nodded acceptance of the task.

"Good. I believe your position in the hills overlooking Placentia should provide an adequate defense to the south and east. Patrols on the north side of the Padus should alert us to dangers from that direction. If there are no further details, Publius?"

The elder Scipio deferred the question to his son.

"No, sir," the decurion said simply.

"Then I will take my leave until further information arrives." Sempronius turned to depart, then paused and said, "By tradition we should alternate days of command, Publius. But you are in no conditions to lead the army. I shall assume full command until you are fit to resume your post."

General Scipio was visibly unhappy at the truth of this statement and said, "Certainly, Tiberius. You will keep me informed of your intentions?" The general knew that with Sempronius's consular rank, no one could gainsay his authority so long as Scipio lay abed wounded.

"Yes, I will inform you of any orders or changes in disposition," Sempronius said. "If that is all, I shall retire until the evening meal."

The men in the room came to attention as General Sempronius departed.

XVII

CLASTIDIUM

As the evening sun fell below the horizon, I walked into the Principia at Placentia. The guard nodded a greeting as I approached General Scipio's chamber, indicating I should go inside. Candles and oil lamps lighted the chamber, and Scipio's servants had placed a stool near the foot of the palanquin for guests to sit.

The general, still pale but looking much better than he had that afternoon, lay upon his cushions, reading a wax tablet that was one of many strewn about him. His eyes glanced up at my salute, and he waved me to the stool as he finished reading the tablet. As he set the report aside, his eyes focused on me. "An eventful journey, Appius."

"You could say that, sir."

"Did you strike his man? I won't ask about the insolence – we both know that is true enough." His eyes twinkled with laughter.

"I did, sir," I said simply. "I have no excuse."

"Let me guess," Scipio said, thoughtfully, "Greek scribe, prideful of his education and position, and wanting to personally hand my message to General Sempronius?"

"An accurate summation, sir."

"And you, having been freshly insulted by every officer you encountered in the camp, could tolerate no more condescension," he said. "Especially from a servant."

"I possibly could have tolerated more, sir. I simply chose not to."

"In front of a politically connected witness, no less." He grimaced. "Unwise, my good Decurion."

"Probably. I certainly thought so later."

"Now I will have to punish you," Scipio said solemnly. "Decurion Asprenas, for the charge of insolence, I find you guilty. Punishment is forfeiture of one day's pay. For the charge of striking a servant on the consul's staff, I find you guilty. Punishment is relegatio for a period determined by the length of this campaign. Until this army is disbanded, you are exiled from Rome unless so ordered into its precincts by consular order or military necessity."

I bowed my head. "I accept your decision without complaint, Consul," I said formally. He had just condemned me to a life in the army. Poor me.

The general, with a hint of a smile, said, "I'll have the documents filed tomorrow. But stay out of Sempronius's sight for a bit, will you?"

"Yes, General." I had no desire to be in the man's company in any case.

"Now tell me what really happened. The whole story – leave nothing out." The general looked younger than he had only a few minutes before, like a child expecting a bedtime story.

I began my tale.

* * *

Two hours later, I was in my quarters finishing my evening meal when Decius and the younger Scipio entered. "I thought you would be at cena, gentlemen," I said, wondering why they were foregoing the elaborate evening meal hosted by Flaminius.

"We've had a messenger from Clastidium," Decius said.

"What news?"

Scipio sat across from me. "The city has fallen. Betrayed by Dasius Brundisius, the garrison commander. He just threw open the gates."

"The grain stores?" I asked.

"Taken to feed the Carthaginians," Scipio confirmed.

"Deodamnatus!" I said. "The garrison?"

Decius grimaced. "Dead to a man, I expect. Or captured and sold for slaves," he said. "The messenger was a civilian, one of the Roman colonists. He was released by Hannibal with the message."

"I guess he wanted to find a way to irritate Sempronius?" I asked.

"And irritate him he has," Scipio said. "It took the better part of an hour for Flaminius and my father to talk him out of an immediate march."

"And now Hannibal has food enough to last the winter," Decius said. "We'll be on half rations soon, if we keep four legions here."

"So, what happens now?" I asked.

"Tomorrow morning, Tribune Torquatus will lead a patrol west across the Trebia," Scipio said. "He's to patrol a day's march, then return."

"How large a force?"

Decius said, "Third Legion."

"That's quite a patrol."

"Indeed," said Scipio. "Sempronius is trying to prove he is a great general. I fear for the army."

"Nothing we can do at this point," I said.

Decius said, "Except pray that Third Legion doesn't find Hannibal's army."

"I'll drink to that," I said, producing a flask of wine. "Here, enjoy. I'm for the baths. I need to wash off a four-day foot march."

"Why don't you bring the wine, Scipio?" Decius said. "I could use a wash myself."

"You two go ahead," he said. "I must see Father after cena."

"Suit yourself," Decius said, grasping the wine. "See you in the morning."

* * *

Two days later, Third Legion returned from their patrol. Their spirits were obviously high, and there were a few bandages evident in the ranks of the legionaries. Decius and I watched from the walls of Placentia as the legion returned to their camp west of the city. A small detachment of riders split from the main force and headed for the city gates.

Decius said, "Tribune Torquatus to report to Consul Sempronius, you think?"

I nodded. "They seem a bit knocked about, but in high spirits. I think they had a run-in with Hannibal and came out the better for it."

"Guess we'll know soon enough," he said.

"Let's go to the Principia and hear first-hand," I said.

We walked down the stairs from the archer's platform and took the brief walk to the administrative building. We arrived just in time to see Torquatus disappear inside. We followed at a sedate pace, not wishing to draw attention to my unpopular presence. We entered the main chamber just as Torquatus began his report.

"… early afternoon yesterday, sir. There were perhaps two thousand infantry and a few hundred cavalry. From our prisoners, they are mostly Iberians. I ordered the cavalry to circle behind them, then had the infantry form line and charge," Torquatus said, his eyes bright. "They were just forming as we hit them. I sent the velites around both flanks to give them a clear field of fire." He paused to take a drink of wine. "Some of their cavalry tried to flee, but our equites intercepted them and cut them down. Then they charged the enemy rear. That's when the rout began. They could not throw down their weapons fast enough."

Sempronius smiled approvingly. "How many captives did you take, Titus?" he asked.

"About two hundred fifty, sir," he said. "The rest were slain and left to rot."

"A good showing, Tribune," General Scipio said evenly.

Decius whispered to me, "I'd expect so, at two-to-one odds and surprise on their side."

"At least we have some good intelligence now," I whispered back, then gestured for silence.

"I'll want your full written report by sundown, Tribune," Sempronius said. "Good work."

"You shall have it, sir. Thank you," Torquatus said.

Sempronius dismissed the tribune and turned to General Scipio. "See, Publius, a bold stroke and our enemy is defeated," he said.

"He was fortunate there were no reinforcements nearby, Tiberius," Scipio said tiredly. "Some of those Numidians would have made his day much more interesting."

"Bah! Numidians! They are but boogeymen to scare children," Sempronius scoffed. "They will be routed just as easily with a properly led army."

Scipio sighed and said, "You underestimate your enemy."

"I defeat my enemy, you mean," Sempronius said. "I believe I shall retire until cena. We should honor our newest hero, no?"

"As you wish, Tiberius," Flaminius said. "I shall prepare a feast in his honor."

"Thank you, Gaius," Sempronius said, standing. "Then I shall see you this evening, gentlemen." He walked from the room followed by a scribe and two legionaries.

"His overconfidence will prove fatal, I believe," General Scipio said.

"He has won our first victory in this war, Publius," Flaminius said. "Let him celebrate a little. Perhaps he will be more amenable to reason in the morning."

"I hope so." Scipio then noticed me and shouted, "Appius! What are you doing here?"

"Observing, sir," I said.

"Saw the tribune returning and thought you would get an edge on the camp rumor mill, eh?" he laughed. "Good for you. But you are lucky Tiberius did not see you."

"The good Consul Sempronius Longus fails to see much," I said. "I felt it was a safe gamble."

Scipio's mood grew somber. "Indeed. There is much he does not see." Then he smiled again and said, "Be gone, Decurion. And be sure not to attend tonight's festivities. I will not have you gamble your life away."

"I have the duty this evening, sir," I said. "No parties and gambling for me."

"Good," Scipio said. "At least one man with some sense will be awake this evening."

Decius and I saluted, then walked from the room.

* * *

"Decurion, signal from the other camp," the duty optio reported, sticking his head into the Guard Commander's tent.

"Come in, Optio," I said, coming awake. I had been dozing fitfully on my stool with my feet propped against the brazier stand and my back against a tent pole. "What do they say?"

"Movement along the river, sir. No word yet on if it's one of our patrols returning," the man reported.

"Acknowledge the signal. I'll be up presently," I said, sitting fully upright.

"Yes, sir," he said, then departed with haste.

I went to our water cistern and pulled out a ladleful. I put a hand in the water and splashed some on my face and drank the rest to clear the last remnants of sleep. Then I walked toward the gate overlooking Placentia and the other legionary camp.

The guards on the tower came stiffly to attention, shivering in the cold night air. It had begun to snow, and the ground was rapidly turning from brownish green to white. I returned the optio's salute and said, "Anything else?"

"Not yet, sir," he said.

"Well, we can wait a bit to call out the guard century then," I said. "Make sure all sentries are alert. I don't want any surprises this morning."

"Right away, sir." The optio rapidly detailed two runners to check the men along the walls. "Anything else, sir?" he asked.

"No, let's just wait a bit," I said. The moon, having been full only a few days before, emerged from behind the snow-clouds, bathing them in a majestic pale light, casting odd shadows across the fields surrounding the city. It was almost exactly a month since our last encounter with Hannibal, I thought. *Hopefully tonight, history won't repeat itself.* From the clepsydra and the marks on the tally slate, it was three hours past midnight. I could see my breath clearly in the cold air. Saturnalia was rapidly approaching, marking the longest night of the year. I doubted we would have much of a celebration here, with Hannibal so close. I pulled my cloak tighter around my body and rubbed my hands together. Damn, it was cold. It began to hail.

"Sir, there!" The optio pointed. "Signal. It reads, under attack by cavalry."

"Acknowledge the signal and call out the guard," I ordered. "Optio, go wake the senior tribune yourself and report."

"Sir, the tribune is in the city with the general," the optio reminded me.

"Right, then go wake Decurion Scipio and tell him."

He saluted, then took off at a run. I turned back to the other camp, which was now ablaze in one corner. I watched as silhouettes of men hurried along the ramparts of the wall and threw pila, the heavy, iron-tipped legionary spear, at unseen enemies below.

I watched for about ten minutes, receiving periodic reports from the guard century, before Decurion Scipio and another tribune joined me on the wall.

"Report," Scipio ordered.

"Looks like Numidians, sir," I said. "I've seen a few of them come along the base of the wall with torches. They set the northwest corner ablaze a few minutes ago." I pointed to a tall black column of smoke. "Nothing happening here as of yet. I've had the guard century called out. All artillery is manned and ready."

"Good," Scipio said simply. "Tribune, take command here. Appius, you are with me. We will take the cavalry to the city to request orders and support if necessary."

The tribune nodded and said, "Yes, sir. I plan to rouse the garrison and prepare to march on order."

"I shall so inform the general," Scipio said, and we walked down the stairs toward our horses. Our turma had already saddled our mounts, bless them. "Mount up!" Scipio ordered. Six hundred men climbed into their saddles. "At the walk, forward!" he shouted, and we rode through the camp toward the gate.

I heard the tribune shout, "Open the gate!" as Scipio approached.

Scipio looked up and saluted the tribune as we passed through the still opening gate. As soon as we were clear, Scipio shouted, "Column of twos, at the gallop, forward!" He kicked his mount and we leapt into the gallop with two lines of cavalry streaming behind. We reached the walls of Placentia in minutes. Scipio slowed us to a walk as we approached the city gates. "Open the gate!"

After passwords had been exchanged, the gates were opened, and we entered the city. Scipio left Decius in command of the cavalry and told me to follow him as he rode to the Principia. A moment later, we handed our reins to a legionary standing guard and walked inside.

As we approached the council chamber, we heard shouting. "You can't march out now. That is exactly what he wants you to do," General Scipio yelled.

"He will not burn down my camp and kill my soldiers without response!" retorted Sempronius.

"We will respond, just not in the middle of the night and unprepared for battle!" Scipio said, struggling to regain his composure.

"My men are not unprepared!" Sempronius said, face reddening. "They are fine soldiers who will do Rome proud! It is you, cowering in your camp in the heart of Italy, who are unprepared. What good is there in delay and further waste of time? Is there a third consul and third army marching to our aid? Romans will not be driven from their native soil, from the land on which they were born. We march now!"

"They will walk into an ambush if you lead them out tonight," General Scipio said more calmly.

"Ha! You wish to defeat Hannibal yourself and rob me of the honor," Sempronius said accusingly. "I will not give up my authority over the army before my term is overin March. We will march, now!"

"You are a fool, Sempronius Longus!" Scipio shouted, realizing his temper had gotten the better of him, tried to pull the accusation back. "Tiberius—"

"A fool? You think me a fool? Only if I remain here amongst you women!" Sempronius turned and stormed out of the room, shouting for his horse.

General Scipio stood shakily, mouth open at his slip of the tongue. "Damn," he said quietly.

"Sir, Decurions Scipio and Asprenas reporting for duty," the junior Scipio said.

"Son, there is a lesson for you," the general said. "Never call a man a fool when he is acting foolishly. It does not allow the fool to reconsider his actions."

"So you have told me, Father," the decurion said softly.

"Report, Decurion," his father said.

"First and Seventh Legions are preparing to march. All of our cavalry is present in the city. Tribune Marius commands the camp and will lead the infantry as ordered," the younger Scipio said.

"Good," the general said. "Take your turma and report that to Sempronius. Stay with him. When it turns bad, provide him with some good options, son. Perhaps we can salvage something from this debacle."

"Yes, sir," the younger Scipio said. We saluted and walked from the chamber in pursuit of General Sempronius Longus.

XVIII

TREBIA

We reached the marching camp in time to see Roman cavalry chasing the Numidians across the Trebia. Third and Fourth Legion's equites and alae cavalry chased twice their number of nimble horses and their black-skinned riders across the shallow river. The water was four feet deep, maybe deeper in some places, but it wasn't a problem for horsemen. As we entered the gate, I saw the Numidians veer north toward the Padus, easily staying out of reach of the Roman heavy cavalry.

We reached the Principia just in time to hear Sempronius dismiss his officers with orders to parade the men. The sun had yet to climb above the horizon, but the sky was lightening to the east. Hail and snow flecked the armor of men readying themselves for combat. I stayed with the men while Scipio reported to the general. A few minutes later, he returned.

"We are to attach ourselves to the general's staff," Scipio said. "Our men will be used as messengers to relay reports back to Placentia and General Scipio."

The buccinators sounded blasts from their horns. "That will be the signal to parade then," I said.

"Let us move to the gate," Scipio said.

We maneuvered our mounts through the press to a position near the gate closest to the Trebia. The gate doors were open. In front of the First Century, a group of four legionaries guarded the aquilifer, who carried a spear shaft topped by a small golden boar, beneath which was a banner with the number III, the standard of Third Legion. He marched at the head of the legion and would guard that standard to the death. Behind him marched the signifier of the First Century, carrying the century's standard, a smaller version of the legion standard with the number I emblazoned in gold on its crimson field. In battle, the First Century would stand at the legion's far right, the place of greatest danger, and anchor the line. Beside the signifier rode the senior tribune of the legion, who was a deputy commander to General Sempronius in charge of this legion while his counterpart commanded Fourth Legion. At another blast from the buccinator, the army marched through the gate.

"These men have been woken from a dead sleep, had nothing to eat, and now march into battle against an unknown enemy," I said. "This is madness."

"It may be madness, but we have no choice but to obey," Scipio said. "Decius, pick a man. Report to General Scipio that we have attached ourselves to General Sempronius's staff and will act as messengers between the consuls."

Decius shouted to one of his men and relayed the message. The cavalryman raced through the gate and toward the city. "Done, sir," he reported.

"Let's be off then," Scipio said as Sempronius's staff marched through the gate into the blustery morning snow.

* * *

A few minutes later, the army stretched itself into a line of battle in the classic triplex aces used by the manipular armies of Rome. At the forefront were eight thousand velites, armored in their traditional pelts and leather and carrying javelins and short swords Behind them marched three lines of heavy infantry.

The legionaries in the first line were the hastatii. These were young men, citizens wealthy enough to purchase armor and weapons, but still inexperienced in war. They wore a lorica hamata, a tightly woven mail shirt that offered protection to the shoulders and torso. They also wore a bronze galea or helm that flared to the rear to protect the neck from chopping blows. They carried two or three pila, the heavy iron-tipped javelins, behind their scutum, which was a long, rectangular shield, curved to protect the legionary from the front. Their other weapon was the gladius, a short steel sword that in the press of battle was more useful than the Gallic long swords. These men would be the first to close with the enemy.

In the second line marched the principes. These were equipped similarly to the hastatii but were more experienced men who had the wealth to equip themselves with the best equipment. Some wore lorica squamata with bronze or steel scales in place of the mail of the hastatii. They too carried the pilum, scutum, and gladius. These men would step forward to fill gaps in the lines of the hastatii, and their experience would steady their younger comrades during battle.

The third line of men were the triarii. These were the wealthiest and oldest of the infantry soldiers. They wore very fine lorica hamata or squamata with intricate designs engraved on the plates or buckles. They carried scutum. They were armed with both the gladius and a long spear called hastae. Many wore brightly dyed horse hair or feathers atop their galea. These men would only be committed to battle if all seemed lost.

To either side of the legionaries marched the alae troops. These men, similarly equipped to the legionaries, were members of the socii or independent city-states on the Italian Peninsula loyal to Rome. They more than doubled the number of troops of the legions, providing much-needed manpower to Rome's forces. In total, Sempronius Longus commanded nearly forty-two thousand men. Four thousand cavalry, eighteen thousand legionaries, and twenty thousand alae infantry. It was an impressive force.

I rode beside Scipio, followed by Decius and the rest of the turma. We trailed the general staff by a hundred yards or so. I watched as the velites plunged into the icy water that was chest high on a tall man. Some of the shorter soldiers were neck deep. The passage was quick as the river was only about forty yards wide at this point, but I saw the men wince as the cold wind began to dry the water from their wet bodies. By the time all had crossed, and it was our turn, I could see the infantry were shivering and concentrating on blocking the wind with their shields rather than the enemy. I saw more than one man drop his weapon from numb fingers only to scramble to retrieve it under the verbal blistering of a centurion.

I brought my heels up to avoid the water but had to kick my horse to force him into the river. He had no more desire for an icy bath than did any of the rest of us. In the end, my boots were soaked, and I hoped I wouldn't lose any toes to frostbite. But the infantry were infinitely worse off, having been nearly submerged.

The sun rose behind the clouds but offered no warmth. The sleeting rain blew into our faces, doubling every man's misery.

Scipio said, "Look there" and pointed across the field.

Along the low flat floodplain stood men in armor waiting and ready for battle. I recognized the Gauls in the center of the formation with their round shields and long swords. Their beards were shaggy and unkempt, and they were lightly armored, if at all.

On the enemy right stood the swarthy men of Carthage and their Libyan allies. Their conical bronze helms and breastplates contrasted with the oval hoplite shields painted white. The shields had designs of gorgon heads, serpents, and other mystical creatures in black or blue. Those men were armed with spears and swords that could defeat any legionary in man-to-man fighting.

On the left, Hannibal placed his Iberian allies. I could see their iron javelins protruding above their round shields, decorated with bronze and iron bosses. Each carried a falcata, a sword with a heavy axe-like head that was particularly good at crushing bones, even through armor. They seemed a mix of heavily armored and lightly armored men, but their projectiles would likely cause some damage before they closed with the Roman line.

"Gods! What are those?" Decius asked, seeing the looming gray shapes towering on either side of the Carthaginian infantry line. "I thought they were boulders, but they move!"

"Those are elephants," I said. I saw fifteen or twenty on each side of the battle line, each ridden by two men. One, the mahout, was the driver and attempted to keep the beast pointed in the right direction. The other was an archer, who could fire down into enemy infantry with a plunging fire that could pierce armor.

A few of the elephants trumpeted and Decius shivered, but I didn't think it was from the wind. "I want no part of them. How would you even attack it? They're as big as a mountain!"

"From behind, Decurion," Scipio said, loud enough for the men to hear. Then, more softly, he said to Decius, "Remember yourself, Decurion. The men watch you."

Decius had the grace to lower his head in shame.

Just then the Numidian cavalry raced between the two armies, followed closely by the Romans sent to pursue them.

"Signal them to fall back!" I heard Sempronius order. "They'll never catch them in any case."

A short time later, the buccinators sounded the recall, and our cavalry returned to take up positions on either flank. The Numidians joined their Carthaginian and Iberian heavy cavalry allies on either flank of the enemy formation.

The stage was set for battle.

The floodplain provided good, solid ground to support armored men and horses. The cold weather had frozen any soft mud to rock hardness. To our right was a series of low hills over which lay the River Padus, just out of sight. To our left was a marsh covered in tall brown grass. After the river crossing, none of the Romans wanted to chance getting stuck in the icy mud the marsh promised, so we stayed clear.

"Torquatus, have them sound the advance," General Sempronius's voice called. And the battle commenced with a sound of horns and the trumpeting of elephants in response.

The velites dashed forward with their shields held aloft, each with a veretum ready to throw. A low whirring sound came from the enemy line.

"'Ware the slingers!" a centurion shouted just before a hail of lead bullets crashed into the light infantry. One of the oval-shaped lead balls crashed into the shin of a velite, and he screamed as the bone smashed into splinters and blood erupted from the wound. Around him other men fell even as they hurled their javelins into the ranks of the enemy. Now screams of pain sounded from the packed ranks of the Carthaginian lines as the iron-tipped shafts fell from the sky into feet, shoulders, necks, and heads. If an enemy was fortunate enough to catch the javelin on his shield, the heavy iron tip would penetrate it and likely bend, so it was difficult to remove. That soldier could either take the time to remove the barb or drop his shield. Either way, he was distracted and weakened, before the main battle began.

The velites launched another volley, then began their rapid retreat before the heavy infantry could move out to slaughter them. The Roman light infantry moved toward either flank, taking shelter by the Roman cavalry. Then horns sounded from the Carthaginian lines, and their cavalry charged.

The Roman cavalry was wet and exhausted from pursuing the Numidians. They tried to countercharge, but when the horses neared the elephants, many of them bolted, throwing their riders. Outnumbered two to one, the Romans fought valiantly, but only for a few minutes. Then in ones and twos, and soon by the hundred, the Roman cavalry fled. The Numidians chased them down, hurling javelins into the backs of their fleeing victims.

"Advance the hastatii," Sempronius ordered. And once again the horns sounded. The first line of infantry walked toward the enemy. At twenty paces from the Carthaginian line, I heard centurions shouting, "Halt! Prepare! Loose!" More than a thousand iron-tipped pila flew toward the Carthaginian lines. On the right, came a few hundred javelins in return. Screams sounded in both formations, then the centurions yelled, "Charge!"

With a crash and clatter, the main lines engaged.

Sempronius moved his horse toward the main battle. He stood between the principe and the triarii. His staff followed and so did we. From our vantage point, we could see the Gauls flailing their longswords against the interlocked shields of the hastatii.

"That's it, men, push them back! Push them back!" the general encouraged.

Soon the Gauls were giving way in the center, and both flanks were holding. The alae troops were having a much harder fight against the better-armored and equipped Libyans and Iberians. Then the cavalry returned.

Carthaginian horses sliced into both flanks and killed several hundred velites. The light infantry fled to the safety of the alae legion formations on the flanks. Alae troops in the principe line moved out to provide some support under the guidance of their prefects. The horsemen were forced to retreat to re-form for another charge.

The lumbering elephants finally reached the flanks of the Roman formation. Strapped to their tusks were swords or spears that slashed into the hapless infantry. Arrows rained down on upraised scutum from the archers atop the great beasts. Armor on the ungainly beasts' heads and flanks deflected javelins and spears. Swords were useless against the tough hide. Soldiers screamed as bodies were crushed beneath ponderous feet, and the trumpeting bellows of the elephants terrified the men on the flanks.

Sempronius Longus finally noticed the threat. To his waiting messengers, he ordered, "Have them use their javelins on the legs. The animals are vulnerable in the knees from behind." The messengers ran off to relay the order to prefects and centurions on the flanks. "Keep pressing forward, men! We have their measure!"

The elephants continued to wreak havoc in the closely packed alae formations on the flanks. Their tusks sliced back and forth, bowling over lines of men as if they were scythes through wheat. The velites fled deeper into the infantry formation, clogging the gaps between units and slowing the cavalry messengers.

Soon though, whether from Sempronius's orders or experienced legionaries taking charge, the velites began to dash out behind the elephants - dodging the deadly arrows - to use their remaining veretum as spears. They attacked the elephants from all sides, distracting the mahouts and archers. Many of the principe broke ranks to join the light infantry. Finally, one or two brave men cut into the tendons of one of the beast's legs. The elephant bellowed in agony and tried to rear, but its injured leg collapsed and the animal fell. Immediately, the rage and helplessness of the infantry unleashed itself on the mahout and archer. The giant gray beast was covered in men, stabbing until it lay an unmoving block of bloody flesh and bone.

One by one, the behemoths fell. Only two of the beasts managed to escape, fleeing back toward the Carthaginian camp, trampling Romans and Carthaginians alike in their pain and terror.

Then the enemy's cavalry returned for another charge. Clumped in indefensible masses around the elephants, the infantry were cut down by the nimble cavalrymen. The alae principe line rallied to establish a new line behind the dead and dying elephants, which held against the cavalry onslaught.

From behind the Carthaginian main line sounded another horn.

Like demons from hell, men rose from the tall grass behind the Roman left. A thousand heavy infantry and a thousand heavy cavalry fell upon the Roman rear. The triarii, surprised but nearly unflappable, turned to face the new threat.

"Sir, do you see?" I said to Scipio, pointing to the triarii engaging the enemy infantry attacking from the rear.

"Yes. But Sempronius does not," he said. "Come, let's inform him he is surrounded. Perhaps we can lend a hand."

The general had committed the Roman principes to the battle against the Gauls. He was directly behind the infantry line shouting encouragement as the Romans pushed the Gauls back and extended his penetration into the enemy line.

Scipio came to a halt and said, "Sir, infantry and cavalry attack from the rear! We must consolidate and withdraw."

"We shall do nothing of the sort. I shall have a penetration of the main line in moments, and we will roll them up!" he countered.

"Sir, all of your forces are committed. You have no reserves to exploit a penetration!" Scipio argued.

"Silence, boy!" the general snarled. "Do not think to lecture your betters."

The alae troops were hard-pressed on all sides but holding steady, I saw. "Sir, if you break their line, you open our backs to attack from their cavalry," I said.

"And you should be under arrest, Decurion!" Sempronius shouted, then wheeled as a shout went up from the Roman infantry. "Forward, men, forward!"

The combined force of the hastatii and principe had broken the Gallic line. After the early morning, the hunger, the icy river crossing, the snow and the freezing cold, the Romans wanted vengeance. They pursued the fleeing Gauls, leaving the rest of the legion behind.

Sempronius, realizing what was happening, shouted at the running legionaries, "Halt! Halt, you men!" and spurred his horse in pursuit.

The Roman legionaries were already a hundred yards from the battle and rapidly gaining on their fleeing foes. But for the alae infantry, this was too much. They began to back away from the pressing Carthaginian forces.

Just before the gap in the line caused by the Gauls' collapse closed, Scipio shouted, "Follow me!" and spurred his horse in pursuit of Sempronius and the legionaries. The turma followed at a gallop, forcing their way through the Carthaginians trying to get around the alae line.

I looked over my shoulder to see a ring of infantry attacked on every front. They were edging toward the river, but I feared they would never make it back to camp.

XIX

THE HOLLOW SQUARE

Scipio pulled up atop a small rise overlooking the Padus and wheeled back toward the battle. The rest of us followed his lead and reined our horses to a halt.

"Defensive perimeter!" I ordered. The men quickly obeyed and created a circle around the officers.

"Oh gods," Decius said, his face becoming pale.

I looked back then. From our vantage, we could see into the fight we had just left behind. The triarii formed a solid wall along the far side. The alae infantry, equipped almost identically to any Roman legionary, had managed to close the near side where we had just managed to force our way through. Thousands of Roman soldiers formed a hollow square and fought against twice their number.

"Look there," said Scipio, pointing. A centurion's transverse crest rose in the center of the square and began gesturing and, though we couldn't hear him, shouting. "They have too far to go."

I didn't understand what he meant until I saw that the square had begun moving in slow, measured half steps, toward the river. The centurion was sounding a cadence, timing the entire legion's steps, to move them toward the Trebia and the marching camp.

The triarii slammed their shields into the Carthaginians on their side of the formation, forcing them back. Half step. The men on the flanks took a half step to the side. The men on our side of the square took a half step back. This process was repeated over and over. They were a hundred yards from the river. Then fifty. Then thirty.

Bodies lay strewn across the battlefield in heaps and mounds of blood and viscera. The legionaries had to step over or sometimes on their fallen comrades. And for every step, more and more fell.

The Carthaginians were pushed to the river's edge. It was too much for some of the alae soldiers who had borne the brunt of the fight today. Some of them broke from the formation and ran into the river, trying to get across and flee to the safety of the marching camp. Most were cut down by Numidian javelins. But their absence in the line left gaps – gaps that doomed the rest of the brave men below.

The Iberians on the left pushed into the center of the square. Four of them attacked the centurion timing the march. He didn't even see them coming. An Iberian spear in his back put an end to the Roman army's disciplined flight.

Behind the Iberians poured the Numidian cavalry. Once inside the square, their javelins and short swords turned a fairly even melee into a rout. Then the slaughter began.

"Come on," Scipio said. "We must catch Sempronius and the rest of the legion." He pulled hard on the reins and spurred his horse after the Roman infantry.

* * *

Nearly two miles up the Padus, we finally caught up with Sempronius. The legionaries had stopped in a village, over which rose hills to the south covered with dormant vines. Barrels of wine lay empty in the streets.

"Roma invicta!" shouted a group of hastatii, raising bowls, cups, and goblets liberated from the Insubres houses. A dead Gaul warrior sat on the ground, leaning against the barrel into which the men dipped for their wine.

One of the legionaries clapped the dead man on the shoulder and said, "You can't fight, but you sure can make good wine."

The other men laughed and added their own comments about Gallic fighting skills.

We passed any number of similar groups until we found the general trying to rally his men.

"You men, we must march on!" Sempronius shouted ineffectually to a legionary who was pouring a flask of wine into his mouth.

His staff officers were having an equal lack of success.

The legionaries broke down doors and searched for more wine. One group of about sixty principes had found a storehouse filled with flasks and guarded it with jealous fury against all comers. Then the fire started. One of the legionaries in a drunken rage knocked over a brazier left behind when the villagers fled from the approaching Romans. The glowing embers immediately ignited the straw strewn across the floor and spread throughout the dwelling. A tower of black smoke rose as the thatch and wood hovel burned.

"Sir, we can't stay here," Torquatus said to the general. "We must flee."

Sempronius ignored him and tried to cajole another group of legionaries into forming.

"Decius, Appius," Scipio shouted, "form a line. We will start with that lot there." He drew his sword and pointed it at a group of legionaries led by a centurion at the edge of the village.

We quickly arranged our horses into a twenty-nine wide cordon and approached the hovel the legionaries were looting. The soldiers were surrounded and at sword point before they knew what was happening.

"Centurion!" Scipio placed the point of his sword at the man's throat. "I would appreciate your assistance in restoring some order in the ranks," he said in a calm and steady voice.

Blanching a bit as the cold steel touched his skin, the centurion answered, "Yes, sir! At once, sir." He stepped back a pace, turned, and snarled, "Now, you lot! We're done sucking at Murtia's teats here," invoking the Goddess of sloth and laziness. "Form up!"

Any of the legionaries who thought about disobeying were soon persuaded by a combination of invective from the centurion and the swords held by the grim-faced cavalrymen. In minutes, the centurion had a century at his command again.

"Orders, sir?" he asked politely, ignoring the fact that he had no idea who the officer he addressed was.

"Form a line two deep. Surround the next building and enlist the aid of all inside your circle. If no officer is present, appoint one an optio and restore military discipline," Scipio said, sheathing his sword. "My men will assist."

In very little time, we had enlisted the help of another four centuries of men. As we moved toward the market square, I saw one of Sempronius's tribunes pointing at us as he tried to get the general's attention.

We were close enough by this point that I could hear their conversation.

Sempronius Longus ignored the man dumbly for a few moments, then realized what he was saying. He said in a steady voice, "Let's see what this is all about" as if he were investigating a new item at the market.

When the general arrived at Scipio's impromptu command post moments later, he found centurions from Third and Fourth Legions making reports to the young decurion.

"What is this?" the general asked.

Scipio ignored the comment until the centurion before him had finished his report, then said, "Carry on, Centurion. Report back once the north side of the village is secure."

The centurion saluted, turned sharply, and marched off as if on a parade field.

Scipio saluted the general, who ignored the gesture. "Sir, I have regained control of approximately a quarter of Third and Fourth Legions. I am in the process of restoring order to the remainder. We should be prepared to march in less than half an hour."

The general's mouth fell open wide. Whatever response he was expecting, a formal report on the state of his command was not on the list. "You have what?" was the best he could manage.

"Sir, I have centuries surrounding and restoring discipline to troops that have lately become disorganized due to battle," Scipio said in an even tone. "I expect the men to rally once it becomes evident that military discipline has been restored."

The general shook his head as if trying to clear out cobwebs. "Very well, Decurion. I will assume command now," he said formally.

"No, sir, you will not," Scipio said coldly. "You will confine yourself to staying out of the way of officers performing their military duties. Is that understood?"

"How dare you—"

"Centurion! Place this man under arrest." Scipio addressed a nearby guard, gesturing at Sempronius Longus.

"Yes, sir," the centurion replied at once and jerked his head at two of his soldiers, who grabbed Sempronius by his arms.

"Confine him in the building," Scipio ordered. "Ignore anything he says. Bind and gag him if he becomes annoying."

Sempronius, who had started to berate the two legionaries, paused for a moment at that threat. "You would not dare."

"General, you have lost two thirds of your men, perhaps more, due to your own foolishness and pride. You will be charged with high treason at worst, negligence at best. Remain silent and perhaps you will survive this debacle. Try my patience and you surely will not," Scipio said in a voice of cold steel. "Take him away."

The legionaries nearly lifted Sempronius as they dragged him toward a small building, formerly a stable, for his confinement.

* * *

A short time later, the surviving men of Third and Fourth Legions formed into marching order and headed west along the banks of the Padus. Between the two legions rode Scipio and his turma, who guarded General Sempronius Longus. The general, none the worse for wear from his confinement in the barn, sat atop his impressive white stallion with a sour look on his face. Torquatus rode at his side. Neither spoke, fearing the wrath of the decurion who had usurped their command.

A few minutes later, Decius rode in from the west. He had taken his section on a scouting patrol. He saluted. "Sir, we've found a bridge," he said, not waiting for Scipio to return the salute.

"Where?" Scipio asked.

"About two miles upstream. It's rickety, but if we cross in small numbers, we can get across the Padus, sir."

"Good work, Decius," Scipio said. "Take a century at double-time. Secure the bridge on both sides. Once we are across, destroy the bridge."

"Yes, sir," Decius said with a grin. He shouted for the century in the van to increase pace and soon they were trotting out of sight into the distance ahead.

Forty minutes later, we marched into sight of the bridge. Decius wasn't exaggerating about its flimsiness. The bridge was made of lashed-together wood and spanned the narrowest point of the River Padus. Still, half the legionaries Decius had taken ahead had crossed it and were waiting on the far side. It would be stable enough. And when it came time to destroy the bridge... well, that wouldn't be a problem.

Decius rode up. "We'll have to lead the horses, sir," he said. "The bridge sways a bit, especially in the middle. The horses don't like it much."

"I don't think I like it much either," I said.

Scipio shot me a quelling glare. "Good enough, Decius. Get the horses across first. Then we will start sending men across by sections." He turned to me and said, "See General Sempronius Longus across the bridge. Take command at the far side until I can get everyone across. I'll be the last man."

"Yes, sir," I said. "Scouting parties?"

"Once two centuries are across, send Decius east along the Padus. I expect we'll find no resistance to our passage, but let's not walk into another ambush, eh?"

"Very good, sir." I turned to Sempronius and with a polite tone said, "General, if you will please accompany me. I'll see you safely across the river."

The look he gave me could have melted steel.

* * *

An hour after noon, one of Decius's scouts returned at a gallop. His horse, snorting and blowing, strained against the reins as the man reported, "Sir, there's a Roman outpost in sight. Three miles ahead. No sign of any trouble, but Decurion Decius maintains an observation post as the section scouts around the castra."

Scipio nodded and said, "See to your mount. I'll have a message for Decius when you return. Carry on."

The equestrian soldier saluted, then turned to lead his horse toward the river. After he was a few paces away, I said, "Hannibal could have taken the outpost, sir."

"True enough," Scipio agreed. "But we need some information about things on this side of the river."

"And if it's bad news?"

"Then we retake the outpost, leave a garrison, and move on," Scipio said with determination. "We cannot cross back here. We are still on the wrong side of the Trebia."

"So we march on?"

"We march on and get back to Placentia and Father," Scipio said.

When the messenger returned, Scipio said, "Tell Decurion Decius to continue observing the outpost until we arrive. I'll want to know if we can take it quickly if we must. Scaling ladders only."

The man repeated back the message. Once Scipio was certain his instructions were clear, the man mounted and was off at a rapid canter.

"I'll get one of the centuries to start constructing ladders, then, shall I?" I asked.

"We'll do that at our next halt," Scipio said. "The men can do it when we stop for water. We'll take half an hour. Send men foraging for wood. We'll carry it with us and build ladders if we need them."

"Good enough," I said.

We came to Decius's position an hour later. The army rested behind a small hill while Scipio and I conferred with the decurion.

"Report," Scipio said.

Decius smiled and said, "I think Hannibal hasn't been here, sir. Haven't seen much in the way of activity, but there's a small Gallic village on the far side of the outpost. The river sort of bends back toward us here." He motioned to the north and continued, "The village is there on the banks of the river. No alarm or worry in the village. Just people going about their day, farming or whatnot."

"Anything from the castra?" I asked.

"Like I said, not much," Decius said. "Just a few heads bobbing along the walls on some walking patrols. No one's gone in or out."

"Call in your men – I'll want them for escort," Scipio ordered. "Decius, you stay here and guard the general. Appius, you're with me. Bring the turma."

"Yes, sir," we said in unison.

A few minutes later, Scipio and I rode within bowshot of the gates. Before we could get any closer, a voice shouted from the wall, "Halt! Who's that then?" ——

Scipio said in a voice pitched to carry, "Decurion Scipio, First Legion."

"Advance and be recognized, Decurion. Leave your men there," the voice said.

"Stay here, Decius," Scipio said in his normal voice. "And watch my back."

"Yes, sir."

Scipio rode up to the gate and the sally port opened. A centurion stepped through with two legionaries. After a brief consultation with the centurion, Scipio shouted, "Decius, bring the turma. All is well."

We rode forward and the gates opened. The centurion saluted and said, "Welcome to Ad Lambrum, gentlemen."

"Thank you, Centurion," Scipio said. "Appius, send a man back for the rest of the army. We'll gather some provisions here and be off. I want to be moving within an hour."

EDWARD GREEN

"You've had some troubles then, sir?" the centurion asked.

"You could say that," Scipio said. "Hannibal is loose in the area. You are wise to maintain such a vigilant guard."

"Thank you, sir."

Scipio nodded his response, then said, "I need information. What lies downstream from here along the Padus? Is there a bridge?"

The centurion said, "There's the outpost of Ad Rotas about three miles from here. Then you'll want to turn southeast back toward the Padus." We walked into the fort and toward the wooden building the centurion used as a headquarters.

"Ad Rotas is similar to this place?" Scipio asked.

"Yes, sir. Almost identical. We both have about a thousand men and are stationed near Gallic villages. Both communities grow crops and fish the river."

"And you've had no troubles with the local Gauls?" I asked.

"No, sir. They seem peaceful enough. Of course, we do spend our pay in the village, so that tends to help endear us to the locals."

Scipio interrupted this commentary. "What is further on then?"

"Well, if you go southeast like I said, you'll find the river bends back to the south. If you keep on that way, you'll come to the bridge just downstream from Placentia. That's where our headquarters is."

"Good. And the terrain?" Scipio asked.

"Gentle hills, lots of little farms. From the tops of the hills you can see down the river pretty well. Not good terrain for an ambush," he said.

"Good." Scipio turned to me. "Appius, I want you on the march as soon as the horses are fed and watered. Stop at Ad Rotas and make sure all is well there. Then press on to the bridge. We will catch you up in—"

"About six hours march, sir," the centurion said.

"Thank you. Six, maybe seven hours," Scipio finished.

"We build a camp tonight, sir?" I asked.

Scipio shook his head. "Not tonight. We'll march on to Placentia. These men can sleep in their own camp tonight."

"That's a long day for them, sir," I said.

"Better a long day than getting caught in the open," he said. "Speed is our ally. If we stop and Hannibal finds us, we are finished."

"I'll not argue that with you," I said, then rose to depart. "The general?" I asked over my shoulder from the door.

The centurion looked confused but said nothing about this non sequitur.

"I will let Father deal with him," Scipio said.

I saluted and said, "May Fortuna watch over you, sir."

"And you, Appius," Scipio said, returning the salute. "See you in a few hours."

XX

RETURN TO PLACENTIA

Scipio and I watched Tribune Torquatus march the dejected men of the Third and Fourth Legions into their camp. To a man, they looked haggard and raw. Scipio had marched them along the hilltop as the sun was setting. They had seen the comrades they abandoned to death only this morning. It was a lesson they would not soon forget.

After returning the legions to their place, we rode in silence to the gates of Placentia. There Decius and the turma awaited our arrival. Alongside the tall decurion sat another dejected form, General Sempronius Longus.

Scipio halted his mount at right angles to Decius and the general. "Decius, see the men back to camp. Appius and I will escort the general to his meeting with father and Gaius Flaminius."

"I'll see to the men, sir," Decius said. "Good luck with your report."

"Thank you, Decurion," Scipio said, then turned to Sempronius. "General, shall we make our reports?"

The general just glowered at the young decurion. But he turned his horse to enter the gates. Within minutes we were walking into Flaminius's audience chamber.

"Tiberius," General Scipio said in a much stronger voice than the day before, "we feared you dead when you did not come straight here."

"Publius, Gaius," Sempronius said in an even voice. "I was detained by these officers," he hissed the last word. "I am to face charges, according to Decurion Scipio here."

This declamation was met with stony silence.

Decurion Scipio broke the deadly quiet, "I detained you during a time of crisis. You did not seem yourself after the trauma of the battle. I

138

assumed command of the army to restore good order and discipline only. You face no charges from me, sir."

Flaminius barked a laugh. "You seem to make a habit out of assuming command of armies, boy."

Scipio had the good grace to redden a bit. "I only did what was necessary, sir."

General Scipio said, "Perhaps we shall both face charges before this is over, Tiberius. Between us we have lost something like thirty thousand men." He paused, letting the number hang in the air.

There seemed to be a lot of uncomfortable silences in this conversation. I decided to ask a question. "Where is Hannibal now?"

"He moved west after you, we thought," Flaminius said.

"We never saw him," I said. "We destroyed the bridge west of Ad Padum after crossing. But we never saw an army passing west."

"We shall send out patrols tomorrow morning to locate him again," General Scipio said. "He will not go far."

"You seem much improved since this morning, Publius," Sempronius said. "Are you quite recovered from your woundsthen?"

"Hardly," said General Scipio. "The surgeon gave me a foul potion that has dulled the pain a bit. I'll not ride a horse for a few days yet."

"You are fit to command here though?" Sempronius asked.

"Fit enough," Scipio said. "I do not plan to chase Hannibal through the snow and sleet, in any case. We must retire to winter quarters until the weather improves."

"Certainly," Flaminius said. "His Africans cannot be familiar with these colder climes and will suffer unless he finds shelter for them."

"One of us must return to Rome to oversee the elections, Publius," Sempronius Longus said. "In your current state of health, I suppose I should be the one traveling."

"I can certainly oversee the training of the legions until spring," Scipio said.

"We cannot hold four legions, no matter how depleted" – Flaminius gazed accusingly at Sempronius – "here in Placentia for the entire winter. We have not the food stores and other supplies necessary to support such numbers."

"I shall march my army to Cremona and winter there," Scipio said. "That should alleviate the problem."

"And we can split Third and Fourth between the two marching camps already constructed until quarters can be finished inside the city for them," Flaminius suggested. "That will provide security for the colonists here as we build up the colony while Scipio guards our line of communications to Arriminium."

"Who will command the legions here then?" Sempronius asked.

"Your man Torquatus is Senior Military Tribune, no?" Flaminius said.

"He is." Sempronius nodded. "And he would be my choice in my absence."

"It is your choice, Tiberius," Scipio said. "No one has removed you from office."

"I think your son made a bold attempt to do so," Sempronius said with cold venom. "He should be severely reprimanded for usurping my authority so."

"If you had held any authority over those men at the time, I would not have been able to do so, Consul," Decurion Scipio said with an emotionless voice.

"Publius!" General Scipio scolded. "Keep your tongue civil or I will see you broken."

The decurion lowered his eyes at the rebuke, but remained otherwise still.

Sempronius Longus seemed to wilt for a moment, then admitted, "The boy is correct. I had lost control. I can see that, however much I dislike the thought." He turned to the younger man and said, "I apologize for threatening you. You acted appropriately in restoring order."

"Sir" was Scipio's only reply.

"I would have you remain here to act as Torquatus's second and commander of cavalry, if you are amenable?" Sempronius said with a hesitant smile.

"A splendid recommendation." Flaminius beamed, eager to put all unpleasantness behind them. "Do say yes, young Scipio. It is the proper thing to do."

Scipio looked at his father and raised an eyebrow.

"You and your turma are detached for duty at Placentia," the general said. "Assist Torquatus in the training of the legions here and guard the colony. First and Second shall march tomorrow, and I will go with them."

"Yes, sir," said the younger Scipio.

Sempronius's smile of approval never reached his eyes, I noted. When I looked at my decurion, I saw only a mask of impassivity.

"I will spend a few days organizing things here, I think," Sempronius said. "I will depart for Rome by the end of the week. Then I leave it to Torquatus and young Scipio here to manage until I return."

"Then it is settled," said Flaminius. "Now let us see to our wounded and care for our dead."

* * *

I started awake as something slapped my feet. I rolled out of bed and into a fighting crouch, then I saw Decurion Scipio standing at the foot of my pallet.

"Good to know your reflexes are still good, old man," he said, smiling. "Get dressed. We must see Father before he leaves." Scipio pulled his armor over an expensive-looking tunic.

"What troubles you?" I asked, reaching for my harness.

"Did you not think that Sempronius Longus agreed a little too fast last night?" Scipio asked.

"It was rather strange, given the circumstances," I said. "But he did have lots of time to think during our trip down the Padus."

"Exactly. And do you think he would give up on vengeance so easily? He plots something. I want to know what."

"So you seek advice from your father?" I said. "He's likely planning something too, knowing that sly son of Dolos and Fraus."

"That would make me the grandson of trickery and fraud?" Scipio asked with humor in his eyes.

"Yes, by Cerebos's balls, it does. You're a clever one too," I said.

"If mother heard you swear like that, she would have your balls served for dinner." Scipio chuckled.

I laughed and said, "She might at that. She's got no sense of humor, your mother." We walked toward the consul's office. Light from lamps and candles lighted the passages and poured from Scipio's chamber. We heard low voices as we knocked to announce ourselves.

"Ah, young Scipio. Good," Flaminius said. "Do come in. And you brought your man Appius. Perfect."

"Father, Gaius. You were expecting us?" Scipio asked.

"I expected you to notice when someone lies to your face, yes," the general said. "And, yes, I expected you to seek me out to gather intelligence before you acted."

"Then you already have a plan?"

"I told you he was quick, Gaius." The general smiled. "Yes, boy, I have a plan and it involves all of us. Take seats, gentlemen. We have little time."

* * *

"Safe journey, Father," Scipio said to the man who lay on the cushioned palanquin.

"Thank you, son," the general said. "Keep your wits about you, boy. Send Laelius with any messages. He can be trusted."

"He or Decius, sir," the decurion said. "Both have proved themselves. I will do as you say."

The general grasped his son's arm and said, "Jupiter strengthen your arms and Minerva give you wisdom. You shall need both soon, I believe."

The younger man's face grew solemn. "I believe you are right, sir."

The general shouted for his bearers to lift the palanquin. "When you are ready, Plinius. Get them moving," he said to the primus pilus.

"Yes, sir," Plinius said, then turned to the column of men. "By centuries, forward march!" His command echoed down the column of soldiers, and Scipio's army marched through the gates and eastward toward the colony of Cremona.

We watched them from the ramparts until the palanquin bearing Scipio's father disappeared over a distant hill. Scipio turned to me and said, "Let's transfer our belongings to a chamber here in the castra. I don't want to be a mile away, if something happens."

"I'll see to it, sir," I said, understanding the need to be at the center of authority. Proximity to the senior officer gave others the impression of power and authority. Scipio understood the reality of appearances. "You should meet with Torquatus and Sempronius, I think."

Scipio nodded. "Good idea. Find me in Flaminius's chambers."

"Very good, sir," I said and walked to our quarters. Along the way I found a centurion from Fourth Legion. "I need a detail of eight men at my quarters. See to it," I ordered.

The centurion looked perturbed that I, a decurion commander of cavalry, was giving orders to the infantry, but thought better of arguing. "Yes, sir. Where exactly?"

I gave him directions and I continued on to my quarters. By the time the eight men arrived, I had our gear packed and ready for transport. "Take these to the city Principia. Ask the guards at the main entrance to the building. I'll have a servant there to guide you to the correct chamber."

The optio in charge of the detail said, "Yes, sir." If he were upset at having such a menial task assigned him, he hid it well. "Will there be anything else, sir?"

"Only our tack and mounts. I'll see to that personally," I said. "Feel free to requisition a cart, optio. You don't have to carry all of this by hand."

"Yes, sir. Thank you, sir," he said, turning to the men. "Garbo, go get a cart. Make it quick."

The man named Garbo acknowledged the order and ran from the tent.

"See you at the Principia, Optio," I said, walking to the stables.

Within an hour, we were established in chambers next to Gaius Flaminius.

XXI

EMPORIUM

The next day, priests of Mars and Jupiter performed the rites to send the fallen across the River Styx. Pyres burned, and the stink of burning flesh and the pall of smoke lay heavy over the floodplain of the River Padus. Gaius Flaminius and Sempronius Longus led the procession to the evening parade, walking from the city to the camp by the Trebia. They wore full armor, dazzling in the setting sun, and were followed by the surviving officers of the legions.

Sempronius Longus climbed onto the dais to address his men. His slow steps and lowered head gave dramatic weight to sorrow. He gazed out at the men of two legions, raised his right hand, and spoke in a clear voice.

"The fallen feel no more. They feel no pain, no remorse, no regret of failure. They feel no love, no passion, no comradeship with their fellow man. No, these things are left to the living to endure. Another burden, heavy upon our souls. Today we take upon ourselves a heavy burden. One of our own devise."

Sempronius spoke slowly, allowing the cadence of his speech to strike the raw emotions of the men gathered before him. "For we who survive must carry the burden of continuing this life of strife and war. We must stand strong as a shield to our people, deflecting the blows of our enemy until our sword falls to end this war. You and I together bear the burden these brave souls cherished in life. They now journey to the Elysium Fields as surely as the sun shall rise on the morrow. We must face our hated foe and drive him from our lands, destroy his ability to fight, and sap his will to oppose the Senate and People of Rome!"

144

The outpouring of rage and sorrow from the men was a profound sound – a roaring wail that echoed through the valley. Sempronius Longus had given them a purpose again, a meaning to their lives that all would strive to fulfill. He had regained command of an army, bent to his will and purpose and ready to face any threat for the sake of Rome.

I watched the men who had despised General Sempronius Longus now shouting for him to lead them into battle again. He was a good orator and, ever the politician, took any chance to persuade the masses to his cause. Veritas would strike me down if I did not admit it – he persuaded me too. Finally, he yielded the dais and Flaminius stood alone before the legions of Rome.

As had Sempronius, Gaius Flaminius raised his hand, and the crowd quieted to hear his words. "Legionaries, men of Rome, hear me. For we honor your brave comrades who fell in defense of this very city that their fellow Romans could live. My fellow colonists, many of whom served as you do now, give thanks and praise to you and your fallen brothers. For our very lives and the lives of our families were saved by your sacrifice. We honor that sacrifice and share your grief and pain at the loss of so many brave souls. Know that their spirits journey with Charon across the great River Styx to a far better place, where there is no pain or fear."

Flaminius bowed his head and paused for a moment before continuing, "Rest assured that their feats of martial prowess shall not go unremembered in this, the newest city of Rome. This day shall be forever commemorated in honor of those who died here. Thus I, Gaius Flaminius, Patron of Placentia, command." A low murmur of approval rumbled through the legions. "Let there be erected a monument to the fallen that all who pass shall know of the heroic deeds of Roman valor that occurred in this hallowed place. A shrine to Mars and Jupiter, that both gods and men may remember."

The formal ritual complete, officers dismissed their men. I joined one of the lines that formed before the tables laden with food of all kinds. This feast of remembrance would be an affair of food and drink that would leave most of the legions incapacitated for hours unless officers maintained some control. At least Sempronius had doubled the guard centuries at both camps and all the legions' cavalry had been moved to Placentia. I filled my board with roasted meat, olives, and bread and walked toward a table holding flasks of wine.

"A good spread," said a familiar voice from behind me in line.

"Indeed," I said, hailing Decius. I allowed the two legionaries between us to pass and said, "And paid for out of Sempronius Longus's own purse."

"That was a good touch," Decius agreed. "He gave a good eulogy. Really put a fire back into the men."

"Yes, he's a fine orator," I said. "But I wish I were certain what he intends."

"With what?"

"He's planning something back in Rome. This," I said, gesturing to the men feasting on Sempronius's largesse, "is just a part, I'm sure."

"Surely he just wanted to regain the trust of the men after such a defeat." Decius lifted an empty cup in salute. "Honoring the fallen and providing good food to the men is a good start on that, I'd say."

"There is that, of course," I said. "But I think there's more to it. Let's just say I don't trust many senators."

"Well, you've a sour disposition most of the time." He chuckled. "It's one of your more charming features."

I smiled at the joke and said, "Just make sure your men are ready at all times. Even tonight."

"You fear an attack?" he said.

"No, I fear an inattentive guard now that Hannibal has disappeared again. He has a way of striking the unprepared that never goes well for us."

"I'll see to the men then, shall I? And you?"

"I'll watch Scipio's back, as always," I said.

"Where is he?" Decius asked. "I thought he'd be here."

"He's speaking to Praetor Manlius, I believe. He'll be along shortly, I am sure."

"Share some wine with me then." Decius lifted a pitcher from the table we had finally reached and filled our cups.

"Over there." We walked to some benches arranged along the edge of the street. We sat and enjoyed our meal and the company of our fellow soldiers, thankful for our survival.

* * *

A few hours later, Decius and I walked along the quay wall of the emporium. The bones of several future warehouses lay exposed, awaiting builders that had been diverted to the completion of the city walls. The sun had just set, but the clouds were still lighted with orange and red, reminiscent of the fires that had burned the dead.

"How did your report to Tribune Torquatus go?" I asked.

Decius shrugged. "Well enough. It doesn't take long to report we didn't see anything."

"Mmph," I said. Decius had just returned from patrolling up the Padus. "It'd be nice to know where the son of Dolos has taken his army."

"It would at that," Decius agreed. "Maybe Sempronius Longus scared him off."

I threw him a dark look. "Hardly," I said. "More likely Hannibal's recruiting Gauls so fast that he'll be back with an army twice the size of ours."

"Let's hope not. He was bad enough when the numbers were even."

We walked onto a dock and sat on the end. It was nice to have a bit of privacy, a luxury in any military camp. I produced a jug of wine and two cups. "Here, have a drink to wash the dust from your throat," I said handing him a cup and pouring.

"To Hannibal," he said raising his cup. "May he grow boils on his backside."

I laughed. "Good enough for me." We drank in silence and watched the stars emerge from behind the clouds.

"The elections are in three weeks," Decius said. "Shouldn't General Sempronius be leaving soon?"

"Scipio said he's going at the end of the week. He sent Manlius and Atilius back to their cities, I heard. Now he's busy drawing up orders for Torquatus and the other tribunes to keep them from doing anything too stupid in his absence."

"Any idea when he'll be back?"

"A few weeks after the elections, I'd imagine," I said. "He can't lead the legions from Rome."

"If you ask me, he can't lead the legions from here either," Decius said sourly.

"We didn't do so well facing Hannibal ourselves, you know."

"We didn't kill over half the army either."

A silence grew between us for a few minutes.

"More wine?" I asked, trying to restart the conversation.

He nodded and extended his cup. The moon had yet to rise. The stars shone through breaks in the clouds, but the only real light was reflected from the torches along the walls behind us. A splash made both of us jump.

"What was that?" Decius asked, standing and looking out over the river.

"It came from that direction," I said, pointing downstream.

We stared out over the water, looking for any more movement and listening for more noise. We waited another two minutes, then Decius said softly, "There." His arm was extended toward the far side of the river. "Do you see a shadow moving?"

I stared hard. "I don't see anything," I said finally.

"Maybe it was nothing," he said.

"Still, let's go tell the guards on the wall to be alert," I said. "Can't hurt, eh?"

We walked east toward the nearest wall projecting out into the water. As we approached, we met the guard commander coming down the stairs.

"Centurion," I said in a terse greeting.

"Decurion," he said coming to attention. "Were you just throwing rocks into the water by chance?" he asked.

"No," Decius said. "You heard it too then?"

"A loud splash and a grunt of pain it sounded like," the centurion said.

"I thought I saw something across the river," Decius said. "Just a shadow, but from the direction of the noise."

"Where are you headed, Centurion?" I asked.

"The west wall," he said. "Wanted to see if they heard anything before I called out the guard."

"Send a messenger," I said. "Call out the guard quietly and alert the cavalry to be ready to sortie."

He looked taken aback at my suggestion. "Sir?"

"If someone's coming in for a raid, let's not scare them off," I said with an evil grin. "It's time to get some of our own back, eh?"

"Right, sir." He climbed back up the stairs and within moments two men raced along the wall back toward the city. "Done, sir," he said, coming back down the stairs. "Shall we alert the other wall now?"

Decius smiled. "A pleasure, Centurion. After you." He stepped aside to allow the man to pass ahead of us. "Hannibal has a way of ruining our celebrations, doesn't he?" Decius asked.

I shot him a grin and said, "Maybe we should invite him next time."

"Let's move right along then, shall we, gentlemen?" The centurion stalked down the stairs and onto the quay wall at a brisk pace. His studded sandals left small divots in the frozen dirt backing the wall but made no noise. We hurried past the wooden shed serving as a warehouse. Baskets of grain and wood stacked to season filled the building to the rafters. We were perhaps twenty yards past when I heard a low whirring sound.

"Down!" Decius and I shouted at once, throwing ourselves to the ground.

The centurion was a moment late in reacting and one of the dozens of lead bullets struck him in the shoulder as we hit the ground. He screamed an incoherent oath as Decius and I grabbed his harness and dragged him back to the shed.

I looked up to see dark shapes climbing onto the quay wall. Men, carrying short swords and small round shields, clambered quietly from twenty or so large rafts. I saw two more anchored twenty yards into the river.

We slid the centurion behind a pile of lumber and took positions on either side. Both of us knew that a sound would mean our deaths. Two hundred enemy soldiers now controlled the quay wall. We watched them as they split, each heading for a wall.

I chanced a quiet whisper. "Any chance we can make it back to the city gate?"

"More rafts coming ashore," Decius said, ducking behind his pile of lumber. "We can't stay here."

"Cerebos's balls," I swore. "Stay in the shadows – we'll try for the next foundation."

We each grasped the centurion's shoulder straps, and Decius warned, "Not a sound."

The centurion nodded as we helped him to his feet. He swayed a little, but with our help he stayed upright.

I looked over my shoulder. "Now!" We ran for the pile of blocks that would serve as the foundation of a stone warehouse some day in the future. It was perhaps thirty yards from the shed. It took two eternities, but we reached the large stone blocks and hid ourselves behind them.

Decius looked back around the corner and hissed. "They saw us!"

"Centurion," I said, "you must make it to the gate and get help. We'll delay them here." I grasped his shield. "Here, give this to Decius."

"Run fast," Decius said hanging the shield on his arm and testing its weight.

The centurion nodded and staggered toward the wall at a fast trot. Then we had no more time for him as thudding footsteps warned us of approaching men.

"Topple the wood?" I asked.

"Why not?" Decius and I both went to the opposite side from the approaching footsteps and pushed at the top of the stack. It swayed for a moment, then toppled over amid a clatter of wood and shouts from the other side.

"That does it. They've certainly seen us now," Decius said.

"Over there," I said, running toward another pile of stone blocks stacked at the far end of a three-foot-wide trench that served some unknown engineering purpose. We reached the pile just as some slingers' bullets whizzed past us and ricocheted from the stone. I ducked my head around the corner and back again. "Ten or so. Coming right for us."

Decius nodded as we drew our swords. "Jupiter strengthen your arm."

"And yours." Then they were upon us.

XXII

ACROSS THE RIVER

Decius and I stood back to back, waiting for the enemy. I heard his breathing, deep and slow. We were ready for the end.

The Carthaginians came in a rush from both sides of the block. One stabbed blindly around the corner, hoping for a lucky cut or at least a distraction, but missed me completely. Two more rushed me as I ignored the wild thrust. I had only my gladius and armor, while they were fully armed with sword and shield. I threw myself into their shields, stopping their charge, then leaped back as their swords slashed air. I felt Decius's warm body inches from my back.

The attackers approached more slowly now, swords held high over their shields. All three spread out, increasing my threat. I heard a sword strike Decius's shield behind me and a grunt. Then I slashed at my leftmost opponent, forcing his shield high. I reversed direction and thrust straight into the eye of the man on my right as he lowered his defenses to attack my open back. The third man made a slashing cut that hit the armor on my back but sliced a bloody strip from my side as he drew the blade back.

The wound was not serious, but it stung. I heard more running steps and knew we had only moments to live. My enemies were more cautious now, but I was desperate. I lunged at the center man's eyes, but he merely stepped back, never lowering his guard. I heard Decius struggling behind me and risked a glance back.

He was choking one of the enemy soldiers with his sword arm while fending off blows with his shield from another. A third lay dead at his feet, his throat a ragged, bloody mess exposing bone and cartilage.

I stabbed into armpit of the man Decius held, then knelt to retrieve the dead man's shield. Decius whirled to fend off the two men that had attacked me. I came up and slammed my shield into Decius's remaining attacker, forcing him against the pile of blocks. I thrust low, finding his stomach with my gladius. I smelled his foul breath as the point of my sword sought his heart. After a moment he went limp.

Four more men came around the blocks, and I jumped back to clear my blade for the next attack. All of them charged at once, and I was hit in the face with a shield. I felt Decius's back hit mine, and we went down in a heap. I slashed blindly with my sword, trying to clear my vision of the tears from the blow to my nose. When I could see again, I watched the last Carthaginian disappear around the corner.

A moment later I saw why. The guard century ran past our position in pursuit of the Carthaginians. Eighty armored men led by a centurion ran headlong for the quay wall. It was a good start. Then I heard the rumble of hooves. The cavalry had made it through the gate.

"Can you get off me now?" Decius grumbled.

I had landed across his legs and back. I rolled to one side and knelt on both knees, looking at his prone and bloody form.

He grunted and rolled onto his back. "Well, that went well," he said.

"Better than I expected."

He sat up and looked at me. "Your nose is ruined. Is all of that blood yours?"

I looked down for the first time and saw my armor and tunic were covered in blood that darkened the shiny armor in the dim light. "Most of it is that fellow's, I think," I said, pointing my sword at the man I'd stabbed in the guts.

Decius stood and helped me to my feet. I was a bit unsteady, but finally managed to stand. I shook my head to clear the cobwebs and then realized that was a mistake. I nearly swooned and found myself leaning against the pile of blocks for support. Once the world stopped spinning, I said, "Let's go report in."

Decius nodded and put his arm around my shoulder to help steady me as we walked toward the city gate.

A few minutes later, we reached the gates to find our centurion friend sitting on the stairs leading up to the parapet. A legionary was helping him doff his armor. He winced as the mail shirt passed over his head.

"Here now, you think you're done just because your arm's a bit sore?" Decius chided the man.

The centurion looked up with a grin. "I see you're still in one piece, though your friend looks a bit worse for wear."

"Most of it is from the poor fellow I gutted, fortunately for me," I said a bit nasally. "You are sound?"

"I'll live," said the centurion, clutching his right arm close to his body. "Broken bone in my arm, I think. Damn slingers."

A clatter of hooves rang out, then Sempronius Longus rode up with Torquatus and Scipio in tow. "What passes? Report!" he said.

"Sir, Carthaginians in the emporium," I said, wishing I could breathe through my nose. I inhaled and continued. "Came across the Padus on rafts. Decius and I heard them and alerted the guard commander here on the east wall." I gestured to the centurion who was now standing at attention. "We were attacked by slingers and infantry as we attempted to reach the west wall. Came here instead."

"How many of the enemy?" Sempronius asked.

"We saw a few hundred, sir," Decius said, taking over the report. "Maybe twenty rafts, maybe more. We were driven off before we could see much more."

"Sir, they'll have a force to attack the walls from the outside too," Scipio said.

"I agree, General," Torquatus said.

Sempronius inhaled and turned his mount toward the two senior officers. "Torquatus, take charge here. Retake the emporium. Get me some prisoners," he ordered. "Scipio, assemble the cavalry at the west gate. We'll see if we can't rush the ambuscade party. Meet me there."

Torquatus dismounted and said to the legionary, "Go have the buccinators rouse the camp. Assembly will be here."

The man who had been attending the centurion dashed toward the guard commander's office.

Scipio looked over his shoulder and said, "You two meet me at the west gate. I'll bring mounts for you."

"Yes, sir," Decius said for both of us.

I was testing my nose and breathing through my mouth stupidly.

Sempronius was riding away, and Decius said, "Centurion, our thanks for the timely aid. But we must be away. Our master and duty call."

"May Fortuna watch over you," the centurion said then laughed. "Though she seems to have her hands full with you two."

We laughed and walked toward the west gate.

* * *

Horns had been alerting the garrison for several minutes, and Sempronius Longus sat agitated in his saddle. Scipio had managed to assemble most of the garrison's cavalry at the west gate. There were two turma already in the emporium that would not be recalled. We watched as a century of legionaries engaged Carthaginian soldiers atop the wall overlooking the emporium.

"Damn, they're in the camp," said an alae cavalry prefect.

"They are on the wall, Prefect," Sempronius said. "This is our chance. They are committed to the assault now." He turned to the gatehouse and shouted, "Open the gates!" Then he aimed his mount at the opening gate and ordered, "Follow me!"

I had just climbed into the saddle when Scipio spurred his mount after the general. I kicked my horse and followed gamely after. Two columns of cavalry streamed through the gate and into the night.

On the other side of the gate, I saw Sempronius leading us at a gallop. He rode at a slight angle toward the river, allowing the cavalry behind him to form a skirmish line. Scipio, Decius, and I were just behind him, forming the vanguard and galloping straight toward a cluster of infantry that were rushing toward the emporium wall. I could see that four ladders had been laid against the walls. Each had men struggling up it, but there were no defenders to welcome them. All the fighting was at the guard tower connecting the emporium to the city.

Sempronius Longus raised his sword and yelled an incoherent shout as he plunged into the infantry without slowing. His blade came down onto the helmet of a Carthaginian soldier who tried too late to flee. Blood exploded from his head as the steel sword sliced through the bronze and into his skull.

I aimed for another man and skewered him with the tip of my blade, then drew back with a twist. The rest of the cavalry closed on the Carthaginian soldiers running for the wall. It was a slaughter. Formed infantry could stand against a cavalry attack, as horses will not charge into a solid mass of men. But the sight of infantry running to assault a wall was a cavalryman's dream. Unprotected backs or clumps of individuals were easy targets for our speedy mounts and flickering swords. In minutes, the only Carthaginians left alive were atop the wall of Placentia.

I rode up beside Scipio and Decius. "That should do it," I said.

Legionaries were pouring out of the west gate now and trotting along the wall toward the ladders. "That should handle those bastards attacking the walls," said Decius.

Sempronius rode up, a bloody sword in his hand and a bloody smile upon his face. "Scipio, take the cavalry across the bridge. See if you can smash whatever force is on the other side of the river. If you encounter more resistance than you can handle, retreat back to the city. I want to bloody their nose, not run into another ambush."

"Yes sir," Scipio said and rode toward the equestrian buccinator to organize the assembly.

"You two, go with him," Sempronius said. And then added grudgingly, "Good work tonight."

"Thank you, sir," I said as we followed Scipio.

Soon we were headed for the bridge to the south of the city at a trot. Once we reached it, we had to dismount to get the horses across the rickety wooden structure. By the time we were across the river from the emporium, nearly an hour had passed.

"There, sir," said Decius, pointing toward the river's edge.

I saw it then too. A small force of men, struggling to push ten huge rafts into the water from the muddy riverbank.

"Form a wedge," Scipio ordered quietly. The order was passed quickly, and we fell into the inverted triangle that would mass all of the cavalry's weight on a single point and hopefully smash the Carthaginian formation. "Right flank, be wary of cavalry coming from our right. Follow me." He led us forward at a walk.

It was two hundred yards to the river's edge. We covered half the distance before the Carthaginians noticed us. A shout and the infantry forming to clamber aboard the rafts began to turn to face the unexpected threat.

"Charge!" Scipio ordered and kicked his horse into the gallop. In seconds, we covered the remaining distance and slammed into the still-forming ranks of the Carthaginians. I rode to Scipio's left and slashed down into the mass of enemy as our horses forced a path through the men. The ponderous weight of two thousand horses forced a hole in the enemy formation. I felt blows on my shield but ignored them, trying to keep up with Scipio. I stabbed a man in the face only to feel my sword ripped from my hand as another sword slashed it. I used my shield as a battering ram, slamming men aside. In moments we were through the infantry and racing away. I looked over my shoulder to see most of the cavalrymen still in formation.

"Circle right!" Scipio shouted. I followed as his mount angled slowly to the right for another pass. This time we charged straight toward the river. Carthaginian infantrymen threw down their weapons and leapt into the water, trying to escape our bloody swords. I kicked my horse until I rode even with Scipio and used my shield to protect his left side.

As we cut a path through the infantry, I heard Decius shout, "Enemy cavalry to the rear!"

Scipio led us left, parallel to the river bank. We raced for the trees, our horses lathered by exertion.

I saw them now, Numidians on their fast little horses. They were approaching us on a converging course a hundred yards away. I could see the javelins held ready to throw as shadows against the night sky. If we could get to the trees, we could turn and fight them.

They closed slowly, their horses fresher than ours. Just as we reached the edge of the trees, they launched a volley of their tiny spears. I heard a horse scream behind me and a clattering rumble as several more horses collided with the unfortunate animal.

Then we were in the trees, and the advantage was ours. "Turn and fight!" Scipio ordered, whipping his mount around with a lash of his reins. I turned to guard his side and kicked my horse after him.

He chose a Numidian that was drawing another javelin from a quiver strapped behind his saddle. Scipio rode to the horse's right side and thrust his sword at the rider's eyes. I darted to the other side and, as the rider drew back to thrust, I grabbed the spear shaft and jerked him from the saddle. In his surprise, he let go of the spear. I stabbed down. The point of the javelin found the man's belly. I jerked it clear and looked up to find Scipio grinning at me.

"Get to work!" I snarled. "Stop standing about like Murtia's children."

He smiled and looked around. "Doesn't seem much else to do at the moment."

I scanned the forest for the enemy. All around me were Roman cavalry. The Numidians had fled.

"Let's get back to the city before Hannibal sends more men after us," Scipio said.

"Form up!" I shouted and heard the order echoed through the darkness.

The men formed two lines and we rode back to the city.

XXIII

VICTUMULAE

"You did well, young Scipio," Sempronius Longus said in a not too condescending tone. "I will sing your praises in the Senate when I return to Rome." It was early evening the day after the attack on the emporium.

"I seek no praise, General. My men Decius and Appius should be rewarded for alerting the garrison though," Scipio said modestly.

I schooled my face to remain solid as stone. I saw Decius do the same. *Gods, no more awards. They tend to put you in more positions to get yourself killed.*

Torquatus entered then with a wax tablet in his hand. "Hannibal has retreated further west," he said, holding up the tablet. "A report from a patrol sent out yesterday. He is camped near Clastidium again."

"Tiberius, we are very exposed here," said Flaminius. "What happens if he attacks again in force?"

"Stay behind your walls and endure," Sempronius said. "Help will come in spring. We can recombine the armies and destroy that Carthaginian demon once and for all."

"Should we not raise more legions?" Flaminius asked.

"I think not," Sempronius said. "Replacements for our losses certainly, but no more. Hannibal cannot endure the winter, feed his men, and pay his mercenaries if he cannot take our fortified cities."

Sempronius frowned, then said, "As much as I hate to admit it, Scipio, your father was correct. We should have stayed behind our walls. The Gauls will tire of hunger and low pay and defect from Hannibal's army soon enough. We must endure. Time is on our side."

"What will you do now, sir?" Scipio asked.

"I will leave for Rome tomorrow. If you have any messages for your father, please have them ready by dawn," Sempronius said. "I will stop by Cremona on my way and see how General Scipio fares."

"I will bring my missives to your man then?" Scipio asked politely.

"Certainly," Sempronius said. "I'll take an escort of cavalry as well. Two turmae should suffice."

"I will see to it, sir," Scipio said. He inclined his head and lifted his chin as he caught Decius's eye.

Decius nodded acknowledgment of his new assignment. *Great, let Decius escort the pompous ass to Cremona. I'd rather stay here anyway.*

"We should keep an eye on Hannibal," Flaminius said, prudently.

Scipio turned his head to face the older man. "Appius will lead a patrol to scout his location tomorrow," he said. "He will relieve the current surveillance patrol and report back anything pertinent." His eyes looked back toward me, with a twinkle of humor.

Caught me gloating about Decius's misfortune, did you? I smiled a small smile and nodded.

"Tiberius, your defense of the city was masterful," Flaminius said with no hint of irony.

"Thank you, Gaius, but I only did what was necessary," Sempronius said. "It was a bold stroke by Hannibal, to be sure. But destined to fail."

"Why so?" asked Flaminius.

"Even if he had taken the emporium, we had enough stores to last until help could reach us from Cremona," Sempronius explained. "The key was stopping them from taking the wall into the city. That is why the cavalry charge into their reserves was necessary."

"I see," said Flaminius. "Still an ingenious defense, to be improvised so rapidly."

"Titus, what of the garrison?" Sempronius asked his senior tribune.

"We lost eighteen legionaries and seven equites," he reported. "We suffered forty-seven wounded, but only two will muster out. The rest will recover from their wounds."

"And the enemy?" Flaminius asked, interested in the totals.

"We killed over three hundred in the emporium or on the wall. I estimate another four hundred in the cavalry charge or across the river. Double that in wounded," Torquatus said.

"Finally, a victory to be proud of." Flaminius beamed.

"We also captured twenty-three men in the emporium," Torquatus said.

Sempronius cleared his throat, "See they are interrogated as soon as possible. I want to know anything about conflicts in the ranks of our enemies, weaknesses, and total numbers."

"Yes, sir," Torquatus said. "The interrogations began last night. We should be receiving reports shortly."

"Good," Sempronius said approvingly. "Keep up the good work, Titus." The general stood and yawned expansively. "Well, I'm for bed. I will see you all in the morning."

A chorus of good nights sounded around the room as the general departed, trailed by Torquatus and other members of his staff.

"Scipio, see me in my chambers in an hour," Flaminius said, rising.

"Yes, sir."

"And you two, keep your heads down," Flaminius said as he passed us for the door.

We both came to attention and saluted.

Scipio motioned us back to our seats. "Once we see the general off tomorrow, I will need an appreciation of Hannibal's intentions."

"He knows we're likely to hole up until spring," I said.

"And he'll know the Gauls better than we do," Decius said.

"I agree. But what will he do about it?" Scipio asked.

"I think that's my job," I said. "I'll follow the Padus until I find him, then I'll stick to him like a leech."

"Good enough," Scipio said. "Make sure you take enough men to set up relays of messengers. I want consistent updates. This once-a-day reporting is maddening."

"I think three turmae should manage, sir," I said.

"Take what you need. Ask for more if you think it necessary. You have the highest priority right now."

"What worries me is Hannibal's knowledge of what is going on inside these walls."

Scipio nodded. "Our Gallic allies, no doubt. We are fighting against their relatives and friends. We must be leaking information like a sieve."

"That should work in two directions, sir," I said.

"I will suggest that to Titus once the consul departs," Scipio said.

Decius said, "Anything private for your father, sir?"

"Yes, I will give it to you in the morning. Come to my quarters before assembly."

"Didn't you have messages that you were going to give to Sempronius Longus?" I asked.

"Yes," Scipio answered. "It will be interesting to see if there are any differences upon their delivery." He flashed a smile. "General Sempronius will be decidedly curious about Father's plans for the upcoming election. I expect his curiosity will get the better of him."

"I'll be careful, sir," Decius said.

"The only important message is the one that I give you now. The written ones are for show," Scipio said, lowering his voice. "Flaminius departs in three days."

Decius looked as confused as I felt. "Where's he going?"

"Rome," Scipio said.

"Ah. A voice of reason and eyewitness to prevent Sempronius Longus from twisting the facts too far, eh?" I said.

"Correct, Appius," Scipio said approvingly. "Now both of you, keep that to yourselves. "Decius, you may tell my father only. He wanted to know the timing of Flaminius's departure."

"I understand, sir," Decius said.

"Alright then. Let us be about our tasks. Dismissed, gentlemen."

* * *

We passed Clastidium without incident. The town looked untouched by the Carthaginians, though there were armed Gauls patrolling the village. The traitor Dasius Brundisius had given the city and its grain stores to Hannibal without so much as a stubbed toe in defense.

Now we circled further west. Not far past Clastidium, my lead scout motioned for the group to halt. I dismounted and moved forward. I had to crawl the last twenty yards, up a small hill into dense brush.

"What do you see?" I said, not wanting to raise my head yet.

The scout motioned for silence, then pointed to a nook in the brush beside him.

I slid slowly into the gap and lay still, letting my eyes adjust to the light. We were looking into the setting sun, making it difficult to see. Then I saw a Gallic town, surrounded by a Carthaginian army. I tapped the man beside me and signaled he should continue observing. I slid back down the hill until I could stand unseen. I walked back to my horse and took the reins again. To the two closest men I said, "Message for Decurion Scipio." I pulled a map from a case attached to my saddle and examined our location.

They pulled wax tablets from their saddlebags and opened them. Each had a stylus ready to imprint my words into the soft wax.

"We have found the Carthaginian army. They besiege a Gallic town, I believe it to be Victumulae," I said, referring to the map. "Enemy numbers appear to be undiminished. Any losses suffered have been more than made up by Gallic recruits. We will continue to observe and report." I had them both repeat the message back to me, then I chose two more men as escorts. "Each of you take a different route. Two-man teams. Make sure this report gets to Scipio, and whoever reaches him first tell him to expect the other team."

"Yes, sir," said the men, saluting.

"On your way then." I turned to my optio, Quintus. "That hill is our observation post. I want a two-man team up there at all times with another team hidden down here. When a messenger comes down the hill, another goes up. Rotate them as you see fit," I ordered.

"Yes sir," said the optio. "And the other men, sir?"

"Find us a nice hidden place to make a cold camp, then send four men to refill all of our water bags. Another four to forage for some straw for the horses."

"Anything else, sir?" Quintus asked.

"Post a guard on the camp and make sure everyone knows the sign and countersign," I said. "We may be here a few days. I'll go back up the hill for now. See to everything and report to me when it's ready."

"Yes, sir."

I climbed back up the hill to observe the Carthaginian army.

* * *

The next morning, just before dawn, I slid back into place beside the observation team. I had a good view of the Carthaginian camp, which was perhaps two miles from the town walls. The town rested along the Padus and seemed substantial. A low haze of wood smoke hung over it and floated eastward. The brightening sky revealed the gates opening just as the sun rose above the horizon behind us.

A mob of Gauls streamed through the gate and from the far side of the town around the walls as well. The formed a mass, variously armed, that must have been every man and boy in the settlement. Some wore conical helmets and carried shields; others wore leather helmets. All carried some sort of sword or spear, though it seemed no two matched. Two men stood in front of the mob and gestured, trying to organize the citizens into a disciplined army, it seemed.

I tapped the closest man to me and motioned for him to report to the optio. I knew Quintus would wait for more details before sending a messenger. I turned back to the scene before me.

There were now thousands of men forming up. I looked toward the Carthaginian camp and watched as the army prepared itself for battle. Their camp was a rambling affair, with tents placed wherever the occupants had decided to pitch them. But it was surrounded by a picket force of infantry and cavalry. These had alerted the general with enough time for the army to form properly before the town's makeshift army could approach.

Then I saw Hannibal again. His shaved head and flowing, black beard stood out as he donned his cloth-covered bronze helmet and climbed atop one of the few remaining elephants. The men around him cheered as the elephant trumpeted. He looked like a king on a throne.

They formed a battle line again with the Gauls in the center and the African and Iberian infantry to either flank. Slingers and cavalry moved to the outside as the Carthaginian army prepared to meet its foe. Hannibal had a perfect vantage from which to observe the battle, atop his elephant throne.

The town army marched forward. I quickly divided the mass into quarters and began to count. After five minutes, I decided there were thirty to thirty-five thousand men to face a like number of Carthaginians.

Another Roman scout joined us, and I motioned him to come closer. I whispered the count of both the Gauls and Carthaginians to the man. I told him to take that information to Quintus and for the optio to send the messenger now.

He nodded and crawled back down the hill.

By the time another man had joined us, the two forces had closed to a few hundred yards of one another. The Carthaginians stopped, awaiting the inevitable charge of the Gauls. The Gauls, surprisingly, continued to march forward slowly, foregoing the usual shouting and keening.

The Gauls came forward another hundred yards. I saw the Carthaginian slingers begin to whirl their slings, and a moment later the battle began. The lead bullets slammed into the packed ranks of the Gauls and many went down. As if an order had been shouted, the Gallic army charged forward to throw themselves onto the Carthaginian shields.

The Carthaginians shouted and slammed themselves forward into the charging Gauls. The forces seemed to stop and spread out as they met. It was a shoving match, punctuated by men falling to quick stabs or slashes past shields. It seemed equal for a few minutes as the two armies struggled for the center.

Then I saw Hannibal gesture to some men standing behind him. One slowly waved a red banner side to side. At that signal, the slingers withdrew, and the cavalry charged.

The Numidian javelins flew by the thousand. The packed ranks of Gauls provided an ideal target as the sharpened steel spikes fell from the air into flesh and bone beneath. In moments the rear of the Gallic mass began running back to the town. Without that weight, the front line was pushed back. First one step, then another, until the entire army was running for the town gate.

Hannibal controlled his infantry and pulled them back into formation before pursuing. But the cavalry slashed through the townsmen who were fleeing in utter terror now. Thousands fell to the flickering steel blades. Within half an hour, a full third of the Gallic fighters lay dead or dying on the battlefield. The remainder reached the safety of the town gates and slammed the doors behind them.

I watched as Hannibal rode his massive elephant to just beyond bowshot from the town walls. He gestured at the town, clearly shouting something to the townspeople, but we were not close enough to hear. He stood erect on the back of the elephant for a few more moments, then slowly turned the beast and rode back to his camp. The Carthaginian infantry began felling saplings and small trees to construct ladders as the cavalry stood watch over the town.

I slid back down the hill to send another messenger to Placentia.

* * *

The following morning, Quintus walked up to me and saluted. "Sir, there's something happing at the town. You should come see," he said.

"What did you see, Optio?" I asked as we began to walk.

"Three men came out of the town and stood a bowshot from the wall," he said. "That's when I came to get you."

As we reached the base of our little hill, I said, "Stay here, Optio. I'll want a good man here to handle anything that happens."

"Yes, sir. Thank you, sir," he said, his chest swelling at the implied compliment.

As I slid back into my observation point, I saw that the delegation from the town had been answered. Hannibal, on his elephant, flanked by two men on horseback, had just reached the townsmen. Hannibal slid down the side of the giant beast and approached the three men, who were obviously explaining something to the Carthaginian as I could see his helmet bob as if he were nodding at some point the Gauls had made. They spoke for another ten minutes or so, then Hannibal shook each of their hands in a formal gesture of respect. He remounted the beast with the assistance of the animal's raised front leg. Then the townsmen walked back to the gate, and Hannibal rode back to his camp.

An hour later the Carthaginian infantry formed up in a broad column. Hannibal's elephant trod to the side of the column as they marched to the town gate. At their approach, the gates opened, and a stream of men came out.

The Carthaginians marched into a broad line, stretching the length of the town walls, a bowshot away. They watched as the townsmen created a pile of weapons. Each Gallic warrior added a sword, axe, or some other weapon to the pile, then moved to one side to make room for the man behind. For an hour or more the Gauls built a pile of weapons. When the stream finally ended, the three men who had spoken to Hannibal came forward again.

Hannibal rode his elephant forward to greet the delegation. They kneeled before the Carthaginian general with their heads bowed low. Hannibal raised both his hands into the air as if in benediction. Then he slammed them down in a fierce gesture. At that signal, the infantry charged.

I watched in horror as the infantry attacked the unarmed men. Some tried to run, but they were surrounded. Armed and armored men met the unarmed Gauls and slew them with abandon. Some of the Gauls tried to wrench weapons away from their attackers or fled toward the pile of weapons only to be cut down. None of the men survived.

The three town elders near Hannibal had been seized by his bodyguards on his signal to the infantry. They were brought before the general and forced to prostrate themselves. Then a familiar face approached the elephant – a man with a bushy red mustache, holding a massive axe. Ducarius. He spoke at length with Hannibal and the elders who had been allowed to raise their heads. Then Ducarius walked behind the kneeling men.

He raised his axe as if testing its weight. Then, as fast as lightning, he struck. The first elder's head sailed across the grass to land inches from the elephant's feet. The other two tried to run, but Ducarius made two more slashes and both lost their heads as well.

The cavalry charged through the open gates into the town. Soon the infantry, finished with their bloody work, followed the cavalry. From the smoke that soon began to billow from the town, I knew it would soon be razed to the ground. I motioned for the observation team to follow me, and we slid down the hillside.

At the bottom, Quintus asked, "Well, sir?"

"The town surrendered," I said. "Then they died. All of them. Every last man."

The optio's face paled.

"Get everyone in the saddle now, Optio," I said, walking toward the camp. "We make for Placentia at once."

XXIV

ROME

"The entire town, you say?" Gaius Flaminius asked after I finished my report.

"Yes, and I saw our old friend Ducarius among the Gallic allies of the Carthaginians," I said.

"I thought you killed him?" Scipio asked.

"Apparently not," I said and described the executions. "He translated for Hannibal."

"Ducarius?" Flaminius asked, eyes wide. He stood and paced across the room. "Large Gaul, ruddy hair, and a shaved chin?"

"Yes, sir," I said, not understanding the senator's sudden change in demeanor. "Bushy red mustache and no beard. Likes to collect heads."

"Gods. I know this man," Flaminius said. "I killed his father and brother. I wear his brother's scalp on my helm in memory of the battle." The old man's eyes went distant. "The brother was a giant and nearly killed me when I was a legate. Ducarius seeks my head in revenge, so I am told."

"He grows in favor with our enemy then," Scipio said.

"From what our Ananes allies say, most of the other tribes in this area have either fled or now support Hannibal," Flaminius said. "Victumulae paid the price for defying Carthage. And it was a lesson well taken, it seems."

"What will you do now, sir?" Scipio asked.

"Go to Rome as we discussed," Flaminius said. "The Senate must be informed of the true events occurring here in the north."

"You will need an escort," Scipio said.

166

"I will take a turma of cavalry," the older man said. "We will move quickly down the highway while Hannibal is occupied in the west."

Scipio looked at me and said, "Appius, you will lead the turma."

"Me, sir?" I said startled. "My job is to be at your side."

"And watching my back." Scipio smiled. "I know your orders from Father. I'll be safe enough here with the legion. Besides, Decius is back. He can keep me out of trouble." His smile faded as he continued, "Gaius Flaminius will need a good pair of eyes and a strong arm at his back. Protect him as you would me. And come back with him when he returns."

I started to protest but his calm gaze silenced me. "Very good, sir" was all I could manage.

"Good," Flaminius said. "That is settled. Get your things together, Decurion. We leave in an hour."

"Yes, sir," I said and left to assemble the escort. The thought of leaving Scipio and Laelius alone made me shudder. Those two could contrive the most insane plans before rational adults could stop them. I would have to have a word with Decius before I departed.

* * *

Ten days later, we descended from the Apennine Mountains toward the end of the Via Flaminia. I could see the Grotta Oscura not a mile to our left. The road leading to the great quarry converged with our own path ahead. The quarry, though still in operation, was used for more mundane purposes now. Great blocks of tufa had been hewn from the earth and transported six miles to rebuild the walls of Rome two hundred years ago, after the sacking of the city by the Senones Gauls. The endeavor had taken twenty-five years and resulted in a thirty-foot-high wall encircling the seven hills of Rome. Such was the Roman fear of Gauls that a generation would be spent building a wall that even now could not contain all of Rome's inhabitants.

We rode on in silence, seeing the countryside and knowing a good meal and soft bed awaited us this night. As we rode over the wooden bridge spanning the River Tiber, Gaius Flaminius said, "Would that I were censor again. I would have this bridge rebuilt in stone."

"You were censor, what, two years ago, sir?" I asked.

"Yes. It took all my efforts to build that road to Arriminium," he said resignedly. "Bridges were too expensive, according to the Senate."

"It was nice they named the road for you, sir," I said in an attempt to soothe this obvious sore spot.

"Hmph! They fought about that too. Some wanted to call it Via Arriminium – others wanted to name it after one or other of the consuls. Finally, Paullus stood up and told them, 'Name it after Flaminius – he is the only man who wants the damn highway anyway.'" He laughed at the memory. "I never knew if he did it as a favor to me or just to get the others to move on to a different topic."

I smiled, not wanting to interrupt his reminiscence. We rode a few miles more until the wall built by King Servius Tullius came into view. We headed for the Porta Fontinalis, the fortified gates opening onto the northern slope of Capitoline Hill, the seat of political power in Rome. We rode through the massive center gate whose doors were flanked by two smaller gates. The morning traffic had slowed as the midday sun climbed to its zenith.

The buildings along the city streets were mainly wood and brick constructions. The stone and wood gave the impression of earth and industry. There was a cacophony of sound as we made our way to the Forum. Merchants hawked their wares to passers-by. Reds, greens, blues, and all the other colors filled the view as the merchants' wares attracted rich and poor alike in the expansive plaza. I found myself looking longingly at a wagon filled with amphorae of wine, having had only water for the past several days on the road.

"Come, Appius." Flaminius spurred his horse. "Down this hill and up the Caelian and we are home." He slowed as we passed through the Forum, but soon we climbed the Caelian Hill to the senator's impressive stone residence. It wrapped around the hillside, providing a wonderful panorama of the city below. The brown stone of its construction was of the same color as the city walls and might have been constructed as long ago. But the house had been well maintained, and I could see trees awaiting the touch of spring to make this place a lush and pleasant home.

Flaminius dismounted and motioned for us to do the same. Servants and slaves flooded into the entryway to greet their master. A man led my horse away toward the stables as Flaminius turned to me and said, "Welcome to my home, Appius."

"And a welcome return to you, sir," I said. "May Tranquilitas bless your home and all who dwell within."

"Well said, Decurion," he said formally. "May Fortuna bless you and all who follow you. Now, will you enter?"

"I thank you for your hospitality, sir."

We walked through the portico and into his home. "Show Decurion Asprenas to his rooms," Flaminius said to one of the slaves. "Appius, join me in the baths once you have cared for your belongings."

"I will, sir. It will be good to be clean again."

A slave showed me my chambers and helped me off with my armor. I instructed him to oil the leather and polish the rings of the mail shirt. Then I allowed him to guide me to the baths.

* * *

The following morning, Gaius Flaminius greeted me cheerfully. "Good morning, Appius. How did you sleep?"

"Very well, thank you, sir," I said. "Your rest was untroubled?"

"I slept, though I must confess to some anticipation for this morning's Senate meeting." He grinned. "It is to be held at the Temple of Belladona as Sempronius Longus will make his report on the progress of the campaign against Carthage today."

"Does he know you are in Rome?" I asked.

"Possibly, but he has been quite busy in the two days since he arrived," Flaminius said. "If not, then perhaps I can advise the Senate of any discrepancies in his report."

"That should be interesting."

"Indeed, it should." He grinned again. "In any case, Tiberius will name the day for the elections. I need to be there for that. And today, you will accompany me, Appius."

"Sir, I am no senator," I said. "I have no place in their deliberations."

"No, but you are a witness I may call to testify before the Senate. You have seen Hannibal's acts at a closer remove than any other surviving Roman." He paused, giving me time to think. "That is why your young master sent you with me."

Damn Scipio and his too agile mind. He would set me up to testify before these wealthy men who control the lives of all Romans. They could buy and sell the likes of me on a whim. "I see," I said. "Then I have no choice but to accept, Senator."

"Good," Flaminius said, satisfied. "Then let us break our fast and be off."

* * *

The columns on the Temple of Belladonna were festooned with streaming ribbons of scarlet. The banner of the Senate and People of Rome
hung over the entrance, announcing today's political session. I followed
Flaminius up the steps, wearing the unfamiliar white toga he had loaned
me. I had worn such garments on rare formal occasions, but never one of
such luxurious cloth. Flaminius had said it was one of his old togas, but
the cloth looked new and blindingly white in the cool morning sun. His,
of course, bore the broad purple stripe of a Roman senator. He greeted
several colleagues by name and made his way into the main chamber.

Inside, the vast room held chairs formed in an open-ended rectangle.
At the open end stood two empty seats. Flaminius strode to his chair in
the front row of the seats facing the two empty chairs. At my wide-eyed
expression of consternation, Flaminius took pity on me.

"Appius, what ails you?" he asked.

"Where do I stand?" I asked in a small voice.

"Oh, you will sit in the seat behind me," he said. "Those two chairs are
for the consuls," he said, pointing to the two chairs facing the formation
of seats. "And these are for former consuls, proconsuls, and censors." He
indicated the front row facing the consuls' chairs. "Quaestors, aediles, and
tribunes sit there." He gestured to the two vertical sides of the rectangle.

I recalled that Gaius Flaminius had occupied all three of those high
offices. "And behind these men, sir?"

"The other senators, lower magistrates, and witnesses," he said. "We
call them the pedites… the walkers. They are unimportant and will not
object to being shifted. You will be quite unremarkable until you testify
to what you have seen. Trust me, Appius." He motioned me to sit, and he
turned to greet more of the arriving senators.

I sat quietly, trying not to look out of place. I watched as the senators arrived, greeted their fellows, and made their way to seats. The lesser
men greeted the greater with varying levels of obsequiousness. Flaminius
seemed to enjoy the interplay as younger men greeted him with flat-
tery and respect. His eyes danced as each conversation, no matter how
mundane, seemed to fascinate him. I was watching closely when his eyes
flared brightly and his smile widened. Then I followed the path of his
gaze and saw that Tiberius Sempronius Longus had arrived.

Sempronius walked to his seat, followed by the twelve lictors, guards carrying the fasces of their office. This symbol was an axe surrounded by a bundle of wooden rods that demonstrated the consul's authority to pass ultimate judgment on any person outside the walls of Rome. Sempronius Longus himself wore the purple-bordered tunic of a senator over a white tunic emblazoned with two vertical purple bars and carried the ivory baton topped with a golden eagle – both signs of his imperium. Since he was the senior magistrate present, he held fasces, the power to conduct official meetings. He brought the session to order and stood, one arm raised until the members of the Senate quieted. His eyes scanned the important people in the front row. I could see the flare of his nostrils as he saw Flaminius's face smiling at him, but he gave no other reaction.

"Senators. Hear me, hear me. I bring news on the progress of the war against Carthage," he began. "As you know, Hannibal has brought an army across the Alps into the Padus Valley. My fellow consul, Scipio, met this army near the River Ticinus with a force of infantry and cavalry. Unfortunately, Hannibal routed this force, and Scipio himself was wounded during the battle." Most men in the room knew of these events, but there was a low murmur as the consul made the report official. "Scipio, facing an untenable supply situation, fell back upon the new colony of Placentia. During this retreat, Hannibal took measures to see to his own supplies. He bribed the commander of Clastidium's garrison, Dasius Brundisius, who surrendered the town, its people, and the grain stores within."

There were cries of outrage and disbelief at this news. The commander of the town, a southern Italian from his name, would be vilified and, if caught he would be executed if the shouted comments I heard were anything to go by. Sempronius held up his hand again and waited patiently for silence.

"These facts are known to most of you. Now I make my report of what has transpired since this august body ordered my recall from Sicily to support my beleaguered friend, Scipio," he said with solemn dignity. "My army marched to Placentia and encamped at the confluence of the rivers Padus and Trebia. Upon consultation with Scipio and our colleague Gaius Flaminius" – he paused to grace Flaminius with an acknowledging smile – "I ordered a patrol to the west to investigate reports of barbarism against our Gallic allies. I am pleased to report that Titus Manlius Torquatus, Senior Tribune of the Third Legion, led the patrol and defeated a force of Carthaginian cavalry that was savaging a Gallic town."

Cheers erupted at this news. It was the first reported victory of the war. I looked at the back of Gaius Flaminius, but he seemed unconcerned about this report. I focused my attention back on the consul.

"A short time later, Hannibal's cavalry struck my encamped troops in the early morning hours. I ordered a cavalry force to drive off the enemy while I assembled my legions to march. Scipio, though wounded, retained command of his consular army, acting through his seventeen-year-old son, encamped to the south of Placentia. He refused to march forth to support my actions."

At this statement, there were shouts and hisses. Sempronius held up his hand in supplication again. Once the room quieted, he continued.

"I led my army forth, across the River Trebia, to face the Carthaginian force. Hannibal chose to meet me on field near the left bank of the river, his camp to his rear. I recalled my cavalry, as they had succeeded in driving off the enemy, until I could position my infantry. Scipio, relenting slightly, provided me with a turma of cavalry led by his son to act as liaison between his headquarters and my own. This gesture, I suppose, was an attempt to free my cavalry from any messenger duties."

I could feel the scowl on my face deepening. Flaminius sat unmoving as he listened to Sempronius's recitation. I felt the urge to shout down the consul but held my tongue.

"I engaged Hannibal's center with my best infantry. He responded by attacking my flanks with cavalry and elephants. My light infantry made short work of the elephants, and my flanks held against all attacks. Then my center crushed the Gauls at the center of the Carthaginian formation and forced them into a rout. Hannibal attempted an ambush to my rear, but the triarii held firm and my forces pursued the Gauls back to a village along the River Padus perhaps three miles distant. From there, I reorganized the men and marched back to Placentia."

As the room applauded, Gaius Flaminius turned to me and whispered, "What do you think, Decurion? Was that how it happened?" He smiled at my appalled look and said, "Let us provide another perspective on the day's events, shall we?"

One of the senators two seats from Flaminius stood and said in a stentorian baritone, "What of your losses, Tiberius?"

Flaminius winked at me and whispered, "Let us see how he answers this question."

"They were grave, Lucius. Especially amongst the alae infantry,"

Sempronius Longus said. "As you would expect from a force attacked from all sides."

Flaminius exploded from his seat. "They were total!" he shouted. "Tell them how many men you lost, Tiberius," he said, regaining some composure.

Sempronius paled as he had not realized that pleasant old Flaminius would dare contradict him. "There were grave losses, as I said, Gaius."

"Thirty thousand men. I think you shade the truth more than a little," Flaminius said. "And what happened to your legions pursuing the Gallic center?"

"They re-formed and marched home, as I said," Sempronius said.

"They looted a Gallic village and had to be brought to their senses by young Scipio. You lost control of them."

"Scipio the Younger assisted me in restoring order in the ranks. The men's blood was up after the battle."

"His turma led you across the river and back to Placentia so you could avoid facing Hannibal's victorious army, which controlled the field, you mean," Flaminius said coldly.

"By then, the men were exhausted and could not be expected to fight through Hannibal's remaining forces," Sempronius said.

"In fact, after losing three quarters of your army, you blamed General Scipio for not coming to your aid," Flaminius said. "When you failed to heed his warning that the initial cavalry attack was bait to lure you from the protective walls of your camp. You marched into the very ambush that Scipio had warned you about."

The room erupted as senators shouted questions at the beleaguered consul. Flaminius sat once more in his chair and looked with cold blue eyes at Sempronius Longus. It took Sempronius several minutes to restore order in the chamber.

"Gentlemen, if I may continue," he said calmly. Then he explained the attack on the emporium and his role in defeating the attackers. Flaminius contradicted none of his assertions this time.

"And in summation, Hannibal maneuvers to the west of Placentia with a force of thirty to forty thousand men, seeking shelter for the winter."

Flaminius stood again. "I have news of events that occurred after Consul Sempronius Longus departed Placentia."

Sempronius frowned at this unexpected statement but said, "Please, Gaius, tell us your news."

"Victumulae has fallen to Hannibal's forces," Flaminius said simply. "I have here the decurion that led the patrol. He witnessed the battle and the events that followed." He turned to me with a hand extended. "Decurion Appius Curtius Asprenas, please tell us what you witnessed."

I stood awkwardly then said, "The townsmen, obviously loyal to Rome, fought with numbers equal to that of Hannibal's forces. But they were no match for his hardened veterans. In much less than an hour, half the men of Victumulae lay dying on the field and the rest fled back within the town walls." I looked at Flaminius, who nodded encouragingly. "The following morning, three men emerged from the town gates to parley with the Carthaginians. Hannibal himself met with them. Beside him, translating I suppose, was a Gaul I am familiar with named Ducarius. He is a traitor, a leader in the Mutina rebellion. I was much too far away to hear their conversation, but they spoke for several minutes."

Flaminius asked, "What happened next, Decurion?"

"The townsmen emerged, lay down their weapons in a great pile, and stood to one side," I said. "Then, when the last man had disarmed himself, Hannibal gave a signal and his forces fell upon the unarmed men and killed every one of them."

Gasps and shouts of horror echoed through the chamber.

"Ducarius personally beheaded the three men who had surrendered the town. Hannibal's men then entered the town and destroyed everything inside before razing the town. I watched it burn as I led my men away," I said.

"It seems that Hannibal does more than maneuver," Flaminius said. "Victumulae was one of the Gallic towns that supplied Placentia with grain and other foods. Hannibal has supplied himself well for the winter, with Roman grain."

"Thank you for that report, Decurion." Sempronius said in an icy tone. He turned and regained his seat. "That concludes the report on the war, gentlemen. The Assembly of the Centurionate will vote in two days' time upon the Campus Martius. Tribunes, make the announcements. This meeting is adjourned."

XXV

ASSEMBLY OF THE CENTURIONATE

Flaminius returned from the next day's Senate meeting with a curious look upon his face. I stood and saluted as he entered the salon where he conducted the business of his house.

"Please, Appius, enough military proprieties," he said with good humor. "I have news."

I dropped my salute and allowed him to sit before I resumed my seat on a comfortable bench near his desk. "What news, sir?"

"I have been nominated as a candidate for consul," he said with a smug grin. "Against all tradition, I might add."

"How so?" I asked.

"Tradition dictates that ten years must pass between consular terms. My last term as consul was only five years ago," he said.

"Then how can you be nominated, sir?"

"Due to the crisis in the north, the Senate voted to allow more experienced senators be considered for the post." He chortled then continued. "It seems Sempronius's faction is out of favor after yesterday's events, and the more conservative among my colleagues would like a firmer hand at the reins."

"Who else was nominated, if I may ask, sir?" I said.

"Gnaeus Servilius Geminus, a good man. Quintus Fabius Maximus Verrucosus, ambitious but wants to hide away from the world. And Marcus Atilius Regulus, noble name but a bit too old now, I believe."

"So you think to have a good chance then, sir?"

"Quite good, I would imagine," the senator said. "The bribes have been flowing quite freely."

"Well, sir, you will have my vote."

"Thank you, my boy."

I didn't take offense at this, because to this elder statesman, Scipio's father was still a boy. "What will you do until tomorrow?" I asked.

"Meet with men. Persuade, threaten, and bribe," he said with a grin. "Politics."

"Scipio charged me to guard you, sir," I said. "If you leave this residence, I should accompany you."

"Certainly, Appius," he said. "I would enjoy your company. But you must school yourself to reveal no reaction to any conversation you may overhear."

"I believe I can manage that, Senator."

"That is probably true. You might be one of Zeno's stoics for all your face reveals." He chuckled. "You will be an admirable guard and companion."

"I shall prepare myself for battle then," I said to more laughter from the old man.

* * *

The mist hung low over the Campus Martius, the plain along the River Tiber to the northwest of the walls of Rome. Legend told of the first king of Rome, Romulus, standing on this field as he neared death. The gods summoned a storm cloud, which lifted him into the heavens and to everlasting glory. It was the field where countless Roman men gathered each spring to martial into the legions of Rome. I had stood on this field every year since my sixteenth year as an equite, a cavalryman of Rome.

Today it was the place of ultimate political power in Roman society. The voting blocks, giant pens into which the classes of Roman society divided themselves, had been erected at Sempronius Longus's direction. There were 189 of these pens, the largest of which was filled with the landless poor, the proletarii, and was furthest from the dais on which the consul now stood. Closer was the line of thirty blocks of the fifth class, who also provided the velites of the legions. Then there were twenty blocks each of the fourth, third, and second classes, which provided the hastatii and principes. Then the eighty blocks of the first class, including the wealthiest Roman citizens, which provided the triarii. Each of these lines of voting blocks was arranged in order of wealth, with the wealthiest being closer to the consular dais. Then came the twelve voting blocks for the equites, my own class. And finally, the six blocks of the senators, the wealthiest and most noble of Roman families.

The basis for these voting blocks was wealth and property, which was determined by the censors. It was their function to divide Roman society into these groups, determining their respective political power. Today, I would once again see the exercise of that power.

At dawn, a stout ram was led by an acolyte of the Temple of Jupiter into the shrine of Mars. The gathered citizens could hear the nervous bleating of the animal as the sun climbed above the horizon. Then the bleating stopped. The sacrifice had been made. The Pontifex Maximus emerged from the shrine and walked to Sempronius Longus, his bloody hands raised. They conferred for a few moments, then Sempronius turned to the gathered assembly and announced, "The spleen ran clear. It is a sign the gods favor Rome and this Assembly of the Centurionate. Voting may commence." The crowd cheered at this proclamation. After waiting for the crowd to quiet, he said, "The first office is for consul of Rome. The nominees are: Gnaeus Servilius Geminus, Quintus Fabius Maximus Verrucosus, Gaius Flaminius, and Marcus Atilius Regulus."

Each senator stepped forward as his name was called. Servilius was a short stout man with only a ruffle of hair around his shiny bald pate. Fabius Maximus's dark features were marred only by the wart over his lip, just to the right of his nose, that gave him the cognomen Verrucosus, or wart-face. Flaminius's white mane shone as bright as his chalked toga in the morning sun. And Regulus, tall and proud, looked the image of his ancient ancestor, the founder of Rome.

Sempronius motioned to one of his assistants, who ran to one of the voting blocks in the first class. "You have the honor of casting the first vote today. May Minerva grant you wisdom."

Then the chosen group began to vote. There were perhaps a hundred men in this block, and their conversations were animated as each tried to convince their neighbor of the superiority of their favored candidate. In truth, most of these men would vote for the man who had paid them the most. But after only a few minutes, the results were announced.

"Servilius and Flaminius," intoned Sempronius from his podium. "The first class may commence voting." At that point, the true voting began. Each of the remaining seventy-nine voting blocks in the top tier voted simultaneously. Each block held only one vote, but since two consuls needed to be elected, each block voted for two men. The first two men to reach a majority of ninety-eight votes would become consuls for the next year.

I cast my vote for Gaius Flaminius and Servilius and watched the vote tally. Sempronius kept track of reported votes through the assistants, while the lictors guarded the dais. Within an hour the first class concluded their voting.

Sempronius Longus returned to his position at the center of the dais. "The votes have been tallied. The count stands at eighty-seven for Servilius, forty-nine for Fabius, forty-six for Flaminius, fourteen for Regulus." He paused to allow the crowd to ponder the results so far, then he said, "The second class may commence voting."

The line behind the first class began the same process of voting for the two men who would become consul. Having only twenty voting blocks, the second class had completed their voting in half an hour. The assistants reported the numbers to Consul Sempronius.

He stepped back to his speaking position and announced, "Gnaeus Servilius Geminus is elected consul of Rome." The crowd cheered but waited to hear the next statement, as one office remained to be filled. "The tally now stands at seventy-three for Fabius, seventy-one for Flaminius, nineteen for Regulus." He paused again before saying, "The third class may commence voting."

As he turned back to the candidates, I thought I saw his eyes lock with Fabius Maximus for an instant. Flaminius was in trouble if Sempronius had allied himself with Fabius Maximus. And somehow, I knew he had done just that.

Another line of twenty voting blocks began to vote. Because the race to ninety-eight votes was so close, as each block completed voting, its vote was announced to the assembly. The men in these blocks were younger and poorer than those who voted earlier, beginning the recruiting pool for the hastatii. Sempronius Longus motioned for silence as he said, "The tally now stands at eighty for Fabius, seventy-nine for Flaminius, twenty-four for Regulus." Again, he paused before saying, "The fourth class may commence voting."

The fourth-class voting blocks repeated the process of their wealthier colleagues. And again, as each voting block finished, their vote was announced to the assembly. Sempronius announced, "The tally now stands at eighty-nine for Flaminius, eight-eight for Fabius, twenty-six for Regulus." He inhaled a deep breath and said, "The fifth class may commence voting."

The thirty blocks of the fifth class would likely decide the day. These were the poorest of Roman citizens, the source of the velites in the legions. *It would take only a little gold to sway these men,* I thought, imagining the sums of money spent to buy votes during this one election.

Each pen containing the voters in the fifth class turned into vicious shouting matches as votes were cast among the poorest of Rome's property owners. The assistants began announcing the voting results. First one for Flaminius, then another. A vote for Regulus, then a vote for Fabius. Finally, Flaminius was only one vote away from the necessary ninety-eight, with Fabius trailing by two with thirteen votes remaining.

"A vote for Fabius," announced Sempronius. Only twelve votes remained to be reported. Another of Sempronius's assistants reported. "A vote for Flaminius." He paused, with a sour look on his face. "Gaius Flaminius is elected consul of Rome."

I exhaled, not realizing that I had been holding my breath. Voting was not normally so exciting. And I had wanted Flaminius to win.

Sempronius quieted the cheering crowd. "Now the office of Praetor..."

And the voting continued.

* * *

"Congratulations, sir," I said to Flaminius. "It was a close victory."

"Bah!" he said scornfully. "Sempronius Longus made a mistake. He wanted old wart-face to win."

"Sir?"

"One of his assistants reported in with too much alacrity on the final round of voting," Flaminius explained. "It was a mistake. He was supposed to wait for a block voting for Fabius Maximus to report and just barely fail to report the vote that gave me victory."

"It was planned so then?" I asked.

"Yes, of course," he said as if the question were childish. "You have been a soldier too long, Appius. Politics eludes you." He sat on a luxuriously cushioned bench. A slave brought a platter with several choice delicacies from which he chose a honeyed dormouse covered in dried sesame seeds.

"Of course, my plan failed as well. I thought I had paid quite enough to the voters in the third and fourth classes to give me the victory, but I am glad I did not stop my efforts there."

The slave brought the platter to me. I chose a quail egg filled with some combination of minced meat and olive oil. It was quite savory. "You won, sir. That is the important thing," I said.

"Yes. Tiberius will leave soon to resume command of the army at Placentia," Flaminius said. "I met with Servilius briefly as the other magistrates were elected. We agreed that I will take command of that army. That should drive the narrow-faced ass quite insane."

"So, back to Placentia then?" I asked, drinking some delicious wine.

"Yes. Very soon. I must confer with Servilius, and the auspices must be taken." He frowned at that thought. "I am loathe to give my enemies the chance to befoul my consulship with a poor augury though."

"I don't understand, sir," I said.

"In my previous term, my enemies held up my confirmation by creating an incident during the augury. It put a pall over everything I tried to accomplish during my year."

"And you fear a repetition?"

"Yes. My political enemies will stop at nothing, save allowing the sacking of Rome perhaps, to discredit me." He drank deeply of his wine. "I must ensure the new colonies are preserved and Hannibal is defeated this year."

"When will you depart for Placentia?"

"Not for a week or more, but as soon as possible." He turned as we heard voices from the outer chambers. "Ah, good. Paullus is here." He rose to greet his guests.

A tall man, his hair dark though graying at the temples, entered, wearing the purple-trimmed robe of a Roman senator. I stood to attention as his retinue followed him into the room. "Good evening, Gaius," he said, smiling, in a deep and rich voice.

"Lucius. How nice of you to come," Flaminius said, greeting his friend with a warm embrace. "And who do we have here?" He turned to allow his gaze to fall on the young woman and boy who followed Paullus.

"My son, Lucius Minor, and my youngest daughter, Aemilia Tertia," Paullus said.

"Welcome to my home, young ones." He embraced each with a kiss on their foreheads. The boy looked annoyed, but the girl received the kiss with a serene grace. "Let me introduce my stern young friend here. Paullus, may I make known to you Appius Curtius Asprenas, Decurion of the Second Legion."

"Good evening, Decurion. You are far from Cremona, where I hear your legion is based now," Paullus said, taking my hand.

"Yes, I am, Senator. I was detached to escort Senator Flaminius back to Rome."

"And you stayed for the elections?" he asked.

"I am assigned to Gaius Flaminius until he returns to Placentia," I said.

"I see." Paullus turned to Flaminius. "You have a noble bodyguard, Flaminius."

"I have a deadly bodyguard," Flaminius said. "Asprenas has survived every battle with Hannibal so far and was decorated for valor in the War with Illyria. Do not underestimate him."

Paullus examined me closely. "Lucius, come here. Greet our friend, Decurion Asprenas."

The boy pushed his curly black hair out of his face and looked up, revealing a pair of dark inquisitive eyes. "Hello, Decurion," he said. "May I see your horse?"

I laughed and said, "Perhaps after dinner, if you are still awake."

Paullus took Aemilia's hand and presented her. "My daughter."

"Good evening, Lady Aemilia," I said bowing over her hand. Her locks were as golden as the boy's were dark.

"Are you happy to be back in Rome, Asprenas?" she asked.

I looked into her pale blue eyes and said, "It has its pleasures, but I go where my duty takes me."

"Perhaps it will bring you home soon," she said in a soft voice.

"We will see, my lady."

"Good, now everyone is acquainted," Flaminius said. "We can begin the meal." He motioned for the servants to bring food and wine.

Young Lucius did not get to see my horse. He was asleep on his couch long before dinner finished.

XXVI

THUNDERSTORM

"Sempronius Longus has gone then?" Flaminius asked. "The elections are only nine days past."

"Yes, two days ago," Paullus said. "He will be back in Placentia before the Ides of March."

"I must leave soon then," Flaminius said. "I will not wait for the augurs to thwart me again."

"The Senate will recall you," Paullus said in a worried tone. "It will be seen as a bad omen. And during a war? You must wait, Gaius."

"If there were a chance the augurs were not bought and paid for by Sempronius Longus and Fabius Maximus, I might agree." Flaminius paced across his chamber. "I cannot allow them to stop or delay me. They did the same to Scipio, diverting half his army before he could meet Hannibal in Gaul, and they have done the same to me."

"Five years ago, we were not facing an invasion of Italy," Paullus said.

"And six months ago?" Flaminius retorted. "No, Paullus. Those men will do anything to thwart those who oppose their political ambitions. I will not play their game and sacrifice Rome in the process."

"The people will turn against you," he said, pleading.

"The people will remember that I am the one who passed the law allowing Roman settlement in the Gallic lands of the Senones, and they will remember my victory over the Insubres despite the Senate's orders to lay down before the enemy. The people will support victory."

"Appius," Paullus said, turning to me, "talk some sense to him."

"I would if I saw the sense in allowing politicians to manage the war from behind the safety of Rome's city walls," I said.

"You forget yourself!" Paullus shouted. "You are both mad."

"No, old friend," Flaminius said soothingly, "we are not mad. We see the situation quite clearly. Hannibal is out there, ravaging the countryside." He embraced his friend. "He must be stopped. Allowing politics to prevent us from stopping him is madness. I must reject it."

Paullus bowed his head. "You will not wait?" he asked.

"No, I will not," Flaminius said with finality in his voice.

"Then I will seek a way to prevent the Senate from issuing a recall order on your behalf," Paullus said with resignation. "I can manage it with some assistance from the Aemillii and Cornellii I think."

"I will speak to Scipio on my way to Placentia," Flaminius said. "I believe you may count on his support."

Paullus brightened a bit, then asked, "When will you leave?"

He turned to me and said, "Appius, what do you think?"

"Day after tomorrow, at dawn," I said, after a moment. "That gives me enough time to organize a proper escort."

"And it will give me time to meet with some men to provide for additional troops this year," Flaminius said. "Paullus, can you push for four additional legions to be raised?"

"Four?" he said.

"Yes. We will need overwhelming numbers to face the Carthaginians. Their veterans are blooded and have followed Hannibal through the snowy passes of the Alps and defeated every Roman army thrown against them. They will be tough and motivated. Only numbers will daunt them at this point."

"I will see what I can do, Flaminius."

"Good. I will make sure Servilius knows my intentions. He will support you, Paullus. And we will not forget you."

"I will do as I must, Gaius."

"As must we all." Flaminius faced the garden and watched the sun setting over Esquiline Hill.

* * *

Two weeks later, I led my turma, reinforced with two hundred alae cavalry appropriated from the garrison at Arriminium by the newly elected consul, into Placentia under an overcast sky. The temperature was near freezing and the air dry as the guards opened the gates to the familiar city. Gaius Flaminius was home.

Scipio and Torquatus greeted us on the steps of the Principia. "Welcome back, Consul Flaminius," Torquatus said formally.

"Thank you, Tribune," he said, gazing about the city from the tops of the steps. "You have done well finishing the castra in my absence."

"The men needed little motivation to finish their own barracks, sir. The weather saw to that," Torquatus said. "Other than snow, nothing impeded their progress."

Indeed, nearly every building inside the fortress walls had been completed. Only a few lacked roofing or exterior trimmings, and those looked to be nearing completion. The engineers had been busy. Every wall had artillery platforms, filled with ballistae or mangonels. The fortress looked ready to withstand any assault.

"I expected to see Sempronius Longus here. Is he at the legion camp then?" Flaminius asked.

"Yes, sir. The general thought to give you time to settle in before conferring," Torquatus said diplomatically. "We expect him for cena this evening. I am sure there will be much to discuss given the upcoming transfer of authority." Torquatus turned to Scipio. "Of course, you remember Decurion Scipio."

"Of course, Titus." Flaminius embraced the young officer. "Your father sends his love, young man. And he made sure to ask me to tell you he is up and walking now. He will be able to ride back to Rome at the end of his term as consul."

Scipio smiled at the news. "Thank you for the message, sir. And congratulations on your election victory."

"Thank you. I believe we can save any other formalities for later, gentlemen." He clung to Scipio's arm. "Decurion, would you escort me to my chambers. It will be good to bathe and get this road dust off my body."

"Of course. This way, sir." Scipio walked arm-in-arm with the new consul.

"I will see you at dinner, Tribune," Flaminius said, walking away.

I dismissed the escort and followed Flaminius and Scipio, with a look at Torquatus, who appeared unruffled at the prospect of this evening's dinner between political opponents. *He's a cool one, our senior tribune.* But the thought of a bath pushed the matter from my mind.

* * *

"I am glad your journey was swift and untroubled, Gaius," Sempronius Longus said. "I worried you may have been slowed by snow in the Apennines."

"No, the weather was cold and unpleasant," said Flaminius, "but no impediment to travel on horseback."

The two men had cordially avoided any conversation about the election or war so far. A chattering of voices in the hall drew our attention. Seeing the mud-spattered man coming through the entrance to the council chamber told me that cordiality was about to end.

The cavalryman came to attention and saluted the general. "Sir, Decurion Decius's compliments."

"Yes, go on, soldier," the general said.

"Hannibal follows the River Trebia southward. His army is somewhat reduced in number. The Gauls have returned to winter quarters. The decurion estimates his strength at twelve thousand infantry and eight thousand cavalry, sir."

"Decius follows him?" Sempronius asked.

"Yes, sir," answered the young soldier. "He moves parallel with the main force and seeks a concealed, elevated position from which to observe the enemy."

"Refresh my memory, Scipio." The general turned to the decurion. "How many men does Decius have?"

"With the return of this messenger, fourteen, sir," Scipio said.

"He will need reinforcements then," Sempronius said.

"I will see to it at once, sir." Scipio stood and motioned me toward the entrance.

Meeting at the door, he spoke in a low tone. "Appius, glad to have you back," he said.

"I'm going to find Decius then?"

"The pair of you seem to do well together."

"Orders, sir?"

"Take this messenger with you. He should have some indication of where Decius went to ground. Report at least twice a day."

"I'll need more than my section, sir."

"Take the messengers that Decius has used so far," Scipio said. "And take thirty men from Laelius. That will give you enough to report for more than a week, and he has no need of them. I am sending him off to take my place with Father. By the week's end, hopefully something will have happened, or we can reinforce you."

"Leave in the morning?"

"Yes. Get at least one good night's sleep," he said. "I'll expect a report by midnight tomorrow."

"I'll go alert the men," I said, saluting.

"Fortuna shield you from harm, Appius," he said with a clasp of my shoulder.

"Thank you, sir."

I watched him make his way back to the dinner party. I waited until the messenger was dismissed by Sempronius Longus. I gathered him by eye as he strode toward me, and together we walked toward the barracks.

* * *

The next afternoon, the messenger led my reinforced turma into a deep draw in the foothills of the Apennine Mountains. The sky was still overcast, but the air was warming considerably. We found a guard of four men watching the horses in the small, concealed clearing at the base of the tiny valley. The guards told us where to look for Decius and the observation team.

I chose three men and climbed up the steep gorge at the head of the draw. It was a vertical chimney, perhaps thirty feet high. One of the first men up had dropped a knotted rope, so the climb was only challenging, not impossible. I rolled onto the ridge at the top and lay on my back, breathing heavily for a moment. Then I turned to help the next man up. Within a few minutes, we were walking along the ridgeline, keeping low so as to not reveal our position to any who might be looking. The tall trees and deep underbrush helped to conceal our movement.

Finally, I heard a finger snap, followed by another. I made two quick snaps in reply.

A low voice said, "Come forward and be recognized."

Still keeping low, I walked forward until I met the three-man patrol wearing dun-colored cloaks over their cavalry armor. "Decurion Asprenas with messages for Decurion Mus," I said softly.

One of the men saluted from his crouch, then motioned for one of the men to lead me onward. I turned to see my three men following close behind, then followed my guide.

A few moments later, we entered a shallow cave that must have once been a bear's den. I had to crawl to enter, though I could crouch after I got inside. I told my three men to wait outside. My guide nodded approvingly.

"Appius," said Decius, smiling broadly, in a low voice. "Welcome to Casa Mus."

"Impressive," I said with a wry smile.

A bronze brazier provided some heat and a soft red-orange light, which was the only source of illumination in the cave. A woolen blanket covered the entrance, pinned in place by two wooden spikes driven into the walls. Decius sat on his camp stool and leaned against one wall.

"It has a wonderful view," he said. "I'll show you tomorrow."

"I have to send a report back by midnight," I said.

"Good enough." He looked at my guide. "Magnus, take one of our men and head down the chimney. Ride to Placentia and report to Decurion Scipio."

The man nodded. "Message, sir?"

"Hannibal is marching into the pass near the Temple of Minerva along the Trebia. I expect him to camp shortly. That puts him a day's march from Ebovium."

The soldier repeated the message, then left quietly.

"You have orders for me?" Decius asked.

"Same as before. Watch and report," I said. "Stay out of sight."

"Good. We're a bit outnumbered here," he said. "How many men did you bring?"

"I brought back your sixteen and thirty of my own," I said. "We report twice a day or more."

"I don't think our little pasture will support the horses for that long," he said. "We'll have to send a patrol looking for another pasture tomorrow."

"If he's only a day away from Ebovium, I doubt we will be here that long," I said.

A rumble sounded in the distance.

"True," Decius said. "It won't take him long to storm the village. Then he'll be coming back this way."

"Unless his troops are mountain goats or grow wings," I said.

"Still, I'll send out a patrol tomorrow morning anyway."

"Suit yourself," I said. "How are you deployed?"

"Two three-man teams," he said. "One watching the enemy from cover and one watching the back. The rest are back in the draw. I usually keep another man here to run messages."

"Very well," I said. "Let's stay with your deployment. I'll want to see his army in the morning."

Another rumble echoed down the valley. "What is that?" Decius and I said together.

With a shrug, Decius said, "Let's go see."

We crawled out of the cave and moved south in the darkening shadows of twilight. The clouds in the sky grew darker. Toward the west, where the sky would normally be bright with the setting sun, was a gray-black mass of clouds. We had crouch-walked about twenty paces when the sky flashed a brilliant white and I stumbled. A few seconds later, the crack and rumble of thunder echoed down the valley.

"Faex!" Decius said, blinking the spots from his eyes.

"You get some shit in your eyes?"

"I can't see."

"You kiss your wife with that mouth?" I asked. I braced myself against a tree, blinking my own sight back into focus. "Let's get the men into the cave."

"Right," he said, leading us to the team a hundred yards down the ridge. "All of you, back to the cave," he ordered as the rain began to spit from the sky.

By the time we made it to the cave, the rain was falling steadily, punctuated by brilliant streaks of lightning and peals of thunder. I said to Decius, "I'll send the rest down the chimney before it gets too bad. I think we're in for a bad night."

"Yeah, but the Carthaginians will have it worse." He grinned.

I slapped him playfully on the cheek and moved back down the trail to the northern patrol. I ordered them into the chimney, they moved with as much speed as they could, sliding down the rope. I walked back to the cave and stood outside a moment looking up into the rain. A ball of ice struck me on the nose. "Ow!" I said ducking under the blanket and into the cave. I probed my injured nose, but it seemed to be in one piece.

"What was that?" Decius asked.

"Hail," I said.

"Oh, Hannibal's in for a very rough night."

Decius, I decided, had an evil laugh.

XXVII

THE CONSUL'S GAMBIT

I woke at a kick to my foot, sitting up rapidly. Decius and I had slept on the floor wrapped in our cloaks, while the three soldiers rotated as guards through the night. One of the men stood over me with a cup of warm tea. I drank, nodding my thanks.

Decius sat up beside me, wiping the sleep from his eyes. I handed him the cup.

"Thanks," he said after draining it. "What time is it?"

"Hour or so before dawn," said the guard, waking the other men.

After the others were up, I said to one of the men, "Get down to the pasture and get six men to relieve you all."

The man nodded and crawled toward the cave entrance.

"The rest of us will go see how the Carthaginians fared," I said, motioning the man closest to the entrance to head outside.

A few minutes later, we were laying prone behind several trees, obscured by brambles. Below us, perhaps two miles distant, was the Carthaginian army. Some of them were lighting smoldering fires with their wet firewood.

"Now that's a miserable bunch down there," Decius said.

I had to agree. The Carthaginians had tried to put up tents when the storm began, but not one was standing. I could see men lying flat in the mud beneath the canvas and pelts of the Carthaginian shelters. Some had tried to hide beneath their horses or the carts used to carry tools, supplies, and fodder, but most had spent the night, miserable and cold, in the mud, pounded by ice and rain.

I turned to Decius and said, "What do you think?"

"I think they had a bad night," he said.

To one of the other soldiers, I said, "Take your friend here and ride to Placentia. Report, Hannibal's army stopped by thunderstorm in the mountains. Continuing to observe." I added, "You can elaborate on what you have seen of the results of last night's storm, but don't over-embellish."

"Understood, sir," he said, then gathered his companion and crawl-walked back toward the chimney.

Decius and I continued to watch the soaked and muddy Carthaginian army crawl out of the muck and begin organizing for the day's march.

"After that night, I don't think they'll want to try attacking anything," Decius said.

"You're probably right," I said. "But let's keep an eye on them anyway."

A few minutes later, we let the new team of guards take over the observation of the enemy.

By the time the sun was up, we had made a breakfast of warm porridge for the men. One of them crawled into the cave and reported, "They're forming up for a march, sir. They've got everything loaded, but it looks like they're headed back north."

I scooped a cup of porridge and handed it to the man. Decius grabbed two more cups, and we crawled back outside to see Hannibal's army march. Decius handed the cups over to the two men as we slid in beside them. The sun was just breaking through the clouds behind us, so we had a wonderful view of the Numidian and Carthaginian cavalry riding north along the Trebia. Eight thousand horses dug muddy trenches into the soft ground by the river, marching ten abreast. After an hour passed, the infantry followed the cavalry. Two hours later, other than the morass of mud and muck, the only indication of the Carthaginian's camp was the carcass of a lone elephant, lying beside the river's edge.

* * *

We climbed down the chimney and saddled the horses. An hour later, we rode at a gallop toward the River Padus, trying to get in front of the Carthaginian cavalry scouts. In two hours, we had reached the river and paused to let the horses drink and the men refill their water bags.

"After you've watered your horses," I said to two men, "ride back to Placentia with this message for Decurion Scipio." I waited for them to focus their attention on me. "Hannibal marches north. He is coming out of the hills toward the River Padus again. I will continue to observe and report." Once the men repeated it back to me, I dismissed them to continue caring for their mounts.

"What do you think he'll do?" asked Decius.

"Fall back on Clastidium or another of his Gallic allies' towns perhaps," I said. "That would be logical."

Decius shook his head with a wry grin. "He hasn't done much that was logical so far, has he?"

"No, he hasn't," I agreed. "Still, he doesn't have the numbers to attack Placentia. And if he goes past toward Cremona, he'll be between two armies."

"Time for more hiding in the shrubs and running away if they get too close?" he asked.

I grinned. "It seems our lot in the army."

"Well, let's get to it then," Decius said. "Mount up, lads. We're off to see up Hannibal's ass. I want a report on how many boils he has."

The men groaned at the awful joke but climbed into their saddles with some jests of their own. It was good to see them smiling as we rode west in search of Hannibal once more.

* * *

I peered through the tree limbs at the side of the road to Clastidium. "We need to get out of here," I said in a soft voice.

"Right, sir." Decius said. "How do we do that?"

"I haven't the faintest idea," I said.

We had ridden for two hours, westward parallel to the Padus. Only the keen hearing of my lead scout had saved us from riding headlong into Hannibal's vanguard. There was infantry to our west, cavalry to our south, and a river to our north. The only problem was the open floodplain to our east. We had no place to hide from the cavalry once we came out of the trees. The mid-morning sunshine gave us no time to hide and wait. My men were good, but hundred-to-one odds were a bit much to ask of them.

"Swim the river?" Decius suggested dubiously.

"It's that or make a run for it."

"It's twenty miles to the Trebia."

"Swim it is then," I said. "Dump the water, men. Use the bags as floats." We led the horses toward the river, which bent away from us in a small oxbow. We reached the edge in a few minutes. I pulled off my breastplate and helmet and quickly strapped them to the saddle. My horse tried to turn and bite me, the ungrateful brute.

"Everyone ready?" I asked.

A few nods and grunts of assent were my only answers.

"Into the water then," I said and led my unpleasant mount toward the river's edge. The water was icy, and I gasped as the water climbed up my legs quickly. In moments, the water was over my head. I wrapped the reins tight around my wrist and pulled the horse into the deep water. He resisted for a moment, then his hooves slipped in the slimy mud and he fell in, pulling me under. I came up gasping, and the horse, wide-eyed with terror, began struggling against the reins. I pulled hard, and he followed me into the deep water.

Around us, my men were all having similar struggles. Some, who could not swim, grasped the inflated water bags with white knuckles and terror in their eyes. The river was over a hundred yards wide at this point, and the current strong toward the east.

I heard a cry behind me, and I looked back to see black-skinned men on short horses along the river's edge. The Numidians had found us. Javelins flew. I heard a hoarse scream behind me and knew one of my men would never make it across. I put my head down and pulled hard for the other bank.

It took nearly ten minutes to cross the river. My hands were blue and shaking as I pulled myself through the marshy grass on the far side. The air bit my wet skin as I crawled onto the muddy riverbank with desperate, gasping breaths. I rolled over to check my mount; his shivering hide flicked away the water in the cool afternoon air. He stood over me, snorting displeasure. I pulled on the reins to help myself to my knees and looked back to see the last of my men coming ashore.

Across the river, perhaps two bowshots distant and a quarter-mile upstream, the Numidians were riding parallel to us. I made a quick count. A hundred, maybe one hundred and twenty of the fast little horses the desert men preferred. I noticed that none of them chose to follow us into the water. I looked around, doing a head count of my own men. Only forty of forty-three. I had lost three men in the crossing. One of their mounts was cropping the dry grass at the river's edge, but there was no sign of her rider.

"Decius," I said with a croak. I cleared my throat and tried again. "Decius?" I said in a clearer voice.

"Here," came the response.

"Get the men and horses dried as best you can," I ordered. "We ride in ten minutes."

"Yes, sir," he said, then shouted for the optios to get the men up and moving.

I grabbed a handful of long, dry grass from the riverbank and began brushing down my horse. It took fifteen minutes, but soon we were in the saddle and walking toward Placentia.

* * *

"Open the gate!" shouted the optio from the guard tower at Placentia. "Patrol coming in, sir," I heard him report to the centurion who crested the wall a moment later.

My forty men trotted through the opening gate to be met by a full century of legionaries with pila ready to deal with any attack by cavalry. I slowed to a walk and moved to one side to allow my men to ride past. Decius joined me.

"Go see the horses seen to, the men fed, and get a change of clothes. Bring me a new tunic. I'll be at the Principia," I said.

"Right, sir," he said. "And you'll give the general the good news?" He shot me a sardonic grin.

"You want to do it?" I asked.

"Better you than me, sir," he said, kicking his horse into motion.

I rode down the Via Praetoria to the back side of the Principia. I handed the reins of my horse to one of the legionaries guarding the entrance. "Have him taken to Decurion Decius. He should be at the Third Turma's quarters."

"Yes, sir," the man said with a salute.

I returned the salute and walked into the stone structure. A few moments later, I was at the entrance to the council chamber. The pair of guards came to attention and saluted.

"Is General Sempronius inside?" I asked.

The legionary on the left said, "No, sir."

I waited for the man to elaborate, but he retreated into stubborn silence. "Consul Flaminius?" I asked.

"Yes, sir," he said.

"Let me pass. I have a report for him."

The two spears returned to order arms, and I strode past the two men and into the chamber.

"...he must be mad," Flaminius was saying to Decurion Scipio.

"Sempronius wants a victory before his term is complete," Scipio said.

Flaminius noticed me and came to his feet. "Appius, what in the name of Mercury happened to you?"

I looked down at my mud-caked tunic, legs, and sandals and imagined my face looked much the same. Only my helm and decurion's crest had gotten me through the guards, it seemed. "Had to swim the Padus to avoid some Numidians."

Scipio said, "Well, you are just in time. Hannibal has arrived."

"Damn, I was trying to beat him here," I said.

Gaius Flaminius called for some wine. Then he motioned me to a bench and said, "What happened?"

"Hannibal came out of the mountains and turned east," I said. "We nearly rode straight into his vanguard."

"How many men?" Scipio asked.

"He had about eight thousand horse and ten, maybe twelve thousand infantry this morning," I said. "No sign of Gauls though. It seems they returned home for the spring plantings."

"Why did you have to cross the Padus?" Flaminius asked.

"Got caught on open ground with Numidians on top of us," I said. "They would have overwhelmed us if we had tried to run. I lost three men in the crossing. Either to javelins or drowning."

"Well, your news is a bit late. Hannibal arrived on the other side of the Trebia a little over an hour ago," Scipio said. "He establishes a camp as we speak."

"What are we doing about it?" I asked.

"Sempronius Longus marches with three legions to confront Hannibal," Flaminius said with scorn. "It seems he wants one last attempt at glory before his term as consul is over in three days."

I blinked in astonishment.

"We have orders to march across the Trebia and build a marching camp before sundown," Scipio said.

"That's in less than an hour," I said.

"Yes. I must depart. Join me once you've changed and seen to your men," Scipio said, standing. "I fear I will need your help in the morning."

Decius came through the entrance carrying a new tunic for me.

"Decius. Glad to see you had a good swim," Scipio said.

Decius barked a laugh. "I was getting a bit ripe, sir." He took an exaggerated sniff in my direction.

Scipio smiled then slapped the larger man on the shoulder. "See you across the Trebia." He walked out, pulling on his helmet.

"Across the Trebia?" Decius asked uncertainly.

I chuckled, realizing that for once barracks gossip had failed to beat the official word down to the troops. "Hannibal is here. It's time for us to go greet the man."

"Filius canis!" Decius swore.

"Thanks for the tunic. I'll go take a bath," I said. "Get us something to eat and meet me there. I think we'll have a long night."

Decius swore again.

"With your permission, Consul?" I said.

Flaminius waved his dismissal.

XXVIII

HANNIBAL'S CAMP

The dawn's light broke across the grassy plain near the Roman marching camp to the sight of a Carthaginian army arrayed for battle. A Roman army marched to greet them. Both sides arranged their heavy infantry in the middle with cavalry on the flanks and skirmishers in front. I rode at Scipio's side, positioned on the army's right along with a thousand other cavalrymen.

I saw the rose-colored light reflecting on the bronze helmets of the infantry, not yet bright enough to be painful to the eye. The morning mist hung low against the ground in wisps of white that hiding nothing from view. The air, warm after the previous day's rain, felt still against my face.

"Let's see how they do in a fair fight this time," Decius said, breaking my reverie.

Scipio said, "Appius says there is no such thing as a fair fight."

I ignored the comment and examined the enemy soldiers intently.

"I suppose," Decius said. "But this looks to be fairer than most."

"The numbers are nearly even, it seems," Scipio agreed. "But they have quite a bit more in the way of cavalry. Could be hard work for us today."

"We lead the Numidians on a merry chase, then let the boys in the middle push them back to Iberia," Decius said.

"Like last time?" I asked without shifting my gaze.

Scipio lowered his head at the memory of half the turma being slain as we fled down the Ticinus. He inhaled sharply and said, "I should hope not. Let us see what the gods bring us this day."

The buccinators sounded the advance, and we marched into battle.

The two armies had formed on opposite sides of the grassy field, about two miles apart. I saw the Carthaginians marching toward us slowly, and I could see their camp a short distance behind. Hannibal had erected a crude palisade around it. A change in tactics.

"Hannibal builds fortifications of his own," Scipio observed.

"He's learning from us," I said. "After Sempronius's men chased those Gauls through his camp…"

"They did slow long enough to start some fires," Decius said. "Maybe they burned some of Hannibal's robes. He likes to look presentable on the battlefield."

"He does stand out," I agreed. "But I think that's more the throne on top the elephant than the clothes."

Decius chuckled. "Look at the one he rides today. One tusk and sheets of scale covering the head and flanks."

Hannibal wore flowing gold and white robes today, his head covered by a simple bronze helmet. His black beard stood in stark contrast to the bright cloth. At his waist was a small sword. The elephant strode ponderously forward behind his infantry. From his vantage point, Hannibal could see the entire battlefield, and in turn he could be seen by both armies.

"More likely he wanted to secure the mercenaries' pay," Scipio said, ignoring our banter.

Our own camp, completed as night fell yesterday, stood a mile behind us. It was a comforting presence of security should we need it. It held a small garrison to man the gates and guard towers and would provide a fortified place to retreat if the battle went poorly.

We marched forward, silent but for the cries of centurions and optios to dress the lines of the marching soldiers. I could hear shouts from the Carthaginians. They taunted or cheered as their officers encouraged them forward. I could see smiles on many faces. This enemy did not fear the Roman legion.

A low whirring sound drew my attention. "Slingers!" I shouted, to be echoed by officers throughout the army.

I could see a thousand or more dun-colored figures a hundred yards to the front of the Carthaginian formation. They stood motionless save one upraised arm, whirling above their heads. At a shouted command, the arms came toward us and the rain of lead began.

"Testudo!" sounded the shouts of centurions throughout the army.

The marching legionaries seemed to collapse inward as each century moved into the testudo. The front rank of men interlocked shields to make an impenetrable wall to the front. The men behind raised their shields overhead and overlapped the front-facing shields. The men on the flanks turned their shields outward. The lead bullets of the slingers clattered against the shields like hail but found few targets. In moments, the legions were marching forward again, if a little slower. Only among the skirmishers could cries of pain be heard as men fell to the devastating impact of lead on bone.

Then it was the velites' turn. Nearly four thousand of the nimble skirmishers hurled their javelins at the unarmored slingers, who were reloading as fast as possible. But the iron tips of the short, throwing spears found unprotected flesh of the relatively compact formation of slingers. I saw men fall, impaled in the chest and stomach. Occasionally, an especially high throw would come down onto an unfortunate man's head or foot. But most nimbly dodged the barrage. The slingers soon retreated behind the oval shields of the Carthaginian infantry, but their bullets had found targets as the unarmored velites carried only a small shield for protection. Several hundred men lay wounded or dead on the ground between the armies. The velites expended their last javelins on the fleeing slingers just as a shouted order from the Carthaginian lines sounded. Behind the compact infantry formation flew a hail of arrows onto the unarmored men. The arrows found upraised shields, but mostly the unarmored backs of the now fleeing velites. Hundreds of them fell, impaled by the relentless barrage.

Cries of "Withdraw!" and "Retreat!" sounded from the centurions who were responsible for the velites. Not that those men needed encouragement to run toward the shields and armored safety of the heavy infantry now only a few hundred yards to the rear. The surviving velites fled to the rear of the Roman formation as the arrows shifted their fire onto the heavy infantry.

Arrows fell from the sky and impacted the upraised shields of the marching legionaries. A few unlucky men felt the bite of an arrowhead slam through their shield and into their arms. But there were few fatal wounds from the rain of Carthaginian arrows. The wounded men either stayed in formation or fell back to the rear, their places filled by the man behind. I saw a few prone and bloody forms behind the marching soldiers, but none moved.

The armies were only a hundred yards apart now. The Roman lines had wide gaps between each of the testudo formations.

"Well, Hannibal has his tactical advantage," I said just as a shouted order sounded from behind the enemy's lines, and the Iberians and Africans surged forward in a rush toward us.

"Halt!" came the order from the primus pilus and echoed across the formation. "Form line!" he ordered. And before the Carthaginians could close the distance, the Roman formation shifted into a battle line again.

The Carthaginians met a solid wall of Roman shields. The impact of shield on shield sounded like a thousand hammers pounding at once. Then the Roman shields slipped apart, and the short gladius thrust through the gaps and into Carthaginian flesh. The battle was joined.

The Carthaginian and Numidian cavalry hung back, waiting for an opportunity to exploit some weakness in the Roman line. I could see they outnumbered us four to one, but we were content to await their charge. If they delayed long enough, perhaps our legionaries could rout the Carthaginian infantry.

We rode a hundred yards to the rear of the triarii, guarding the right flank of the army. From this vantage, I could see Hannibal, atop his elephant, surveying the carnage before him. The archers – there were only a thousand or so – stood in two ranks in front of the immense gray armored beast, but they had ceased firing when the Carthaginian infantry charged. Around Hannibal rode several officers, identifiable from their plumed and decorated helms.

One had to be Mago, who had been the commander of the ambush force during the previous battle near here. I wondered which man he was. The Carthaginian prisoners had described him very well, but I could not pick him out.

All seemed very alike in countenance from this distance. Their dark skin, from a life spent in the sun, and thick black beards contrasted with the bronze of their armor. Other than small variations in armor or underclothes, all the Carthaginian officers could be brothers. In fact, many were.

* * *

For three hours, the armies pushed, shoved, and stabbed at the other, but both sides seemed equally matched. Other than some feints by the Numidians, the Carthaginian cavalry remained behind and to the flanks of the enemy army. I had an uninterrupted view of the fight in the center. Scipio and I scanned the battlefield for signs of a Carthaginian surprise, but all attention seemed focused on the infantry fight.

The Carthaginians, fighting with falcata and short spears, lashed at the impenetrable Roman shields. Every few minutes, the centurions would blow their high-pitched whistles and the legionaries would thrust their swords into the mass of Carthaginian soldiers, then step back as the man behind stepped forward, offering only an instant of vulnerability as the front line withdrew to the rear to rest and drink before rejoining the battle line. The principes had stepped into the fight to give their hastatii brothers a chance to rest in this fashion. The Carthaginian left could not wrap around the right of the Roman line for fear of the cavalry waiting to charge their exposed flank, so the battle became a struggle of which army would tire first.

I saw Centurion Septimus, with a few of his hastatii, gathering more javelins, brought forward by the quaestor's men, to hurl over the heads of the men fighting in the front line. I caught his eye and nodded to him. His eyes brightened in recognition, and he came to attention briefly before returning to the fight.

I'm not sure exactly what happened next, but there was a cry from the far side of the battle, then the Roman line pushed forward a step, then two. It seemed as if the line would stabilize again after some mistake by the Carthaginian right. Then the Roman line surged forward again. This time the line moved forward several paces.

Horns sounded from behind the enemy line. I could see Hannibal gesturing to his commanders. One of them rode toward the cavalry on their left and another to the right.

"Prepare to charge!" Scipio shouted.

A few heartbeats later, the Carthaginian heavy cavalry spurred into the gallop, straight for us.

"Charge!" Scipio cried and spurred his horse toward the enemy.

I kicked my horse after him and held the point of my sword toward the onrushing enemy. We leapt forward from the cavalry formation, but soon all the equites followed, seeing the danger of an unopposed Carthaginian attack. Still, we were thirty facing thousands until the rest could catch us.

Scipio aimed for the leading Carthaginian officer, and I pulled my horse to his right. In my periphery, I could sense Decius on the decurion's left, and I knew our men were arrayed properly on our flanks. In seconds, we crossed the open ground between the two cavalry forces. The Carthaginian cavalry commander's sword was high in the air as we crashed together. Scipio stabbed low, and I slammed my shield into the man, knocking him off balance. Scipio's sword impaled the man's leg, ripping a bloody gash as we sped past.

I ducked a sword coming from my right and lashed out with a back-hand blow that connected with a Carthaginian helmet. I raked my spurs down my mount's side and he jumped forward, crashing into a dismount-ed man trying to pull Scipio from his saddle.

Scipio stabbed down, and the man died with a sword in his mouth. Then he shouted, "Push through! Push through!" He turned his horse toward Hannibal's elephant, looming over the battlefield. The beast's single tusk swept everything in its path as it turned to follow the cavalry streaming past.

I echoed the command and with the arrival of the rest of the Roman and alae cavalry, we drove a wedge straight through the enemy. On the far side, I saw what Scipio meant. The Carthaginian infantry, routed, fled toward the Carthaginian camp. The cavalry charge had covered a retreat. "Press forward, men!" I shouted. "They're running!"

We slashed and fought free of the Carthaginian cavalry. Scipio or-dered, "After them!" and leaned into the gallop in pursuit of the fleeing infantry.

The Roman buccinators sounded recall. I looked over my shoulder to see most of the Roman cavalry pull up. The heavy infantry stood still, watching the enemy they had just routed flee before them. Scipio contin-ued his charge. Decius and I followed. The recall sounded again.

Scipio pulled up. His eyes blazed as he turned to us. I saw the Carthaginian cavalry turning wide to avoid any contact with us or the legionaries.

"Hannibal is right there!" Decius shouted, reining in his horse. "We can get him."

Scipio regained his composure and said, "We may kill him, but we would die in the process, Decius."

The rest of us gathered around Scipio. "Orders, sir?" I asked.

"Let us see what the general decides," he said. "Back to our lines."

The thirty men of our turma walked our horses back toward the Roman lines while the Carthaginians fled to the safety of their camp.

* * *

"We must assault their camp now!" shouted Torquatus as Scipio, Decius, and I joined the impromptu command conference behind the Princeps.

"You forget yourself, Tribune," Sempronius Longus said. "I alone am responsible for the actions of this army."

"They flee before us, and we halt the attack?" Torquatus asked in a more reasonable tone.

"They set a trap," Sempronius explained. "Hannibal intends to trap us between the infantry behind the palisade wall and the cavalry behind us."

"What are your orders, sir?" Scipio said, focusing the general's attention elsewhere.

Sempronius Longus, surprised at the source of this interruption, thought a moment, then said, "Bring ladders forward. We shall move forward in testudo to the walls of the camp. Then we will assault the walls. Triarii will form a protective spear wall to the rear. Velites to support them. Cavalry to screen the flanks."

In ten minutes, the army had re-formed according to the new orders. We marched in deliberate silence toward the Carthaginian camp, a mile away.

The soldiers in testudo moved at a half-step pace due to the encumbrance of the interlocked shields. Behind the legionaries, the velites carried scaling ladders that they would pass to the hastatii, before the final charge to the wall. The triarii marched in normal columns, being far enough behind to avoid any missile fire from the Carthaginian camp. The equites stayed close to each flank of the triarii columns. We moved forward at the pace of snails on a cold day.

Before we covered half the distance, the Carthaginians opened their gate and poured forth to form a battle line spanning the length of the camp wall. Sempronius Longus had given Hannibal time to reform his army. Now they were prepared to fight again.

"Deodamnatus!" Decius cursed. "We had them running and now we're back to this."

Scipio turned his head and said in an icy tone, "Control yourself, Decurion. The men watch you."

Decius at once schooled his face to hide his frustration. "Sorry, sir."

Scipio nodded and turned back to observe the battle.

"Form line!" shouted centurions across the Roman army. The

turtle-shell formations spread instantly into the more maneuverable formation. In moments, the two battle lines faced off once again. The Roman hastatii and principes readied pila for the charge. At a hundred paces, the buccinators sounded double-time, and the entire army accelerated into a trotting jog that doubled their normal marching pace. The Carthaginians, not wanting to wait for the Roman charge, raced forward.

The buccinators sounded a different note, and every legionary stopped. "Loose!" came the orders from every centurion in the formation. A rain of iron-tipped javelins arced through the sky to fall upon the running Carthaginian infantry.

Men screamed as the heavy iron points pierced shield and armor to find vulnerable flesh. Blood spurted from deep wounds in men across the Carthaginian line. Either by wounds or distraction, the pila reduced the Carthaginian charge to a meager trickle of individuals instead of a massive hammer blow.

The Roman shields were locked together and ready for the Carthaginian assault. Then each man's gladius slipped through the small gap to thrust toward the enemy's vitals. Soon, the shoving match from earlier in the day resumed. Neither side seemed to have an advantage. And midday passed into memory as the fight wore on.

* * *

The cavalry forces watched each other once again, neither side willing to commit to battle until the infantry showed signs of wavering. Afternoon faded toward twilight, while men struggled to kill each other with sword and shield in the muddy ground before the Carthaginian camp. Scipio made several trips to General Sempronius's command post for orders.

Every time he returned with a cold and intense, "We remain here unless enemy cavalry threatens the infantry."

As the light faded, a messenger from the general arrived.

"Sir, General Sempronius's compliments and would you prepare your men to withdraw to camp," he said.

Scipio stared at the man. After a moment, he shook himself and asked, "Did the general give any instructions other than prepare to withdraw?"

"No, sir." The messenger swallowed, unnerved by the intensity of Scipio's gaze. "Just that all commanders should prepare to withdraw back to camp."

"Very well," the decurion said. "Carry on."

The messenger saluted, then hurried off toward another turma to deliver his message.

"What do you think, sir?" Decius asked.

"I think we will have a long night," Scipio said. "We will rotate sections. One forward, two back. We will leapfrog over each other as the infantry withdraws. As the triarii reach us, that section will withdraw toward camp. All men be prepared to turn and charge if enemy cavalry threaten. Any questions?"

"What do we do if the infantry rout?" I asked.

"Reform on the line closest to camp," Scipio said. "Once we are thirty men again, I will decide if we attack enemy infantry or cavalry or flee altogether."

"Understood, sir," I said. "We cover the retreat then."

Decius nodded and went to pass the orders to the men.

Scipio and I watched the infantry fight until the call to withdraw sounded from the buccinators.

Decius and I turned and kicked our horses into a trot. At fifty yards, Decius halted his section and turned to face the battle again. At a hundred yards, I halted my section. I turned to see the infantry stepping back in short steps while still fighting the Carthaginians to their front. Scipio's section turned and accelerated toward my men and soon passed me to take up a position fifty yards behind mine.

It took half an hour for the infantry line, thrusting, stepping back a pace, thrusting again, to reach Decius. He turned his section to move behind Scipio's. Now I waited for the slowly retreating infantry to reach my men. All the while, I watched the enemy cavalry, standing on either side of the camp watching the battle in the deepening darkness.

We repeated this pattern endlessly it seemed. The now cloudless sky revealed the boundless stars of the heavens, and the infantry stepped back, thrust, stepped back and thrust. Men died if they suffered a wound and could not be dragged away from the front line before the line stepped back. The Carthaginians were merciless to any Roman left behind. Still the Carthaginian cavalry remained unmoving in the deepening darkness.

And the infantry moved back another step.

It was nearly midnight by the time we had crossed half the distance to camp. We had lost sight of the Carthaginian cavalry long ago. Now we spread the cavalry screen wider, in case the enemy tried to move around and behind us.

Then, without any warning, the Carthaginian infantry stepped back from the fight. The Roman infantry, wary of a trick, continued to pace backwards, their shields facing the enemy. The Carthaginians did the same until they faded from view into the darkness.

After several minutes, we heard centurions shouting orders to form marching columns. A messenger rode to Scipio, halted with a salute, and said, "General Sempronius's compliments, sir. Your men are to form a rear guard along with the alae cavalry."

"Form a rear guard. I understand," Scipio replied. He returned the messenger's departing salute and said, "Get the men into skirmish order."

"Skirmish order!" Decius and I shouted. In minutes, we rode behind the marching army, senses straining to hear any approaching enemy attack. None came.

An hour later, we rode into camp.

Scipio's energy seemed boundless. As we rode towards our tents, he shouted orders. "Feed and brush your mounts. Officers, inspect your men's kit and animals."

There were groans as we all wanted no more than to untack the beasts, throw some hay into their ricks, and fall into a bone-weary sleep.

Decius and I looked at each other. With a deep breath I ordered, "Optios, inspect at the turn of the watch. Decurion Scipio will review the men at assembly. All frogs to be cleaned, horses groomed, and ricks and troughs filled. Tack will be oiled and inspected for wear."

Decius said, "Any man whose kit is not perfect will stand duty until dawn." He whispered to me sotto voce, "That should motivate them."

"You are an evil man," I said with a half-smile.

"Right, and let's get these horses groomed," he said. "I've no wish to be standing guard tonight."

In less than an hour, the men had seen to their horses and tack. None were found wanting by Decurion Scipio's inspection. He inspected my mount last and with a clean finger traced along the seat of my saddle, pronouncing, "Good work, men. I will see you after the morning meal. Sleep well."

The men scattered toward their barracks. Decius and I escorted the decurion to the Principia and to his room.

Decius asked, "Sir, did that all seem a bit pointless today?"

"What do you mean?" Scipio asked.

"Well... what did we accomplish?" he asked finally.

"Appius, why don't you give him the lesson you gave me?" Scipio said as we reached his quarters.

"Yes, sir. Good night," I said.

"Good night, sir," Decius said.

"Good night, gentlemen. Good work today," he said and walked into his chamber.

Decius and I walked two doors down to the chamber assigned to our use.

"What did he mean?" Decius asked.

"Every battle is pointless, and every battle is important," I said. "It is a waste of lives and resources to fight and fail to win, but to those who fight and suffer wounds or die, it is the most important moment of their lives."

"So what is the point?" he asked.

"You have to fight to win. If you fail to fight, the only resolution is death. Which is better?" I asked.

"Appius," he said with a groan, "you make my head hurt."

"Good night, Decius," I said.

The only response was snores. Decius had fallen into his pallet without even removing his armor. I threw a blanket over him and turned to my own bunk.

I pulled off my armor and hung it on a stand made for the purpose. Then I fell into my pallet and darkness took me.

XXIX

ARRETIUM

Gaius Flaminius strode into the council chamber flanked by twelve men in armor, each carrying bundled rods with axe heads affixed, his lictors. They were the bodyguard of a consul. Scipio, Decius, and I stood in conference with Torquatus at the side of the room as he entered. Flaminius wore armor and carried his helmet under one arm. There was a stony silence as he approached the council dais, but the unspoken message was clear. Flaminius was taking command.

Flaminius stopped five paces from Sempronius Longus and said, "Good morning, Tiberius." He smiled broadly and continued, "The Ides of March have come, and your consular year is at its end."

Sempronius's nostrils flared, but he held his temper in check. "Indeed, Gaius. It is now the Year of Servilius and Flaminius. Though the auspices have not been taken nor the rites completed for you to hold the office of consul."

"I take no stock in augurs paid by you and your colleagues to tell my future, Tiberius," Flaminius said. "I find their interpretations somewhat suspect."

"You mock the gods?" Sempronius said.

"No, Tiberius, I mock you and your attempts to retain power when Rome itself is at stake," Flaminius said with ice in his voice.

Sempronius shook himself and said, "You call down the wrath of Jupiter, Castor, and Pollux upon all of Rome with your sacrilege."

"I merely accept the office for which I was elected. You and your friends in Rome failed. Failed to win the war and failed to steal the election."

"And you" – Sempronius pointed to Flaminius's helmet – "famous slayer of Gauls. Will you now slay Carthaginians in the thousands?"

Flaminius held up the helmet in both hands. Instead of the traditional horsehair crest, the helmet plume was a long and fine run of blond hair, still attached to the skin. "I killed this man, this Gallic warrior in battle. I wear his scalp as an honor won in the cause of the People and Senate of Rome. And I swear by Mars and Minerva that I will kill as many Carthaginians as it takes to defeat Hannibal and his masters in Africa."

"You are a fool, Gaius. You invoke the gods even as you insult them. You invite ruin for all of Rome."

"I am consul," Flaminius said, voice rising slightly. "And you will remove yourself from the trappings of that office and relinquish your Imperium, or I will have you exiled."

"Take the auspices, Gaius," Sempronius pleaded. "I will wait."

"You will do as you are ordered, Senator."

Sempronius's shoulders fell, and his head came forward. "I plead with you, Gaius. For the sake of Rome, do not affront the gods."

"Your time is at an end." Flaminius turned to his lictors. "Senator Sempronius Longus is no longer consul and no longer holds Imperium. See him to his chambers. He will leave this city by noon tomorrow."

"Yes, Consul," said one of the bodyguards. He gathered two of his fellows by eye and approached Sempronius Longus. "Senator, if you will be so kind." He gestured toward the doorway.

"Gaius, I yield to you the title, duties, and responsibilities of consul," Sempronius Longus said stiffly. "May the gods bless your year." With that proclamation, he strode from the room with all the haughty dignity he could muster.

Flaminius waited for the room to quiet then walked to the dais and slowly sat in the chair Sempronius had just vacated. "Let us see about winning this war, shall we?"

* * *

Two days later, Flaminius held a conference of all senior officers. The main council chamber was the only room large enough for the gathering. Men stood in dense clusters discussing training, supplies, and other preparations for the new campaigning season.

Flaminius sat on his consular chair at the front of the room, speaking with Tribune Torquatus and Decurion Scipio.

"If we fall back to Arretium, Placentia and Cremona will be vulnerable to attack," Torquatus said.

Flaminius shook his head then said, "If we leave a strong garrison in each, they will be safe enough." He raised his hand to forestall argument. "Half a legion, alert and behind these walls, can stave off the entire Carthaginian army long enough for aid to come. And the same for Cremona."

"What happened to concentrating force?" Torquatus asked.

"Servilius is raising new legions even as we speak," Flaminius said. "Four new legions in addition to the current four will bolster our numbers well enough."

"You will combine eight legions into one army?" Scipio asked.

"Minus the garrisons for the walled colonies and cities of the north, yes."

"And what will this mighty army eat?" Torquatus asked. "No city can supply an army so vast for long."

"We build sixty quinqueremes at Ostia," Flaminius said. "We shall supply the army with grain shipments from southern Italy and Sicily. Our men shall eat well."

"So we fall back to Arretium to combine forces with Consul Servilius?" Scipio asked.

"Yes, Scipio. And we will place four legions in Arriminium under him," Flaminius said. "Whichever of us makes contact will call upon the other for aid. We will face Hannibal with the full might of Rome."

Torquatus rose again to make another attempt. "Consul, first you say we concentrate, then you say we divide our forces," he said gamely. "Hannibal has outmaneuvered our armies at every turn. What makes you think you can bring him to battle?"

Flaminius paused a moment – to collect his thoughts, it seemed. Then he said, "Hannibal must defeat every Roman army to win, Torquatus. He must engage us, or his own men and the Gauls will turn on him." He waved a hand at the maps on the table. "The key to victory is to destroy their trust in him. One victory by Rome can accomplish that task."

"He will never fight on Rome's terms," Torquatus said.

"He need only fight," Flaminius said. "Our numbers and discipline will defeat him."

Torquatus conceded the point and sat.

Scipio asked, "How do we lure Hannibal into a fight we can win, sir?"

Flaminius looked at the young decurion with raised eyebrows and a frown. "You too, young Scipio?" The consul faced all the officers and said, "Hannibal will come to battle of his own accord. We must wait until his new allies and mercenaries annoy the Gauls enough by their pillaging that he is forced to move or suffer rebellion in his ranks." He raised a hand as if he were on the Senate floor. "In that moment, he will be vulnerable, and we will strike him down. We shall end his occupation of Roman land, and Roman soil will taste his blood. Jupiter, Mars, and Minerva will grant us victory if we have but the patience to await our chance."

There was only silence in the room.

Flaminius gathered himself and walked to the center of the chamber. "Gentlemen, we march for Arretium. Prepare your men. We depart at first light." He paused for a moment, then said, "Torquatus, stay a moment. The rest of you are dismissed."

I followed behind Scipio as we made our way from the room back to our own quarters.

Once we'd reached them, Scipio turned and said, "Torquatus is correct. Hannibal will never fight on our terms. We must lure him into a battle that we can win."

"How do we do that?" I asked.

"Well, I doubt he will attack any force that outnumbers his three to one," Scipio said. "At least, not if he knows he is outnumbered."

"Shall I inform the turma of our departure, sir?" I asked.

"Yes." He held up his hand to stop me from leaving. "And the other decurions. Make sure the men know we will be receiving reinforcements at the end of the march. That should keep up their morale during what could be perceived as a retreat. I expect we will have our share of scouting duties. Make sure every man has a full bag of grain and a net of forage for his mount."

"I understand, sir," I said.

"On your way then," Scipio said. "I will see you back here for dinner. Bring Decius. I will want to discuss the state of the men and animals. Bring the optios as well."

"Yes, sir." I walked out of the office, gathering my thoughts on the men in my section and the readiness of the turma as a whole.

* * *

Scipio's turma led the army through the gate and onto the road to Arretium. Three turmae would scout the road ahead for any threat to the marching legions. It took nearly an hour for the army to pass through the gates, until the rear guard, another three turmae, finally departed Placentia.

Scipio, Decius, and I watched the line of soldiers climb onto the high road and march dejectedly south. We could feel the men's despair. Roman men, raised on stories of victories against Etruscans, Samnites, and Carthaginians in the past, now faced the fear that they were not the men their fathers and grandfathers had been. Shoulders slumped, heads down, the infantry marched.

"Let us be away from here," Scipio said seeing the somber faces of his men. "We have a mission to accomplish." With that statement, he spurred his horse to the gallop.

Startled by the sudden departure of the decurion, it took a moment for the rest of us to follow. We raced along the road for three miles before Scipio relented. Pulling up sharply at a slight bend in the road, he looked back at his men. "A good gallop on a spring morning makes the spirit soar, does it not?" Scipio asked as we caught him at last.

Breathing a bit hard, Decius said, "Yes, Decurion. A fine morning for a run."

Scipio dismounted and patted his horse's glistening flank. "Good work, my treasure," he said to the stallion. "Lead the mounts for a bit. Decius, you take the road. Appius, left side – I'll take the right."

"Yes, sir," we replied in unison and signaled the dismount. I led my men into the verge along the road's edge, noting that Scipio took his men into the much tougher terrain, rocky hills. All the horses were blowing hard and white sweat foamed in their hair. Within half an hour, I was out of sight of the road and turned to walk parallel to its course.

Optio Quintus led his horse beside mine. "Decurion," he said hesitantly.

"Quintus, I see you've regained your breath," I said.

He grinned and said, "It was a good ride, sir. I was worried he wouldn't stop until one of the horses came up lame."

"That's why he wanted all of the mounts checked so thoroughly last night, if you recall?" I said.

Quintus nodded. "True enough. Still, I think a few of them will be a bit footsore tomorrow."

"Perhaps," I said. "But we will be in Arretium soon enough. There will be enough remounts for everyone."

"And four new legions, sir?" he asked.

"And four new legions, yes," I said. "The Senate authorized the additional legions and replacements for our own losses."

Quintus gazed into the forest ahead for a few minutes. "Some of the men thought the Senate might sue for peace."

I looked into his eyes and saw the fear and doubt that Hannibal raised. "Quintus, Hannibal is not a demon sent from Hades to plague us."

"It is said that he swore an oath to Ba'al, the Carthaginian god of war, to destroy Rome and all its people," Quintus said in an awed voice.

"He may have," I said. "But what do we have to fear? Is Jupiter not supreme among gods? Is Mars to cower before a foreign god? I don't think so."

"But he wins battles," Quintus persisted.

I grimaced and continued my theological argument. "That is because Minerva has yet to bless us with the general to lead the legions." I forced a laugh. "Perhaps it is you, Quintus, or someone you know."

He thought for a moment, then said, "You might be right, sir. But until she does, must we continue to lose?"

"Gods are fickle," I said, glad he had begun to think. "Flaminius seems a good leader. Let's give him a chance to earn Minerva's blessing."

He nodded, satisfied. "Where will we camp, sir?"

"Decius will choose a site for the army. I'm certain the engineers have already joined him." We came to a small clearing, and I decided I had had enough walking. "Mount up!" I ordered.

Quintus echoed my command and we rode ahead, looking for signs of the enemy.

* * *

We finished our patrol close to sunset, and rode back along the high road, seeking the marching camp. We found it three miles back, on a small hill overlooking the road. A small stream ran in a gully at the base of the hill. I ordered Quintus to see to the horses as I handed him my reins. I walked through the main gate toward the Principia seeking Scipio.

Decius met me at the entrance to the headquarters building. "Anything?" he asked.

"No sign of the enemy," I said. "Found a couple of unlucky hares."

"I'd leave that part out of the report," Decius said. "Flaminius is overly fond of rabbit."

I laughed. "I'll just do that. Any word on Scipio?"

"He reported in about ten minutes ago," Decius said. "None of the patrols have seen Hannibal. Looks like we stole the march."

"That's good." We reached the consul's chamber. I entered, made my brief report, and was dismissed in turn.

Scipio was waiting for us at the entrance. "Good patrol, Appius?" he asked.

"If by good you mean that we saw nothing, then yes, sir," I said.

Scipio nodded. We fell in beside him as we walked toward our tents. "How are the men?"

"My optio has some fears of evil foreign gods." I relayed my conversation with Quintus.

"You may be more correct than you know, Appius," Scipio said. "Minerva, daughter of all-mighty Jupiter, has yet to choose her champion among Roman leaders. We should sacrifice to her and ask her blessings."

"That's just what I told him, sir." I glanced at Decius knowingly. "You just made it sound better."

Decius asked, "The turma?"

"Yes," Scipio said. "Let us embrace the piety of our men. It will help them bond with each other and their officers."

"When should we do it?" I asked.

"The day after we reach Arretium," Scipio said. "Tell the optios that they will plan the ceremony with all propriety. As senior officer, I will perform the sacrifice. A priest of Minerva will be present to read the augury. I will see to that detail myself."

"We will inform the men, sir," I said.

Decius smiled. "The optios will be beside themselves with pride. They'll know this ceremony isn't political if they plan it themselves."

Scipio smiled a small smile. "Precisely. And working together, without interference from us, trains them to trust themselves, each other, and us."

* * *

The legion arrived at Arretium with no incident and no sighting of Hannibal. The next day, Decius and I woke before dawn, bathed, and dressed in our pristine, white togas. We walked to the temple district and joined the men who gathered near an altar that the optios had erected the day before. Atop the altar sat a brazier, filled with coals that glowed a dull orange in the morning mist. No one spoke, for fear of giving offense to the gods with an inopportune remark.

We circled the altar in a slow line, with our right hands raised. We stopped on the west side of the altar. The sun would rise over the altar to light our sacred rite. We waited for the arrival of the priests and the chief celebrant, Scipio.

Within minutes, we saw the formal procession walking slowly toward the altar from the shrine of Minerva. Scipio, dressed in a chalk-white toga, led a male goat slowly to the steps of the dais on which the altar sat. The goat's head bowed and stayed low as Scipio led it up the steps to stand before the altar. An elderly priest and twelve acolytes followed Scipio up the stairs and arrayed themselves around the dais.

The priest stood between the goat and the altar, turned to face east, then began the invocation. "Janus, Jupiter, Mars Pater, Quirine, and Minerva, we seek your blessings this day." His right hand reached toward the rising sun, fingers splayed and bent back so that his palm seemed to touch the fiery circle on the distant horizon. As the name of each god was spoken, an acolyte placed a votive offering into the brazier, then stepped back to his place on the dais. The fragrant smoke rose into the morning sky, a good beginning to the ceremony. When the priest spoke the name of Minerva, all the soldiers slapped their chests in the sign of respect for the goddess.

The priest shifted his voice and intoned, "O Minerva, daughter of Metis and Jupiter, Goddess of wisdom and poetry, healer and warrior, weaver and crafter, gladly we give thanks and rightly praise you and all the gods." He raised his head higher and continued, "Proud, warlike Goddess, in the great honor and wisdom of Your Father, powerful in war are you. Upon your head, the grim helmet is borne with its frightful dec- oration, won by Jason, the Gorgon's blood that glows brighter with your increasing fury. None have, with her pilum, inspired more ardent calls to arms on the buccina than you. May you with your grace and wisdom accept this sacrificial offering. You come from Mount Pandion to our rites by night. The winged axle of your biga carrus, with its paired purebred horses, carries you astride the morning sun's beaming light. Shouting aloud, now, to you, we dedicate the blood sacrifice of these virile men and their war-torn armor."

Incoherent cries breached the morning peace as the men shouted to the eastern sky for Minerva to accept their offering.

The priest now turned to face Scipio. "Do you order me to make this sacrifice to Minerva?"

Scipio responded in a clear voice, "I do so order, holy one."

The priest said, "I demand of thee, Decurion Publius Cornelius Scipio, a sprig of rosemary."

Scipio nodded to an acolyte. "Take those that are pure," he said.

The acolyte placed the fresh rosemary into the brazier.

The priest drew forth a bronze knife and trimmed a tuft of hair from the goat's fetlock. Then he turned back to face Scipio. "Do you constitute me as the representative of the Third Turma, First Legion, sanctioning also my vessels and assistants?"

Scipio lifted his voice in response, "So far as may be without hurt to myself and the Third Turma, First Legion, I do."

The priest raised the tuft of goat hair and touched it to Scipio's forehead. Then he slowly turned and placed the first portion of the sacrifice into the brazier. The smoke continued to rise in a column into the morning sky. A falcon cry sounded above the city. "Jupiter blesses the offering to his daughter!" the Priest cried.

The priest motioned to another acolyte, who came forward with a small bowl. The priest began to chant as he dipped his hand into the bowl. He sprinkled the spelt and salt over the goat, sanctifying the sacrifice. At the end of each chant, he invoked the name of Minerva.

The men slapped their chests in respect for the goddess with each mention of her name, then reached their right hands toward the flame in the brazier.

The priest continued to chant as another acolyte approached with a small jug. The priest raised the jug toward the rising sun, again invoking Minerva's blessing. Then he slowly anointed the goat with the wine in the vessel. The amber liquid doused the head and neck of the beatific animal, which continued to wait in placid contentment.

The final two acolytes approached. One took the lead line from Scipio's hand, then used his other hand to fasten it along the staff he held, until he could control the head of the goat.

The priest, continuing his chant, made a small slice down the goat's spine with the bronze knife. The animal, now sanctified by blood, could no longer be touched by human hands. The acolyte with the loop and staff controlled the animal as it tried to escape the pain caused by the priest's blade.

The other acolyte carried a bronze hammer. With impressive strength, the acolyte struck the goat on the forehead, and the animal toppled to the ground. At once the priest knelt, chanting, beside the now-still animal and sliced through the neck. Blood poured from the wound, and he gathered it in a bronze bowl. An acolyte came forward to hold the bowl, and the priest moved around the animal to make a long slice down the animal's stomach.

Entrails poured forth from the open belly. None had been pierced by the priest's deft blade. Acolytes brought forward tools to butcher the animal, presenting the spleen and liver to the priest on bronze platters. He examined both closely, continuing his chant. Finally, his voice rose in a shout. "Minerva accepts your offering and blesses your leader!" Both organs slid from the platters into the brazier.

The priest raised his right hand to the sun again. "Minerva, we thank you for accepting this blood offering. Janus, Jupiter, Mars Pater, Quirine, thank you for the blessings and bounty of Rome. Vesta, sister of Minerva, we close the ceremony with an offering of salt cakes for you." An acolyte presented another platter on which rested three small loaves. The priest placed each into the brazier. Then he knelt beside the remains of the butchered goat and touched the bloody heart. "Let this sacrifice now be a blessing of strength and nourishment to the men of the Third Turma, First Legion of Rome." Acolytes carried the meat, now profaned for consumption by men, to the cook fires to be prepared into a feast for the soldiers.

XXX

GAIUS FLAMINIUS

"I require information, young Scipio," Flaminius said.

Scipio grimaced. "May I dispatch cavalry patrols to discover Hannibal's location, sir?"

"Can they stay out of reach of the Numidians?" Flaminius asked.

"My men have become expert at scouting the enemy, sir."

It was Flaminius's turn to frown. "I do not wish to be drawn into a battle unless Servilius is able to support my army."

"I understand, sir. But unless we patrol, at some risk of a skirmish, battle will be forced upon us."

Flaminius's frown deepened. "Very well then. See to it."

"At once, General." Scipio turned to leave.

"You will hold yourself here, Decurion, as my advisor and cavalry commander," Flaminius said. "Your man Asprenas can lead the patrols."

Scipio turned and saluted the general. Then he motioned us to a corner. "You heard him," Scipio said. "Appius, organize four patrols. Northwest, north, northeast, and along the Via Cassia."

I nodded and said, "Decius will be with me. I need a good second."

"Fine. Just find Hannibal for me," Scipio said.

"What route do you think he'll take?" I asked.

Scipio thought a moment. "He likes to do the impossible or at least what any normal general would consider impossible. The terrain to the north is difficult swamp and mountains. No sane man would bring an army along that route."

"So, we'll scout that direction then, eh?" I suggested.

"I doubt he will march down the Via Cassia. That puts him between

217

the armies at Arretium and Arriminium. He is no fool to give us that opportunity."

"And the coast road?" I asked.

"It is a possibility. But it would be obvious. Has he been obvious yet?"

"North it is then," I said.

"On your way," Scipio said. "Messengers daily or more often if you find Hannibal."

I cocked my head in askance.

"Very well, old soldier. You know your task. On your way."

"See you in a week." I saluted then walked toward the exit.

* * *

"These damn mosquitoes are going to eat me whole," Decius cursed.

We were all covered in insect bites. "The warm weather woke them early this spring. They're all a bit hungry, it seems. Rub some honey on your skin," I suggested.

"What good will that do?" Decius asked.

"None, but it will attract them to you. Maybe they'll leave the rest of us alone."

"Very funny," he growled. "This marsh is no place for a man."

"That's why the decurion thinks Hannibal will come this way." We had left Arretium three days before, and we were deep into the swampy gorge that passed through the Apennine Mountains to the north.

"He'd be a fool to come this way," Decius said, swatting another insect from his neck. "His army would have no drinkable water, little food, and no supply line."

"Yes, but he'd be on Arretium's doorstep. If Flaminius won't fight, then it's straight on to Rome. We're the only army between here and there."

"So you've said," Decius admitted. "Still, his army would be a festering bug bite."

"Get a couple of men up on the heights." I pointed toward the rocky slopes of the small valley. "Maybe they can see something from up there."

Decius detailed two optios to lead three-man teams up the hills to either side of the swamp.

"Let's rest here while we wait," I ordered. "Dismount!"

We busied ourselves tending the horses. I checked the pickets and came back to find Decius holding a bowl in either hand. "What's this?" I asked.

"Puls," he said. "Left over from the morning."

I took the bowl and sat on a convenient log. "Thanks."

We ate the bland boiled emmer with little gusto. I glanced toward the hills again, just in time to see one of the optios barreling down the hill, his men close behind. I dropped the bowl, standing. "Mount up!" I ordered.

The optio ran up to me, saluting as he skidded to a halt. "Carthaginians, sir!" he gasped. "They're about four hundred yards that way. You just can't see them because of the trees." He pointed to a dense copse about two hundred yards distant.

"Get your men mounted." I turned to Decius. "Signal the other team to get back here," I ordered. "We need a concealed place to watch from."

"There was a goat path up into the hills about half a day back," he suggested.

"Right," I said. "Pasture for the horses, hidden by rocks. Get them moving. I'll wait here for the other team."

I grabbed the reins my optio held for me. "Thanks. Detail a man to stay with me and take the rest with Decius."

Quintus saluted and carried out my orders. Minutes later, the other team joined us. "We're the rear guard, men. Don't get seen." We led the horses after Decius. As we found cover, I left two-man teams to watch our rear. I didn't want to get a nasty surprise from behind without some warning.

We moved on, leapfrogging our way back toward the path we had found the day before. In three hours, we found the base of the path and had Numidian scouts rustling in the brush just behind.

"Alright. Quietly now. Lead the horses. Up the path," I said. "Watch your step."

We made it to the first big rocks, just as the Numidians broke through the underbrush. Behind them came twenty thousand Carthaginian mercenaries. I tapped my optio's shoulder and mimed that he should watch the advancing army. I left two men with him and continued up the path. At the top, I found Decius already organizing a defensive perimeter.

"I need two men to report to Arretium," I said to Decius.

"They're guarding the horses," he said. "I didn't want to send them without your order."

I nodded then walked to the horses. I found three men waiting; one was the signifier, the standard bearer for the turma. The other two were my messengers. "Report for Decurion Scipio. Hannibal's army located forty miles north in the Apennine marsh. He will be at Arretium in two days. At least twenty thousand infantry and five thousand Numidians in sight. I intend to continue observing, moving back toward Arretium as circumstances allow. I will report daily unless otherwise warranted."

They read back the message, and I dismissed them. The men led their horses across the goat pasture to another path on the far side of the clearing that led downhill toward Arretium.

Decius walked toward me. "They are on their way?"

I nodded. "Any way to get ahead of them?"

"I don't think so," he said. "Unless they don't head for Arretium."

"Getting messages back to the decurion will be difficult if they patrol," I said.

Decius nodded his agreement. "Still, one or two may pass where thirty cannot," he said.

"Keep scouts posted," I said. "I want an accurate count of enemy troops by type for my next report."

Decius said, "If we come out of these hills, the Numidians will be on us before we go a mile. I don't fancy a three-day gallop back to the city."

"I know," I said. "Our job is to gather information and get it back to the decurion. We will stay here as long as we can. Then we head east. Servilius should be marching to Flaminius's aid as soon as he knows Hannibal is over the Apennines. We can join him on the march."

"Very good, sir," Decius said formally. "I'll see to the observers." He walked toward the men I had left watching the Carthaginians.

* * *

I squatted next to the soldier assigned to observe the enemy. The army, encamped at the edge of the marsh, had been there for two days. "Any movement?" I asked, handing the man a waterskin.

"Some cavalry patrols, sir," he said after a long drink. "They headed south. Nothing heading up into the hills."

"Good," I said. "Fighting our way out of here would deprive the legions of a chance to get even."

He smiled at the bad jest. "There's something going on in the center of camp. Lots of officers going in and out of the commander's tent. But nothing happens when they come out."

"When did that start?" I asked.

He continued to respond without turning his head to face me. "About an hour ago," he said. "Right after Hannibal himself arrived."

"Maybe just getting reports from his officers?" I said.

"Maybe," he said. "But there was a lot of shouting, from the way they were waving their arms. It looked like they were calling for someone to come quickly."

"Good eyes," I said. "Anything else?"

"No, sir," he said. "Just normal activity. Sharpening weapons, oiling leather, grooming horses, and the like. No one seems to be in a hurry."

"Let me know if anything changes," I said, then walked back to our camp in a low stoop until I was behind some tall boulders.

Decius met me at the edge of camp. "Any change?"

"No. It seems Hannibal thinks he hasn't been spotted yet. He's planning his advance, I think."

"Well, he can't stay still for long," Decius said. "Someone is bound to see his patrols and tell Flaminius."

"Sir!" called one of the perimeter guards. "Lookout says to come quick." He pointed toward the man I'd just left.

Decius and I walked briskly back to the observation post. The lookout never looked away from the Carthaginians. He waited for us to settle before speaking.

"Hannibal's been wounded, sir," he said.

"What?" Decius said.

"Something happened to his head or eye," the man said. "He's got bloody bandages around his head, and they cover his left eye."

"The commotion earlier?" I asked.

The man nodded. "Must have been calling for the surgeon."

I explained the scout's earlier report to Decius. "But now he's up and about," I said. "They will start moving soon, I would guess."

"You don't think the wound will slow him down?" Decius asked.

"Like you said," I answered, "his army will be a festering wound if it stays here. They have to move."

Decius said, "Well, if they sit still, they'll have two armies attacking them in a week."

I nodded. "Good work, soldier." I swept my hand toward the headquarters tent. "Where's Hannibal now?" I asked.

"Just there." He pointed. "To the left of the horse by the entrance."

I found the distant figure and saw the white bandages covering the left eye and circling the head. Blood seeped through the cloth near the covered eye. I watched Hannibal stroke his horse.

A Gaul rode up to the enemy general. A large Gaul, with a bushy red mustache. I saw the skulls dangling from his saddle.

"Ducarius!" Decius exclaimed. "That bastard, I bet he's been recruiting Gauls from all over the north."

"Very likely," I said.

The two figures conferred for a few minutes. Then Hannibal turned abruptly and made a sweeping gesture toward the camp. Ducarius led his horse away from the general, and the camp stirred to life, the men making the familiar preparations for a march.

"Looks like he wants to get moving," Decius said.

"Can we get a messenger to Arretium?" I asked.

Decius shook his head. "Doubt it. Too many cavalry patrols in the area right now. Maybe after nightfall." It was approaching midday.

"See to it," I ordered. Turning to the soldier, I said, "Let us know when they march. I'll send a man to be your messenger."

The soldier nodded, but never moved his gaze from the Carthaginians.

* * *

Columns of smoke rose into the evening sky. Decius and I looked southward from our hilltop and saw a low shadow on the horizon. Hannibal's army – burning villages, farmsteads, and crops as they advanced.

"Well, I suppose we don't need to send that messenger, do we?" Decius asked.

I tore my gaze from the smoke-filled horizon. "No. I'm sure the general can see the smoke as well as we do."

"What now then?" Decius said.

"We skirt the enemy patrols and head back to the city," I said. "We ride at night and hide during the day."

"What joy," Decius said. "I always enjoy dodging Numidians."

"Makes life interesting," I said.

"Break camp!" Decius ordered the men. "We ride at once."

Half an hour later, we reached the bottom of the hill and rode southwest, avoiding, we hoped, any enemy patrols.

* * *

We arrived at the eastern gate to the city three days later. Scipio met us at the gate.

Decius and I saluted. "The other patrols?" I asked.

"All back yesterday," Scipio said. "What of Hannibal?"

"Came through the marsh," I said. "Did our messenger get through?"

"Yes, but I'm afraid Flaminius didn't believe him," Scipio said. "He said it was impossible to bring an army through that swamp."

Decius snorted. "Did the fires change his mind?" he asked, dismounting and leading his horse toward the headquarters building.

Scipio and I followed. "Yes," Scipio said, "he sent messengers to Servilius two days ago. Flaminius refuses to march out until Servilius arrives."

"Sensible," I said. "Hannibal outnumbers him right now. We counted nearly fifty thousand men. Gauls are coming from all over to fight against their Roman oppressors."

Scipio nodded. "Thank you for the new estimate. But I fear that will make Flaminius even more hesitant to fight."

We reached the general's headquarters. Guards lifted the curtain covering the entrance, and we walked into the main chamber. Flaminius stood, red-faced, surrounded by staff officers. I sent Scipio a questioning look, but he only shrugged and shook his head.

The general noticed our arrival and said, "Scipio! He's moved around Arretium."

Scipio's face remained calm. "Where are the Carthaginians now, sir?"

"Burning every village and farm around the city, I expect," Flaminius said, his hands clenching into fists then relaxing. "We have not the numbers to face him without Servilius."

"I agree, sir," Scipio said. "Perhaps a force of cavalry to harass and delay their advance?"

"His cavalry would sweep them aside. No, we remain here until Servilius arrives."

"General, these men are the last patrol," Scipio said. "They report Hannibal has fifty thousand men now."

"From where?" he asked.

"Mainly Gauls, sir," I said. "More seem to arrive every day. We saw Ducarius among them."

"Bah! Gauls." Flaminius turned back toward his seat at the head of the room, ignoring the comment about Ducarius. "Fickle and foul they are. Well, there's nothing for it then. We cannot face Hannibal outnumbered nearly two to one."

Scipio tried again. "Still, some cavalry to harass Carthaginian detachments—"

"No!" Flaminius cut him off. "We remain in camp until reinforcements arrive." He sat on his camp stool and drank from a wineskin slung over its shoulder. "The villages will have to endure."

"Yes, sir," Scipio said.

"General," I said, "Hannibal has been wounded."

"Wounded? How?" the general asked.

"I'm not sure, sir. He rode into camp three days ago. When he came out, his head was wrapped in bandages that covered his left eye."

"He is still in command?" Flaminius asked.

"Yes, sir," I said. "Once the surgeon finished with him, he began issuing orders and his army moved south."

"Very well. He is wounded. It seems not to interfere with his ability to command."

"General, may I see to my men?" Scipio asked.

"Yes, of course," Flaminius said. "Good work, gentlemen. Scipio, I will see you back here for an evening meal and to review more of these reports."

"I will be back shortly, sir."

We all saluted, then trooped out of the office and back to our quarters.

XXXI

PURSUIT

"General, you must do something," the villager complained. He was a Roman citizen by his dress, though a plebian. "Hannibal is burning our property, stealing our livestock, and destroying our livelihoods."

Flaminius sat on his camp stool in the headquarters and listened to the seemingly endless stories of Hannibal's outrages on the Romans in the area. "Good Roman, I shall march upon Hannibal when my reinforcements arrive. Until then, you and your family are safe within these walls."

"But General, Hannibal destroys everything in his path. There will be nothing left but ashes if you don't attack him now."

Flaminius, exhausted from the long day of similar stories, finally lost his patience. "Enough of this nonsense. I have important matters to see to. You may depart at once." He motioned for the guards to escort the protesting man from the chamber.

"Not very politic, sir," Scipio said.

"No, perhaps not," Flaminius agreed. "I know the people suffer. But I can do nothing until Servilius arrives."

"The cavalry could harass the raiding parties, General," Scipio said.

Flaminius smiled a tired smile. "Leave off. You have been pushing that course for days now. I will march with a concentrated force, or not at all."

Scipio nodded and said, "I advise only the best course of action I see, sir."

"And the fact that you are the cavalry commander has no bearing on that advice?"

"Only that I would see the mission executed as efficiently as possible," Scipio said earnestly.

Flaminius laughed. "Boy, you are so much like your father at this age. Idealistic and noble to a fault. Servilius will be here in two, perhaps three days. Your honor can await another chance at glory for that long."

"Sir, I meant nothing of the sort!" Scipio protested.

Flaminius waved a hand to calm the decurion. "Yes, I know. Be at peace. I meant no insult."

Scipio controlled himself with icy discipline. "With your permission, sir, I will walk the perimeter and see to the change of the guard."

"Of course. A good walk and some duty will take your mind off the suffering of the people. If there were not thirty more important petitioners awaiting my attention, I would join you."

"Thank you, sir." Scipio saluted and turned to leave. "Appius, join me," he said as he passed my post by the doorway.

I fell in behind him. We walked in silence until we reached the guard headquarters by the east gate. Scipio said, "Inspect the reserve force. Join me atop the gatehouse when you finish."

I nodded and entered the building. Inside I found an optio playing dice with two of his men. They came to attention as they noticed my rank.

"Good day, sir," said the optio with a salute. "What can I do for you?"

"Have the reserve force fall in outside. I will inspect them at once," I said.

"The centurion took them to the north gate, sir," the optio said. "There was a fire in one of the sheds there. He used the men to help put out the fire."

"Why was headquarters not informed of this?" I asked.

"Dunno, sir," the optio said nervously. "We three are all that's left here."

I nodded. "Have the centurion report to Decurion Scipio the moment he returns, Optio."

"Yes, sir," the optio said. "Where will the decurion be?"

"On the wall, inspecting the guard positions," I said. "Ask the guard at the gatehouse which way we went."

"Yes, sir." The optio saluted again.

I returned the salute and left the building. Black, sooty smoke filled the air to the north. I could see orange traces of embers as they arced through the billowing column. I walked to the stairs by the gatehouse and climbed up to find Scipio staring into the eastern distance.

"Sir, the reserve force is putting out a—"

"Fire near the north gate," Scipio finished. "Yes, the guards here informed me."

"Very good, sir. Shall we continue the inspection?"

"Hannibal must know that Servilius is coming by now."

"I suppose so," I said, not knowing where the decurion's thoughts were taking him.

I saw the black clouds of smoke at the north gate turn to gray. *The soldiers must have put out the fire.*

"He will not allow himself to be trapped between two armies, nor will he allow us to join together," Scipio continued. "This," he waved to the columns of smoke on the horizon, "is provocation."

"And if that is the case, sir?" I said.

"Then Flaminius is correct to stay behind these walls and await Servilius's arrival."

"That is what the general said we would do, isn't it, sir?"

"Yes." Scipio thought for another minute. "Hannibal knows that too. He knows Flaminius and knows the proper course of action."

"What is the problem then?" I said.

"Hannibal cannot allow us to join forces with Servilius," Scipio said. "He has to provoke Flaminius into a mistake."

"If we stay behind these walls, he can't do that, sir," I said.

Soot-smeared infantry marched toward the guard headquarters from the north, distracting both of us. A moment after dismissing them and entering the headquarters, the centurion commanding the guard climbed the stairs and saluted Scipio. "You wanted to see me, sir?" he said.

"I was going to inspect your men, Centurion. But they seem to have had a busy afternoon. Let them eat, drink, and rest. I will see them after my inspection round."

"Yes, sir," the centurion said. "Thank you, sir. Putting out that fire was some thirsty work."

"What burned?" I asked.

"Barracks," the centurion said, scowling. "Someone knocked over a pot of drippings, and the cook fire spread into some laundry. The cook was napping and didn't sound the alarm until the fire was going along quite nicely it seems. He'll be on a charge. Nearly burned down the whole barracks block."

"Anyone injured?" Scipio asked.

"No, sir," said the guard commander. "Barracks were empty, save the cook and the servants doing laundry out back."

"Very well. Make sure there is a full report made to headquarters. Dismissed."

The centurion saluted then clambered back down to his office.

"What now, sir?" I asked.

"We inspect the guard," Scipio said and led the way north along the wall.

* * *

That evening, Decius and I sat with the decurion at a low table in the Principia offices assigned to Scipio. We ate a simple meal and discussed unimportant matters, distracting ourselves from the carnage outside the city walls. A knock at the chamber entrance caused us to turn. Marcus, Scipio's optio, stood in the doorway.

"What is it, Optio?" Scipio asked.

"Sir, I was out leading a section of cavalry escorting villagers into the city," he began. "I saw the Carthaginian army on the high road."

"Where was this?" Scipio said.

"South, sir," Marcus said. "They were passing between the two hills southwest of the city. The road to Rome."

"Cerebos's balls," I swore. "There's nothing between him and Rome."

"Quiet," Scipio said. "Marcus, go on."

"That's about all, sir. They had a cavalry screen watching the rear, and the infantry was marching in column."

"Come with me," Scipio said, walking swiftly to Flaminius's chamber.

"Young Scipio, welcome," Flaminius said. "You are here again to per-suade me to use the cavalry to harass Hannibal?"

"No, General." Scipio stopped a few paces from the older man. "My optio here has a report you need to hear."

"I see," Flaminius said. "Report, Optio."

Marcus saluted and again described what he had seen.

Flaminius paled, then looked away. "I should have listened to your counsel, Scipio," Flaminius said. "It would have tied him to us until Servilius arrived."

"You could not have anticipated this, sir," Scipio said.

"You did," Flaminius said. "Why else try to persuade me to harass him?"

"I did not anticipate that Hannibal would leave two intact armies behind him while marching on Rome. That course makes no sense."

"Therefore, he has a plan. A trap for us," Flaminius said. "And I have no choice but to react."

"As you say, General. It may be a trap, but we do not have to step into it."

"We will do our best not to, of course." Flaminius motioned to one of his runners. "Get a message off to Servilius to speed his advance. Tell him what the optio just reported."

Scipio said, "Sir, we can trail him. Harass him with cavalry raids, until we can pin him against the walls of Rome."

"My intentions exactly, Decurion. All staff officers to report to headquarters at once. The army will march at daybreak."

Young boys, messengers for the general, scampered out the door to carry the message to every barracks in the city.

"Scipio, you may get your chance at glory yet," Flaminius said with a wry smile.

* * *

The army marched south along the high road. Scipio and I rode near General Flaminius at the head of the First Legion. Cavalry screened the army to all sides as the patrols attempted to locate Hannibal's army.

It was approaching noon when Decius galloped through the screen of cavalry and reined in beside Scipio. He saluted then said, "General, they've turned southeast. Making for Corito, looks like."

"You are certain it is the main force?" Flaminius asked.

"I had a good view from above them, sir. Thirty to forty thousand infantry and several thousand cavalry."

"Good work," Flaminius said. "Get some water and fall in with the rear screen."

"Yes, sir."

"Inform the vanguard we march toward Corito," Flaminius said to one of his tribunes. "We will camp outside its walls tonight."

The tribune rode forward with the message.

"Scipio," Flaminius said, "what do you think?"

"Corito is not worth the delay in taking," Scipio said. "Hannibal will not be there when we arrive."

"Agreed," Flaminius said. "Supplies from the fishing villages along Lake Trasimenus's shores?"

"A good wager, General," Scipio said.

The general nodded, then fell silent for a few minutes. When he spoke again, it was with a harsh voice. "He toys with us. I will stay with him, but just out of reach. Let him feel frustration like he caused me."

* * *

Thirty thousand Roman soldiers marched as the sun brightened the eastern sky. Decius and I led the cavalry guarding the supply wagons at the rear of the army. We choked on the dust raised by the nail-studded sandals worn by the infantry. By midmorning we had passed through the hills guarding the road south to Rome, then turned southwest for Corito.

Decius handed me a waterskin and said, "Ever been to Corito?"

"No. You?"

"Once. It's on a mountainside. Stout walls, very defensible."

"Not a good place to attack if you have an army behind you?"

"I wouldn't want to."

"Maybe Hannibal will try to storm the place and we can besiege him."

Decius laughed. "And maybe Venus will visit me in my bedroll tonight."

I chuckled and said, "Well, if she does, keep it down. I need my sleep."

"We'll try, but no promises." We both laughed, knowing the chances of a fight today were slim.

After a few minutes, I said, "We could be fighting in front of Rome in a few days."

Decius nodded. "True. Think of all of the eligible women who will be watching from the city walls."

I shook my head. "Do you ever think of anything except sex?"

"Not if I can help it. I'm married, not dead," he said, nearly choking on his laughter. "You're the prude, Appius. With you around, I don't have to be the role model for the men."

I rolled my eyes and made a show of swatting him with my reins. "The men need more than one example, but you are incorrigible, I think." The look of mock horror in his eyes was enough to make me laugh again. "How long until we get there?"

He controlled his laughing and said, "Three, maybe four, hours. Well before sunset."

"Check the men. I'm going to report to the decurion and see what's happening up ahead."

"Yes, oh mighty Decurion. I shall follow your orders to the letter," he said mockingly.

I chuckled again as I spurred my horse forward to the general's position at the head of the army.

* * *

Scipio sat his mount with all the dignity a young Roman noble could muster. I could see the tension in his spine as I approached the command party. I pulled my horse beside his and saluted. "Sir, all is well with the supply wagons. Any orders?" I asked quietly.

"No, Appius. Thank you for the report," Scipio said, voice controlled as ever. "We will continue the march until the enemy encamps for the evening. Please inform the men that we will in all likelihood not be stopping at Corito."

Surprised, I asked, "Why is that, sir?"

The cold reply came instantly. "I am not in the habit of explaining my orders. Please carry them out at once."

"Yes, sir," I said immediately. I saluted and turned my horse sharply to the rear, kicking him hard. We leapt toward the rear of the formation, leaving the decurion behind in an instant.

In minutes, I rode beside Decius again.

"What news?" he began.

"We'll not be camping at Corito."

"Oh. Why not?"

"I'll be damned to Hades if I know," I said. "The decurion nearly took my head off for asking."

"That's not like him."

"I know that better than anyone. He is not happy about something, and I would guess it is the general's decision to pursue Hannibal."

"He fears a trap?" Decius asked.

"I don't know," I said. "But it has him worried, whatever it is."

"Well, I'll tell the men. Take a drink of wine and eat something. You look as pale as a toga."

I nodded and reached into my saddlebag for some dried meat to chew. I knew Decius was right. Seeing Scipio nearly lose control shook me. I hadn't realized how much I depended on the boy's unnatural calm to allay my fears. Now I looked at the situation clearly. We were pursuing the greatest general in the world, who commanded nearly two men for every one of ours, and he was between us and our home. It was not a good feeling.

XXXII

LAKE TRASIMENUS

A quarter-moon had risen over the mountains to the east by the time we camped that night. A cool breeze blew in from Lake Trasimenus to the south. Along the eastern edge of the lake, I could see the cook fires of Hannibal's army. They were in the hills, fifteen miles distant.

"A beautiful night for a stroll by the lake with a beautiful woman," Decius said.

"Too bad all I get to do is walk beside you," I said.

He chuckled as we continued walking the perimeter set by the cavalry. The infantry busied themselves building camp for the night. The walls were up; only the gates remained to make the defenses whole. Then they could set up our tents and sleep for the night. We watched as the heavy wooden doors were fitted onto the iron hinges.

"Bring them in, Decius. Get the horses watered and fed. I'll report to the decurion," I said.

"Let me know if you find someone to take that stroll with." Decius mounted his horse. "And see if she has a friend."

"Be off!" I said. Then I rode into the camp to look for Scipio.

* * *

I found him at the Principia, which a century of infantry had raised while their fellows dug the footings for the perimeter wall. He listened as cavalry scouts reported to General Flaminius. I walked quietly to stand next to him, and he motioned me to remain silent. We stood around a large box filled with sand in which had been sketched a rough overview of the terrain around Lake Trasimenus.

"Hannibal camps at the northeast corner of the lake, sir," the scout said. "We see cooking fires in the hills from there to there." He drew a line along the shore of the lake with a stick. "We observed from here, along the shore," he said, pointing to a position half the distance from our camp to the hills where Hannibal's camp lay.

"We might be able to catch him if we march before dawn," Flaminius said.

One of the tribunes said, "The lake fog is thick in the mornings this time of year, according to the villagers."

"That could hide our approach," Flaminius said. "We could be on him before he knows we are near."

"He still outnumbers us, sir," Scipio said.

"Surprise could tip the balance in our favor," a decurion from First Legion said.

"Servilius will be here soon," said another tribune.

I could see the tension in Scipio's back as he said, "If we attack, we wager Rome's safety on a role of the dice."

Flaminius's eyes hardened. "Not so. Servilius can still follow Hannibal to Rome's walls if we fail."

Scipio lowered his head in submission. There were several other arguments for and against, but I could see Flaminius had persuaded himself into attacking. The debate was for show, as the decision had been made. We would attack in the morning.

* * *

"Good morning, sir," I said to Scipio as he walked to the head of the formation, leading his white mare. I saluted, and he returned the gesture.

"Have the men form up at the rear of the army," Scipio said quietly. "We march in fifteen minutes."

"Yes, sir," I said. "Would you care to inspect the men, sir?"

"No, Appius. I am sure you and Decius have seen to everything," he said, loudly enough for the front rank to hear. "The men are ready. I am proud to lead them today."

I could see the effect his words had on the men. Backs straightened, heads came up, and eyes filled with pride. "We'll make you proud, sir," I said.

Decius rode up from the Principia. "Orders confirmation, sir," he said.

"We are the rear guard today?" Scipio said.

"Yes, sir."

"General Flaminius said if I were so certain that this would be a mistake, I could guard our retreat," Scipio said in a voice pitched only for our ears.

"So your counsel is dismissed and you are in disgrace, sir?" I asked.

"Something like that. We keep the door to Corito open, gentlemen. Those are our orders."

Decius and I nodded understanding. "We will do our best, sir," Decius said.

"I know, Decius. I know your dedication and loyalty well. You and the men are a testament to Roman discipline and skill."

Decius gazed at him, dumbstruck by the compliment. It was the first time I had ever seen the man at a loss for words.

Scipio saved him. "Decius, please lead us into formation."

Decius spun his horse and shouted, "At the walk, by twos!" The optios echoed the orders. "Forward, march!" he commanded.

Thirty horses moved forward in two columns to follow the end of the army marching through the gate into the foggy morning. Scipio and I fell in behind the last two men. Scipio motioned for the signifer to move to the head of the column near Decius.

"He is using hastatii to scout ahead of the army," Scipio said quietly. "The infantry is in column behind the first two maniples."

"We try to form line after we make contact?" I asked.

"He expects to be in the hills and overrunning Hannibal's guards before the sun is over the horizon."

"A bold plan," I said.

"If it works." Scipio's voice had gone even quieter. "Hannibal is no novice. He will be prepared for an attack."

We rode on in silence as the fog thickened. We could barely see three horses ahead. The damp air muffled the horses' hooves on the soft earth. The moon barely brightened the sky above us, and we could see no stars.

We rode at a walk for over an hour. We could hear the water lapping on the shore to our right. Finally, Scipio spurred his horse. I followed. We caught up with Decius in minutes.

"Any news, Decurion?" Scipio asked.

Decius seemed surprised by our appearance. "No, sir," he said. "Just having a wonderful time trying to keep contact with the unit ahead of us. Turn your head at the wrong time, and they just disappear."

"It is to be expected," Scipio said. "I am sure the army is a long line of independent units at the moment."

"The fog will burn off when the sun comes up," I said.

"It may, but not quickly," Scipio said. "Be prepared for an attack from our left."

"I'll tell the men," I said and headed back down the line to talk to each pair of men. By the time I returned, the sky was brightening to the east. The effect was blinding as the golden light surrounded us. Then the line halted. We nearly rode into the infantry unit to our front, they stopped so suddenly.

Scipio acted at once. "Anchor our line on the lake. Face rear and form line," he ordered.

Decius and I got the men in order. We formed a line angling across the line of march, facing to the rear. Decius gathered the rest of the turmae commanders for a quick conference with Scipio.

"Decius is in command," Scipio told them. "Appius and I will go see what the problem is in the front."

All the cavalry was now facing to the army's rear. But the infantry had not moved. Scipio and I rode past the men, who rested their shields on the ground and enjoyed the halt as only soldiers on the march could. We passed unit after unit, standing unconcerned by the unexpected halt. After ten minutes, we finally came to the general's party.

"Send another messenger," Flaminius was saying to one of the tribunes shifting uneasily around him. "I need to know why the infantry halted."

"Right away, sir," the man said, dispatching a waiting messenger a moment later.

Scipio turned his horse toward the lake side of the party, staying out of Flaminius's sight. The general was focused on the horizon to the east. But the blinding sun, refracting though the fog, made seeing anything in that direction impossible.

We waited for the messenger to return along with the rest of the general's staff. Five minutes passed, then ten. Our eyes ached and watered as we tried to see past the dazzling fog to the east. Then an inhuman howl sounded from the hills to the north.

I gazed into the fog and saw shadows now. In seconds, the shadows became men. "'Ware the left!" I shouted.

Most of the infantry didn't have time to even turn before the first Gauls attacked. Hundreds died in the first onslaught. Roman discipline failed as units became individuals fighting against men with longer swords and surprise on their side.

I saw a bushy red mustache on the face of a man I had seen up close on a riverbank months ago. Ducarius rode at the head of a group of twenty Gauls. They charged straight at Flaminius's standard. The charge overwhelmed the general's guards, and the staff officers were still stunned by the unexpected attack. "General! Flee!" I yelled, kicking a Gaul trying to pull me from my saddle. I stabbed down at the man as he stumbled back and felt my sword impact bone.

I looked up toward the general to see Ducarius leaping from the back of his horse and sweeping Flaminius out of the saddle. None of the tribunes were mounted as clusters of Gauls surrounded those still alive. Flaminius stood groggily and made a wild thrust toward the Gaul. Ducarius batted the general's sword aside with contempt and stepped forward. With a massive fist, he punched the general in the face. Flaminius's knees buckled, and he stumbled back with glazed eyes. Ducarius grabbed the Gallic scalp attached in place of the general's crest and yanked. Flaminius, off balance, fell to the ground. Ducarius held the scalp aloft as a trophy and screamed his triumph into the sky.

Flaminius slashed with his sword at the Gaul's legs, but Ducarius dodged the blow. The Gaul then stepped on the general's sword arm with nail-studded sandals, immobilizing the still supine man. With his left hand, he grasped Flaminius's helmet, forcing the general's face into the mossy turf of the lake shore. Then he slashed down with the sword in his right hand, severing the general's head from his neck. He held the head into the sky and roared again. Cheers and shouts erupted from the Gauls nearby. He remounted his horse and rode into fog to the north with Flaminius's head dripping gore down his arm. He had another Roman skull to add to his gruesome collection.

Scipio drew his sword and yelled, "Appius, with me!" He spurred his horse westward, bowling over Gauls with bloody swords seeking new targets for their rage. We raced through the carnage, ignoring Roman and Gaul alike as we made our way back to our men.

We passed the Gauls' line of attack, where Roman infantry stood silent in the fog listening to sounds of battle, but not knowing which way to march. Scipio shouted orders to the centurions for them to prepare their men for attack from the north, but we spared no more time for them. In less than three minutes, we reached the turma.

"Form line, echelon right," Scipio ordered.

Decius and I echoed the orders, and the rest of the cavalry followed our lead. Now we had a line of cavalry perhaps two hundred yards long, slanted to the northeast, anchored on the lake. Our turma was somewhere in the middle.

"At the walk, forward!" Scipio said in a perfect parade ground voice. "March!"

We all nudged our horses into a walk. We moved west, away from the battle. As we came to the narrowest part of the shore, we heard a familiar rumbling sound.

"Ware cavalry from the north!" I shouted, not seeing them but knowing they were coming.

Scipio waited a heartbeat then shouted, "Charge!" He raked his spurs savagely along his horse's flank. The white hair was stained pink, but she leapt forward into an immediate gallop.

"Charge!" I repeated and followed Scipio. In seconds, we met the Numidian charge at an angle. The fog made everything more chaotic. Men hacked and slashed and died, and the melee was uncontrollable.

I pointed my sword at a man in black leather armor and kicked my horse into his mount. I missed my first lunge, then had to twist in the saddle to parry his slash at my back. I hooked the left rear pommel of my saddle behind my knee and leaned almost horizontal to slash his girth strap. His animal, startled by the sharp pain near the belly, jumped forward, dumping the man onto the ground, stunned. I sat up and looked for Scipio. I heard his voice shouting in the fog. I trotted toward it, wary of Numidians in the mist.

I found Scipio surrounded by three Numidian horsemen. He was turning his horse and keeping them from tangling him up in a grapple. I charged my horse into the nearest man, slashing at his neck. The Numidian died as my blade found an opening and sliced through muscle and cartilage.

Scipio saw an opening and stabbed low into another man's stomach. The remaining Numidian decided to find better odds elsewhere and fled into the fog. Scipio pulled up and nodded his thanks. "We must break through now, before they have time to regroup," he said.

"We abandon the army?" I asked.

Scipio nodded. "Hannibal has us surrounded and outnumbered, and our general is fallen," he said. "This battle is lost. We can hope to salvage some survivors, nothing more."

"Yes, sir," I said, lowering my head in shame.

Scipio rapped my shield with his sword. "None of that!" he said with brows lowering. "We are all that remains of the command structure of this army. We have a duty to survive and report to Rome. We may be all the warning they receive of this disaster."

I raised my head and said, "Sir, what of the men back there in the fog?"

"They are dead or captured," he said with ice in his voice. "Though those that are captured will wish for death soon enough, I think." He lowered his voice to a more reasonable tone. "Appius, we can do nothing more. Your first rule of battle, survive. We must make sure our men survive."

Decius arrived with the signifier. "There he is. Don't lose him again!" he said to the standard bearer. "Over here, men!" he shouted. Soon we were surrounded by our soldiers who, to a man, looked to Scipio for orders.

"We move west at once," Scipio said. "Gather any survivors and tell them to move west as fast as possible. Corito is the rally point. Inside its walls, we will be safe enough tonight. Teams of four. Stay together and watch your backs. I will see you all at the evening meal tonight."

"Spread out!" I ordered. Then the turma headed west, gathering the remnants of Flaminius's Consular Army.

XXXIII

SURVIVAL

We moved westward along the shore of Lake Trasimenus. The water, I noticed, shimmered a pinkish-red in the morning light. It was not yet mid-morning and the sounds of battle were diminishing behind us. We walked the horses, knowing that if the Numidians came, we would have to run hard to evade them.

Decius came alongside me and said, "We're almost back to camp."

I saw he was correct. We were approaching our campsite from the night before. The only thing that remained was the turned earth where the camp walls had been erected. "Too bad we took everything with us on the march."

"Indeed. But at least we are out of the trap," he said.

"We should leave a team here to guide any survivors toward Corito," I said.

"Volunteering?" he said with a wry smile.

I returned the smile. "I've been in the army for fifteen years now. I learned long ago never to volunteer."

"Good. I was thinking along similar lines."

"Let's go suggest it then."

"You know what he'll say."

"He'll say, 'Decius, pick two men and stay here.'"

"Why not Appius?" he said.

"Because he needs me more than you," I said, laughing. We were still chuckling when we pulled alongside Scipio.

"What do you find humorous today, gentlemen?" Scipio said.

We silenced ourselves, and I said, "Nothing sir. Merely some black humor."

"Well, if you can find anything to laugh about today, Jupiter himself must be watching over you. What have you for me?"

"Sir," I began, acknowledging the gentle rebuke, "we should leave a patrol here to guide any survivors toward Corito and to watch for enemy patrols."

"I thought of that already," he said. "I detailed Marcus and two men to hide themselves in the forest to the north."

Decius and I looked at each other with raised eyebrows. Then with a sinking feeling, "Marcus, sir?"

"Yes. He is a good man. Reliable. And I have other duties for the two of you."

Mercury chose that instant to deliver Minerva's insight to my mind. With a sinking feeling in my stomach I asked, "What duties, sir?"

"I need the two of you to lead some men back toward the battle site. Round up survivors and point them in this direction," he said as if the idea were not pure madness. "If any of the infantry survived, they will have followed us through the Numidian lines."

"And then catch up with you at Corito, sir?" Decius asked.

Scipio nodded. "That is correct. The fog should burn off in another hour or so. That gives you time to get into position without being seen," he said. "If nothing else, I need to know what Hannibal is doing now. I need information, gentlemen. And I need you to get it for me."

"We will pick two men, sir," I said. "See you at Corito this evening."

"Good." Scipio smiled grimly. "I knew I could count on the two of you. Best you leave at once. Until this evening, gentlemen."

We saluted, then turned back toward the rear of the column. Decius muttered, "I should have joined the navy."

* * *

An hour later, I was in the forested hills overlooking Lake Trasimenus's northern shore along with a decidedly unhappy Decius and two messengers. We watched as the last wisps of morning fog faded in the bright sun and gentle breeze. On any other day, it would have been a breathtaking view. Today, it revealed only carnage.

Along the shore of the lake lay thousands of Roman soldiers, dead or dying. Clusters of Carthaginians moved through the remains, looting the corpses. "That's how they pay their soldiers," I said. "Robbing the dead. Plunder as payment for their services," I shifted my body to get a better view. "One of the disadvantages of a mercenary army."

"It seems to be working for Hannibal," he said.

"All too true," I said.

"Sir," one of the messengers said, pointing, "what's that floating in the water there?"

I saw dark objects bobbing in the water along the lake's edge. "I don't know," I said. "Decius, any idea?"

He shook his head. We watched for a few minutes.

"Those Carthaginians on the shore nearby aren't moving," Decius said.

He was right. On the shore opposite the objects was a large group of Carthaginian soldiers. Then one of the objects moved, and I understood. "They're legionaries," I said.

"What?" Decius said.

"They're Roman survivors standing in neck-deep water," I said. "They probably can't swim and can't come ashore without being killed, or worse, captured."

"He's right, Decius," said one of the messengers. "You see there? One of the Carthaginians just threw something at them, and they ducked beneath the water for a moment."

One of the Romans moved toward the shore. As he reached the shallower water, he fell to his knees. A small knot of Carthaginians rushed forward, seizing the man and dragging him out of the water. In moments, he was bound and led away toward where the Carthaginian camp must lie to the north. The rest of the men in the water remained still.

Numidians rode the length of the shore, stabbing corpses they suspected of still being alive with their javelins.

"You'd think they'd be looking for any Romans that escaped their ambush," Decius said in a low voice. "Have you made a count of the dead?"

I nodded. "I make it close to fifteen thousand."

"That's what I came up with too," he said. "Half the army dead. Where's the rest?"

"We need to find out," I said.

Decius rolled his eyes. "You want to go closer to their camp?"

"Want to, no," I said. "Have to, yes."

"I swear, he gets it from you," Decius said. "Castor and Pollux, both trying to get me killed."

I laughed a silent chuckle. "Let's go. I'd hate to disappoint you." To one of the messengers I said, "Go to Corito. Report to Decurion Scipio, we have seen fifteen thousand dead. I intend to scout the enemy camp, then return to Corito."

The man repeated the message and led his horse down the hill away from the lake.

We climbed higher into the hills, seeking Hannibal's lair.

* * *

An hour later, we lay on moist leaves deep in the underbrush overlooking the Carthaginian camp. It was much closer than the campfires we had seen the previous night would have indicated.

Decius placed his lips to my ear and said, "They must have sent cavalry ahead to light fires, while the army stayed here on the hill."

I nodded agreement. Below us we saw thousands of Roman prisoners gathered in stout wooden pens surrounded by Carthaginian soldiers. "What do you think? Nine, ten thousand?" I asked.

"Romans?" he asked. At my nod, Decius said, "Nine thousand."

Screams of pain and terror came from the camp as the Carthaginian torturers plied their trade. Men were roasted slowly over fires while Carthaginian soldiers threw small stones at them. Others had the skin flayed from their bodies while crowds watched. It was all quite sickening.

Hannibal sat with a group of his officers in a half circle near a large tent facing us. As he turned his head to speak, I could see the patch covering his left eye. It was dark leather and held in place by a simple thong tied around his head.

A few minutes later, the one-tusked elephant was led toward the general from the center of camp, avoiding the prisoner pens. The gray beast still carried Hannibal's throne atop its back. The mahout sat across the neck and tapped the animal's shoulder with a long stick.

"What are they doing there?" I asked, pointing toward the elephant.

Decius observed for a moment, then said, "Oh no," with a voice devoid of any emotion.

"What?" I asked.

"Watch" was all he would say.

Then I noticed what lay by the fire in front of Hannibal. A legionary had been staked to the ground. I watched as the elephant was forced to step forward onto the helpless man. Several of the officers applauded and laughed.

"Gods!" I said. The bloody pile of flesh and bone lay still before the one-eyed general. The fire lighted his face with the glow of Hades.

"Look there," the remaining messenger said.

I shifted my gaze to the east and saw Romans. "Cerebos's balls," I cursed. "It looks like most of the vanguard."

"It is," Decius said, shaking himself free of the macabre scene. "Look, you see the standard that Carthaginian bastard is holding?"

I saw the standard. "First Legion. Second Century," I said.

"There will be more," Decius said.

"Make a count," I said. We counted as the survivors of the vanguard were marched to the waiting pens, surrounded by their captors. A few minutes later, we had our total.

Decius said it first. "Six thousand."

"We must get back to Corito," I said. "Hannibal has killed or captured the entire army."

"Thirty thousand men, dead or captured." Decius said in awe.

"Yes, and I don't want to join their number," I said. "So, if you please, lead the way."

Decius nodded and slid himself back to the copse of trees hiding the horses. Minutes later we were mounted and riding away from the horrors of the Carthaginian camp. As the sun passed its zenith, I changed our course.

"Let's head north and approach Corito from the east," I said.

"Sounds good to me," said Decius.

I kicked my horse into a trot as the three of us descended into a draw.

* * *

"There's Corito," Decius said, with a lift of his chin.

The city lay about two miles west of us. The walls were lighted by torches, but we could see little else.

"Let's push on for another hour. Then we'll head in," I said.

Night had fallen, and the moon was up, but it was only a quarter-moon. Illumination was sparse, especially in the trees where we rode. Farm buildings surrounded by ripening crops covered the visible countryside. Hannibal's raiders had not reached this far in their pillaging.

"What's that?" the messenger said.

"Where?" I said.

The man lifted his arm toward a low shadow north of the city.

"I see it," Decius said. "Looks like cavalry."

"A lot of cavalry," I said. "Servilius's vanguard maybe?"

"Or Hannibal's reinforcements," Decius said. "With our luck lately, do you want to cast dice with Fortuna?"

"Better us than Corito," I said. "We're scouts. Let's scout."

"You are determined to get me killed," Decius said with a grin.

"Let's get to that tree line on the north side of the city," I said. "Then we can observe unseen."

With trees and hills at our back, the approaching force could not see our movement. I kicked my horse into a gallop and made for the trees separating two fields. In very little time, we arrived.

"Dismount," I said. "Soldier, watch the horses and stay quiet. Decius, with me."

We moved low through the underbrush, partially hidden by the wheat growing in the field in front of us. When we reached the edge of the trees, we knelt so our eyes could just see over the tops of the grain.

"There, sir." Decius said. "About thirty up front."

"I see them," I said. There was a group of horsemen spread into a loose line, walking across the field parallel to the main road to Corito. A mile behind them, I could see the shadow growing against the horizon. The near group were several hundred yards from us, but still just shadows.

"How do you want to do this?" Decius asked, keeping his voice low.

I thought for a moment. "They'll get a bit closer. When they reach about there" – I pointed to a low stone wall bordering the road about fifty yards away – "I'll walk out and greet them."

"Mad plan, as always," Decius said. "But at least you're just going to get yourself killed." He showed me all his teeth in a canine smile.

"They are most likely equites sent ahead of Servilius," I said.

Decius nodded. "True, but if they aren't, the two of us are going to have a hard time getting you back."

"I want you to have my horse ready to come get me if they turn out to be Carthaginians," I said with a smile of my own. "Or get into Corito and get help. Use your best judgment, Decurion."

"I knew you'd try to get me killed," he said, then lifted himself to a crouch and moved back to get the horses.

I waited a few more minutes. Decius returned with the horses. The near group was almost in position.

"Here I go," I said.

"Fortuna watch over you," Decius said. "You madman," he whispered under his breath.

The skirmishers, for that had to be their role, didn't see me at first. That was good, as it gave me some separation from the trees where the horses hid. I walked thirty yards before the nearest horseman saw me and sounded a warning.

"Infantry to the left!" he shouted in crisp, clear Latin before turning his horse and aiming his javelin at my chest.

"Hardly infantry, soldier," I said in my best Roman officer's voice.

The man's charge abruptly halted as he pulled on his reins. "Advance and be recognized," he ordered as several of his companions closed the distance and pulled in beside him.

"I am Decurion Appius Curtius Asprenas, Third Turma, First Legion," I said, walking forward slowly.

"Decurion!" the man shouted over his shoulder. "He says he's a Roman officer."

A moment later, I was speaking to the commander of the skirmish force. "What are you doing here?" he asked.

"Scouting for my commander, who's in Corito – there," I said, tilting my head toward the city.

"Who's your commander?" he asked.

"Decurion Scipio," I said.

"You're with First Legion, General Flaminius's army then?" he said.

I nodded. "Correct, but the general is dead," I said. "He was killed in an ambush this morning."

"Dead?" he said in an unbelieving tone. "He was to wait for us to arrive before moving on Hannibal."

"Unfortunately, he didn't," I said. "Why don't you take me to your commanding officer, Decurion? Then I won't have to tell this story twice." I was bone tired and this man was annoying me.

"This is not the First Legion, Decurion," he said with a curl in his lip. "And you do not give the orders here. Your story is a bit odd. Decurions do not perform scouting missions alone. I think you are a deserter."

I rolled my eyes. "Your paranoia is getting the better of you."

"So now I'm a paranoid, am I?" the cavalryman said with a sneer. "What proof do you have you are not a deserter?"

"Your supposition is easily disproved, sir," I said. "Corito is less than a mile away. We can knock on the door and talk to what's left of Flaminius's army."

"And let you lead us into a trap? I think not," the decurion said. "Bind him. Put him on one of the spare horses."

Two men grabbed me roughly and wrapped two leather cords around my wrists, securing my hands behind my back. Someone unbuckled my belt and took my weapons. They lifted me onto a horse and wrapped another cord around my waist, securing me to the saddle.

"Decurion, stop this! I am an officer of the First Legion," I shouted.

"Gag him!" the decurion ordered.

A knotted rag was wrapped around my head, covering my mouth. The knot tasted of foul grass and slime. *Great, I'm sharing a snaffle bit with one of the horses*, I thought.

"Message to the commander," the decurion said to one of his men. "Have taken a prisoner. Possibly a Roman deserter or traitor. Corito may be taken. Possibly a trap waiting inside. Recommend we skirt the perimeter and move on toward Rome."

When the man repeated the message back, the decurion sent him on his way. Then the rest mounted and we rode east, circling wide around the town.

After he is done falling off his horse laughing, Decius is never going to let me forget this.

XXXIV

RESCUE

In the morning, I struggled against my bindings to sit up. A guard had thrown me under a tree at our cold camp around midnight. Now my muscles ached from the cold ground and tree roots. A guard pulled down my gag and shoved a piece of hard, salty meat into my mouth. Then he helped me to my feet and walked me to my already saddled horse. After a few seconds of struggling, we managed to get me atop the beast. And once again, I was tied to the saddle. At least he left the gag off this time. I guessed they weren't worried about me making noise now.

Minutes later, the order to march came and we moved south again. At least this time, we rode along the east shore of Lake Trasimenus. In the night, the rest of the cavalry had joined us. I rode with the main body now. I was surrounded by four thousand Roman and alae cavalry from Servilius's army. I saw the commander, riding ahead of me. From the look of his expensive bronze armor, he was of Senatorial rank. I could only see the back of his helmet, so I could not identify him. But having been in Proconsul Scipio's household for years, there was a good chance I had seen or even been introduced to him. I took a chance.

To my guard, I said, "Who leads these men?"

My only response was silence.

"Not fond of conversation, I see," I said, trying to moisten up my parched mouth and throat. "Any chance I could get some water? That salted pork was enough to dry a lake into a desert."

He didn't say anything but pulled a waterskin from the far side of his saddle. Awkwardly, he held the bag aloft and dribbled water onto my face and into my eager mouth. After a few moments, he pulled the bag back and refastened it to his saddle.

"Thanks," I said earnestly. I hadn't had a drop of water since well before midnight. "What's your name?"

Again, the soldier made no response.

I turned my attention back to the senator in command of this cavalry force. I looked for any identifying features. I prayed to Fortuna that he was someone I knew, and better yet, someone who knew me. Stubbornly, the man refused to turn to look back over his shoulder.

We rode on for another hour or so. We were near the southern end of the lake now. The commander had to make a decision soon. Turn right to get back on the Via Cassia, the main road to Rome. The other options, left or straight, took us into the hills and eventually to the Via Flaminia. I expected a halt to rest and water the horses, but I was disappointed.

My guard shoved another piece of salty leather into my mouth as we continued to ride south. I chewed on the tough meat, trying to wet it with the saliva that had only recently been restored to my mouth. It occupied my thoughts as my frustration grew at my circumstances.

We had passed many farmsteads throughout the morning. Now we reached the base of the hills and some dense forest. Finally, the commander called for a halt.

The commander turned. And my stomach turned queasy. It was Gaius Centenius. I knew him well. The elder Scipio cordially loathed the man. His gaze passed over me and stopped. I could see that he couldn't quite place me. He turned to one of his officers and spoke too low for me to hear. But it wasn't hard to guess the question. Who is that prisoner?

Receiving the reply obviously jogged his memory. He kicked his horse into a walk toward me. "Why Decurion Asprenas, whatever brings you here? My man tells me you are a deserter," he said in an unctuous tone.

"Senator Centenius," I said politely, "your men wouldn't believe me when I told them my commanding officer was in Corito."

"It is Propraetor Centenius now. And who is your commander?" he asked. "Marharbal, Mago? Or do you work for Hannibal himself?"

"I am Roman, sir," I protested. "My commander is Decurion Publius Cornelius Scipio, as ever."

"The boy Scipio is now a decurion?" he said, surprised. "I remember him as an awkward boy who could barely hold a sword without toppling over."

"He's grown, sir," I said. "If you will permit me, sir, I have intelligence that you should know."

"Oh by all means, do share it," Centenius said. "I long to hear a good tale."

"I swear by Jupiter and Minerva that what I say is true, sir," I said. "Hannibal ambushed General Flaminius yesterday morning. His army was defeated or captured. I was detailed to observe the enemy as the survivors made their way back to Corito. I observed Hannibal's men guarding fifteen thousand Roman prisoners. The rest of the army is dead or in Corito. Most are dead."

"Amazing. Hannibal killed or captured Flaminius's entire army?" he said with a polite smile. "And how is it that you escaped such a massacre, Decurion?"

"I was with the cavalry screen at the rear of the army. We broke through and marched back to Corito, gathering the remnants of the army as we could."

"So you ran away," he said coldly. "That is desertion. You admit it with your own tongue."

"I did not desert, sir," I said. "The general was killed at the beginning of the attack. The army was in disarray and surrounded, with their backs to the lake. We did what we could to survive and assist other survivors."

"And General Flaminius was with the rear guard, I suppose?" Centenius said scornfully.

I spoke, knowing that the conversation was doomed. "No, sir. He marched at the head of the main force. I was making a report there when the attack began. I saw the general fall before I made my way back to my men."

"Again, you admit that you ran from battle. In fact, you ran the entire length of the army during an ambush, which I find difficult to believe. More likely, you led Flaminius into the trap yourself. And now you try to do the same to my men." He snarled at the soldier escorting me, "Take this coward traitor from my sight." He jerked the reins of his horse so hard it nearly fell over as it turned.

"Come with me," said my escort. They were the first words he had spoken to me. I had no choice in the matter, since he held the reins of my horse and was riding away toward the rear of the formation before I could protest.

"That went well," I said to no one in particular, then resigned myself to a short life, unless I could get back to Corito.

* * *

Propraetor Centenius chose to continue south, crossing the hills toward the Via Flaminia. It was the more direct, if rougher, path to Rome. As evening approached, we climbed into the low, forested hills south of the lake. The men around me began looking into the trees surrounding us with wide eyes that sought to penetrate the growing gloom as the sun dipped behind the hills to the west. Every sound seemed to jerk their heads from side to side. Most of these men had never been on a patrol, I realized. They were showing all the signs of green troops in the field for the first time.

The moon, which was slightly fuller tonight, still provided scant illumination when it rose. Finally, Centenius called a halt and the men began establishing a hasty camp.

My escort led me to a large tree and tied my horse to a low limb before dismounting. Then he helped me down. He guided me to the tree and pulled a small rope between my tied hands before looping it over the same limb that he had tied my horse to. He made sure it was long enough for me to sit against the trunk, and began caring for the horses. His hands concentrated on the menial tasks at hand, but his eyes never left me. He was a good soldier, it seemed. Quiet and professional, with all the conscientiousness required to perform his duty to the utmost. I was not going to escape under his watchful eyes.

After he had seen to the horses, he fed and watered me. That is to say, he gave me a drink of water, then broke a hard biscuit into pieces and fed them to me. Every time I tried to start talking, he shoved another bite into my mouth. He followed that with another drink and some salted meat that was indistinguishable from the leather of my belt. While I chewed this, he ate a quiet meal of his own.

A shout from the south and a clash of metal on metal jerked both of our heads around. He stood and immediately saddled his mount again with a quick efficiency of a veteran cavalryman. He slid the bridle over his horse's head and then pulled himself into the saddle.

"Hey!" I said, "you can't just leave me here."

He ignored me and kicked his horse into a trot toward the commotion. I listened but still couldn't see anything. The noise was getting louder, and I felt the queasy feeling that Centenius was finding out how good the Carthaginians were.

More sounds of fighting came from the east. Shouts and screams now. Men were dying, and I could do nothing but strain against the damn tree. I nearly ripped my shoulders out of their sockets trying to free myself, but the old veteran had tied his knots well. My horse was becoming excited by the commotion and my efforts to escape, so I calmed down and began whispering to the nervous beast. All I needed now was a kick from my own horse to injure me.

The fight seemed to move in every direction. Nearby, men were shouting and pointing, but the dense forest made coordinating the fight impossible.

I sat down in the dirt and struggled to get my hands past my feet. I exhaled all the air from my chest and squeezed into the tightest ball I could manage. Finally, the rope slide past my boots. My hands were now in front of me at least.

I examined the knots, looking for a place to bite that might loosen the restraints. I gnawed at the leather, but it was too tough to bite through, and the rope was too thick to saw through without a knife. But I had to get free. The sounds of fighting were coming closer. I searched the ground for a sharp rock or piece of metal.

"At least you're not dead," a familiar voice said from behind me. "It would have been a shame to risk my life if they'd hanged you."

"Decius!" I said. "Cut me free. What's going on?"

He walked his horse a bit closer, and I proffered my hands up to his knife.

"It is traditional to be captured by the enemy, you know?" he said with a snort.

I rubbed my raw wrists before grabbing my saddle and bridle for my horse.

"Marharbal is attacking," he said, identifying Hannibal's senior cavalry commander. "He has a few thousand infantry in the hills ahead and cavalry on the flanks."

"We have to get out of here," I said as I jumped into my saddle. "Which way?"

"Follow me," Decius said, and led the way north.

I saw mounted Numidians and Carthaginians fighting with Italians and Romans in dozens of individual melees. We rode into the top of a draw and descended into the dense underbrush without being opposed by either side. Being unarmed, I thanked Fortuna for our good luck.

In minutes, we reached the widening bottom of the hill, and the trees thinned to reveal more enemy cavalry waiting to attack.

"We'll have them on us in a moment if we try to run past," I said.

"All is well," Decius said. "Wait a minute." He fumbled with something in his saddlebag, then lifted a small whistle. "It's for my son. But I may keep it after tonight." He blew two sharp blasts.

Nothing happened. But several of the Numidian cavalry began peering into the dark trees behind us. Then about thirty Roman equites swarmed into the Numidians from behind. Without hesitation, Decius kicked his mount into a gallop. I followed behind as fast as I could. In moments we passed the enemy line and Decius blew two more blasts on his son's whistle.

I looked over my shoulder to see the Romans turning to flee back into the woods. Several Numidian horses now had no riders, I observed with grim satisfaction.

When we had put some distance between us and the battle, I pulled in beside Decius and asked, "What was that?"

"I assumed you'd get yourself killed or captured when you met with your friends back there," he said. "I sent the messenger to Corito and followed after. Scipio sent three turmae to assist me. When they caught up, I had some of them scout around. That lot," he tilted his head toward the Roman camp, "didn't even see the Carthaginians circling ahead of them."

"And you decided not to warn them?" I asked.

"I've grown accustomed to your total lack of humor. They annoyed me by arresting you." he said without remorse. "So I used the Carthaginian attack as a diversion to come get you."

"And the whistle?" I asked.

"I assumed that the Carthaginians would have an outer cordon for their attack. I left a turma in position to give us a chance to get away. The other two were waiting in ambush for when they disengaged," he said. "We'll rejoin them at the base of the lake."

I looked at Decius, who said all of this with as little emotion as if he'd been planning a training patrol for his men. "Good job," I said.

He just nodded.

"And thank you," I said. "I think Centenius was going to hang me."

"That's what I thought," Decius said. "What do you say we pick up the pace? I want to sleep in a bed tomorrow."

"I agree," I said.

We spurred our horses and rode north into the waiting darkness.

XXXV

THE MARCH TO ROME

"Centenius is dead then?" Servilius asked.

"He must be dead, sir," I said to the remaining consul of Rome. "Though I did not see him fall. Marharbal had his forces completely surrounded by the time my scouts overtook him."

"Four thousand men, gone," Consul Servilius said to no one in particular. "Hannibal is an evil magician in league with Ba'al."

The elderly man's face cast about the chamber for someone else to speak. His remaining cavalry force consisted of those who had escaped from Flaminius's ambush. His infantry were green conscripts. And Hannibal was between him and Rome. No one wished to add to his misery, so he found no solace.

"General," Scipio said, "we can make it to Rome on the Via Cassia. My men are experts at scouting. We can avoid a battle and reach Rome."

The council chamber in Corito remained quiet while Servilius considered this advice. The staff officers from his legions and the remaining officers from Flaminius's waited to see what the general would decide. Servilius looked into the eyes of the young decurion for some spark of hope.

"Rome needs our protection," he said after an achingly long pause. "We shall march to her defense at once. All officers are to make preparations to march in two hours."

The decision released the tension in the room. Men began to speak amongst themselves and move toward the chamber exit. Scipio tilted his head in that direction. Decius and I followed him out, and we walked toward the stable where our horses rested.

"We will likely be at the vanguard of this army," Scipio said. "I expect to be tasked with ensuring no Carthaginians lie between us and Rome."

"Scout the road ahead?" I asked

"And the hills beyond," he said. "Decius, I want you to take your section and find Hannibal's main force."

"That should be fun," Decius said.

"Stay out of sight and report back at least once a day," Scipio continued. "I'll send you replacements at two-day intervals."

"And if Hannibal splits his forces?" Decius asked.

"Report and use your best judgment." Scipio placed his hand on the older man's shoulder. "I trust you."

Decius's cheeks reddened, but he nodded gravely at the young decurion.

"Gentlemen, we are ten days' march from Rome. Consul Servilius will need us to keep him informed. Once again, you are the eyes and ears of the legion. You will do your duty and do it well, I have no doubt. I need no heroes this week. We need information, not confrontation."

"That we can do," I said. "But what of the army once we are in Rome?"

"This army is too terrified to face Hannibal at the moment. It needs reinforcement, and I dare say, new leadership," Scipio said quietly. "I expect the Senate will have something to say about that when we arrive."

"Can we raise more men?" Decius asked.

"Yes," Scipio said. "But equipping them will become the problem. We have bled the citizenry dry with our ineptitude and fallibility. The state will have to pay for much of the arms and armor for the new legions."

Decius looked grim. "More taxes then," he said.

"Yes. But that is a better alternative to slavery or death. That is the fate of any Roman that yields to Hannibal."

"We'll get the men ready, sir," I said.

"Leave me Marcus and three others," Scipio said. "Split the rest of my section between you."

"Yes, sir," I said. The morning sun had burned away the last of the fog. We would be marching before midday.

* * *

Eleven days later, I led the vanguard of Consul Servilius's army onto Campus Martius. "Dismount!" I ordered. Then I looked toward Capitoline

Hill, which overlooked the Field of Mars. Atop the hill I could see dozens of figures in chalk-white togas.

"Watching our arrival or planning an assassination?" Decius asked, noticing the direction of my gaze.

"Both probably," I said. "I would not wish to trade places with Consul Servilius."

"They'll blame him for not moving fast enough to support Flaminius?" he asked.

"They'll blame him for losing. Because there's no one else left to blame," I said.

"Bad luck," Decius said.

I turned to see that the men were caring for their horses, noting with approval that all were unsaddling and grooming their mounts with no need for instruction. "They will say Flaminius flouted the will of the gods by refusing to wait for the omens. Servilius is guilty by association," I said.

"What do we do now?" Decius asked.

"You made the report to Scipio and the general," I said. "Hannibal marches for Apulia. He cannot be allowed to sway our Italian allies to his side."

"We follow him?" Decius said.

"We follow him," I said. "If whoever the Senate puts in charge has any sense."

I picked a stone from my horse's forehoof. "Scipio should be here before nightfall," I said. "I'm certain he will have a better appreciation of the political situation than either of us."

"He will that," Decius agreed. "He's one of them," he said pointing with his brush toward the men in togas.

"Yes, but fortunate for us," I said, "he's also a good soldier."

Decius grunted as his horse's tail flicked him. "He gets the job done and keeps us alive." He killed a horsefly that was troubling his mount with a meaty thwack of his hand. "That's good enough for me." He brushed the messy remains off his hand with the back of the brush.

A dark-haired man wearing a tunic of fine weave and expensive sandals walked purposefully through the Porta Fontinalis. He moved directly toward the turma. A few moments later, he spoke in a cultured voice, "Decurion, who commands here?"

"At the moment, me," I said, ignoring the man's rudeness at not introducing himself.

"You will go at once to the Forum and make your report to the Senate," he commanded.

"No," I said.

"You have your orders, Decurion. I suggest you obey them," he said.

"You are correct," I said. His face, which had been tensing for a confrontation, relaxed. "I have orders from General Servilius to scout ahead of his line of march and find a suitable place for his army to camp. I also have orders to report only to General Servilius, through my decurion, until his arrival later today."

The man sputtered, "The Senate's orders supersede those orders. You will report to the Senate at once."

"I will not," I said. "The Senate can wait a few hours for the general's arrival. Now if you will excuse me, I have work to do." I turned my back on him and began brushing debris and dirt from my horse's mane.

"How dare you!" he shouted. "You will turn and obey my orders."

I ignored the man and continued grooming my mount.

"Sir, perhaps you should run back to the city now," Decius said. "I'd hate if something untoward happened to you. These horses and men have been hunting Carthaginians for the past year. They're a bit wild."

"What?" said the man uncertainly.

"You should leave," Decius repeated. "Before you annoy them. They're liable to stampede and hurt you if you don't. Them being half-wild creatures and all." Decius put a friendly and immensely strong arm around the man's shoulder, all the while keeping up a patter describing his concern for the man's safety. Decius pulled the man back to the city gate as if he were a mule and the messenger a plow.

The man, unable to free himself from Decius's embrace, walked, unwillingly but inevitably, back toward his masters atop the hill.

When Decius returned, I said, "Thank you."

"He was an annoying little fellow," he said. "I worried for his safety here."

"Your concern for a citizen of Rome is quite noble," I said.

He grinned.

We waited for the army to arrive.

* * *

A few hours later, Servilius's column arrived. He rode at the head, surrounded by the tribunes and decurions of the legions. The infantry marched into the Campus Martius and put on a good show for the men in white togas on the hill above. The prefect of engineers had his men preparing the field for a marching camp by the time the rear of the column halted.

Servilius sat upon his black horse, observing as his army made camp. Decius and I made our report, then found Scipio near where the headquarters tent was being erected.

"Hello, sir," Decius said. "Welcome home."

"Thank you," Scipio said. "Though I doubt we will be here long."

"Servilius will follow Hannibal south then?" I asked.

"I doubt Servilius will be in command much longer," Scipio said. "The Senate will meet in the morning. The general must give a personal account of recent events. I expect the report will not be well received."

"Then the army will march under a new commander?" Decius asked.

"I think, yes. But the political situation is uncertain. We will wait for the outcome and then do our duty."

"Of course, sir," I said. "Will you visit your father's house then?"

"I shall, once I have seen to the men. You will both join me. I may need your services before we march again."

"I'd prefer to stay with the men, sir," Decius said.

"I would prefer to remain with the men as well," Scipio said. "Unfortunately, our duty lies elsewhere now. I will need six men as messengers and a commander for that detachment. That would be you, Decius."

"And me, sir?" I asked.

"As always, Appius," he said, "you serve my father as my bodyguard and advisor. You would find some excuse to remain close to me, no matter what I ordered. So I order you to remain close to me and advise me."

I bowed my head to acknowledge the truth of his words. "We call upon your father's allies in the Senate then?" I asked.

"Yes. Tonight, if possible," he said. "I have prepared messages to several. I will need them delivered by trusted men." He looked meaningfully at Decius.

"I'll pick the men myself, sir," he said.

"Good. Let us get the men settled then. We have a long day ahead of us." Scipio led his horse to the where our men had the turma's horses picketed while they built their tents. With practiced efficiency, the legion was at work building a marching camp under the lee of the walls of Rome.

* * *

"Father!" Scipio said as the older man embraced his son.

"Publius. Welcome home, son," the elder Scipio said. "When news of Lake Trasimenus arrived, your mother and I worried."

"My messages?" the decurion asked.

"Arrived and allayed our worst fears," Scipio said. "Though the reality gave us all enough to fear."

"Flaminius died bravely," the younger man said. "Appius and I saw him fall to Ducarius."

"He died and put the Senate into a panic," Scipio said scornfully. "He affronted the gods and paid the price for it."

"Yes, Father. I know."

"Appius," the older man said, "welcome home to you as well. Thank you for brining Publius safely home."

"It is I who thank the decurion, Senator," I said. "He saved my life as well."

"Oh?" the senator said. "There was nothing of this in your letters, Publius."

"There was nothing to tell. Appius exaggerates."

"Then I surely wish to hear the tale," Senator Scipio said with a smile.

"You are looking much better than when last we saw you, sir," I said, noting only a slight limp in the older man's stride.

"I am riding again," Scipio the elder said. "Perhaps I can convince the Senate to let me join Gnaeus in Iberia next year. I am fit enough."

"A picture of health, Father," Scipio said. "But I think Uncle Gnaeus can manage without you for a while yet."

"Laelius sends his greetings from Cremona in a letter that arrived a few days ago," Senator Scipio said. "He's been named prefect and now commands the city's garrison."

"Good for him," Scipio said, smiling. "I must send him a message of congratulations. We did not get the chance to serve together long enough. Perhaps his next posting?"

The elder Scipio smiled at this thought and then swept his hand in expansive invitation, "Come in, bathe and relax. Appius, you can regale us with the heroic deeds of the young decurion here over a meal and wine."

"Thank you, sir," I said and followed them into the massive townhouse.

* * *

"So, you see, son, Flaminius's failure to take the auspices and his subsequent defeat has thrown much support behind Fabius Maximus," Senator Scipio said, taking a sip of wine.

"What will happen with Servilius?" the younger Scipio asked.

The senator thought a moment, then said, "Fabius hates him. I would expect he would insist Servilius be stripped of the consulship at the very least."

I sat on a blue cushion in a worn but comfortable toga while Scipio and his son discussed politics. I listened while really concentrating on the dormice the slaves carried in on silver trays. They were stuffed with cheese and bread. They seemed to explode with flavor on my tongue. Followed by sweet Falernian wine, they were an antidote to too many weeks of salted pork or beef and thin gruel.

"We should concentrate on mitigating his authority then, Father."

The older man nodded. "Nominate a political opponent as co-consul at the very least. I doubt there is a way to prevent his election this time."

"Flaminius was his most vocal opponent. Who could replace him?"

"Paullus, if you could get him to stand forth. Everyone allows that he is wise and a superb military mind. Varro, perhaps."

"Oh, is he returned from his embassy to Carthage finally?" asked the younger Scipio.

"By way of Syracuse, it seems. There was some irregularity in the security arrangements for his ship. It sank with all hands off the coast of Sicily. Fortunately, Varro had himself smuggled out on a Greek ship the night before."

"Very clever," I said.

"Clever indeed," Scipio agreed. "He made his way home from Syracusae, then?"

"Yes. He had to walk from Syracusae to Massana to find a ship home. But he made it," the older man said.

"Who else is a possibility?" I asked.

"Marcus Minucius would be the only other candidate, I think," the senator said. "He refuses to even contemplate any military policy that is not aggressively confrontational."

"Not the best choice as a general, perhaps," I said.

"Oh, he is a good field commander," the elder Scipio said. "But he thinks that the attrition of men and resources is an acceptable trade for victory."

"As one of the prospective men and resources, I would rather not be attrited," I said, noticing the interplay between father and son. The elder man was treating the younger with the respect as an equal.

"Let us concentrate our efforts on the other two, then," said Scipio the younger.

Senator Scipio called for parchment and ink. A few minutes later, invitations were sent to Paullus and Varro for an urgent conference before the Senate session at noon.

The conversation turned to news involving family and friends. I returned my attention to the delicacies on silver trays until the senator bade us a good night. I followed his example and made my way to my former quarters in the residence. I slept and thought no more of politics and war. It was good to be home.

XXXVI

DICTATOR

"Thank you for coming so early, my friend," the elder Scipio said to the familiar dark-haired man.

"Good morning, Scipio, though there has not been much good lately," said Senator Paullus, embracing his friend. "Young Publius, you have grown much since I saw you last."

The younger Scipio received his own engulfing embrace from the towering man. "Thank you, sir. Army life seems to agree with me."

"And I hear good things of your deeds," Paullus said.

"Thank you, sir. But I did no more than my duty required." Scipio lowered his eyes, glancing to the Senator's side.

Paullus left the young man dangling in the discomfort of his approbation before relenting. "Aemilia, come greet our friends," he said to his daughter.

"Hello, Senator, Decurion," the golden-haired girl said in her soft, clear voice. She embraced each and bowed her head. She was every inch the Roman lady, dressed in a dazzling blue dress trimmed in pale red. Her hair was held up with two ribbons that perfectly matched the colors of her dress. "Is that Decurion Asprenas, father?"

I became the focus of everyone's attention as Paullus said, "I believe it is, Aemilia."

Decurion Scipio, whose eyes had not left Aemilia since their greeting, turned to face me. "Indeed, this is Decurion Asprenas. He is my second-in-command," he said formally.

"Senator, Lady Aemilia. It is good to see you both well," I said with a bow as formal as I could manage.

"My brother still complains that he did not get to see your horse, Asprenas."

I chuckled. "It was a very late night and he is a very young boy. I am sure there will be other opportunities for him."

"Yes, I am certain," she said with firmness. "Would you be so kind as to escort me inside?" she said, taking my arm. "I fear this morning's conversation will be all politics."

Looking over her head to Senator Scipio, who nodded, I said, "Of course, Lady Aemilia. It would be my pleasure."

Decurion Scipio bowed stiffly as we passed into the residence, following us with his eyes until we disappeared inside.

"How have you been, Asprenas?" Lady Aemilia asked.

"As well as could be expected, given the setbacks the legions have suffered recently," I said, leading her into a garden on the east side of the main building.

She paused to admire some white flowers in full bloom and enjoy their fragrance. "It must have been truly awful. Gaius Flaminius dead, and most of his army."

"Yes. Decurion Scipio witnessed his death," I said.

"What happened?" she asked. "How did it happen, I mean?"

I thought for a moment, trying to think of a way to describe the events without distressing her. "We were marching in a thick fog. The head of the column stopped, but we could not see why. I assume the Carthaginians had attacked them, but I never found out for sure."

"And then you were attacked?" she asked.

I nodded, not wanting to remember. "Scipio and I had just joined General Flaminius's staff and were riding at the rear of the group when a Gaul named Ducarius led a force to ambush the command party," I said. "They were cut down to a man. Ducarius slew General Flaminius with his own hand."

"I see," she said softly. "He was such a nice man."

"I should not be speaking of these things to you, my lady," I said.

"I am a Roman woman," she said. "I am quite capable of coping with death in the defense of the people of Rome."

"I see that you are, my lady," I said. "I would spare you the pain of knowing, if I could, so that your face could remain untroubled by such concerns."

"You are quite noble, Asprenas. But I would have the knowledge still," she said, looking me straight in the eyes. "I would always have you tell me the truth, no matter how painful."

"If that is your wish, my lady," I said. My heart constricted in my chest, and I felt a warm flush cross my face. This girl, not yet fourteen, was as strong and forceful as a summer storm. I wanted to protect her, keep her safe from the world. I had to change the topic. "My lady, can I get you some refreshment? A drink or some fruit, perhaps?"

"Some juice would be nice. Thank you," she said, letting me retreat into the mundane task of ordering servants.

"They will bring us some juice and a light meal," I said. "We can rest there." I pointed to a set of cushioned benches arranged by the garden wall.

"That will be lovely. We can enjoy the morning sun together."

"Um... yes, my lady," I said.

We walked to the benches and made ourselves comfortable. We chatted about nothing in particular until the drinks arrived. A slave placed a platter of fresh fruits and another of cheese between us, then left to stand by the entrance to the house.

"What is Decurion Scipio like?" Aemilia asked.

"I'm not sure what you mean. He's a good commander, very calm under pressure," I said.

"No, though that is a good quality," she said. "As a man. What is he like?"

"Ah. Hmm. He is very reserved," I began. "I suppose that is from his upbringing. He is very intelligent, and, for his years I think, wise."

"Is he a strong warrior?" she asked.

"Strong enough. More important is that he never stops thinking about what is happening around him. He seems to be aware of everything, even when focused on staying alive in a fight. That is a difficult feat for most anyone."

"So, you like him."

"I can't say I like him. But I admire and respect him. He is my master's son, not my friend. We are not equal, nor shall we ever be."

"Does that prevent you from being friends?" she asked.

"My duty is to follow his orders and protect him from harm," I said. "Friendship doesn't come into it."

"How sad that his closest companion is not a friend."

"He has friends, my lady. Gaius Laelius, for example."

"But you are closest to him?"

"I have been his tutor and protector for many years. I expect I will remain his advisor and bodyguard for the foreseeable future. But I doubt we will ever become friends."

"Perhaps you are correct, Asprenas. But I hope that you will become friends. And I hope that you will remain my friend."

I was certain my face had become bright red. "My lady, I will always be your devoted servant."

"No!" she said, nearly shouting. "You and I are friends, Asprenas. I will have us be nothing else." Her voice calmed as she spoke. "I will need good friends who will tell me the truth. I see the sycophants surrounding my father and mother. I know that as I grow older, marry, and begin a family, there will be those who seek to befriend me for political purposes. I need friends like you, who will tell me the truth."

I looked at this girl who was wise beyond her years in stark admiration. "I will be your friend, my lady. You have my word."

"Good," she said with a slight nod of her head. "Then I shall call you Appius and you shall call me Aemilia."

"In private, Aemilia," I said, and she smiled. "In public, you shall always be Lady Aemilia."

"The fate of all who bear my family name." She took my hand. "Appius, my good friend, tell me what has happened to you and Publius since we last met."

* * *

I stood by the younger Scipio at the entrance to the family residence as evening fell. Lady Aemilia waited with us, having spent most of the day talking with the young Scipio scion. Decius stood, uncomfortable in his linen tunic and sandals, looking decidedly out of place in the luxurious home of his commander. We could hear a rising murmur of voices over the wall surrounding the courtyard, moving toward the heavy wooden gate. We couldn't understand the words, but the voices sounded excited from their tone.

Senators Scipio and Paullus, and another man, broad in shoulder but of refined features, walked through the open gate. I did not recognise him

"Father, welcome home," the younger Scipio said in greeting. "Senators Paullus and Varro, welcome to our home," he said to the other men.

"A pleasure, Publius," Varro said. "It is good to see you again and looking so fit."

"I could say the same for you, Senator, after your late embassy to
Carthage," the young man said. "You must tell me of your escape, sir."

"Another time perhaps," Varro said. "Tonight, we have weightier matters to discuss."

"Indeed, we do," said Paullus, his olive complexion marred by splotches of red at his cheeks.

"Then allow me to escort you inside, gentlemen. Cena awaits," the
younger Scipio said with a graceful bow.

Decius and I followed the senators and their children into the house.
In a broad, open-air room, benches covered in intricately woven cushions
sat in a wide circle. Slaves stood at the walls, bearing platters of food and
decanters of wine. As the nobles arranged themselves, more slaves came
forward with bowls of water and towels. A brief silence ensued as the new
arrivals washed their hands and wiped away the road dust. Decius and I
imitated the nobles awkwardly, but finally the food and wine began to
circulate through the room.

"Father, what happened at the Senate? Will there be a new election?"
the younger Scipio asked, broaching the topic.

"No, there will be no elections for six months at least," Senator Scipio
said.

The younger man looked surprised. "Then Servilius remains the sole
consul?" he asked.

Varro said, "No. We have appointed a new Dictator instead."

"Dictator?" Aemilia said. "What is a Dictator?"

Paullus answered, "Daughter, a dictator is a man with absolute authority appointed in an emergency when debate and deliberation could cause
death and destruction."

"And who has the Senate appointed this task?" the younger Scipio
asked.

"Fabius Maximus," Paullus said in a gruff voice.

"He railed that Hannibal passed only five miles from the walls of
Rome," Varro said. "He demanded to know where the legions assigned
to protect us were."

"He gave Servilius little choice but to nominate him as Dictator,"
Scipio said. "Very smooth for a wart-faced ass."

"Fabius Maximus had no love for Servilius before the elections, and now he loathes the man," Paullus said. "He demands Servilius present himself to the new dictator tomorrow after the investiture."

"With no lictors as escort, while Fabius will have twenty-four, carrying fasces with axe heads affixed," Varro said. "It is a vile insult to the dignity of Servilius, whose only crime was to oppose Fabius in an election and win."

"What is the significance of the axe heads, father?" Aemilia asked.

"It means that he has the authority of life and death over all citizens, even inside the walls of Rome itself, unlike the power of a consul," Paullus said. "Servilius risks his very life by walking before Fabius tomorrow."

"What will Fabius Maximus do, Senator?" the younger Scipio asked.

Paullus paused to take a drink of wine, then said, "He says he will follow Hannibal, but refuse to fight except on the most favorable terms."

"He proposes to force Hannibal to pillage the countryside and annoy our Italian allies or starve," Senator Scipio said. "While we reinforce garrisons in every port and city to prevent him from receiving reinforcements and supplies from Carthage."

"We know he marched south to keep from annoying his Gallic allies," I said.

"Indeed, Appius," the elder Scipio said. "Fabius Maximus intends to turn the local population against Hannibal and starve him into submission."

"A long-term strategy, if it works," the younger Scipio said. "What is to prevent it from working?"

"Reinforcements from Spain and Gaul. Our Italian allies turning traitor. Or Hannibal capturing a port. Any of those would spell disaster for Rome," Varro said, taking a drink of wine.

"But Fabius Maximus with ultimate power?" Paullus asked. "What of the danger in that alone?"

"We did the best we could, Paullus," Varro said with a soothing gesture. "Minucius will be Master of Horse. Fabius will not be able to sway him nor amass enough power to become King."

"King?" the younger Scipio said. "Who said anything about king?"

The elder Scipio raised his hands to prevent the others from answering. "When ultimate authority is given to a man, there is always the possibility he will become corrupt and attempt to make that authority permanent. The Senate is sworn to prevent that from ever happening again," he said. "We have kept that vow for nearly six hundred years. We must continue to keep it even under the threat of Hannibal."

The room fell silent for several moments. It was Varro who spoke first. "Minucius is a good man. The legions know he is a great commander and he will have the respect of the cavalry."

"Our new commander, it would seem," the younger Scipio said in my direction.

"Yes," Senator Scipio said. "You will meet him tomorrow, after he takes office. He will need your help in organizing the new cavalry formations."

Decurion Scipio looked at Decius and me. I nodded once, acknowledging the new task ahead.

"What of the new legions, do you think?" Paullus asked. "How long will it take to raise them?"

"Not long, I would think," Varro said. "The plebes are scared to death right now, with Hannibal so close."

"Weapons and armor will be the problem," Senator Scipio said. "The smithies will have to work day and night to manufacture enough to equip all the new infantry."

"And new taxes to pay for it all," Paullus said.

"Better new taxes than a poorly equipped army facing Hannibal," Scipio said.

Paullus nodded a grudging agreement. "Finding more cavalry will also be a problem."

The discussion went on until the candles burned low. Tomorrow, we would meet the new cavalry commander and see what sort of General Fabius Maximus would be.

XXXVII

FABIAN STRATEGY

Decius and I stood behind our decurion on the steps of the Forum. Our position allowed us to guard his back, and each other, from the thousands of Roman citizens crammed into the area to hear the first words of the new dictator.

"You feel it, don't you?" Decius asked in a voice pitched for our ears over the roar of the shouting crowd.

"What?" I asked, shoving another citizen off the steps. Some in the crowd held signs, others shook their fists in the air, and everyone was shouting, it seemed. It would only take the right incident and these people would riot, I thought.

"They are scared," Scipio said.

"Cerebos's bone, they're scared," Decius swore. "They're about to hang us all and surrender to Hannibal."

The buccina and cornu sounded a sharp blast, announcing the arrival of the new Dictator. Quintus Fabius Maximus Verrucosus walked out of the pillared building where the Senate met, stopping at the edge of the steps. His toga bore the purple trim and two broad stripes marking his imperium, his command over life and death for all Roman citizens. The white of his hair matched the blinding white of his toga, which had been carefully chalked for this day. He was painful to look at as the sun struck him full in the face as he stood before the angry crowd.

Twenty-four hulking men, each bearing fasces with axe-heads at-tached, followed the new Dictator. They formed a semicircle behind him and ensured no senator or citizen had a position above them on the

Forum steps. These men were veteran soldiers, all sworn to protect Fabius Maximus unto death.

He let the crowd roar for a minute or more. Senators, standing now on the steps below the man at the center of the storm, began shifting uneasily and glancing around as if searching for an escape from certain death if the crowd erupted into violence. The decurion moved to place himself behind his father, and Decius and I followed, jostling and shoving our way through the crowd.

Fabius Maximus raised his right hand as if about to speak on the floor of the Senate. The crowd quieted, though a sullen rage lurked beneath the calm. I could see the reddened faces, the clenched fists, and eyes fixed on the new object at the center of their distress, the man at the top of the stairs.

"People of Rome, hear me," Fabius Maximus said in a booming voice accustomed to projecting across shouting men. "I, Quintus Fabius Maximus, this morning appointed as Dictator of Rome, order Consul Gnaeus Servilius Geminus to appear before me now."

Twelve of the lictors moved forward, clearing an area before the Dictator in preparation for the arrival of Servilius. From the far side of the Forum came a jostling as the consul approached. He was surrounded by his own escort of twelve lictors, with fasces of their own, though these bore no axe head. Servilius entered the clear area to stand before Fabius Maximus.

"I appear as ordered, Magister Populii," Servilius said, using the older and more formal name for the office of Dictator.

"People of Rome, let us not disparage this man. We elected him and his now-deceased colleague Gaius Flaminius. He performed the office to the best of his ability. But his actions and those of his co-consul offended the gods," Fabius Maximus said.

The crowd roared their disapproval at the man they had overwhelmingly elected only a few months earlier.

After a few moments, Fabius raised his hand again to quiet the crowd. "To be turned from one's course by men's opinions, by blame, and by misrepresentation shows the signs of a man unfit to hold office," he said. "This man held his course through contravening opinion. He answered blame with truthful and honest testimony of his failures to the Senate. He made no misrepresentations to the Senate and People of Rome, I say." He paused, the crowd hushed into complete silence. "And yet, he is unfit for the office to which we elected him. His offenses against the gods require recompense and sacrifice."

The crowd erupted into cheers of approbation.

Again, the raised hand silenced the crowd. "Consul Gnaeus Servilius Geminus, dismiss your lictors and surrender the symbols and duties of your office," Fabius Maximus said in a solemn voice.

With as much dignity as he could muster, Servilius turned to his escort and said, "Lictors, surrender your fasces to these men." He indicated the twelve men holding open the circle in which they stood. "You are hereby dismissed from the office of consul." He turned back to face the Dictator. "I surrender my office to you, sir."

"Servilius, I will find an office more suited for your talents," Fabius Maximus said in a calm, quiet voice. "For now, you are dismissed as you have dismissed your men and shown the proper forms of respect for the laws and traditions of Rome."

The former consul lowered his head in acknowledgment and turned to join his fellow Senators on the steps of the Forum.

"Marcus Minucius Rufus, come forward," Fabius Maximus said once Servilius had reached the safety of his peers.

A short, squat man, with dark, thinning curly hair stepped into the circle. He looked up at the Dictator with a pugnacious glare. "I am here, Magister Populii," he said.

"Minucius, we have had many disagreements in policy, but I need your aid during this time of crisis," the older man said with patient dignity. "Will you accept the role of Magister Equitum?"

Minucius continued to glare at his political opponent, but said, "I will, sir."

Fabius said, "You have the thanks of the Senate and People of Rome, in addition to my own. Please confer with me this evening at my head-quarters on the Campus Martius."

"Of course, sir," Minucius said, saluting and then striding into the crowd.

Fabius watched his newly appointed second-in-command leave the Forum, then said, "We must appease the gods' righteous anger and ask their support in the coming days. To this effect, I order the following: first, every landowner will sacrifice a cow, a goat, a sheep, and a pig to the gods with all appropriate ceremony." He paused, allowing the crowd to understand the enormity of this sacrifice. "Second, I declare a festival for the next three days, to be paid for by the Senate of Rome. Music and feasting shall be devoted to the gods' pleasure."

The crowd cheered, causing Fabius Maximus to pause until he could be heard again.

"Finally, during the festivities, each citizen must spend exactly three hundred thirty-three sestertii and three hundred thirty-three denarii in honor of the gods."

The crowd cheered again, and Fabius Maximus opened his arms to the crowd, basking in their relief and joy that Rome would be safe once more under his care. He stood there for several minutes, enjoying their confidence in him and approval of his actions. Then he motioned to his escort and, surrounded by twenty-four lictors, strode from the Forum toward the Capitoline Gate and his new headquarters on the Field of Mars.

* * *

I walked across the smooth stones of the Circus Flaminius with Scipio and Decius.

"I still say it was an amazing piece of oration," Decius said. "He had the people eating from his hand."

Scipio, reserved as always, said, "He said what needed to be said to calm the people and bring order back to the streets of Rome."

"I thought they'd kill Servilius before he could leave," Decius said.

"He gave them another focus for their terror and rage," Scipio said.

Decius cocked his head and asked, "Who?"

Scipio stopped at the entrance to the command tent and exchanged salutes with the guards before replying, "Himself. Who do you think they will blame if Hannibal wins another victory?"

Scipio's political sense was far better than my own. "He risks much, then," I said.

Scipio's lips thinned, and he said, "He risks his life, as do we all for the glory and honor of the Senate and People of Rome. Come, let us find the answers to all of our questions from the Dictator's own lips." With an uncharacteristic flourish of his cloak, he strode into the tent.

Decius growled, "He's in a mood, isn't he?"

Deciding to poke his pride a bit, I imitated Scipio's flourish and said, "Not at all," entering the tent with a rigid imitation of a nobleman's walk.

"Everyone's a comedian tonight," Decius said, following us inside.

We found our places to the left of the commander's stool and fell in behind Scipio. A few moments later, Fabius Maximus and Marcus Minucius entered from the back of the tent. The primus pilus ordered, "Atten-SHUN!" and the officers snapped forward and stiffened.

Fabius moved to the stool but simply stood before it and turned to face his officers. "At ease, gentlemen."

Everyone relaxed, but their attention remained focused on the white-haired man. He was dressed in a white tunic trimmed in purple and garnished with a polished, black leather belt which held a small dagger at his left hip.

"Tonight will be a general overview of my strategy and some basic assignments in preparation for march," he said. "Hannibal, by all reports, is marching for Apulia. We will follow him in four days' time. This delay will provide us with an opportunity to honor the gods, attend to our current organizational problems, and raise additional troops."

Minucius received a nod from the Dictator, and he said, "At the conclusion of this meeting, I will see all cavalry commanders outside. I will have orders for some of you and task others with messenger duties." He turned back to Fabius Maximus.

The new general said, "Gentlemen, we face a crisis of confidence. Our soldiers have been defeated time and again. We must train them, build their confidence, and train them some more. Unfortunately, we have a war to fight as well. These two tasks may appear diametrically opposed." He paused, observing the faces of his officers. "I say they are not. We will march on Hannibal. We will remain as close to him as possible. If he makes a mistake, we will take the opportunity to strike. But most of all, we will wear him down. We will deprive him of easy resupply and reinforcement. We will garrison our cities and build our navy. Hannibal will find no additional forces and will have to feed and pay those he has from the land he occupies."

The faces of the officers in the room remained impassive. Flaminius had said as much, they remembered. It would take more than words to sway them to enthusiasm for this plan.

"Servilius Geminus will be in charge of fleet construction at Ostia, with the rank of proconsul," he said.

There was a slight murmur as some of the officers of the former general realized that Fabius Maximus was trusting the fate of the naval blockade to Servilius.

"Rome and our allies are depending on us to protect them. We must not fail in that task. I ask you now to support me. We can prevail, we must prevail, we shall prevail."

"General," called one of the tribunes near the front.

"Yes," Fabius said. "There is a question?"

"How will we defeat Hannibal?" came the voice again, hidden from view by the mass of bodies in front of Fabius Maximus.

"Through a long war of attrition," said the general. "There will be hardship and setbacks. But we must never lose sight that we are defending our people, our homes, and our way of life."

"An honest answer at least," I whispered to Decius.

Scipio turned his head to glare at me.

"Sorry, sir," I said even more quietly.

Fabius Maximus said, "We march in four days. Prepare your men. Inspect everything. Report all deficiencies in supply to the quaestor. I will have the primus pilus issue all necessary orders to the infantry commanders."

"Atten-SHUN!" came the stentorian voice of the senior centurion.

"Dismissed," General Fabius Maximus said.

* * *

A few minutes later, we stood outside in a circle of decurions around the Master of Horse. Minucius still had a pugnacious scowl on his face, but now looked approvingly at the men around him. "Gentlemen, we have the task you all want. Find Hannibal and stay with him. We will be the eyes of the army. Decurion Scipio," he said, looking for an unfamiliar face.

"Here, sir," Scipio said, stepping forward a pace.

"Your turma has the most experience shadowing Hannibal's army," Minucius said.

"I believe so, sir," he said.

Minucius nodded. "Good. Go find him. Leave at first light. I expect at least two messages a day once you locate him. I want to know where he camps, what he eats, and when he farts."

Several of the younger men laughed at the coarse language.

"We will be on the trail at first light, sir," Scipio said.

"Do what you have proven so good at, Decurion. Be a scout and stay out of contact. The legion will be with you in a few days."

Minucius detailed a few other officers with scouting duties toward Campania and to the north. The rest were detailed to hold men ready as messengers for General Fabius. A few minutes later, he dismissed us.

"Well, sir, we're back in the saddle then," Decius said.

"It would seem so," Scipio said. "Tell Marcus to draw rations for a week from the quaestor. I will inspect the men two hours before dawn."

"Yes, sir," Decius and I said in unison.

"Get some rest once the men are bedded down for the night. Wake them an hour before inspection. I will be at my father's residence tonight if you need me."

"Sir, would you like an escort?" I asked.

"Yes, detail two men," he said. "I will use them as messengers if need be, otherwise, they can have a good meal and a comfortable bed tonight. They can find me in the stable."

I looked at Decius and he nodded, already knowing which men would be assigned to see the decurion home.

"Good night, sir," Decius said.

"Good night, gentlemen," he said and walked toward the stables to check his horse personally.

I gathered Decius by a tilt of my head, and we walked toward the tents of our turma.

"Away from Rome and the comfort of my wife's arms again," Decius said ruefully.

"Away from Rome and its bloody politics, you mean," I said. "We are far better off chasing Hannibal through Apulia."

"Appius, you need a wife," Decius said with a laugh.

For some reason, an image of Aemilia came to my mind. I shook my head, and said, "I need a softer saddle. Mine could be used as a torture rack."

Decius laughed again, and we walked through the camp to find our men. Tomorrow would begin a new phase in the war against Carthage. There was hope again.

AUTHOR'S NOTE: ON THE ROMAN ARMY DURING THE SECOND PUNIC WAR

The Roman Legions in Scipio's time bore some resemblance to those most readers will be familiar with. Television, movies, and most literature focus on Julius Caesar and his descendants after the creation of the Roman Empire. Scipio lived in the Roman Republic, which had quite different standards from the professional legionaries of Imperial times. With this thought in mind, I decided to write this guide to the legions of the Roman Republic.

Infantry Task Organization (Pedites)

Let's start with the basic organizational unit of the Roman Legion, the century. This formation consisted of two maniples of sixty men each, totaling one hundred twenty men per century. Each maniple was divided into ten sections of six men. Each maniple was commanded by a centurion, supported by an optio (perhaps two), a tesserarius, and a signifier. The maniple was the smallest independent infantry command in the legion, but nearly always operated together as a century. All the soldiers were citizens of Rome and were required by law to bring with them weapons and armor appropriate to their position in the battle line.

These legionaries were further divided by wealth and experience into three lines with attached skirmishers called velites. The velites were the youngest and poorest Roman citizens. They wore padded cloth or leather armor if they wore any at all. Some would wear animal skins over their heads to denote their prowess in battle. They carried from five to seven light javelins called veretum as a primary weapon. Their only protection was a small shield called a parma. Most carried a short sword called a gladius as a backup weapon for use after the veretae had been expended. These men were usually the first to engage the enemy. They formed a loose screen in front of the heavy infantry and used their speed and agility to stay away from the enemy. The velites's javelins served to distract or wound enemy soldiers. The iron tips were designed to bend on impact, rendering shields useless until the offending point could be removed. Occasionally the velites did kill enemy soldiers, but this was not their primary purpose. Their goal was to distract enemy soldiers and disrupt enemy formations. Once their ammunition had been used, these skirmishers fell back through the waiting gaps in the hastatii lines. Sources differ on their role after skirmishing. Some say they formed with the triarii at the rear, and others say they moved to the wings. I prefer to believe it depended on the tactical situation.

The first line of infantry, the hastatii, were citizens, usually younger ones, who could afford the arms and armor necessary for heavy infantry. These men carried lorica hamata or squamata (mail or scale armor respectively), a scutum (shield), pila (heavy iron-tipped javelins), a galea (helmet), and a gladius. Being young men, they tended toward vigorous attack. After loosing their pila, the hastatii charged into the enemy with their shields and, on command, thrust with their gladius. Roman commanders used them as shock troops to tire the enemy front-line soldiers.

The next line were the principes. These men carried the same equipment as the hastatii, although their weapons and armor tended to be of higher quality. These men were veterans whose experience would stabilize hastatii morale if they wavered. These were the main-line troops of the Roman army and served as the model for legionary soldiers in Imperial times.

The final line were the triarii. These were the wealthiest, oldest, and most experienced troops in the manipular legion. They carried hastum (long spear) and scutum. They protected the rear of the formation and served as a steady reserve if the hastatii and principes needed to retreat and regroup. These centuries were half the size of their hastatii and principes counterparts at thirty soldiers per maniple, totaling sixty per century.

The senior centurion of the legion was known as the primus pilus, and commanded the First Century. He also served as an advisor to the legion or army commander on the administration of the marching camp.

All centurions made reports to the primus pilus, who consolidated their reports for the commander. This obviated the commander from having to take ten or more reports from individual centurions.

Centurions who served well in battle could hope for elevation to the equestrian ranks, assuming they could amass the wealth necessary to attain such status.

Cavalry Task Organization (Equite)

Roman cavalry came from the equestrian (horse rider) rank of society. Technically, all Romans of the senatorial class were equestrians. In practice, a few very powerful families held the wealth and influence necessary for election to the Senate. However, all equestrians were wealthy individuals from the upper classes, who could afford the best equipment and the care and feeding of a horse. Each wore lorica hamata or squamata and carried a gladius. Some sources say they also carried a spear or lance. Again, I prefer to believe that their weapon choice depended on the tactical situation. They were organized into turmae of thirty men each and subdivided into ten-man sections. Each section would be commanded by a decurion, elected from within their number. Since all these men were equestrians, any equitum (cavalryman) would outrank any peditum (infantryman), no matter the rank of the foot soldier. The decurion was therefore the senior officer in a unit comprised of officers of equal rank. The senior decurion doubled as the overall commander of the cavalry.

Equestrians could hope for advancement to Senatorial rank through the patronage of tribunes, praetors, or consuls.

Roman Legion 217 BC

	Hastatii Century (Heavy Infantry) 120 men
	Principe Century (Heavy Infantry) 120 men
	Triarii Century (Spear-armed Heavy Infantry) 60 men
	Velite Detachment (Light Infantry) 240 men
	Equite Turma (Cavalry) 30 men

Alae Legion 217 BC

	Alae Century (Heavy Infantry) 120 men
	Alae Velite Detachment (Light Infantry) 240 men
	Alae Cavalry Turma (Cavalry) 90 men

Officers

The lowest rank officer in the Roman army was the optio. Equivalent to a corporal or junior sergeant, these men would command detachments, guard details, or other small forces as assigned by their centurion or decurion. They served as assistants to the junior officers and maintained order and discipline in the battle line while their superiors led from the front.

The tesserarius was a veteran legionary, trusted by his centurion. To him was given the task of receiving and relaying the daily watch word and number to his century. The password and number were engraved on a block of wood called a tessera, hence the title. While there is little in the historical record, I chose to give the tesserarius the role of supervising the century in the absence of a centurion and managing details at the centurion's direction. He would fight in ranks as a legionary, taking command if both centurions were slain.

The signifier carried the century's standard or signum. In battle, he would stand in the middle of the formation and provide a visual focus for the men to rally around. Additionally, he could relay messages for the centurion with the signum about the tactical disposition of the century. A signifier was appointed from each maniple, but only one would carry the standard. The other would take up the staff if the first fell to the enemy. Traditionally, these men wore bear skin over their heads to set them apart.

Each century was divided into two maniples commanded by a centurion. Equivalent to a reinforced platoon leader or a company commander, the centurion stood in the front rank and fought alongside the legionaries in the century. Centurions were veteran soldiers who were responsible for training their men to stand in the line of battle and fight with the discipline that dominated the ancient world. As noted above, centurions who served bravely could be elevated into the equestrian rank, assuming they could afford to sustain such a station.

Decurions, as stated earlier, were elected by the equestrian-ranked soldiers who served as cavalry for the legion. Cavalry were the eyes and ears of the infantry-focused legions. With a total of only three hundred men, Roman cavalry tended to be swept from the battlefield by Carthaginian forces, which had more and better horsemen. That is not to say that their flight from the battlefield served no purpose, as the ill-disciplined Carthaginian, Numidian, and Iberian cavalry tended to follow the Roman horsemen on a long chase rather than engaging the vulnerable rear of the infantry. The decurion ranked above the centurion, being of a higher social class, but lower than a tribune. If they could gather enough money, influence, and patronage, equestrians could advance into the senatorial ranks. Technically, all senators were equestrians, but not all equestrians were of senatorial rank.

Military tribunes were men from senatorial or equestrian families, usually on their first military service. Not to be confused with the political office, these men were elected to serve as staff officers for each of the annually recruited legions. Sixteen of these positions were filled in elections by the Assembly of the Tribes each year. Each consul also appointed two tribunes to serve as military deputies, making a total of twenty. These men served as staff officers to the commander of the legion or army. Sometimes they were entrusted with the command of an entire legion. Each legion would have four to six of these men who were there to learn how to command a legion from a more experienced praetor or consul.

Prefects were commanders of allied units. They were Roman citizens appointed by the consuls and assigned to each alae legion. They normally numbered twelve per legion, which coincided with ten infantry legions, a cavalry commander, and a senior prefect to command the rest. The remaining subordinate officers came from the allied units themselves. These prefects would also choose the best soldiers from the alae legions to serve as a bodyguard to the general.

Additionally, the consul would appoint prefects to command specialty units, such as engineers or artillery. While they could take command if necessary, they tended to command only their specialists and security detachments.

Commanders

Two consuls were elected each year by the Assembly of the Centurionate to serve as Rome's political and military leaders from March to March. Their authority, called Imperium, allowed them to command armies and garrisons throughout the Republic. These men would have experience as tribunes and be at least forty-three years of age. Elections were held, usually in winter, and the winners assumed their new office during the Ides of March, or mid-March. During the Punic Wars, consuls normally led armies in the field consisting of two legions for each. These double-strength armies were the primary offensive force of the Roman Republic. With attached socii (Italian client states of Rome) legions, each consular army swelled to over twenty thousand infantry and twelve hundred cavalry. When both consular armies combined, very few contemporary military forces could withstand their attack. When both consuls were present in a military camp, they normally alternated supreme command daily. Often they remained separated to retain command of their respective armies. During the Second Punic War, the consular armies grew to as many as four legions and associated allies each. Most of these soldiers were spread across the Italian Peninsula to garrison the walled cities and towns. This stopped Hannibal from capitalizing on his military victories by preventing him from establishing a base of operations in Italy. Still, the size of army that could be sustained in the field by the Roman Republic was impressive.

At the end of their term of office, consuls were named as proconsul by the Senate to a specific region or army and given a limited Imperium to command armies in that region or as assigned by the Senate. Usually, the army would be one legion or half the size of a consular army. During the Second Punic War, these armies grew at a similar rate to the consular armies. Proconsuls would lead legions in Hispania, Sicilia, Gaul, and other regions occupied by Carthaginian forces.

The quaestor, elected by the Assembly of Tribes, was the supply officer of the Roman legion. He also served as the paymaster. This was a critical position for the Roman Consular Army as thousands of men depended on him to sustain them with food, water, pay, and other military necessities. Because of the importance of this office, candidates had to have a minimum of ten years of military service. During the Republican period, there were twenty quaestor positions, but only two were assigned as military adjutants, one to each consul. As such, when a consul left office, the quaestor also left office. If the consul were later appointed as a proconsul and governor of a province or commander of a legion, the former quaestor would be appointed as proquaestor and follow the proconsul for his term of office. During the Punic Wars, Rome raised many more legions than normal, and proquaestors must have served with the proconsuls leading armies in Hispania and Sicilia.

Praetors were elected officials who also held Imperium. They too were elected by the Assembly of the Centurionate, and the minimum age for the office was forty. Normally they served as judges in civil matters, but during times of war they could command armies in the field. They could assume command of local garrisons or single legions. Their authority was only superseded by a consul or proconsul. Once their term of office was complete, they could serve as propraetors with limited Imperium to command armies in the field if needed.

AUTHOR'S AFTERWORD

The events of this book read like an action movie script. I am a fortunate author in that most of the far-fetched events described in this book actually happened. As the cliché goes, truth is stranger than fiction.

While there is no record of Scipio scouting up the River Rhodanus (the Rhône) to witness the destruction of the Volcae, he did indeed ride to the rescue of his father at the Battle of Ticinus, then refused the award for his bravery. Scipio had to have been nearby for the Battle of the Trebia, if not directly involved – although I am quite sure he did not usurp the authority of Consul Sempronius Longus. A writer must take some liberties for the sake of drama. He certainly witnessed the utter disaster at Lake Trasimenus (Lake Trasimene), before returning to Rome.

I quite enjoyed creating the election scene. Roman voting was incredibly complex and corrupt to modern eyes. I hope you enjoyed the contrast to modern elections. It is a good reminder to all of us that it could always be worse.

Hannibal did achieve the ultimate ambush at Lake Trasimenus. He managed to establish an ambush using an entire army. As far as I can find, this battle is the only time in history where a general achieved such a feat. The battle is still studied in military academies today.

Any accuracy in the events I described, I must attribute to others. I am certain I have forgotten to acknowledge many contributors. Any errors, alas, are entirely my own. Some were intentional for the story, but far too many were due to my failure to absorb the words of experts far more intelligent than me. I leave it to you, dear reader, to decide which is which.

I hope you have enjoyed the story so far. Appius and Decius will follow Scipio to Spain next, and take the war to Carthage. Roma Invicta!

Edward Green
Bonn, Germany
September 2018

ABOUT THE AUTHOR

Author is the latest in a long list of Edward Green's job titles, that include Navy Rescue Swimmer, Air Intercept Controller, Test Engineer, Firefighter, Transportation Officer, Battle Captain, and Garrison Commander. His current job is the culmination of a life of adventure and romance. And he has the bone and joint pain to prove it.

Born the son of a Navy Corpsman and a high school teacher, he grew up in the Commonwealth of Virginia. Joining the United States Navy at seventeen, he soon became a precocious smart-ass who should have been kicked out of the military. Instead, he thrived and excelled, becoming a rescue swimmer (working out and getting great suntans) and a tactical air controller (playing the best video game in the world). After twelve years, he decided to leave the Navy and go to college. Working as a test engineer for a government contractor and later a 911-Telecommunicator and Firefighter, he finally graduated college after six years with a degree in Information Technology. Then, he joined the United States Army Reserve. He deployed to Iraq, then Afghanistan, then taught ROTC for a couple of years, and then deployed again to Afghanistan before finally retiring from the military after twenty-four years of service.

Now he lives in Bonn, Germany, where he pretends not to understand German to amuse himself and fails to understand German to amuse others. Perhaps in a future version of himself, he will actually learn the language. One can only hope.

READ MORE BOOKS
BY EDWARD GREEN:

HANNIBAL'S NEMESIS
(JANUARY 2019)

HANNIBAL'S FATE
(MAY 2019)

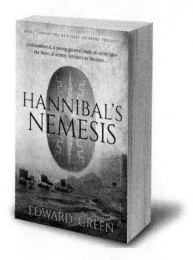

HANNIBAL'S NEMESIS

BOOK TWO IN THE REPUBLIC OF ROME TRILOGY

EDWARD GREEN

218 BC, South of Rome

Hannibal has crossed the Alps, destroyed three armies sent against him, and now threatens to sway Rome's Italian allies to side with Carthage. He has dispatched his brothers Mago and Hasdrubal to Carthage and Iberia to recruit reinforcements to support his campaign in Italy. Rome's confidence is shaken, and experienced generals are in short supply.

A young man, not old enough to be a senator, much less a general, volunteers to lead what older and wiser men perceive as a suicidal attempt to invade Iberia. With less than 30,000 soldiers, he will lead a desperate attempt to intercept 100,000 Carthaginian reinforcements. The outcome will decide the fate of western civilization in …

Find out more about Book Two at:
http://windheimpublishing.com/hannibals-nemesis/

Please join my series mailing list at:
http://windheimpublishing.com/hannibals-foe/

Or visit my author page at:
http://windheimpublishing.com/home/authors/
edward-green/

Dear Reader,

I am an independent author. Your reviews are the best way to help me tell stories that you love.

Please leave a review and tell me what you think about my work.

Thank you,

Edward Green

Made in the USA
San Bernardino, CA
04 January 2020